THE
COMPLETE
PLAYS
OF
SOPHOCLES

ALSO BY ROBERT BAGG

Madonna of the Cello: Poems (Wesleyan University Press)

Euripides' Hippolytos (Oxford University Press)

The Scrawny Sonnets and Other Narratives
(Illinois University Press)

Euripides' The Bakkhai (University of Massachusetts Press)

Sophocles' Oedipus the King
(University of Massachusetts Press)

Body Blows: Poems New and Selected
(University of Massachusetts Press)

The Oedipus Plays of Sophocles with Notes and Introductions by
Robert and Mary Bagg (University of Massachusetts Press)

Niké and Other Poems (Azul Editions)

HORSEGOD: Collected Poems (iUniverse)

Euripides III: Hippolytos and Other Plays
(Oxford University Press)

The Tandem Ride and Other Excursions
(Spiritus Mundi Press)

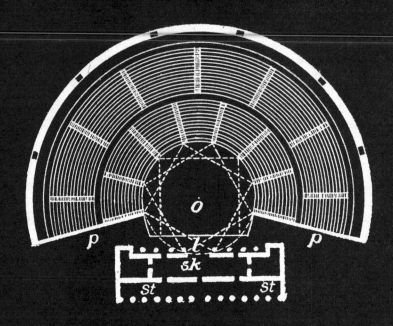

THE
COMPLETE
PLAYS
OF
SOPHOCLES

A New Translation

ROBERT BAGG AND JAMES SCULLY

HARPER  PERENNIAL

NEW YORK • LONDON • TORONTO • SYDNEY • NEW DELHI • AUCKLAND

HARPER PERENNIAL

HarperCollins books may be purchased for educational, business, or sales promotional use. For information please write: Special Markets Department, HarperCollins Publishers, 10 East 53rd Street, New York, NY 10022.

FIRST EDITION

Designed by Justin Dodd

Library of Congress Cataloging-in-Publication Data is available upon request.

ISBN 978-0-06-202034-5

11 12 13 14 15   DIX/RRD   10 9 8 7 6 5 4 3 2 1

We dedicate these translations to the memory of three didaskoloi,
the classicists John Andrew Moore, Thomas Fauss Gould, and Charles Segal.
They inspired not only their students but also a new generation of classical
scholars—many of whom provided, through their own works or comments on our
translations-in-progress, a constant source of insight and forward momentum.

CONTENTS

WHEN THEATER WAS LIFE: THE WORLD OF SOPHOCLES

I

Greek theater emerged from the same profound creativity that has propelled the institutions and innovations of ancient Athens, through two and a half millennia, into our own era. Athens gave us epic poetry, painting and sculpture based on the human form, democracy, philosophy, history, anatomy and medicine, experimental science, trial by jury, grand civic architecture, and state financing of the arts, including (and especially) drama. Athenians also took pleasure in two forms of high-spirited social interaction that, in more subdued forms, remain in vogue: the symposium and the bacchanal.

Historians have tended to emphasize Athens' glories, showing less interest in the brutal institutions and policies that paid for and enforced its wealth and dominance: its slaves, for instance, who worked the mines that enriched the communal treasury; and its policy of executing the men and enslaving the women and children of an enemy city that refused to surrender on demand.

Athens' raw and unbridled democracy became, during its war with Sparta, increasingly reckless, cruel, and eventually self-defeating, in part because Athens vested enormous decision-making responsibility in its impulsive assembly. But inherent in its questing, risk-taking energy, and the vesting of its fortunes in its male citizenry, was critical examination of its own actions, policies, principles, and beliefs. Drama, both comic and tragic, played an influential part in this search for self-recognition. The mantra "Know thyself" stared down from Apollo's temple at the pilgrims seeking advice from the oracle at Delphi. Playwrights, known to the Athenians as *didaskaloi* (educators), used their art to enlighten audiences of thousands about themselves, both individually and collectively.

Athenian tragedy did not have the restrictive meaning it does at present: plays that end badly for nearly every character. Several Athenian "tragedies" conclude with positive resolutions of their major conflicts. In *Aias, Philoktetes*, and *Oedipus at Kolonos*, for instance, the surviving protagonists achieve resolutions or reconciliations that emerge from the play's action, usually in some suspenseful or unexpected way. Will Odysseus and Neoptolemos succeed, in what seems a mission impossible: delivering Philoktetes and his bow back to the war against Troy? If so, how? What circumstance or argument, what measure of grit, human character, or divine intervention, will carry the day?

Sophocles' plays all possess a distinct attribute of Athenian creativity: critical engagement with life, not just the life preserved in heroic legend but also that taking place around him in Athenians' homes, the city's agora and assembly, its temples, law courts, and battlegrounds. Plato, through his character Socrates, personalized this imperative, holding that for individuals "the unexamined life is not worth living." Other Athenian intellectuals, including Thucydides, Euripides, Plato himself, and Aristophanes, widened the view by explicitly examining and judging the actions and morality of their contemporaries. At stake was not only the life of the individual but also the viability of the polity as a whole. Aristophanes, as a comic playwright, was free to pillory not only policies he didn't like but also the conduct of living persons including, in *The Clouds*, the forty-year-old Socrates, a relentless interrogator notorious for challenging established wisdom and for proposing concepts thought preposterous by hoi polloi, "the many" whose votes and opinions outweighed those of the aristocrats throughout most of the fifth century BCE.

Virtually every Athenian theatrical innovation—from paraphernalia such as scenery, costumes, and masks to the architecture of stage and seating and, not least, to the use of drama as a powerful means of cultural and political commentary—remains central to our own theatrical practice. We thus inherit from Athens the *potential* for drama to engage the most controversial and emotional issues people face. The fusion of dramatic narrative, poetry, acting, music, song, and spectacle moved Athenian audiences, as Aristotle tells us, to the pity and fear, but also to the enlightenment they experienced in the theater.

Through the plays of Sophocles, in common with those of Aeschylus and Euripides, thousands of theatergoers could witness and contemplate human life at its most extreme and meaningful. Sophocles' scripts bristle with ironies and implications that suggest his characters do not, or cannot, understand everything that is happening to them. They, and we as the audience, sense that we're in over our heads; the knowledge of who we are and what we are doing is an unfolding mystery. Consider the words of Oedipus' wife, Jokasta, as she enters, unexpectedly, to mediate a quarrel between her husband and her brother Kreon. Oedipus has just accused Kreon of conspiring with the blind seer Tiresias to identify him as the murderer of Laios, Thebes' previous king (and Jokasta's late husband).

> Wretched men! Why are you out here
> so reckless, yelling at each other?
> Aren't you ashamed? With Thebes sick and dying
> you two fight out some personal grievance?
> Oedipus. Go inside. Kreon, go home.
> Don't make us all miserable over nothing. (747–752)

Jokasta demands the men stop behaving like children and get back to the more urgent matter: finding the source of the plague that is ravaging Thebes. Her intervention starts a sequence of discoveries that will prove the seer correct and identify Oedipus not only as Laios' killer, as the prophet Tiresias predicted, but also as Jokasta's own son. The tone she takes toward her husband and brother conveys what we, who have our own theorizations, might recognize as a Freudian irony—Jokasta's motherly dismissal reminds us of her initial relationship to Oedipus. The revelations following her rebuke remind us that attempts to avoid looming trouble can backfire. The consequences of our actions cannot always be foreseen.

Sophocles' remarkably resilient plays have proven themselves as timeless as the experiences they dramatize: human vulnerability to suffering both merited and unmerited, the courage required for a citizen to face down a tyrant, violence inspired by vengeance or sexual passion, the effects of war on combatants and civilians, and the longing of the ill-fated for justification and redemption. Implicit in this timelessness, however, is *timeliness*. The myths that engaged Sophocles' audience originated in Homer's epics of the Trojan War and its aftermath. Centuries later Sophocles reworked material from these epics, which were central to Athenian culture, into dramatic *agons* (contests) relevant to the tumultuous, often vicious politics of Greek life in the fifth century BCE. Today Sophocles' themes, and the way he approached them, correspond at their deepest levels to events and patterns of thought and conduct that trouble our own time.

Even so, though his plays communicate in and through time, translations of them do not. Each generation, in its own idiom and in accord with its own cultural presumptions, renders them into the style it believes best suited for tragedy. This inevitably calls into play the translator's own sense of ancient and foreign linguistic decorum. The catch is that decorum, ancient or current, does not exist in a social or historical vacuum. At the very least, any contemporary translation must begin by trying to convey both *what* that literature seems to have been communicating and *how* it communicated—not only in its saying but also in its doing. These plays were not just entertainments. They were social, historical events. Recognizing this basic circumstance doesn't guarantee a translation's success, but it is a precondition for giving these works breathing room. They were not made of words alone.

Victorian translators tried to match the elevation they believed essential for Greek drama. Increasingly, however, the 'high tone' once expected from gods and heroes sounded affected or bombastic. Worse, it glossed over the foibles and occasional playfulness of those gods. In *Aias*, for instance, Athena is unmistakably teasing and flirting with Odysseus, boasting how she has spun Aias around in his own rage. It had been difficult to render nuances of this order until, in the second half of the twentieth century, William Arrowsmith, editor of the Oxford series of Greek Drama in New Translations, commissioned poet-translators to write and publish more natural, idiomatic, and thus more accessible and playable versions.

Some scholars and critics still view the use of modern idiom as not only grating but also as a gratuitous departure from established 'literal' meaning, thus undermining Sophocles' stylistic and 'communicative' intentions. And yet, though patches of literalness are possible and desirable, a consistently literal translation is literally impossible. Not all Greek words correspond exactly to modern English words. Many have quite different spectra of associations and nuances. Depending on context, *logos* can be and has been translated as "word," "language," "theory," "reason," "ratio," "proportion," "definition," and "a saying"—as in the opening line of *Women of Trakhis* ("People have a saying that goes way back"). Of course *logos* is also the basis for the English "logic" and the conceptualizing of biology, geology and every other '-ology.' And then there's "In the beginning was the Logos, and the Logos became flesh and dwelt among us." How does one put that into a hermetic linguistic filing system? In life, in actual production, neither easily nor well.

Greek, in every sense a living language, does not stand still. The ancient Greeks lived with a panoply of dramatic expressions, from the pungency of cut-and-thrust dialogue to exhortation, exultation, and elaborately detailed messenger narratives. Audiences expected chorus members to be capable of conveying sympathy, rebuke, irony, naïveté and wryness, and outbursts of pain and mourning and, between each scene, to perform complex and often highly allusive choral songs. To translate the rich range of expressive modes Sophocles had at his disposal, we need the resources not only of idiomatic English but also of rhetorical gravitas and, on rare occasion, colloquial English as well. Which is why we have adopted, regarding vocabulary and 'levels of speech,' a wide and varied palette. When Philoktetes exclaims, "You said it, boy," that saying corresponds in character to the colloquial Greek expression. On the other hand Aias's "Long rolling waves of time . . ." is as elevated, without being pompous, as anything can be.

Unfortunately we've been taught and have learned to live with washed-out stereotypes of the life and art of 'classical' times—just as we have come to associate Greek sculpture with marble pallor, despite the fact that the Greeks painted most, if not all, of their statues. The statues' eyes were not blanks gazing off into space. They had color: a *look*. To restore their flesh tones, their eye color, and the bright hues of their cloaks would seem a desecration, but only because we've become accustomed to static, idealized conceptions of ancient Greek culture. A mindset that sees Greek statuary as bland marble may condition us to preserve, above all, not the reality of ancient Greek art but our own fixed conception of it—which, ironically, is inseparable from what the ravages of centuries have done to it.

The classical historian Bettany Hughes writes in *The Hemlock Cup* (81) that Greek sculptures "were dressed in real clothes as if they suffered hot and cold like any other human. . . . Statues, monuments, temples . . . were all painted and stained in Technicolor. The stark application and gloopy pigments used would shock most of us today, but these were designed to be seen under the bright Attic sun, and their gaudy glory to be remembered."

As translators we have a responsibility not to reissue a replica of classical Greek culture but rather to recoup its living reality. We recognize that locutions sounding contorted, coy, allusive, or annoyingly roundabout to us were a feature of ordinary Greek and were intensified in poetic theatrical discourse. Such larger-than-life expressions, delivered without artificial amplification to an audience of thousands, did not jar when resonating in the vast Theater of Dionysos, but may to our own Anglophone ears when spoken from our more intimate stages and screens or read in our books and electronic tablets. Meanwhile, where appropriate, and especially in rapid exchanges, we have our characters speak more straightforwardly.

Of course there are no 'rules' for determining when a more-literal or less-literal approach is appropriate. Historical and dramatic context have to be taken into account. The objective is not only to render the textual meaning (which is ordinarily more on the phrase-by-phrase than the word-by-word level) but also to communicate the *feel and impact* embedded in that meaning. When use of the literal word or phrase would obscure what we think Sophocles meant (or what his audience would have understood a passage to mean), we've sometimes opted for a non-word-literal translation, seeking instead a phrase that will communicate a more precise dynamic and significance within a dramatic exchange. Dictionaries are indispensable for translators, but they are not sufficient. The meanings of words are immeasurably more nuanced in life than they are in a lexicon. As in life, where most 'sayings' cannot be fully grasped apart from their social context, so in theater: dramatic context must take words up and finish them off, communicating the felt realities that make the concerns and the actions of the play compelling.

For example, in *Aias*, Teukros, the out-of-wedlock half brother of Aias, and Menelaos, co-commander of the Greek forces, are trading insults. When Menelaos says, "The archer, far from blood dust, thinks he's something," Teukros quietly rejoins, "I'm very good at what I do" (1300–1301).

Understanding the exchange between the two men requires that the reader or audience recognize the 'class' implications of archery. Socially and militarily, archers rank low in the pecking order. They stand to the rear of the battle formation. Archers are archers because they can't afford the armor one needs to be a hoplite, a frontline fighter. This issue generates some of the more heated moments in the play after Aias commits suicide. The point is that Teukros refuses to accept 'his place' in the social and military order. For a Greek audience, the sheer fact of standing his ground against a commander had to have been audacious. But that is not how it automatically registers in most modern word-by-word translations, which tend to make Teuk-ros sound defensive (a trait wholly out of his character in this play). Examples: (a) "even so, 'tis no sordid craft that I possess," (b) "I'm not the master of a menial skill," (c) "my archery is no contemptible science," (d) "the art I practice is no mean one." In modern English idiom, tonally, his negation preempts his assertion (the 'I'm not . . . but even so' formula). It admits weakness.

"I'm very good at what I do," however, is a barely veiled threat: the dramatic arc of the encounter, which confirms that Teukros will not back down for anything or anyone, not even a commander of the Greek army, substantiates that Sophocles meant it as such. Hearing the line in context we realize instantly not only what the words are saying but, more pointedly and feelingly, what they're *doing*. His words are not just 'about' something. They are an act in themselves—not, as in the more literal translations, a duress-driven apologia. Translation must thus respond to an individual character's ever-changing moods and demeanor. The words should reflect states of mind, just as they do in life.

Idiomatic or colloquial expressions fit many situations better—especially those that have a more finely tuned emotional economy—than phrases that, if uninhabited or hollowed out, sound evasive or euphemistic. Many of the words Sophocles gives his characters are as abrupt and common as he might himself have spoken in the agora, to the assembly, to his troops, or to his family and his actors.

We also have chosen a more literal translation in passages where scholars have opted for a seemingly more accessible modern phrase. For instance, at the climactic moment in *Oedipus the King*, when Oedipus realizes he has killed his father and fathered children with his mother, he says in a modern prose version by Hugh Lloyd-Jones: "Oh, oh! All is now clear. O light, may I now look on you for the last time, I who am revealed as cursed in my birth, cursed in my marriage, cursed in my killing!" (Greek 1182–1885). When Lloyd-Jones uses and repeats the word "cursed," he is compressing a longer Greek phrase meaning "being shown to have done what must not be done." This compression shifts the emphasis from his unsuspecting human actions to the realm of the god who acted to "curse" him. To keep the immediacy of the original, we get:

> All! All! It has all happened!
> It was all true. O light! Let this
> be the last time I look on you.
> You see now who I am—
> the child who must not be born!
> I loved where I must not love!
> I killed where I must not kill! (1336–1342)

Here Oedipus names the three acts of interfamilial transgression that it was both his good and his ill fortune to have survived, inflicted, and participated in—birth, sexual love, and murder in self-defense—focusing not only on the curse each act has become but now realizing the full and terrifying consequence of each action that was unknowable *as it happened*. Registering the shock running through him, Oedipus's exclamations convey the shock of his realization: *I did these things without feeling their horror as I do now.*

Finally, translations tend to be more or less effective

depending on their ability to convey the emotional and physiological reactions that will give a reader or an audience a kinesthetic relationship to the text or its performance. This is a precondition for maintaining the fluidity that characterizes any living language. Dante wrote that the spirit of poetry abounds "in the tangled constructions and defective pronunciations" of vernacular speech where language is renewed and transformed. We have not attempted that—these are translations, not new works—but we have striven for a language that is spontaneous and generative as opposed to one that is studied and bodiless. We have also worked to preserve the root meaning of Sophocles' Greek, especially his always illuminating metaphors.

II

Sophocles reveals several recurrent attitudes in his plays—sympathy for fate's victims, hostility toward leaders who abuse their power, skepticism toward self-indulgent 'heroes,' disillusionment with war and revenge—that are both personal and politically significant. It is also significant that all his plays to a greater or less degree focus on outcasts from their communities.

Historically, those who transgress a community's values have either been physically exiled or stigmatized by sanctions and/or shunning. To keep a polity from breaking apart, everyone, regardless of social standing, must abide by certain enforceable communal expectations. Athens in the fifth century BCE practiced political ostracism, a procedure incorporated in its laws. By voting to ostracize a citizen, Athens withdrew its protection and civic benefits—sometimes to punish an offender, but also as a kind of referee's move, expelling a divisive public figure from the city (and from his antagonists) so as to promote a ten-year period of relative peace.

In earlier eras, Greek cities also cast out those who committed sacrilege. Murderers of kin, for instance, or blasphemers of a god—in myth and in real life—were banished from Greek cities until the 'unclean' individual 'purged' his crime according to current religious custom. The imperative to banish a kin violator runs so deep that Oedipus, after discovering he has committed patricide and incest, self-imposes this judgment and demands to live in exile. When he reappears in *Oedipus at Kolonos*, he and Antigone have been exiled in a more or less traditional sense.

Philoktetes, Elektra, Aias, and Herakles (in *Women of Trakhis*) are not all outcasts in the conventional sense, though all have offended their social units in one way or another. They may or may not be 'tragic characters,' but each is punished for a physical condition, a violent obsession, or murder. The personalities at the center of the non-Oedipus plays offend against their social worlds. In these translations we attend to their social worlds as Sophocles presents them.

We have not attempted to fit the action and import of each play into a theory of tragedy—for instance, to conceive it ultimately as a tragedy of character. Rather, we widen the purview to include the breadth and specificity of Sophocles' obvious, fundamental social and historical concerns. In each of the four non-Theban plays, a lethal confrontation or conflict 'crazes' the surface social coherence of a society (presumed to be Athenian society, either in itself or as mediated through a military context), thus revealing and heightening its internal contradictions.

In *Women of Trakhis* a revered hero overreaches, destroying his reputation, his marriage, and ultimately himself. *Elektra* exposes the dehumanizing cost of taking revenge. In *Aias* a heroic soldier's rebellion against his corrupt commanding officers exposes the tyranny of an aristo-military hierarchy. In *Philoktetes* the title character is treated as an inconvenient military asset and shelved, but when recalled to active service he resists the rehabilitation offered by his former betrayers until a god negotiates a culturally mandated resolution.

In our own time aspects of Aias and Philoktetes have been used for purposes that Sophocles, who was the sponsor in Athens of a healing cult, might have appreciated. Both heroes, but especially Aias, have been appropriated as exemplars of post-traumatic stress disorder, in particular as suffered by soldiers in and out of a war zone. Recently, excerpts from these two plays have been performed around the United States for audiences of American service members, their families, and concerned others. Ultimately, however, Sophocles is intent on engaging *and resolving* internal contradictions that threaten the integrity and historical continuity, the very future, of the Athenian state. He invokes the class conflicts Athens was experiencing by applying them to the mythical/historical eras from which he draws his plots.

Modern-day relevancies implicit in Sophocles' plays come sharply into focus or recede from view depending on time and circumstance. The constant factors in his masterpieces will always be their consummate poetry, dramatic propulsion, and illumination of human motivation and morality. But scholars have recognized and documented events in his plays that allude to events in Athenian history. For instance, the plague in *Oedipus the King* is described in such vivid detail that it dovetails in many respects with Thucydides' more clinical account of the plague that killed one third to one half of Athens' population beginning in 429 BCE. Kreon, Antigone's antagonist, exhibits the imperviousness to rational advice and lack of foresight present in the politicians of Sophocles' era, whose follies Thucydides narrates, and which Sophocles himself was called in to help repair. Most movingly, *Oedipus at Kolonos* explicitly celebrates an Athens that no longer existed when Sophocles wrote that play. In it he gives us Theseus, the kind of all-around leader Athens lacked as it drove itself to destruction—this under the delusion that its only enemies were Spartans and Sparta's allies.

Every drama, almost every speech and character, demands we grasp its import both within and beyond the play. That the Athenians revered the wisdom of their playwrights is clear from the name by which they were known—*didaskaloi* (educators, teachers)—and by the massive, expensive, and technologically impressive structures they created in which to stage, watch, and honor their works.

III

Archaeologists have identified hundreds of local theaters all over the Greek world—stone semicircles, some in cities and at religious destinations, others in rural villages. Within many of these structures both ancient and modern plays are still staged. Hillsides whose slopes were wide and gentle enough to seat a crowd made perfect settings for dramatic encounters and were the earliest theaters. Ancient roads that widened below the hills, or level ground at the hill's base, provided a suitable performance space. Such sites, along with every city's agora and a temple dedicated to Dionysos or another god, were the main arenas of community activity. Stone tablets along roads leading to theaters commemorated local victors: athletes, actors, playwrights, singers, and the plays' producers. Theaters, in every sense, were open to all the crosscurrents of civic and domestic life.

The components of the earliest theaters reflect their rural origins and were later incorporated into urban settings. *Theatron*, the root of our word "theater," translates as "viewing place" and designated the curved and banked seating area. *Orchestra* was literally "the place for dancing." The costumed actors emerged from and retired to the *skenê*, a word that originally meant, and literally was in the rural theaters, a tent. As theaters evolved to become more permanent structures, the *skenê* developed as well into a "stage building" whose painted facade changed, like a mask, with the characters' various habitats. Depending on the drama, the *skenê* could assume the appearance of a king's grand palace, the Kyklops' cave, a temple to a god, or (reverting to its original material form) an army commander's tent.

The origins of Greek drama itself have roots in two earlier traditions, one rural, one civic. Choral singing of hymns to honor Dionysos or other gods and heroes began in the countryside and evolved to become the structured choral ode. The costumes and the dancing of these choral singers, often accompanied by a reed instrument, are depicted on sixth-century vases that predate the plays staged in the Athenian theater.

It's not coincidental that the highly confrontational nature of every play suggests how early choral odes and dialogues became fused with a fundamental aspect of democratic governance: public and spirited debate. Two or more characters facing off in front of an audience was a familiar situation, one central to both drama and democratic politics.

Debate, the democratic Athenian art practiced and perfected by politicians, litigators, and thespians—and relished and judged by voters, juries, and audiences—flourished in theatrical venues and permeated daily Athenian life. Thucydides used it to narrate his history of the war between Athens and Sparta. He recalled scores of lengthy debates that laid out the motives of politicians, generals, and diplomats as each argued his case for a particular policy or a strategy. Plato, recognizing the open-ended, exploratory power of the verbal *agon*, wrote his philosophy entirely in dramatic form.

The Greeks were addicted to contests and turned virtually every chance for determining a winner into a formal competition. The Great Dionysia for playwrights and choral singers and the Olympics for athletes are only the most famous and familiar. The verbal *agon* remains to this day a powerful medium for testing and judging issues across the spectrum of civilized life. It is at least possible that superior arguments will emerge from debate and dialogue. And character, as in the debate between Teukros and Menelaos, may be laid bare. But there is no guarantee. Bad or harmful conclusions may prevail when a debater is both eloquent and wrong-headed. Persuasiveness can be, and frequently is, manipulative (e.g., the sophists evolved into hired rhetorical guns, as distinguished from the truth-seeking, pre-Socratic philosophers).

For instance, Odysseus's comment to Neoptolemos in *Philoktetes*—"At your age, just like you, my hand / was quicker than my tongue. / But now I've learned it's words / that move people, not deeds" (108–111)—was considered by one ancient critic to be a slander against Athenian politicians. One famous example of a civic speech crafted to have a dramatic effect, and achieve a political purpose, is Perikles' funeral oration as Thucydides presents it. The speech is not, Paul Cartledge (62) argues, "a simple hymn to democracy"; rather, it is "ideologically slanted . . . to persuade his fellow citizens that wars were good for Athens." Perikles was, however, stating a fact when he said, "Athens was called a *demokratia* because governance was effected in the interests of the many [citizens] rather than the few."

The works of the Greek tragic poets were commissioned and funded via a type of wealth tax on rich citizens who were assigned the role of financing a particular production by the *polis* (i.e., Athens), and staged under the auspices of a civic festival. The playwrights wrote as *politai*, civic poets, as distinguished from those who focused on personal lyrics and shorter choral works.

Plays performed at the Dionysia honored its patron god, Dionysos. The god's worshippers believed that Dionysos' powers and rituals transformed the ways in which they experienced and dealt with their world—from their ecstatic response to theatrical illusion and disguise to the exhilaration, liberation, and violence induced by wine. Yet the festival also aired, or licensed, civic issues that might otherwise have had no truly public, *polis*-wide expression. As we see in *Aias* and *Philoktetes*, a play could even serve a *particular* civic purpose—either by reconfirming (via *Philoktetes*), or by revising or redefining (via *Aias*), the link between military and civic responsibility. This link was on public view when the orphans of warriors who had been killed in battle were given a place of honor at the Festival of Dionysos. The bottom line, however, is that even as *Aias* and *Philoktetes* are set in a military milieu, the issues they engage are *essentially* civil and political. Neither *Aias* nor *Philoktetes* is concerned with the 'enemy of record,' Troy, but rather with Greek-on-Greek conflict. With civil disruption, and worse.

Communal cohesiveness and the historical continuity of the *polis* are threatened from within: in *Aias* by the individualistic imbalance and arrogance of Aias, whose warrior qualities and strengths are also his weakness, and in *Philoktetes* by the understandable and just yet inordinately unyielding self-preoccupation of Philoktetes himself. In both cases the fundamental, encompassing question is: with what understandings, what basic values, is the commonality of the *polis* to be recovered and rededicated in an era in which its civic cohesiveness is under the extreme pressure of a war Athens is losing (especially at the time *Philoktetes* was produced) and, further, the simmering stasis of unresolved class antagonism? In sharply different ways, all three Oedipus plays and *Elektra* cast doubt on the legitimacy of usurped, authoritarian, or publicly disapproved leadership.

Given this sense of their historical sources, we've considered it our job not simply to translate the plays as texts but to communicate their relevance and their urgencies to an audience of our own time.

IV

The Great Dionysia was the central and most widely attended event of the political year, scheduled after winter storms had abated so that foreign visitors could come and bear witness to Athens' wealth, civic pride, imperial power, and artistic imagination. For eight (or, by some accountings, nine) days each spring, during the heyday of Greek theater in the fifth century BCE, Athenians flocked to the temple grounds sacred to Dionysos on the southern slope of the Acropolis. After dark on the first day, a parade of young men hefted a giant phallic icon of the god from the temple and into the nearby theater. The introduction of this huge wooden shaft, festooned with garlands of ivy and a mask of the god's leering face, initiated a dramatic festival called the City Dionysia, a name that differentiated it from the festival's ancient rural origins in Dionysian myth and cult celebrations of the god. As the festival gained importance in the sixth century BCE, most likely through the policies of Pisistratus, it was also known as the Great Dionysia.

Pisistratus, an Athenian tyrant in power off and on beginning in 561 BCE and continuously from 546 to 527, had good reason for adapting the Rural Dionysia as Athens' Great Dionysia: "Dionysos was a god for the 'whole' of democratic Athens" (Hughes, 213). Everyone, regardless of political faction or social

standing, could relate to the boisterous communal activities of
the festival honoring Dionysos: feasting, wine drinking, dancing, singing, romping through the countryside, and performing
or witnessing dithyrambs and more elaborate dramatic works.
The Great Dionysia thus served to keep in check, if not transcend, internal factionalizing by giving all citizens a 'natural'
stake in Athens—Athens not simply as a place but rather as
a venerable polity with ancient cultural roots. To this end Pisistratus had imported from Eleutherai an ancient phallic rep-
resentation of Dionysos, one that took several men to carry.
Lodged as it was in a temple on the outskirts of Athens, this
icon gave the relatively new, citified cult the sanctified air of
hoary antiquity (Csapo and Slater, 103–104). Thus validated
culturally, the Great Dionysia was secured as a host to reassert,
and annually rededicate, Athens as a democratic polity.

As Bettany Hughes notes in *The Hemlock Cup*, "to call
Greek drama an 'art-form' is somewhat anachronistic. The
Greeks (unlike many modern-day bureaucrats) didn't distinguish drama as 'art'—something separate from 'society,'
'politics,' [or] 'life.' Theater was fundamental to democratic
Athenian business. . . . [In] the fifth century this was the place
where Athenian democrats came to understand the very world
they lived in" (Hughes, 213).

Regardless of its political agenda, the festival retained
much of the spirit and tradition of its rural roots. The morning after the parade of young men brought Dionysos' icon
from the temple to the theater grounds, a much larger procession arrived. A cross section of Athenian society, some bearing other phallic images of the god, brought provisions for a

sacrifice and feast. Young virgins of aristocratic family carried golden baskets of fruit; male citizens lugged wineskins and enormous loaves of bread; resident aliens, called *metics*, contributed honeycombs and cakes while their daughters hauled in jugs of water. At the massive altar before the temple, priests of Dionysos butchered (in sacrifice) several hundred bulls that young men of military age had herded into the pageant; the animals' joints and haunches were then wrapped in fat, seared on the altar, and distributed to the vast crowd, who finished roasting the meat on portable braziers. Five days of theatrical competition ensued: day one featured ten fifty-member male choruses singing and dancing in homage to Dionysos; day two offered comedies; and the last three days were devoted to tragic drama.

The occasion offered Athens the chance to display treasure exacted from subjugated 'allies' (or tributes others willingly brought to the stage) and to award gold crowns to citizens whose achievements Athens' leaders wished to honor. The sons of soldiers killed in Athens' ongoing wars paraded in new battle armor paid for by the city. Theater attendance itself was closely linked to citizenship; local town councils issued free festival passes to citizens in good standing. The ten generals elected yearly to conduct Athens' military campaigns poured libations to Dionysos. In the front row (eventually on stone chairs, some of which are still in place today) sat priests and priestesses of the city's chief religious cults. Members of the five-hundred-member city council and the *ephebes*, or newly inducted soldiers, filled ranks of wooden seats, while the city's tribal units congregated in their own wedge-shaped sections. The theater's bowl seethed with a heady, sometimes unruly brew of military, political, and religious energy.

Performances began at dawn and lasted well into the afternoon. The 14,000 or more Athenians present watched in a state of pleasurable anxiety. Whatever else it did to entertain, move, and awe, Athenian tragedy consistently exposed human vulnerability to the gods' malice and favoritism. Because the gods were potent realities to Athenian audiences they craved and expected an overwhelming emotional, physically distressing experience. That expectation distinguishes the greater intensity with which Athenians responded to plays from our more detached encounter with drama in the modern era. Athenians wept while watching deities punish the innocent or unlucky, a reaction which distressed Plato. In his *Republic*, rather than question the motives or morality of the all-powerful Olympian gods for causing mortals grief, he blamed the poets and playwrights for their unwarranted wringing of the audience's emotions on the grounds that the gods had no responsibility for human suffering and banned both from his ideal city.

Modern audiences would be thoroughly at home with other, more cinematic stage effects. The sights and sounds tragedy delivered in the Theater of Dionysos were often spectacular. Aristotle, who witnessed a lifetime of productions in the fourth century, identified "spectacle" as one of the basic elements of tragic theater: oboe music; dancing and the singing of set-piece odes by a chorus; masks that transformed the same male actor, for instance, into a swarthy-faced young hero, a dignified matron, Argos with a hundred eyes, or the Kyklops with only one. The theater featured painted scenery and large-scale constructions engineered with sliding platforms and towering cranes. Greek tragedy has been considered a forerunner of Italian opera.

Judges awarding prizes at the Great Dionysia were chosen by lot from a list supplied by the council—one judge from each of Athens' ten tribes. Critical acumen was not required to get one's name on the list, but the *choregoi* (the producers and financial sponsors of the plays) were present when the jury was assembled and probably had a hand in its selection. At the conclusion of the festival the ten selected judges, each having sworn that he hadn't been bribed or unduly influenced, would inscribe on a tablet the names of the three competing playwrights in descending order of merit. The rest of the process depended on chance. The ten judges placed their ballots in a large urn. The presiding official drew five at random, counted up the weighted vote totals, and declared the winner.

V

When Sophocles was a boy, masters trained him to excel in music, dance, and wrestling. He won crowns competing against his age-mates in all three disciplines. Tradition has it that he first appeared in Athenian national life at age fifteen, dancing naked (according to one source) and leading other boy dancers in a hymn of gratitude to celebrate Athens' defeat of the Persian fleet in the straits of Salamis.

Sophocles' father, Sophillus, manufactured weapons and armor (probably in a factory operated by slaves) and his mother was apparently a midwife. The family lived in Kolonos, a rural

suburb just north of Athens. Although his parents were not aristocrats, as were most other playwrights' families, they surely
had money and owned property; thus their status did not ham-
per their son's career prospects. Sophocles' talents as a drama-
tist, so formidable and so precociously developed, won him
early fame. As an actor he triumphed in his own now-lost play,
Nausicaä, in the role of the eponymous young princess who,
playing ball with her girlfriends, discovers the nearly naked Odysseus washed up on the beach.

During Sophocles' sixty-five-year career as a *didaskalos*
he wrote and directed more than 120 plays and was awarded
first prize at least eighteen times. No record exists of his placing lower than second. Of the seven entire works of his that
survive, along with a substantial fragment of a satyr play, *The
Trackers*, only two very late plays can be given exact production dates: *Philoktetes* in 409 and *Oedipus at Kolonos*, staged
posthumously, in 401. Some evidence suggests that *Antigone*
was produced around 442–441 and *Oedipus the King* in the
420s. *Aias*, *Elektra*, and *Women of Trakhis* have been conjec-
turally, but never conclusively, dated through stylistic analysis.
Aristotle, who had access we forever lack to the hundreds of
fifth-century plays produced at the Dionysia, preferred Sophocles to his rivals Aeschylus and Euripides, considered *Oedipus
the King* the perfect example of tragic form, and developed his
theory of tragedy from his analysis of it.

Sophocles' fellow citizens respected him sufficiently to vote
him into high city office on at least three occasions. He served
for a year as chief tribute-collector for Athens' overseas empire. A controversial claim by Aristophanes of Byzantium, in

the third century, implies that Sophocles' tribe was so impressed by a production of *Antigone* that they voted him in as one of ten military generals (*strategoi*) in 441–440. The classicist Thomas Gould speculates that it was the managerial and inspirational skills on display during the production, rather than any politically rousing sentiments in the play, that earned Sophocles this post. Later in life Sophocles was respected as a participant in democratic governance at the highest level. In 411 he was elected to a ten-man commission charged with replacing Athens' discredited democratic governance with an oligarchy, a development that followed the military's catastrophic defeat in Sicily in 415.

Most ancient biographical sources attest to Sophocles' good looks, his easygoing manner, and his enjoyment of life. Athanaeus' multivolume *Deipnosophistai*, a compendium of gossip and dinner chat about and among ancient worthies, includes several vivid passages that reveal Sophocles as both a commanding presence and an impish prankster, ready one moment to put down a schoolmaster's boorish literary criticism and the next to flirt with the wine boy.

Sophocles is also convincingly described as universally respected, with amorous inclinations and intensely religious qualities that, to his contemporaries, did not seem incompatible. Religious piety meant something quite different to an Athenian than the humility, sobriety, and aversion to sensual pleasure it might suggest to us—officially, if not actually. His involvement in various cults, including one dedicated to a god of health and another to the hero Herakles, contributed to his reputation as "loved by the gods" and "the most religious of men." He was celebrated—and worshipped after his death as a hero—for bringing the healing cult to Athens. It is possible he founded an early version of a hospital. He never flinched from portraying the Greek gods as often wantonly cruel, destroying innocent people, for instance, as punishment for their ancestors' crimes. But the gods in *Antigone*, *Oedipus at Kolonos*, and *Philoktetes* mete out justice with a more even hand.

One remarkable absence in Sophocles' own life was documented suffering of any kind. His luck continued to the moment his body was placed in its tomb. As he lay dying, a Spartan army had once again invaded the Athenian countryside, blocking access to Sophocles' burial site beyond Athens' walls. But after Sophocles' peaceful death the Spartan general allowed the poet's burial party to pass through his lines, commanded to do so, as legend has it, by the god Dionysos.

—RB & JS

Aias

ACHILLES IS DEAD

Achilles is dead. Aias, the next greatest warrior, should inherit his armor, but Agamemnon and Menelaos award it to Odysseus. Enraged, Aias sets out to kill them, but Athena deludes him into slaughtering the war spoil of the Greek army: defenseless sheep, goats, oxen, and herdsmen. When Aias realizes what he has done, his shame is irremediable. He does then what no Greek hero ever does: He kills himself.

Heroic Aias epitomizes the aristocratic ethos of the Homeric world. Sophocles' play, however, was conceived four hundred to five hundred years after Homer's time, in the challenged democratic ethos of fifth-century BCE Athens. To Athenians, Aias's life was legendary. Roughly 10 percent of the population revered him as an ancestor. Homer shows him saving the Greek forces many times over. Accordingly—an occupational hazard of Greek warriors—he's full of himself. His lack of *sôphrosunê*, the wisdom to understand and accept his own limits and those of life itself, looms huge. When realization does come, it's too late. The "savage discipline" he learned as a warrior is so ingrained it has become his nature. He cannot choose to act outside it. He may regain his honor only by killing himself. Yet when he does do that—though he had seemed to be the center of the world, the focus of everyone's consciousness, their hopes and fears—the world doesn't end. Against all expectations, the play goes on over his lifeless body, which must be dealt with.

Aias's family and his sailor warriors are regrouping, preparing the body for burial. First Menelaos and then Agamemnon intervene, both insisting the remains be left as carrion for scavengers. Teukros argues with each in turn—until Odysseus arrives and pressures Agamemnon into letting the burial proceed. The obvious question is, why was it necessary to dwell, at such extraordinary length, on the conditions of Aias's burial?

Let's go back a bit. Between Aias's death and the discovery of his body, the Chorus, divided into two search parties, stumble about, disoriented, calling out to one another. Within this 'hole in time' (literally, a historical void), the play undergoes a definitive shift in historical and ideological perspective.[1] This is confirmed by Teukros, Aias's half brother, a lesser but not insignificant version of Aias himself. His exchanges with Menelaos and Agamemnon bring the tone and concerns of the play down, ingloriously, to an earth less cosmically resonant than the one we'd started out with. On these grounds, the terms of perception become those of fifth-century Athens. The heroic era has undone itself. We have witnessed its tragic end. Why then hasn't Sophocles left it at that?

Sophocles was considered not only a great playwright, but a great teacher.[2] The philosophically and theatrically difficult heart of *Aias* is his brilliant attempt to delimit and resolve a civic and historical conundrum: how does a political system, indeed a culture, adapt to new circumstances without self-destructing? Specifically, how does it make the transition from a monarchical/aristocratic tribal structure, in which the lives of all depend on heroic, bigger-than-life individuals, into an electoral republic sustained by the *inter-dependence* of all—who are not mythic but life-sized, yet who still bear the strains of ancient heroic values? How may this intensely but incompletely democratized culture honor the individualistic heroic legacy that never ceases informing it?[3] There are no final answers, nor is this the only way to frame the issues. Nonetheless, it is concerns of this order that drive the plot of *Aias*.

Aias is caught in the wrong kind of war. Objective conditions have changed; he cannot. Everyone has depended on him for their survival: family, his retinue of Salaminian marines, the Greek forces and their commanders. All have needed him to be a tower of strength—his brutishness not a flaw but, rather, crucial to his heroic stature. He has held the battle line when no one else could. Yet circumstances have rendered his *aretê* (his particular valor) obsolete. The war has become a quagmire. Now it's not the broad-shouldered who are needed, but those with brains—as the blunt-spoken Agamemnon puts it, comparing Aias to a big ox kept on the road by a little whip. The resourceful Odysseus (whose ingenuity ultimately conceived the Trojan horse) is the hero the Greeks really need.

During the original performance—presumably after Aias's death, as the language and social perspective of the play dropped down into an antiheroic, demythifying mode—the audience reacted violently.[4] Small wonder. Imagine that audience engrossed in the fate of Aias, an Athenian cult figure. They have been empathizing with him to his bitter end. The air is still resonant with the stunning poetry of Aias's death, when suddenly—in an extraordinarily irruptive entrance—the long-absent Teukros straggles in too late to save the day. Yet more unsettling, Teukros brings with him the unbeguiled social reflexes of a fifth-century Athenian.[5] Immediately he demythifies Telamon—the legendary hero father whom Aias has spent his life trying to live up to—by exposing him as a sour, aimlessly mean old man. Teukros, like Aias, is combative and courageous, but as a 'barbarian' and a lowly archer he lacks Aias's stature. Nonetheless, in dressing down the Greek commanders he can, and does, demolish the source of their unquestioned authority. And the audience? Given the collision of once timeless myths and current realities—the jamming together of high rhetoric and muckraking plain speech—their outrage seems inevitable. Sir Francis Bacon noted that "narratives made up for the stage are neater and more elegant than true stories from history, and are the sort of thing people prefer." Sophocles' audience expected him to rework a legendary past, not challenge it with a jaundiced view from their own historical moment. Yet that's exactly what Teukros does, subjecting their mythic heritage to a perspective and concerns that are wholly contemporary, mundane, and unresolved—thereby redirecting the focus of the play away from received myth and onto the audience itself. In fifth-century Athens, the sarcasm and insults crackling the air over Aias's remains may have been more shocking than the self-contained tragedy of the mythic Aias. Some spectators,

especially aristocratic and oligarchic ones, must have felt
unease at Teukros's open contempt for the two kings.[6] Others had to have been thrilled at the over-the-top rendering
of Menelaos, the authoritarian Spartan king whom more
than a few Athenian farmers, tradesmen, and warriors must
have loved to hate. All we know for certain is that what
that audience experienced was not 'tragedy' as might be
expected—nor what a modern audience viewing tragedy
through a generalized Aristotelian lens would be looking
for—but a different *kind* of experience: a fundamentally
civic, political, ethos-challenging drama.

The shift from an aristocratic, heroic ethos to a democratic
one—tested and threatened though that might be—would seem
to suggest an overall 'narrative of progress.' Yet there is none.
Within the heroic ethos, Tekmessa, despite occasional checks,
speaks with authority. Her noble lineage, her wife/concubine
relation to Aias, and her own *sôphrosunê*, certified by the Chorus, earn her that freedom. In the relatively democratic air that
seems to sweep in with Teukros, however, she's mute. She must
defend Aias's remains as her child Eurysakes does; they are two
speechless suppliants shielding his body with their own. What
power they presume inheres, now, in their piety. Yet the social
disjunct is so striking we may be reminded that in fifth-century
Athens, where participation in the democratic polity was re-
stricted, women did not have a public voice linked to political
power.

The intrepid Teukros has humanizing depths and reso-
nances of his own, however. He knows something about
mentoring that Aias had no way to envision. Organizing the

funeral procession, Teukros says to the still speechless Eurysakes: "You too, boy, with what strength you / can muster,
and with love, put your hand / on him and help me, I need
your help / to lift your father's body . . ." (1595–1598). That
Eurysakes' help is more symbolic than actual doesn't make it
any less crucial. In contrast, all Aias himself had imagined,
by way of training or nurturing, was putting his boy's hand
into the loop of the monster shield that he alone, a giant
of a warrior, could bear the weight of. Short of that, the
most Aias could conceive of was the play world of a child
who knows neither joy nor grief—a sentimental projection
steeped in the pathos of Aias's own doomed life.

The end Sophocles envisions is neither judgment nor
justification, praise nor blame, but a social/political modus
vivendi. Nothing could be simpler, yet harder, to achieve,
though something of an answer does come from Odysseus
when he feels pity for the deluded, blood-smeared Aias,
despite the fact that Aias has tried to kill him. Later, the
dead Aias no longer a threat, Odysseus again emphasizes
that their commonality as human beings, whose lives are
as "shadows in passing," runs deeper than personal differ-
ences or antagonisms.[7] Consequently, when Agamemnon
grasps at reasons to prevent Aias's burial, Odysseus brushes
them aside. He won't bargain that commonality away. Assuming the authority vested in him by the award of Achilles' armor, Odysseus says to Agamemnon: "However you
put it [*explain it, justify it*], you'll do what is right" (1553).
Though diplomatically posed as a statement of fact, in
context this has the force of a warning. 'Right' means not

what is expedient, but what human beings *as* human beings ought to do. "One day," Odysseus says, "I will have the same need" (1549), thus presuming a socially vested self-interest.

How might this outlook translate into our own world? It was said by Irishman John O'Leary, who had reason to say it: "There are things a man must not do to save a nation."[8] A nation (a society, a culture, a tribe, an army, a *polis*) must have some basis in universally applicable principle; otherwise it's a pit of expediency. Some things are sacred, we say, meaning there are acts one must not commit: like torture. More horrific than 'murdering' defenseless domestic animals, as Aias does, is torturing them, which he also does. More issues and realities are aired in *Aias* than are raised here. Let's just say the play in its entirety hovers uneasily over grounds such as these, grounds no less sacred in this world than in that of fifth-century Greece.

—JS

NOTES

1. The palpable disorientation of the Chorus's search parties, looking to save Aias from himself, is prefigured by the play's opening scene, which has been characterized as "a most unusual dumb show" (Taplin, 40; Hesk, 41). Greek tragedies do not begin as pantomime. Nonetheless, there's Odysseus, in the obscure stillness of early morning, trying to distinguish Aias's tracks from a muddle of others—looking not to

save Aias but to ascertain if he really is the warrior, as suspected, who has slaughtered the livestock, the unsorted war spoil, that is (was) the common property of the entire Greek army.

2. "If we may paraphrase a famous quotation from Shelley and turn it on its head, early Greek poets from Homer (*c.* 700) to Pindar (518–446) were the 'acknowledged legislators of the word.' They were not just arbiters of elegance and taste but articulators, often controversially so, of ideologies and moral values. . . . A very special class of poets is constituted by the writers of Athenian tragedy. . . . Theirs could be an explicitly didactic genre though necessarily an indirect, analogical medium for commenting on current political affairs or ideas, since with very rare exceptions tragedy's plots were taken ultimately from the 'mythical' past of gods and heroes." —Paul Cartledge, *Ancient Greek Political Thought in Practice*

"The fifth century Athenians . . . considered the problem of the state and the basis of its authority . . . These things were discussed and debated both before and after the coming of the sophists; and we catch echoes of these debates in great literature—in Herodotus, naturally, and in the speeches of Thucydides, but also in the *Eumenides* of Aeschylus, the *Antigone* of Sophocles. It could be that the *Ajax* [*Aias*] is an important document for a transitional period of Greek thought." —R. P. Winnington-Ingram, *Sophocles: An Interpretation*

3. This "incompletely democratized culture" was nonetheless more thoroughly democratic than any modern democracy. The *dêmos*, the common people, had something of a handle or grip (*kratos*) on power, not least because their political engagement was relatively hands-on—actively participatory, rather than mediated through layers of putative representatives, though in time their democracy, like ours, also functioned as an empire.

4. Herbert Golder, *Introduction to Aias* (Oxford University Press, 1999).

5. As a barbarian, an outsider, Teukros looks on heroic Greek self-mythification with a colder, more realistic eye than most 'natives' might be predisposed to. In certain respects this applies as well to Tekmessa, another barbarian.

6. Though Menelaos and Agamemnon are brother kings sharing command of the Greek forces, Sophocles goes out of his way to cast them in distinct political roles: Menelaos, though noble, expounds an oligarchic politic, whereas Agamemnon, the superior of the two, bases his authority on his spectacularly sordid 'noble' lineage. (As the fifth century wore on, antidemocratic opposition coming from those of noble birth was taken up, increasingly, by the oligarchs—landowners who were not *aristoi* but who wanted special privileges in a polity of 'rule by the few.' Some strategically minded oligarchs would also try to make common cause with the *dêmos* against the nobles.) For the most part, democracy was not called *dêmokratia*, which could mean anything from "people power" to "mob rule." To forestall negative interpretations, the defenders of democracy preferred to call it *isonomia*, "equality before or under the law."

7. Greek ethos held that one must 'help friends, harm enemies.' Sophocles challenges this not only through Odysseus but through Aias himself, who concludes, with strikingly disabused *sôphrosunê*, that friends and enemies change over time. "I know, now, to hate my enemy / as one who may later be a friend. / My friend I'll help out just enough— / he may, one day, be my enemy" (829–832). Ironically, Odysseus and Aias together constitute a formidable critique of what was, even in fifth-century Athens, a seemingly unchallengeable ethos.

8. John O'Leary (1830–1907). An early member of the Irish Republican Brotherhood and editor of *The Irish People*. Imprisoned for nine years by the British, after which he went into exile in Paris. Praised by W. B. Yeats for his "moral genius," in particular because O'Leary would not allow any special pleading about the needs of a nation (i.e., the need to establish a free Irish state) to blur the outlines of good and bad, whether in action or in literature.

Aias

Translated by James Scully

*Coast of Troy. Murmurous surf. In the obscure silence of early morning,
ODYSSEUS is tracking, pausing over, footprints in the sand. Behind him
the peak of a tent, made of hides, shows above the gated walls of AIAS's
compound.*

VOICE OF ATHENA

Odysseus! Every time I see you
     you're out! getting
the jump on your enemies.

ATHENA appears. ODYSSEUS hears but cannot see her.

Now you're nosing around the tents
Aias and his sailors pitched
here, at the edge of the sea
where all is saved or lost.
     You're looking to see
which tracks are *really* fresh,
whether he's in there or still   10
out here somewhere.
Well, go no further. Your nose
like a Spartan foxhound's
has led you to the right place.

You needn't sneak around to see
what's up. He's in there all right,
dripping sweat and blood spatter
     from his head
and his sword-slashing hands.

Speak. Why are you after him?   20
You might learn something
from one who knows.

ODYSSEUS
Athena? Really? No god
comes nearer my heart than you!
I can't see you but in my mind
I know you, your voice
sounds *through* me

like a bronze-mouthed trumpet!
You're right. I've been closing in
on an enemy: Aias   30
with his monster shield.
It's he, and no other, I'm tracking.
Last night he did something unthinkable.
Or maybe he did. I'm not sure.
We're all still confused.
        I took it on myself
to get to the bottom of this.

Just now at dawn we found
all our war spoil: cattle, sheep, oxen,
even the herdsmen guarding them,   40
butchered! Every last one.
We all think we see in this
the heavy hand of Aias.
Someone saw him charging across
the field, all by himself, swinging
his sword spraying blood.
A lookout reported this to me.
Right away I picked up the trail.
Still, the tracks are mucked up.
Some are his. The rest,   50
who knows?

You got here just in time.
I've always counted on you
to set me straight.

ATHENA

Odysseus, don't I know that?
     For some time now
I've been keeping an eye out,
helping you along.

ODYSSEUS

I'm on the right track then?

ATHENA

Absolutely. He did it.   60

ODYSSEUS

It's crazy. What got into him
he'd do a thing like that?

ATHENA

    MAD!
He felt *he* should be awarded
the armor of Achilles.

ODYSSEUS

But why take it out on *animals*?

ATHENA

He thought the blood smearing his hands
was *your* blood.

ODYSSEUS

This was murder meant for *us*?

ATHENA

He'd have gotten you, too,   70
if I hadn't been watching out.

ODYSSEUS

How did he dare think
he'd get away with it?

ATHENA

By coming up on you
alone, under cover of darkness.

ODYSSEUS

How close did he get?

ATHENA

Near as the flaps
on your commanders' tents.

ODYSSEUS

So close? And bloodthirsty?
What stopped him?   80

ATHENA

I did! I took his own
rush of horrible joy
it was incurable
and spun him round in it!
He couldn't see straight,
hacking at cattle, at sheep,

in the milling pool
of unsorted war spoil, cracking
spines in a widening apron
of blood and carcasses.   90
He thought he'd grabbed
with his own hands
the sons of Atreus—and plunged on
slaughtering one warlord after another,
me drawing him on, entangling him
deeper in misery.
He broke off then, arm weary.
The cattle and sheep still alive
he roped together and hauled
back to his camp here   100
as though they were men! not
beasts with horns and hooves.

He's in there now, torturing them.
See this sickness for yourself.
Then you may tell the Greeks
what you have witnessed.

ODYSSEUS *looks to slip away.*

Wait! right . . . there.
He can't hurt you now.
I'll make sure the light of his eye
won't find you.   110

YOU IN THERE, AIAS! Stop
hog-tying your captives.
Come out here!

ODYSSEUS

Athena, what are you *doing*! Don't.

ATHENA

Shsh! You want to be called a coward?

ODYSSEUS

God no. Just . . . let him be.

ATHENA

Why? He's the same man he was, isn't he?

ODYSSEUS

Exactly. And still my enemy.

ATHENA

(teasing, testing)
To gloat over your enemy,
what could be sweeter?   120

ODYSSEUS

I'm happy just letting him stay there.

ATHENA

Afraid to look a madman in the eye?

ODYSSEUS

If he wasn't mad, I would. Face him.

ATHENA

You could stick your face in his
he still wouldn't see you.

ODYSSEUS

Why not? He still sees with the same eyes.

ATHENA

Open and shining as they are
I'll darken them.

ODYSSEUS

Gods make anything the way they want.

ATHENA

Quiet then. Don't move.   130

ODYSSEUS

I have a choice? I wish
I were somewhere else.

ATHENA

AIAS! Still don't hear me?
ME!? Your comrade-in-arms!

AIAS comes out: blood-smeared, bloody whip in hand.

ATHENA, invisible to ODYSSEUS, is visible to AIAS. ODYSSEUS, in turn, is invisible to AIAS.

AIAS

Greetings, Athena, daughter of Zeus!
You've backed me to the hilt
and yes! on your temple I will hang
trophies of solid gold!

ATHENA

    That's . . . nice.
But tell me: you plunged your sword   140
deep into the blood of the Greek army?

AIAS

That I did. I don't mind saying.

ATHENA

And drove your spear into the sons of Atreus?

AIAS

Never again will those two
dishonor Aias.

ATHENA

You mean they're dead.

AIAS

Yes, dead! That's the last time
they'll rob *me* of Achilles' armor.

ATHENA

I see. And Laertes' son, Odysseus,
what about him? He got away?   150

AIAS

That foxfucker you ask *me*
about *him*?

ATHENA

Yes. Odysseus. The one who's always
standing in your way.

AIAS

Hah! My lady, of all my prisoners,
he's *the* best. In there in chains.
I'm keeping him alive, for now.

ATHENA

For what? What more can you want?

AIAS

First I'll chain him to a post . . .

ATHENA

Poor man! Then what?   160

AIAS

. . . whip the living skin off his back.
Then kill him.

ATHENA

Torture? Do you really have to?

AIAS

Anything else, Athena, you'd have your way.
But *that* one gets what's coming to him.

ATHENA

Well, whatever pleases you,
do it.

AIAS

Right. I've work to do. But
you, be sure to watch my back
the way you did last night.   170

AIAS goes back inside the camp compound.

ATHENA

You see, Odysseus, how powerful
the gods are? Have you ever known
a man more prudent, yet readier
to step up in a crisis?

ODYSSEUS

Never. Yet I feel his wretchedness.
My enemy, yes, but caught up
in a terrible doom. My doom, too.
I see that now. All we who live, live
as ghosts of ourselves. Shadows in passing.

ATHENA

Then think on that, and watch yourself.   180
Never challenge the gods. Don't
puff yourself up when you beat someone
at something, or when your wealth piles up.
In the scale of things, one day lifts
humans up, another brings them down.
The gods love those who take care
but abhor those who cross them.

ATHENA vanishes. ODYSSEUS leaves. The CHORUS comes on, agitated.

LEADER

Son of Telamon, rock of Salamis
towering up from the crashing sea,
        when you do well   190
our hearts surge with joy—
but when Zeus comes down on you,
when Greek rumors come after you,
        we're flustered, like doves
with a quick, scared look!

CHORUS

(severally)

Loud whispers from the dying night
        shame us. They say you tore
across the meadow through sheep
and cattle, the horses
        wild-eyed, panicked!   200

as you with your flashing sword
slaughtered the unsorted war spoil of the Greeks.

These whispers Odysseus
        slips into everyone's ear.
And they believe him! Each one who hears
makes more of it than the one before. It's all
        too believable! They're getting a belly laugh
making a mockery of you.

Sure. Set sights on the man who's bigger than life,
        you can't miss.   210
But say stuff about me, who'd listen?

It's only the great they envy after.
Yet we, down here, can't all by ourselves
like a tower
        defend the walls of a city.
We're better off working with them: the great
depend on us, we depend
on one another.

But fools too thick to learn these truths
understand nothing, they go *on* about you—   220
        what can *we* say
unless you back us up?

LEADER

Out of your sight they chatter like a flock
of noisy little birds—but if you'd just
show yourself! then
                as when the huge
bearded vulture shadows them
suddenly
they'd shrink away. And shut up.

CHORUS

(severally)

That *mother* of a rumor   230
        shames us!
Was it Artemis riding a bull
—or what—
        drove you against
cattle that belonged to everyone?
She helped you win some victory
        or take down a stag
and you gave nothing back?
Or has the bronze-armored War God
you fought side-by-side with   240
        as if he didn't exist
schemed against you in the night?

Aias, in your own right mind
you'd never go so far astray
you'd attack a bunch of cattle.
        It could be

the gods deranged you. But if so
may Zeus and Apollo run these rumors off.

Or if the god-almighty kings are spreading lies
or the bastard son of that hopeless race of Sisyphos   250
        Odysseus is hissing insinuations
don't sit and sit there brooding in your tent
backed against the sea: call them on it!

LEADER

Stand up for yourself!
You've been holed up too long,
        battle fatigued.
Out here the flames of your ruin
lick at the very heavens.
The arrogance of your enemies
        is a wind-whipped firestorm   260
roaring, tongues run amok with insults
and mockery, while we're stuck
in anguish here.

*TEKMESSA emerges from the compound. The gate is left open, exposing the
tent front with its flaps closed.*

TEKMESSA

Shipmates of Aias, blood brothers of Athens,
you who cherish the house of Telamon
        so far away—
now is time for grief! Aias our rock,

our savage giant of a man gritting out everything
is down, dumbstruck. A raging
storm roils his mind!   270

LEADER

Day is backbreaking enough.
                    And night was worse?
O daughter of the Phrygian Teleutas,
by war he brought you to bed
and has loved you ever since—
          you must know
something you could tell us.

TEKMESSA

How speak the unspeakable?
Madness in the night gripped him
          like death—   280
the glory of our great Aias
          it's gone!
There . . . awful things in there.
Carcass corpses, blood-drenched offerings
by his own hand slaughtered!

CHORUS
(severally)
The way you talk about this fire-hardened warrior
we can't stand it!
                    Or get past it.
With Greeks spreading the same rumor

            this looms *huge*.   290
I dread what's next. If his crazed hand
        his dark gleaming sword
slaughtered all together, the cattle with the men
                riding herd on them
he'll die, for all to see, in shame.

TEKMESSA
So that's where he got them!
Some he drags in, slams down,
        cuts their throats.
Others he breaks their backs.
Then he goes after two white-footed rams,   300
cuts the head off one, then
        the tip of its tongue.
And throws it all away!
The other he ties to a pillar
upright, the forefeet up,
grabs a leather harness, doubles it
        and lashes out.
The whip hisses, he's screaming
        curses so awful
no man could think them.   310
It must be a god
came wailing *through* him.

CHORUS
(severally)
Time to pull something over our heads

and steal away quick afoot
> or by ship
on benches pulling on banks of oars
> > go . . . *some*where!
The sons of Atreus so threaten us
we could be stoned to death
> *with* him   320
—caught out in *his* fate—
if we stand by him.

TEKMESSA

No that's past! That lightning crash.
Now is soft southerly breeze
> after bloody rampage.
Now is worse harrowing pain.
He sees what he has done to himself
> all by himself—
nothing eats deeper than that.

LEADER

Then we might pull through this.   330
Bad things seem less bad once they're over.

TEKMESSA

Would you harm your friends to lighten
your own life? Or, as a friend to friends,
share their grief?

LEADER

Lady, grief on grief is worse.

TEKMESSA

His madness gone, then, makes it worse.

LEADER

How so?

TEKMESSA

When he was rapt in bloody fantasy
he was happy! For us, it was horrible.
Now it's over. He's stopped, seen what he's done,   340
and dropped down in despair.
For us it's *still* horrible. Isn't this then
twice as bad?

LEADER

You're right. He's been struck
    by a god.
How else explain he's no happier now
than when his mind wasn't his own?

TEKMESSA

Exactly.

CHORUS

But how did this madness
    fly down on him,   350
tell us! We hurt too.

TEKMESSA

Then I'll tell you what I know.

In the dead of night, when the night-lighting
    torches had burnt out
he went for his double-edged sword
and was slipping out toward the dark
    deserted paths. For nothing.
"Aias!" I called, "what *are* you doing?
There's been no messenger, no trumpet, they're all
asleep out there!" All he said was that old   360
catchphrase: "Woman, silence
    becomes a woman."
I stopped. And said no more.

He'd already gone out alone.

What happened out there, I can't say.
He came back hauling captives
    all roped together:
bulls, sheep dogs, bleating sheep.
Some he hung upside-down
    and cut their throats.   370
Some he broke their spine.
Still others he tied up and tortured
like they were men!

Next I know he bolts outside
talking crazy to something crossing
    his brain out there,
struggling to get the burden of his words out
cursing the sons of Atreus, and Odysseus,

all with little snorty laughs at how much
hurt he'd done them.   380

Suddenly he's tearing back in, and then . . .
       then . . .
slowly, heavily,
    he came to his senses.
And looked. At what he'd done. The blood work.
And beat at his own head, with great
    heaving sounds
sinking down—one more wreck
among the wretched carcasses of sheep.
      And sat there,   390
fingernails digging into his hair.
A long time he didn't move. Or speak.
Then he turned. Threatened me
to tell him everything. What happened,
what had he got himself into.
My friends, I was so scared
    I told him all I knew.
And he cried! Like I never heard before!
Always he taught me only cowards
cry like that. And broken men.   400
When he grieved it wasn't shrill
but low, rolling, like the groaning
of a wounded bull.

But now he won't move: won't eat, drink,
    just sits there

among the animals his sword butchered.
Surely he's brooding on something awful.
It's there, the way he moans his agony.
Friends, that's why I'm out here.
Go in, do something. Stop him. Sometimes   410
when friends say something it helps.

LEADER

Tekmessa! From what you say
his miseries live on under his skin.

Off: stutter babble, muted. AIAS in the tent.

TEKMESSA

And worse to come. Hear it?

AIAS, louder.

LEADER

He's still mad! Or sees
what his madness has done.

AIAS

Son! My boy!

TEKMESSA

Eurysakes! He wants you!
What for? What'll I do?

AIAS

Teukros! Where's Teukros? Still off   420
on raiding parties? And me dying here?

LEADER

Sounds sane enough. *Hey in there*
          open up, come out!
When he sees us, even me, he may
out of respect for our feelings
get a grip on himself.

TEKMESSA pulls aside the tent flaps.

TEKMESSA

Here. . . . See the man
and what he has done.

AIAS exposed, steeped in his carnage.

AIAS

O O
my sailors! friends!   430
     you alone
alone stand by me still—
          look
what a storm surge of blood wrack
breaks over & around me!

LEADER

You were right. Look
how far gone he is.

AIAS

O O
comrades, old hands
who set out with oar blades   440
      blazing through water—
you alone of those who care for me
can help me.
        Come!
slaughter me with these beasts!

LEADER

Don't say that!
Evil doesn't cure evil.
You only make it worse.

AIAS

     LOOK!
at the brave warrior   450
who did not back down—
who had the courage to murder
helpless, unsuspecting beasts.
   See me
laughed at! To my shame.

TEKMESSA

Please, lord, don't talk like that.

AIAS

Still here? Go find somewhere else!
gods o gods

LEADER

For love of the gods, ease
off. Learn something.   460

AIAS

Wretched *fate* twist! to let
     those bastards
slip through my hands, and me grab
   horned bulls, noble goats,
to pour their dark blood out.

LEADER

What's done is done.
Nothing can change that.

AIAS

   You
sneaking spying agent of evil,
   Odysseus! the oiliest   470
     sleaze in the army! I know
you can't stop laughing, gloating over this.

LEADER

Who laughs or cries is for gods to say.

AIAS

Even now, broken, if I could just
set eyes on him ... *o o o o*

LEADER

Don't talk so cocky. Think
what a pit you're in!

AIAS

O Zeus father of my line
   let me just
kill the scheming sonofabitch, his two brother-kings,   480
       and die!

TEKMESSA

If that's your prayer, pray my death too.
How will I live without you?

AIAS

Aiai!
darkness
is my light:
death's shadows
the clearest illumining
left to me.
O take me take me   490

down
to live in that darkness.
I am not fit to ask
help from the gods of forever
nor goodness from men,
the creatures of a day.
Athena great goddess
torturing me
belittles me to death.
Where is a man to go?   500
Where rest?
Where? If all my glory
mortifies among these carcasses?
Where? if mad obsessed
with victory
I disgraced myself?
A whole army gathers out there
to strike me down.

TEKMESSA

Don't! I can't bear hearing such a man
        speak the words   510
he could never bring himself to speak.

AIAS

Surge
of water currents
rushing through the sea,
sea caves, sea meadows,

trees!
a long time, too long, you've kept me
here, at Troy—
but not now, not
now while I still breathe.   520
Let everyone know that.
River Skamander, so kindly unkind
to all the Greeks: this is one soldier
whose face you won't see
float on your waters anymore.
I don't mind saying, with pride,
of all the Greek army
Troy has not seen such a warrior
as this
dishonored in the dirt of earth.   530

CHORUS

This is horrible. What can we do?
Stop you? Let you go on? How?

AIAS

Aiai! My very name, Aias
is a cry in the wilderness.
Who'd have thought
my name would sound my life?
I really can cry out now
aiai! aiai! aiai!
my name in pieces.
I'm the man whose father won   540
the prize of prizes, the most beautiful,

fighting here. And I'm the son
who in Troy won as much,
as powerful as he—for what, to die
in disgrace among the Greeks!

One thing for sure—had Achilles himself
lived to present his own arms
to the worthiest warrior here, I alone
would have got my hands on them. But
when the sons of Atreus procured them,   550
giving them to that schemer who works
every angle there is—they brushed aside
all the victories of Aias!

Let me tell you something. If my eyes
my mind hadn't been seized, *hustled*
away from where they were headed,
that would've been the end of those two
lobbying the judges. Yet the stone-eyed
look of the unbending daughter of Zeus
just as I was about to strike them   560
made me crazy! Stained my hands
with animal blood. Now they're out
celebrating, they got away! no thanks
to me for that. When a god spellbinds
a warrior, even losers may elude him.

                    Now what will I do?
The gods hate me. The Greeks hate me.
The very plains of Troy hate me too.

Should I abandon this beachhead, leave
the sons of Atreus to go it on their own   570
and sail back across the Aegean? I should
go home! Yet how can I face my father,
Telamon? How could he stand to look at me,
stripped of every shred of honor, knowing
he himself stands crowned with glory?
How could he bear it?

              Well then
should I go up to the walls of Troy
single-handed, alone, take on
every last one and go down   580
fighting? But then the sons of Atreus
would be only too happy at that.

I must find a way to show my father,
old as he is, his son wasn't gutless.

To want to live
      longer, when longer
means only misery, is shameful.
What's the joy, day after day, taking
one step nearer, one step back from, death?
I figure the man who keeps on going   590
in hopeless hope isn't worth a damn.
If he's noble he'll live with honor
or die with it. That's all there is to it.

LEADER

Aias, no one says you're doing anything
but telling the truth. The way you feel it.
But hold on. Give your friends
a say in this.

TEKMESSA

My lord, nothing is worse than bad luck
that dooms us. My father in Phrygia
was a free man, rich and powerful,   600
yet I'm a slave. It seems that
what the gods called for
your strong hand made happen.
Even so, now that I share your bed
I wish you well—and I beg you
by Zeus who guards our hearth,
don't leave me to your enemies'
contempt, don't let them get
their hands on me!

The day you die, I'm alone.   610
Helpless. The Greeks
will drag me off, your son too,
to eat whatever a slave eats.
My master, *one* of my masters,
will pelt me with shame
in a hail of stinging words:
"Look at her. Aias's whore.
He was such a big hero,

she had it so good. Now look:
all she does is shitwork."   620
They'll say that. That's how some
demon will get on me. But think
how shameful their words leave *you*
and yours . . .

           Don't do this
to your father, so painfully aged!
Don't! Not to your mother,
so old after so many years
praying night after night
you'll come home alive.   630
           Pity your son
who will pass his life without you,
brought up under the thumb
of guardians who couldn't care less.
           Think what
desolate life you're leaving us.
All I have is you. With nowhere
to turn to. Backed by fate your spear
drove through my country and left it
           gone!   640
My father too, and mother, fate took
down into Hades. What home have I
without you? What means to live?
           You're my life!
Remember me? Haven't we had joy?
A man shouldn't forget that.

One kindness breeds more kindness.
But when a man lets slip away the joy
he's had, there's nothing noble in that.

LEADER

If only you would pity her, Aias,   650
as I do, you'd commend what she says.

AIAS

Sure. I'll commend her—if
she does what I tell her to.

TEKMESSA

Aias, I will always do anything for you.

AIAS

Bring me my son. Now. I want to see him.

TEKMESSA

O. Yes, but . . . I was so afraid
I let him leave the tent.

AIAS

When I had that . . . problem? Or what?

TEKMESSA

Yes. In case he ran into you. And died.

AIAS

The way *my* fate goes, could be.   660

TEKMESSA

Well, at least I stopped *that.*

AIAS

And you did well . . . thinking ahead that way.

TEKMESSA

(stalling)

Now, how else can I help you?

AIAS

I want to speak to him. Face to face.

TEKMESSA

Yes. Servants are watching him. Near here.

AIAS

Then why *isn't* he here?

TEKMESSA

Eurysakes! Your father's calling.
Whoever's got him, bring him here.

AIAS

Not coming? Can't hear you?

TEKMESSA

They're coming! The servant . . . here they are!   670

Servant brings in boy, who holds back.

AIAS

Here! Up, up! Into my arms!
(impatient, waving the servant forward)
Fresh blood won't scare him, not if
he's truly my son. Like a colt
he has to be broken in early on
to become as his father—trained
in the savage discipline of a warrior
so that that becomes his nature.

The boy is in his arms.

                    Dear boy
may you be luckier than I was. If so, if
you're still like me, you won't do badly.   680
For now, I envy you your innocence.
You know nothing of evil. Life is sweetest
before we realize the joy of it, and the grief.
Then it will be up to you, to show
your father's enemies what you're made of
and whose son you are.

But for now, O, graze
on the fizzy air, be a child, a joy
to your mother here. And don't worry.

The Greeks won't dare   690
touch you, or shame you, not
even when I'm gone. I'll leave
Teukros to watch out for you
and bring you along,
he won't let you down

. . . except, he's far away now
hunting down our enemies.

But you, my sea warriors, comrades,
you must care for him too!
Tell Teukros it is my command   700
he take the boy back home
where he may see, and be seen by, Telamon
          and my mother, Ereboia,
to ease them in old age as they go down
into the kingdom of darkness.
And tell Teukros my weapons are not
prizes to be handed out by judges
at war games—not for the Greeks,
not for the one who is destroying me!
(to EURYSAKES)
Look, this is for you, Eurysakes,   710
this shield gave you your name.
Take it. There's *seven* layers of oxhide,
no spear can pierce it. Here, grab hold
by the braided leather loop. Like so.

The other arms and armor will be
buried with me.
(to TEKMESSA)
Quick. Take the child inside.
Batten everything down. No crying!
Women are always doing that.
Shut the opening, *now*!   720
A wise doctor doesn't chant prayers
when the only cure is the knife.

LEADER

Why the mad rush? I don't like this.
Your words are too edgy.

TEKMESSA

Aias, my lord, what are you thinking to do?

AIAS

Don't ask. Just, get hold of yourself.

TEKMESSA

I'm petrified! For the gods' sake,
for your child, don't leave us!

AIAS

Don't worry at me! Don't you know
I no longer owe the gods anything.   730

TEKMESSA

Please! Don't say that!

AIAS

 Save your breath.

TEKMESSA

Won't you listen?

AIAS

 I've heard enough.

TEKMESSA

Lord! I'm afraid!

AIAS

(to servant, indicating the tent flaps)
 Shut them! Now!

TEKMESSA

For the gods, give a little!

AIAS

 Isn't it foolish to think
you can teach me, now, to change my nature?

*The tent flaps are closed over him. TEKMESSA and EURYSAKES retreat into
the compound. The gates are pulled shut behind them.*

Fabulous Salamis, you must be there   740
still
sparkling above the raging battering sea
giving all men joy, for all time—
but I these long years
camped on the grassy slopes of Ida,
I wear down
against the day I will go down
into skincrawling, unknowable Hades.

CHORUS

(severally)

Now I come to grips
with yet more grief: 750
Aias, seized by the gods
with incurable madness.
The man you sent forth in war fever
to do brave things in war
now sits it out, ruminating lonely thoughts
his friends can hardly bear.
All his heroic deeds, his honors won,
the hateful sons of Atreus
let lie *like nothings* where they've fallen.

Think of his mother, her hair   760
white with years!
When she hears how
disease has eaten his heart

she won't cry to herself
with mournful nightingale notes
o no! o no!
she'll howl herself
inside out! beating her hands
on her breast,
tearing her gray hair out!   770

LEADER

He's better off hidden
in Hades . . . this maddened
warrior from the noblest line of warriors
who's lost touch with himself
and all he was bred for,
staggering among strange thoughts.

CHORUS

Wretched father,
not knowing yet!
How will you bear the shame of it,
to hear   780
your line, never doomed before, has ended
in Aias's ruin?

AIAS *comes out, calm, with Hektor's sword in hand.* TEKMESSA *and*
EURYSAKES *also appear.*

AIAS

Long rolling waves of time
bring all things to light

and plunge them down again
in utter darkness. There is
nothing that cannot happen.

Solemn oaths, willpower, go under.
Just now my mind was made up,
tempered, like hot iron plunged   790
into cold water. Even so I felt
the sharp edge of this same mind
soften at that woman's words.
How could I leave her
a widow? my son fatherless
among enemies . . .

        I will go down
to the cleansing pool by the great salt marsh
to wash this filth off. Get out from under
the anger Athena heaps on me. I'll find   800
some place no one passes through.
I'll dig into the earth, bury
this sword, hateful thing,
some place no one ever sees.
Let night and Hades keep it in the dark.
From the day I was given this
by Hektor, my worst enemy, the Greeks
gave me nothing but a bad time.
It's true, the old saying: *gifts
from enemies bring no good*.   810

From now on I'll know how to

give way to the gods and how
to venerate the sons of Atreus.
They give the orders. We're bound
to obey. How could it be otherwise?
Great natural forces know their place
in the greater scheme of things. So
the snowy tracks of winter melt away
before the fruit ripening into summer.
Dark night, making its rounds, makes way   820
for the white horses of day scattering light.
Savage blasts of wind die down, so as
the groaning ocean may sleep. Great
sleep itself, overcoming all, yet lets go.
It's not *sleep* binds us forever. How can
we not learn limits from that vast
natural discretion?

       I have.
I know, now, to hate my enemy
as one who may later be a friend.   830
My friend I'll help out just enough—
he may, one day, be my enemy.
Most men never find a secure
mooring in friendship.

But . . . that will all work out.
You, woman, go in and pray the gods
all my heart desires will come to pass.

TEKMESSA leaves.

And you, my friends, do me the honor
she does. When Teukros comes, tell him
to care for us. And do right by you.   840
I will go where I am going,
but soon, perhaps, you should hear
I've come through this and found
a kind of peace.

AIAS leaves.

CHORUS
(severally)
            Ooo I've got goose bumps, I'm so flat out happy
                        I could fly!
                    O Pan god Pan
                    show yourself,
                you who get the gods to dance,
                    sweep across the sea   850
            from the snow-swirling cliffs of Kyllene,
                    teach me, dance me
                the wild crazy steps of Mysia
                        and Crete
            you all by yourself taught yourself—
                    now *I* want to dance!
            And Apollo, lord of Delos, cross over
                    the waters of Ikaros,
                    kindly join me
            that I may see, face to face, your brilliance!   860

            Ares dissolves his blood-dark threat!

Zeus god Zeus
now in broad daylight our swift ships
can put to sea again!
Aias buries his pain
and goes, in good faith,
to make the sacrifice the gods require.

LEADER

Time darkens all things
and time rekindles them.
I believe anything is possible   870
now Aias no longer
feuds with, nor hates,
the sons of Atreus.

MESSENGER arrives.

MESSENGER

Friends! News! Teukros
is just back from Mysia. In camp,
by the generals' tent. He was
confronted by everybody at once.
The Greeks saw him coming
from way off. When he got near
they surrounded him, shouting insults,   880
things like *he's related to a crazy,
a traitor*—no way could he save himself
from being stoned to shreds. Suddenly
swords were out. In hand. But then
when it got to the breaking point

the elders broke it up. Everyone
calmed down. But where's Aias?
He's the one who needs to hear this.

LEADER

Just left. He's pulled himself together
with a whole new sense of purpose.   890

MESSENGER

NO!! . . . I was sent too late
or took too long getting here.

LEADER

You've done your duty, haven't you?

MESSENGER

He wasn't to be let go out.
Not till Teukros gets here.

LEADER

    Well I'm telling you
he's gone with the best intentions
to do the best he *could* do:
make his peace with the gods.

MESSENGER

That's a dumb thing to say—if there's any   900
truth in what Kalchas predicted.

LEADER

A prophecy? What *more* do you know?

MESSENGER

I know what I heard. I was there.
Some chiefs were gathered around
in conference. Kalchas got up and came
over to Teukros—gave him his hand
and steered him away, out of earshot
of the generals. He insisted Aias
be kept indoors the rest of this day,
otherwise Teukros would never see him   910
see the end of it. Kalchas himself said this.
As for Athena, her anger would end
when this day did.

       He also said,
"The gods have it in for men too
full of themselves, their bodies gotten
too big and stupid—they're only human
but think they're superhuman. Against
them, the gods are pitiless."

       His own father warned him   920
the day he left home. Reckless Aias
rushing to war. "With your spear
go," he said, "for victory! but always
only with help from the gods."
Yet Aias was cocky. Like a fool he said:

"O father, with help from the gods
a nothing could rack up victories!
I can do it without them." He *said* that.

Another time Athena was after him
to counterattack the Trojans. Bloody them.   930
He uttered, then, words too
awful to speak: "My Lady,
go, back up the other Greeks.
Where Aias stands the battle line
will not be broken through."
That did it. Brought down on him
what no one wants: the fury of Athena.
Still, if he can get through this day
with Apollo's help, we might yet
save him. So Kalchas said.   940

Teukros got right up and sent me
here with these orders for you.
But if he's gone, he's gone for good,
or Kalchas is no prophet.

LEADER
(at the compound gate)
Tekmessa! whose life is misery!
Come hear what this man says.
It cuts too close for comfort.

TEKMESSA comes out with EURYSAKES.

TEKMESSA

Haven't I had enough? Why get me out here
again—just as I was finding some relief?

LEADER

Listen. I'm afraid   950
this man has news of Aias.

TEKMESSA

You, man, out with it. Surely not . . . the worst?

MESSENGER

For *you* I don't know. I'm afraid
for Aias. Has he gone out?

TEKMESSA

Out, yes. Why? Why scare me like this?

MESSENGER

Orders from Teukros: this one day
keep Aias in his tent. Don't let him
go out alone.

TEKMESSA

Where's Teukros? Why does he say this?

MESSENGER

He just got back. He believes   960
if Aias goes out today, he'll die.

TEKMESSA

No! Where did he hear this?

MESSENGER

From Kalchas. The seer. He fears
today, for Aias, it's life or death.

TEKMESSA

AI!! Stand, friends, between me and what
follows this foul relentless luck!
You, hurry, go meet Teukros.
The rest split up, east and west, to the far
reaches of the bay. Pick up his tracks.
He deceived me. I see that now.   970
What love he had for me
he's thrown away. My child,
what am I to do? I can't just sit here.
I'll go too, long as I'm strong enough.
Everyone, let's go! We've no time to lose
finding this man who's in a rush to die.

CHORUS

We're gone almost before the words
are out of your mouth.

*CHORUS goes off in two parties. Servant takes EURYSAKES elsewhere. AIAS
on a desolate shore. A sword point sticks up from behind bushes.*

AIAS

This *killer* is set
to do what it does best.   980
If there were time to think
I'd think this the gift
of Hektor, the guest-friend
I hated most the sight of—
sticking up from the enemy earth
of Troy, its edge
fresh off the grinding stone.
I've embedded it with care
for a quick, merciful death.

I have done all I can do.   990
Now it's up to you, Zeus,
as it should be, to help me.
I ask little enough, just
a messenger to break the news
to Teukros—to be the first to pull
me up off the blood-running sword
before my enemies come running
to throw my body to the dogs
and crows. That's all I ask of you.

      From Hermes,   1000
who takes us under, I ask only
a short quick death, a soundless leap
from waking to sleep, as the sword
slips through me.

I call also
on the deathless virgins who see
all human suffering: the dread
ever-overtaking Furies.
Look how the sons of Atreus
have brought my life to a rotten end!   1010
Overcome their vile lives with vile deaths!
O Furies, let your rage drink the blood
of the whole body of the Greek army!

And you there,
Helios, chariot wheels climbing the sky,
as you pass over my homeland
pull up on your gold shimmering reins,
tell my death, my disaster, to my father
so old now, and to the luckless woman
who suckled me. Poor mother!   1020
When she hears this her wailing
will overwhelm the city. But now's
no time for tears. Time now is only
to do, and quickly.

Death, Death! look at me!
We will have words in the otherworld.
And Helios, bright day, this is the last
I will see of you. Not ever again!
O light! O holy Salamis, hearth
of my fathers, and great Athens too   1030
whose people grew up with mine,

and the springs and rivers, the very
plains of Troy, good-bye to all
who have nursed me in this life.

This is the last word Aias has
for you. The rest I will speak
only to the dead in Hades.

AIAS falls on his sword. His body is screened by the bushes. CHORUS in two parties—"hurried and disorderly" (Garvie, 209)—stumble in from opposite directions.

SEMI-CHORUS 1

> Take pains, get pain,
> pain piled on.
> Where haven't I looked?   1040
> Where have I?
> Still no sign anywhere.
> Listen! What's that?

SEMI-CHORUS 2

> Your shipmates!

SEMI-CHORUS 1

> What's the word?

SEMI-CHORUS 2

> We've covered the west.

SEMI-CHORUS 1

And . . . ?

SEMI-CHORUS 2

Nothing. Hard going.

SEMI-CHORUS 1

Nothing on the road from where the sun comes, either.

CHORUS
(severally)

If only some fisherman   1050
out fishing day and night,
or nymph from Olympus or some
stream rushing toward the Bosphoros
could shout to us they've seen
somewhere
a man of ferocious heart wandering through!

It's hard making my way
aimless,
no wind at my back,
to catch a glimpse of that fast fading man.   1060

Off: short, sharp scream.

CHORUS

From the wood! Who screamed?

Off: drawn-out howl.

Disclosure of TEKMESSA, *rising from behind the bushes that hide the body of*
AIAS. *Two parties of the* CHORUS *converge.*

CHORUS
(severally)
Tekmessa!
         His spear-gotten bride . . .
dissolved in her own cries.

TEKMESSA
Now nothing . . . left! I'm lost! My friends . . .

CHORUS
What?

TEKMESSA
Here. Aias. Fresh slaughter.
His sword buried in his body.

CHORUS
(severally)
              Nooo! We'll never get home!
                Lord you've killed us too,   1070
             your own comrades! And you,
                    poor woman.

TEKMESSA
AIAI! his very name, Aias, cries out of us!

LEADER

Who had a hand in this?

TEKMESSA

Himself alone. *He* planted the sword
he fell on. The sword stands witness.

CHORUS

(severally)

And I saw nothing!
Blind, dumb, and you by your own hand
in your own blood
with no friends to watch over you!   1080
Where now is Aias
relentless as the grief sounding his name?

TEKMESSA covers the corpse with a robe.

TEKMESSA

Don't look! I'll wrap him
in my robe. Nothing must show.
None who loved him could bear seeing
the blood gasping up through his nostrils,
darkening from the wound
his own hand opened.

Now what will I do?
Who'll lift you up? Where's Teukros?   1090
If he would just come, give

composure to his brother's corpse!
O Aias, to have from so high
come to this! Even your enemies
must to their sorrow feel it.

LEADER

It had to be, had to,
you were so thick-hearted
you had to push your fate to the bitter end.
All night long,
all day, you'd be groaning,   1100
raging at the sons of Atreus
with inextinguishable murder in your heart.
Yes, the day
Achilles' arms became a contest prize
for the best warrior,
that day began this misery.

TEKMESSA groans.

LEADER

Grief this deep stops the heart.

TEKMESSA, howling.

LEADER

I don't
wonder you cry out over and over,
you've lost so much.   1110

TEKMESSA
You imagine my life. I live it.

LEADER
Yes.

TEKMESSA
Ah child, our new overseers will put
the collar of slaves on us.

CHORUS
Shsh! It's unspeakable
how brutal the sons of Atreus
will be to you in your grief.
Pray the gods stop them!

TEKMESSA
Yet the gods had a hand in this.

LEADER
The gods' burden will break us.   1120

TEKMESSA
Athena, dread daughter of Zeus,
she concocted this. She'll do
anything for her Odysseus.

CHORUS
Sure in the darkness of his heart
that long-calculating man

has to be thrilled!
He mocks this mad frenzy,
he laughs, and with him
the sons of Atreus have a good laugh too.

TEKMESSA

Then let them laugh! *Joy* in his sorrows.   1130
They didn't miss him alive? Maybe they will
when in the thick of it they find he's gone!
Men with no sense don't know what good
they have . . . till they've thrown it away.

His death leaves more pain to me
than joy to them. His own joy is
he got what he wanted. And met his own death
on his own terms. What's for them
to celebrate? His death is between him
and the gods—and not, no way, for *them*.   1140
Let Odysseus mouth off. What was Aias
is gone. And has left me wretched.

VOICE OF TEUKROS

o god o god o aias o god

LEADER

        Quiet!
I think I hear Teukros, shouting something
awful striking the heart of this disaster.

TEUKROS appears.

TEUKROS

Brother Aias, dear familiar face,
what I hear, is it true?

LEADER

He's dead, Teukros. Know that for a fact.

TEUKROS

This falls on me!   1150

LEADER

That's it, for sure.

TEUKROS

The rashness of it!

LEADER

Yes. Let it all out.

TEUKROS

So *sudden* a doom . . .

LEADER

Sudden, yes.

TEUKROS

But his son!
Where will I find him in this *Troy*?

LEADER

Alone. In the tent.

TEUKROS

    Get him. NOW!

before our enemies bag him like   1160
a lion cub whose mother finds it gone.
Go! Hurry! Help him! Others too!
Men can't help crowing over
the dead—once they are dead.

TEKMESSA hurries off.

LEADER

While he lived, Teukros, that's exactly what
he commanded: that you watch over his son.
And you do.

TEUKROS

A worse sight I have not seen
in all my life—the road here
became the worst I ever walked   1170
when I learned, Aias, it was
your death I was on the trail of.
Word of it raced through the Greek army
like a message from the gods. It got to me
before I could get to you. Hearing it I
moaned low my wretchedness. But here
now the sight of this unnerves me

aiai!

(to sailor)

You. Uncover. Let's see the worst.

The sailor does so, behind the screen of bushes.

It's awful to see in the flesh   1180
courage this brutal. What fields of grief
your death seeds for me! Where
will I go now? Who will welcome me
who couldn't help you through this?
Naturally our father Telamon
will be all smiles when I come home
without you—that same man who,
after getting good news, is no less
sour than before. He'll curse me out
as the bastard of a captive girl, war spoil,   1190
a coward who let you down. Or charge that
calculating to get your privilege and power
I betrayed you. Overbearing, foul-tempered,
aimlessly mean old man! He'll say all that
and banish me. His words will brand me
a *slave*. That will be my welcome home.
Now enemies are everywhere, same as
in Troy. *This* your death has left me.

Now what? How can I lift you off
the acrid glint of the swordpoint   1200
that took your breath away? You see

how even in death your enemy, Hektor,
took you down?
(to sailors)
>   Look how fate
bound these two together! With the war belt
Aias gave him, Hektor was gripped
against the chariot rails and dragged,
mangled, till his life gave out. In turn,
Aias got this gift from Hektor
and fell on it.   1210

>   Wasn't this sword forged
by the Furies? And that war belt by Hades,
the savage craftsman who fashions death
for everyone? As I see it, these things
and all such always are ways the gods
set men up. Anyone who sees this otherwise,
think what you like. This thought is mine.

LEADER

Don't drag this out. Think how you'll bury
your brother—and what will you say now
that your enemy's coming up. There!   1220
He's the type that could mock us our loss.

TEUKROS

From the army? Who?

CHORUS

The Menelaos we came all this way to help.

TEUKROS

O yes. This close
there's no doubt who *he* is.

MENELAOS arrives with guards and a herald.

MENELAOS

Hey, you! Don't lift that corpse don't
even touch it! That's an order.

TEUKROS

A tall order. Why waste your breath on it?

MENELAOS

Because I say so. Our commander says so too.

TEUKROS

Then maybe you'd care to tell us   1230
on what grounds you order this?

MENELAOS

We brought him here thinking
he'd be a friend, an ally of the Greeks.
He turned out to be a worse enemy
than any Trojan. With his spear he
plotted to murder us all in the night.

If a god hadn't stopped him, it would be
our doom now to die his shameful death,
exposed to all, while he'd still be alive.
Yet the god drove his mad rage aside   1240
against cattle and sheep. Not a man alive
has the power, now, to bury him in a grave.
We'll haul the carcass out onto damp
yellow sands somewhere, for seabirds
to feed on. So don't puff yourself up
threatening us. We couldn't in life
keep him in line, but like it or not, in death
we will. He will go wherever our hands
take him, and leave him, seeing as in life
he never listened to a word I said.   1250

When a common person defies his betters
it shows he's no good. What city can thrive
where there's no fear of the law? How keep
discreet order in an army camp without
shutting it up in fear and respect? Even
a man grown gigantic, he should watch it!
One little slip, he could go down. No,
the man who lives in fear and shame
is safe. But in a city of no respect, just
insolence and willfulness, though it   1260
enjoy awhile a following wind, one day
it will go under. Fear is in order.
Why dream we can do what we want
without paying for it? One such turn

deserves another. This man flared up, all
hot-tempered and cocky. Now it's
my turn for high-and-mighty thoughts.

I warn you: bury that man, you may
bury yourself with him.

LEADER

You've set down right-minded precepts,   1270
Menelaos. Don't overreach yourself
outraging the dead.

TEUKROS

My friends, it's no surprise that a nobody
of common stock offends, in his own way,
when a supposed noble can talk such trash.

Again now. You say you brought him here
as an ally. He didn't sail here on his own?
His own master? What justifies your claim
to command him and his men? You rule
the Spartans, not us. You've no more grounds   1280
to claim power over him than he over you.
You yourself came under orders; you're not
the commander of these forces. So how is it
you command Aias?

            Lord it over those
you're lord over. Give *them* a tongue-lashing

with your big talk. I'll bury Aias the proper way
no matter what you or that other general say.
Your mouth doesn't scare me. Aias didn't, like
those poor bastards in the ranks, come here   1290
to get you your wife back. He came
because of an oath he'd taken. Not for you.
He wouldn't go to war for the shell of a man.
Next time you come here bring more heralds,
bring the commander in chief! Make
all the racket you want. As long as you are
what you are, I wouldn't bother to notice.

LEADER

Again insulting words! On top of all this?
I don't like it. Even if they *are* called for.

MENELAOS

The archer, far from blood dust, thinks he's something.   1300

TEUKROS

I'm very good at what I do.

MENELAOS

How you'd brag . . . had you a shield.

TEUKROS

Barehanded I'd match *you* in *all* your armor.

MENELAOS

Your courage is all in your mouth.

TEUKROS

A righteous cause is my courage.

MENELAOS

What? It's right to defend my killer?

TEUKROS

Your killer!? You're dead? And still alive?

MENELAOS

A god saved me. But he *wanted* me dead.

TEUKROS

If the gods saved you, why disrespect them?

MENELAOS

How do I disrespect the gods?   1310

TEUKROS

By forbidding the burial of the dead.

MENELAOS

This was our enemy. It's right to forbid him rest.

TEUKROS

Did Aias ever *really* confront you as an enemy?

MENELAOS

We hated one another. You know that.

TEUKROS

Sure. He knew you rigged the vote against him.

MENELAOS

The judges made that ruling. Not me.

TEUKROS

You'd put a straight face on any crooked scheme.

MENELAOS

Talk like that could get someone hurt.

TEUKROS

Not us more than you.

MENELAOS

One last time. He will not be buried.   1320

TEUKROS

I'm telling you. He will.

MENELAOS

I saw, once, a real blowhard make
his crew sail into a spell of bad weather.
When the storm broke, you wouldn't have heard
a peep out of him, scrunched under his robe,
not daring to breathe a word with the crew

running round stepping all over him. So
you. One little cloudburst may set off
a monster storm that will drown you out.

TEUKROS

Me too. I once saw a fool so full   1330
of himself, he made fun of others' misery.
It happened a man like me, the way I feel
it could be me, said something like
"Man, don't disrespect the dead. You do,
you will pay for it." To his face said it,
the face of the fool standing before me now,
Menelaos. How's that for talking double-talk?

MENELAOS

I'm leaving. It would be shameful if anyone knew
I, with so much power, stooped to quibble with you.

TEUKROS

Then get! Shame is in standing still   1340
blasted by hot air from a fool.

MENELAOS and Attendants leave.

LEADER

A big fight for sure. And soon.
Move, Teukros! Find a hollowed-out spot,
some moldy darkness men will hold
famous forever as his tomb.

TEKMESSA reappears with EURYSAKES in hand.

TEUKROS

Just in time, his wife and son are here
to perform the burial rites.

          You, boy, come here.
Stand by the father who gave you your life.
Press your hand on him, clutching locks of hair: 1350
mine, your mother's, your own.
The suppliant's power that is stored there
will go under with him. And if anyone
comes from the army to pull you away,
damn him, let *him* lie unburied out
in nowhere, his people cut off at the roots
the way I cut this lock. Take it. Let no one
move you. Hold on to him. *Don't let go.*

And you, don't stand around like women
but as men! Keep close. Defend him   1360
until I return, after I've made a grave
for this man, no matter who forbids it.

TEUKROS leaves.

CHORUS
(severally)

      When, when will these wandering years
        add up to something, anything

to put an end
to this spear-driving backbreaking work
on the plains of Troy
whelmed in the shame and sorrow of the Greeks.

He should have been sucked up into the sky
or plunged into the black hole   1370
of ever open Hades—
the man who taught Greeks
to combine forces with hateful arms
for making war,
exhaustion reviving exhaustion
to kill men.

The thrill of myrtle garland
brimming shallows of wine bowls
sweet crescendos of flutes
all that that man has taken from me,   1380
taken my sleep
and love making love into the night.
I'm left out here, who cares?
my hair sopping wet, sodden with night dew,
never to let me forget
I'm here, in miserable rotten Troy.

Was a time massive Aias held off
nightmares, and waves of arrows.
Now he is given up
to the brute demon that pursued him.   1390

                    Ahead
                what joy can I see?
            O to be blown homeward
        to the wooded headland towering up
                over the beating sea.
                To sail! under the high
                tableland of Sounion
        hailing all praise to blessed Athens.

TEUKROS returns.

TEUKROS

Watch it! I hurried back seeing
Agamemnon's almost here! For sure   1400
he'll be running off at his mindless mouth.

AGAMEMNON enters, followed by MENELAOS and Armed Attendants.

AGAMEMNON

You there! With the big mouth insulting us.
Think you'll get away with it? Yes, you.
Son of a slave. To think how you'd strut
and sound off if your mother were well-born—
nobody that you are, standing up for
something that's a nothing. And to claim
we have no authority, on land or at sea,
to command you—that Aias sailed here
as his own chief! Dangerous talk,   1410
coming from a slave.

Your great man,
where did he go, where stand, that I did not?
Was he the only man in the Greek army?
It may be we'll regret the day we held
a contest for Achilles' armor—if Teukros
denounces us because he won't accept
the judges' decision, a clear majority,
but keeps backstabbing, tearing us down
the way lowborns do. What laws would hold up   1420
if we overruled judges, replacing the winners
with losers? This has to be stopped.
It's not the burly broad-shouldered who
come out on top, but those with brains.
A big strong ox is kept on the road
by a little whip. You may get some of that
yourself, if you don't listen to reason.
You, who are so insolent defending
a shadow man.

Get hold of yourself,   1430
Teukros, know your place. A free man's
qualified to plead your case. Go find one.
I can't understand your barbarian babble.

LEADER

You should both be sensible.
That's the best I can tell you.

TEUKROS

(turning his back on AGAMEMNON)

Wonderful! That's gratitude for you. You're
dead, and gratitude has turned tail: a traitor.
This man hasn't one word to say for you
Aias, the man you fought for at spear
point . . . put your life on the line for.   1440
It's all gone. Tossed off.

(wheeling round to face AGAMEMNON)

      . . . And you!
going on and on, glib and mindless: you don't
recall backing across the ditch, falling behind
your barricades? You, down to nothing?
Aias only, all alone, came to save you!
With flames leaping up over the sterns
roiling the decks, Hektor striding the ditch
bounding over barricades toward the ships,
and who stopped him? Wasn't this the work   1450
of one who, you say, went nowhere but
where you went too?

      You won't admit
he served you honorably? Not when he fought
Hektor hand-to-hand? Not that he had to.
He cast his own lot into the plumed helmet.
Not wet clay that breaks up, either, but baked
hard and light, so it could rise to the top
when the helmet was shaken up.

That's who *he* was.   1460
And I stood with him. Me, the slave,
the son of a barbarian mother.

Where are you looking? at what?
to go on this way? You don't know
your father's father, old Pelops, was born
a Phrygian barbarian? Atreus who
fathered you fed his own brother a meal
so ghastly—his brother's own children!
Your own mother, a Cretan woman,
was caught by her own father in bed   1470
with a slave! For that he ordered her
drowned in the silence of fishes. That's
where *you're* from. And you talk about
my origins? I
am the son of Telamon. My mother
is royal blood, born of Laomedon. She,
the most precious war spoil, was awarded
to Telamon by Herakles himself,
son of Alkmene. I, as the son
of two such noble parents, cannot   1480
dishonor this man, my own blood,
who died so badly—while you, shameless
would throw his body away unburied.

Now hear this. Wherever you dump him
you'll have to dump our three bodies, too.
There's more honor dying for him

out here, for all to see, than lost in war
for your wife. Or was it your brother's wife?
Watch out! For yourself, not me.
One move toward me you'll wish   1490
you *had* been a coward.

ODYSSEUS *arrives.*

LEADER

Lord Odysseus, just in time! *If* you mean
to loosen this knot, not yank it tighter.

ODYSSEUS

What's going on, my friends? Way back there
I could hear the sons of Atreus shouting over
this brave man's corpse.

AGAMEMNON

Only because, Lord Odysseus, we've been hearing
outrageous rant from this man here.

ODYSSEUS

Outrageous? How so? I'd make allowance
for a man who answers insults with outrage.   1500

AGAMEMNON

I insulted him all right. For acting against me.

ODYSSEUS

O? How did he wrong you?

AGAMEMNON

He says he won't let this corpse lie there,
he'll bury it. To defy me.

ODYSSEUS

As a friend, may I speak the truth
yet keep rowing in time with you?

AGAMEMNON

Of course. I'd be foolish to say no.
Of all the Greeks, you're my greatest friend.

ODYSSEUS

Listen. Keep faith with the gods. Don't,
so coldly, throw this man out exposed   1510
naked to the world. Don't let the violence
so seize you with hate, you crush
justice under your foot. To me, too,
he was an enemy, the worst in the army,
from when I won Achilles' armor.
Yet despite that, I had to admit,
of all the Greeks who came to Troy, none
could equal him. Except Achilles.
There's no justice in disrespecting him,
you can't hurt him more—but you could   1520
break the everlasting law of the gods.
It's horribly wrong to harm a brave man
when he's dead. However much you hate him.

AGAMEMNON

You, Odysseus? Side with him against me?

ODYSSEUS

I do. Yet hated him

when it was honorable to hate.

AGAMEMNON

Then why not step on him, now he's dead?

ODYSSEUS

O son of Atreus, what honor is there

gloating over such a triumph?

AGAMEMNON

For the ruler, it's hard to show piety.   1530

ODYSSEUS

It's not hard to respect friends

who give him good advice.

AGAMEMNON

A loyal man defers to those who rule him.

ODYSSEUS

Easy now! You have the best of it

when you listen to your friends.

AGAMEMNON

Think what man you're standing up for!

ODYSSEUS

That man was my enemy. But a noble one.

AGAMEMNON

What's that mean? Respect a dead enemy?

ODYSSEUS

Yes. His greatness weighs more with me
than our enmity.   1540

AGAMEMNON

The man changes *like that*.

ODYSSEUS

Many men are friends. Then enemies.

AGAMEMNON

You approve such men as friends?

ODYSSEUS

I wouldn't approve an obstinate one.

AGAMEMNON

You'll have us looking like cowards.

ODYSSEUS

No. All Greeks will see us
as brave, and just.

AGAMEMNON

You're saying I should let them bury him.

ODYSSEUS

Yes. One day I will have the same need.

AGAMEMNON

So. In all things man works for himself.   1550

ODYSSEUS

Of course. Who else?

AGAMEMNON

Then this will be your doing, not mine.

ODYSSEUS

However you put it, you'll do what is right.

AGAMEMNON

For you I will do this—and would do
much more, believe me. But *him*,
as in life, so in the shadows below,
I hate. Do what you want with him.

AGAMEMNON, MENELAOS, and Armed Attendants leave.

LEADER

Whoever says you weren't born wise
in your very bones, Odysseus, is a fool.

ODYSSEUS

If I may . . . I want to tell you   1560
Teukros: much as I was his enemy,
now I'm ready to be his friend.
I want to help you bury the dead,
to share your concerns—do what
is necessary, and right, to honor
this towering man among men.

TEUKROS

Noble Odysseus, I salute you for this.
I misjudged you, completely. Of all the Greeks
his worst enemy, you were the only one
to come forward and stand up for him.   1570
You hadn't the heart, here, to heap
the insults of the living on the dead—
unlike that mad, arrogant commander,
him and his brother, who'd filthy up
the corpse rather than bury it. For that
may Zeus, lord of Olympos, and the
unforgetting Furies, and Justice that puts
an endpoint on everything . . . doom them
to the abomination they wished on him.

Except, son of old Laertes, I'm afraid   1580
I can't let you prepare, or touch, the body.

That might offend the dead. Help in
any other way is welcome, though.
Bring others from the Greek army.
Now I have work to do. Just know
you are, to us, a magnanimous friend.

ODYSSEUS

I'd wanted to help. But as that's your
wish, I understand. I will leave.

ODYSSEUS *leaves.*

TEUKROS

We've lost too much time. Hurry.
Some of you dig the grave, others   1590
set the tall tripod for the caldron
over the fire, ready to heat
the holy cleansing bath. Someone else
bring his body armor from the tent.
You too, boy, with what strength you
can muster, and with love, put your hand
on him, and help me, I need your help
to lift your father's body—easy now,
the warm veins are still welling
his black blood out.   1600

         Come
everyone who called him friend,
hurry!

perform this service for this man
who was as noble as they come.

Funeral procession forms.

CHORUS
What men see, they know.
But until the future arrives
no one can see it coming
nor what is in it.

ALL *leave, carrying the body of* AIAS.

Women

of Trakhis

INTRODUCTION
"YOU'VE SEEN NOTHING
THAT IS NOT ZEUS"

In Sophocles' *Women of Trakhis*, Deianeira is an ordinary woman married to Herakles, a canny and violent enforcer who carries the ideal of Greek manhood to its logical (and superhuman) conclusion. To cope with her anxiety about his labors and escapades, yet keep his affection and preserve her marriage, she tolerates his conduct. But ultimately her actions—given her predicament, plus the nature and history of her husband, the most feared and storied hero of the ancient world—destroy not only her but Herakles as well.

By the time Sophocles wrote this play, Herakles had become a widely worshipped cult figure. (As the son of Zeus and Alkmene—the mortal wife of Amphytrion of Thebes—Herakles displayed his strength and resourcefulness at an early age: he strangled two snakes sent by Zeus' revengeful goddess wife Hera to kill him in his cradle.) His reputation as a savior and benefactor of humankind swelled over centuries. Mythmakers invented countless improbable monsters and obstacles for him to overcome. But egomania and vengefulness were also part of the legend. In *Women of Trakhis*, Sophocles undermines reverential accounts of the hero's selfless service to his fellow Greeks by taking equal notice of his crimes and his brutal, deceitful, selfish acts. When Herakles finally appears, he is writhing in a robe smeared with clinging, burning, penetrating acid, yet Sophocles makes it difficult for an audience to feel sorry for him.

Deianeira is a shadowy or absent figure in the earliest versions of the Herakles myth. By making her the driving force, Sophocles succeeds in dramatizing the destructive side of his culture's fascination with hero cults and especially with Herakles himself. He creates in Deianeira one of the most sympathetic and realistic female characters in Greek drama, and presents a Herakles who, though blessed with immense strength and resourcefulness, is also egomaniacal and cruel.

As the play begins, Deianeira explains to the chorus of Trakhinian women how painful it is loving "the best" man alive. "People have a saying that goes way back," she explains. "*You don't know your own life, / whether it's good or evil—not / until it's over. Mine* I know now. / It's unlucky and it's harsh" (1–5). Deianeira has missed Herakles. She resents his latest fifteen-month absence. But until now—when she is confronted by Iole, an attractive and aristocratic young slave whom Herakles has sent ahead to become his third wife—she has tolerated his sexual conquests and his neglect. Sophocles renders, with striking realism, Deianeira's struggle to reconcile passion, devotion, and jealousy as she reacts to the girl's sudden arrival at her house. Pondering how to deal with the threat posed by Iole, Deianeira remembers a "love charm" given her by Nessus, a centaur who was attempting to rape her when Herakles pierced his chest with a poison-soaked arrow. Dying, Nessus promised that the gore from his wound, if carefully preserved, could be used to keep Herakles "from seeing and loving" anyone but her. Deianeira, having saved the gore all these years, will now rub it into a robe and have a messenger take it to Herakles as a homecoming gift. In so doing, she inflicts on him a horrible, unquenchable agony. This epitome of warrior culture is rendered helpless at the hands of a "frail woman, / born with no male strength" (1192–93). "She beat me—only she," says Herakles. "And didn't even need a sword" (1094–95). When Deianeira hears from her son Hyllos what her love potion has done to her husband, whose passion she craves and fears, she plunges a shortened sword into her heart.

Deianeira insists she has never resented her husband's other women, whose number she claims exceeds those of any other mortal. But imagining that she will sleep "under the same blanket" with Herakles and his new bride is more than she can bear. Sophocles could easily have given Iole a chance to speak for herself, thus enlivening the drama with a face-off between the two women. He chose instead to show Herakles' lover as visibly nubile but utterly intimidated, seemingly incapable of speech. In this play, as in most versions of the myth, Iole is brought to Trakhis against her will. Iole's silence and Deianeira's instinctive pity for her allows the audience to focus on the conflict between the loyal wife and the husband wedded to his own legend. The drama thus takes off on a collision course of conflicting passions, Deianeira's to keep her husband's love, and Herakles' to make his latest conquest permanent.

To fifth-century Greeks, the word *heros* (its singular form) had a meaning quite distinct from our own. We think of heroes as people who place themselves at considerable risk to accomplish something dangerous or courageous, often for the common good. The ancient Greeks, however, assumed an unusual capacity for anger and violence to be a common attribute of a *heros*, whether in myth or real life. Simply stated, the difference between our own and ancient Greek attitudes toward heroes is that we want heroic violence to be sanctioned in moral terms. A Greek *heros*' destructive conduct, however, could be appreciated as an impressive, even divine attribute. Consider Kleomedes, an Olympic boxing champion who won his title between the battles of Marathon and Salamis. Enraged and maddened because his title was stripped after his blows caused the death of his final opponent, Kleomedes pulled down the pillars of a school building, killing all the pupils inside. To escape the wrath of the dead children's families, he hid in a large trunk in the Temple of Athena but disappeared before they broke open the lid. When consulted by the townspeople about what to do next, the oracle at Delphi sardonically advised, "Honor him as a hero." To modern readers, a hero's heartless fury marks him as immoral; to the ancient Greeks, a *heros*' anger—a most privileged word and concept in Greek culture—could make him immortal.

Zeus will grant the Herakles of the *Trakhis* immortality. But before this apotheosis, the dying Herakles will evaluate his life experience. In a highly charged conversation with his son Hyllos, Herakles recounts how much it cost him to keep Greece safe from savage tribes of beasts (natural and supernatural), to perform other nasty 'Herculean' tasks for twelve years—and how little peace he has earned. As evidence of the Olympian gods' abandonment, Herakles complains that they did not protect him from Deianeira's lethal gift, nor did they allow him to take revenge on her.

Hyllos patiently explains to Herakles why Deianeira does not deserve his father's wrath:

Hyllos   You wouldn't hate her—if you knew.

Herakles Wouldn't hate her? If I knew what?

Hyllos   Her good intentions hurt you—that's the truth.

Herakles Her "good intention" to kill me?

Hyllos   When she saw the woman who's in our house,
               she used love medicine to keep you. It went wrong.

[. . .]

Herakles O what a miserable creature I am!
               I'm finished. Finished! For me
               there will be no more sunlight.   (1286–1298)

Herakles neither takes responsibility for Deianeira's jealous reaction to Iole's arrival nor expresses regret for his wife's suicide. He's obsessed with his own shame at being destroyed by a woman. Herakles then attempts to impose a set of 'labors' on his son—a series of deathbed commands he forces Hyllos to promise, and swear to Zeus, that he'll carry out. The first command orders Hyllos to transport his father to Mount Oita and burn him alive on a pyre of olive limbs. When Hyllos refuses (which the Greek audience would have attributed to the religious prohibition against kin murder), Herakles proceeds to negotiate. He agrees to let Hyllos build the pyre but find someone else—who turns out, in another play by Sophocles, to be Philoktetes—to light it. He then orders Hyllos to marry Iole.

Horrified, but compelled by his divine oath to Zeus, Hyllos
agrees. As a crew assembles to carry the mighty hero to the
mountain, Hyllos speaks a few final, rebellious words:

> Lift him up, friends. Forgive me
> for what I am about to do.
> But look at the cruelty of what
> the ruthless gods have done
> to us—the gods whom we call
> our fathers, whose children we are—
> and yet how coolly they watch us suffer.
> No one foresees the future,
> but our present is awash with grief
> that shames even the gods, and pain
> beyond anything we can know
> strikes this man who now meets his doom.
> Women, don't cower in the house.
> Come with us. You've just seen death
> and devastating calamity, but
> you've seen nothing that is not Zeus.   (1435–1450)

Hyllos expresses grief for his father's pain, but not for losing him. By condemning the cruelty of the gods—shouldn't they
treat mortals as their children, Hyllos asks, since mortals revere
them as fathers?—he implies distress at his own father's treatment of him. He concludes by blaming Zeus for the calamity
that has struck his entire family. This might not have seemed
blasphemous or impious to Sophocles' audience; the gods' cruelty and capriciousness were universally acknowledged and

accepted. But Hyllos' invocation of Zeus, and this father-god's indifference to suffering, reminds us that Zeus was in fact Herakles' father. In time, the advent of more compassionate deities caused the demise of Zeus and the other Olympians. The *Trakhis* was one of many works written in Sophocles' Athens that eventually eroded uncritical acceptance of the arrogance and violence endemic to heroic culture itself.

At the end of his life, Sophocles wrote *Oedipus at Kolonos*, setting the play on the last day of the life of aged Oedipus, a hero who possessed anger more righteous than Herakles' and whose solemn reception by the gods granted him an honor in death that had been withheld during his prime. Sophocles himself became after death a different breed of *heros* altogether, revered for receiving into Athens and very likely his own house a cult whose mission was to heal the sick.

—RB

Women of Trakhis

Translated by Robert Bagg

CHARACTERS
    DEIANEIRA, Herakles' wife
    SERVANT, a woman of Deianeira's household
    HYLLOS, eldest son of Herakles and Deianeira
    CHORUS of young Trakhinian women
    LEADER of the Chorus
    MESSENGER from Trakhis
    LIKHAS, personal herald to Herakles
    Captive Women of Oechalia
    Iole, daughter of Eurytus
    HERAKLES, heroic worker of miracles
    OLD MAN, senior aide to Herakles
    Soldiers serving Herakles

The play opens at Trakhis, in front of the house in which DEIANEIRA has been living. Its size and façade are impressive, but less than royal. DEIANEIRA and her female SERVANT enter the stage from the house.

DEIANEIRA
People have a saying that goes way back:
You don't know your own life,
whether it's good or evil—not
until it's over. Mine I know now.

It's unlucky and it's harsh.
I know this long before
I'll go down to Hades.
When I was still a girl, living
with my father in Pleuron,
marriage terrified me—like it   10
terrified no other girl in Aetolia—
because a river lusted for me, a river
named Achelous. He kept asking
Father if he could marry me,
each time in a different shape: first
a bull, next a glittering snake,
then an ox-head rising from a man's trunk,
water sloshing from his rank beard.

When I imagined marrying that creature
I was so miserable! I'd want to die   20
before I got near a bed like his.
Then, just in time, joy arrived!
The amazing son of Zeus and Alkmene
battled him and saved me. Exactly
how he won this fight I can't
tell you, because I don't know. If someone
feeling less panic than I felt was watching,
he could tell you. I sat there numb, sure
my beauty would destroy me.

But Zeus the battle god blessed the outcome—   30
if what happened was really a blessing.

Ever since Herakles won me for his bed
I've nursed one fear after another.
There's been no end to my anxiety.
Each night I imagine some new threat
which the next night's threat scares away.

Of course we had children. He sees them, sometimes,
the way a farmer tends a back field, twice
a year—sowing his seed, reaping the harvest.
That was his life: no sooner home than he's   40
back on the road, always working for this one man.

Now that he's put his labors behind him,
I'm more afraid than ever.
                                  From the time
Herakles killed that brave fighter Iphitus,
we've been uprooted, so we live
among strangers here in Trakhis.
Where Herakles is now, nobody knows. He's gone.
That's all I know. And that I ache for him.
No herald's brought news for fifteen months.
I'm all but sure he's mired in more trouble.   50

Then there's this tablet he left me.
I've prayed so often to the gods
that it wasn't meant to bring me grief.

The female SERVANT who has been listening to DEIANEIRA worry out loud
approaches and interrupts her mistress.

SERVANT

Deianeira, my lady, so many times I've quietly
watched while you've wept, suffering with you
since Herakles has been gone. But now
I've got to say—if a slave may advise
a freeborn person—what you should do.
Since you're so blessed with sons,
why not send one to find your husband?   60
Hyllos your eldest is the one to send—
if he thinks news of his father's well-being
matters to us.

                Here he comes now,
jogging up the path. If my advice
makes any sense, why not take it?

*Enter HYLLOS, breathing hard from sport or the hunt. DEIANEIRA stops him
as he runs past. SERVANT goes indoors.*

DEIANEIRA

Hyllos, my son, sometimes even a slave
knows just what to say. She wasn't
born free but speaks as if she were.

HYLLOS

Her words, Mother? May I hear them?

DEIANEIRA

Your father's been gone for so long. She thinks   70
it's shameful you haven't tried to find him.

HYLLOS

But I *do* know where he is. If you can
believe what people have been saying.

DEIANEIRA

Then why not tell me, Son. Where he's living.

HYLLOS

He slaved during last year's plowing season
—seed to harvest—for a Lydian woman.

DEIANEIRA

If he has sunk that low, we can expect
to hear much worse said about him.

HYLLOS

He's gotten clear of it now. So I hear.

DEIANEIRA

Do people say where he is? Alive, dead, what?   80

HYLLOS

They say he's attacking Euboean
territory—the kingdom of Eurytus—
or getting ready to attack.

DEIANEIRA

Did you know, Son, that Herakles left me
prophecies—ones I trust—about that very place?

HYLLOS

What prophecies, Mother? They're news to me.

DEIANEIRA

They say that he'll either be killed, or if
successful in the battle he takes on—
then he'll have peace for the rest of his days.
With his life hanging in the balance, Son,   90
won't you go help him? Our own survival
depends on his. If he dies, so do we.

HYLLOS

Of course I'll go, Mother. If I had known
how dangerous these prophecies were,
I'd be there now. But I never saw
much reason to worry. Father's luck was
never the kind that would make me anxious.
Now that I'm better informed, I will do
whatever it takes to find out the truth.

DEIANEIRA

Then go now, Son.   100
When you've searched out the truth, no matter how
late, it always works to your advantage.

*HYLLOS exits stage left on the road out of town. CHORUS enters from the
town, singing.*

CHORUS

O Sun! The Night
pulsing with stars
gives birth to you
the moment she
reddens into death.
You set, O Sun,
fire to her sky
as she lays you   110
to rest. O Sungod—
where, tell us where,
is Herakles,
Alkmene's child?
Master of flaming light,
find Herakles!
Is he edging
through the straits
of the Black Sea?
Or making landfall   120
where continents meet?
Speak to us, you who see
what no man sees.

Deianeira's heart
aches for this man.
Once a prize won in battle,
she's restless as a bird
who's lost its mate.
She can't still her desire

or stop her tears.   130
Sleepless, ravaged
by fears for the husband
who's gone, she wastes away,
alone on a manless bed,
imagining her own
miserable fate.

Just as you watch
waves surge and foam
over the open sea
under tireless winds—   140
Northwind, Southwind—
so the troubles of a life
wild as the sea off Crete
plunge Herakles under,
then lift him to greatness—
because always some god,
when Death sucks him down,
pulls him back into life.

Lady, I respect you,
but not your despair.   150
I don't think it's right
for you to let hope die.
Zeus makes sorrow a part
of whatever he gives us.
Grief and joy
come circling back

to all of us,
circling as the Bear
retraces her steps
on the starpaths.   160

For the night pulsing with stars
slows for no man, nor does wealth,
nor does pain—they all
speed through us, then they're
gone to some other man
who'll know joy and its loss.
Now I ask you, Queen Deianeira,
to ask this of yourself:
When has Zeus ever been
indifferent to one of his sons?   170

DEIANEIRA

You're here, I suppose, because you know my troubles.
But you cannot know the worry eating
my heart out. I hope you'll never
learn it by suffering what I've suffered.
As young girls we thrive in our own safe place,
where the Sungod's heat doesn't oppress us,
nor the rain nor the wind. You glory there
in your innocent life—until you marry.
Then panic attacks you night after night—
you fear for your husband, your children.   180
Wives know the misery I feel now
when they face what I've had to face.

I've wept—so much—long before this.
But now I must tell you something far worse.
When Herakles embarked on his last journey
he left behind a message carved on wood.
Never before—and he went to fight often—
had he explained its meaning to me.
Always sure that he'd win,
he never believed he would die.   190
But this time he seemed to expect his own death.
He told me how much of his wealth
would be my widow's share, which lands
would go to each of his children—but
this time he fixed the date of his own death.
When he'd been out of the country fifteen
months, that would be his time to die.
But if he survived after that,
there'd be no further trouble in his life.

The gods ordained this destiny, he said—   200
ordained that Herakles' own labors
would cause it. So it will happen
just as the ancient oak at Dodona's
shrine told him it would, when its leaves
rustled and whispered to its sibyls.
Today's the day that prophecy falls due.
I wake in terror from a long sweet sleep, friends,
fearing I must live on without the man
who is—of all men living—the best.

LEADER

Shush. Let go of those mysteries for now.   220
A man wearing laurel flowers
is walking toward us, a sure sign
he brings news we can celebrate.

Enter MESSENGER.

MESSENGER

Queen Deianeira, let me
be the first to reassure you.
Herakles is alive. He's won,
and from that battle he's sent home
trophies to please our native gods.

DEIANEIRA

Old man, what's this news you've just brought me?   230

MESSENGER

That your lord, loved by so many,
will be restored to your house
in all his victorious might.

DEIANEIRA

Who told you this, a stranger or a villager?

MESSENGER

Down in the meadow where oxen graze all summer,
a herald named Likhas is telling everyone.

I heard it from him and hurried here,
hoping that you'd be generous
if I was the first to tell you.

DEIANEIRA

Why doesn't Likhas bring the news himself   240
if fortune's been so good to Herakles?

MESSENGER

It's not so easy for him, ma'am. The whole
town of Malia crushes around him,
asking questions. He's stuck there—everyone
intent on learning what interests them.
They won't let him go till each hears his fill.
That ruckus holds him there unwillingly,
but I'm sure you'll see him in person soon.

DEIANEIRA

O Zeus,
who keeps the highlands of Mount Oita green,   250
you've given us some joy at last! Sing out
your gladness at this news, you women
in the house and come from town, brilliant news
beyond all hope, that dawns on me, on us!

CHORUS

Let the house
that awaits
its bridegroom

sing out in joy
triumphant
from its hearth!

Let shouts from the men   260
in one great voice
go to the god Apollo
whose keen bright
arrows protect us!

Join them, girls,
sing the anthem
to Artemis, his sister, let
your voices carry
to her hunting deer   270
in fields where quail fly!
Sing to the goddess
whose torches blaze
in both her hands, sing
to her neighbors
the nymphs!

I'm soaring!
I won't deny you,
flute, king of my soul!
Ivy is working   280
green magic
through my body—
Haiiiii! Eiiiiiiii!—

ivy whirls me
into the flashing
dance of Bakkhos!
Praise Bakkhos
who heals us!

Look over there,
beloved lady.   290
What I am singing
your eyes can see!

DEIANEIRA

I see them, girls. My eyes
have been scanning the horizon.

*Enter LIKHAS leading several of the Captive Women up the path. The group
includes the strikingly young and sensual Iole.*

You've come a long way, Likhas. We're glad you're here,
if it's true that your news will make us glad.

LIKHAS

Our coming is good news—and the facts I bring
will justify your welcome. When a man's been
lucky, he should be greeted as a friend.

DEIANEIRA

Then tell me, friend, what I most want to hear.   300
Will I see Herakles come home alive?

LIKHAS

Not only was he alive when I left him,
he was robust. Not sick in any way.

DEIANEIRA

Where is he? Home, or still on foreign soil?

LIKHAS

A headland juts west from Euboea. Herakles
is on it making sacrifices to Zeus.
He builds altars and offers to the gods
some of the wealth he's won by making war.

DEIANEIRA

To keep a vow? Or was an oracle involved?

LIKHAS

A vow. He keeps the vow he made   310
when he conquered a country
and stripped it of these women here.

DEIANEIRA notices the Captive Women entering under guard.

DEIANEIRA

These women—who are they? Who owns them?
I feel so sorry for them. Or am I wrong
to think that they'll be slaves?

LIKHAS

He picked them out when he raided Eurytus' city.
Splendid prizes for himself. And the gods.

DEIANEIRA

Was it that raid against a city—which
lasted longer than anyone predicted?
So long I lost all track of the days?   320

LIKHAS

No. He was in Lydia most of that time—
not a free man, he told us, but enslaved.
You won't take offense at the word "enslaved,"
lady, when you hear the reason Zeus willed it.
Herakles was bought by a foreign queen
named Omphale for a full year. He admits it.
He was so mortified by this disgrace
he vowed to make the man who had caused it,
as well as his wife and daughter, slaves themselves.
Not idle words. When he'd done a year's   330
penance for this crime, he hired
an army to lay siege to that man's
city—making Eurytus pay dearly,
the man most to blame for his troubles.

Herakles was an old comrade of this Eurytus,
and had sought refuge—in friendship—under his roof.
But Eurytus abused Herakles, lashing him
with vicious words meant to wound him:

"Your arrows never miss, do they Herakles?
How come my sons beat you in competition?   340
What's more, you're now a mere slave who grovels
when a free man barks at you." When Herakles
got drunk on wine at a feast, Eurytus kicked him
out of the house. Herakles was enraged.
So one day, when Eurytus' son scrambles
high up Mount Tiryns tracking some lost horses,
he drops his guard while his eyes search
the vast plain below him. Herakles grabs
the preoccupied lad and throws him
off a sky-high cliff to his death.   350
This murder disgusted our real king,
Olympian Zeus, father of us all,
who had Herakles sold
as a slave to another country.
With no parole allowed, since he'd
killed Iphitus by deceit—the only
man Herakles ever killed that way.
Had he killed his man fairly,
Zeus would have pardoned him.
Gods don't appreciate insolence   360
any more than we do.
           Now all those men
he killed, so full of themselves, bursting
with arrogant and bitter things to say—
they're down in Hades, their town's enslaved.
Their women I've brought here trade their lives
of ease for a much less pleasant existence.

Your husband ordered this, so I loyally
carry it out. Once he has sacrificed to Zeus,
the god who fathered him, in thanks for his
victory, you can be sure he'll come to you.   370
Of all my news, this last must please you most.

LEADER

It's certain you'll be happy, Queen. Half your joy
has arrived, and the rest is on the way.

DEIANEIRA

Why shouldn't news of my husband's success
make me happy? Such good fortune must
always be celebrated. But a cautious mind
will feel apprehension for any man
who has so much luck. He could lose it all.

DEIANEIRA looks at the Captive Women.

My friends, I feel a strange pity,
looking at these sorry captives—   380
exiles who've lost their fathers and their homes.
Once they were daughters of free men.
Now they'll be slaves for the rest of their lives.
Zeus, decider of battles, grant
me this: don't ever punish my children
the way you are punishing these girls.
But if it must happen, do it when I'm gone.
That's how much looking at them scares me.

DEIANEIRA approaches Iole.

You poor girl! Who are you? Are you married?
Have you a child? You look so innocent.   390
And so wellborn. Who is her father, Likhas?
Her mother—who is she? Out with it!
I pity her more than the other women
because she seems to know what to expect.

LIKHAS

Why ask me? How should I know? Could be
her father's not the poorest man in his kingdom.

DEIANEIRA

Is she royal? Did Eurytus have a daughter?

LIKHAS

I don't know. Sorry. I didn't ask many questions.

DEIANEIRA

Didn't her friends ever mention her name?

LIKHAS

No, ma'am. I had a job to do. No time for chat.   400

DEIANEIRA again approaches Iole.

DEIANEIRA

You tell me then, poor girl. It upsets me
that I don't even know your name.

LIKHAS

It won't be like her if she speaks. She hasn't
spoken a word. She's done nothing but cry
miserable tears the whole way here
from her windswept home, devastated
by what the Goddess of Luck
has done to her. Let's respect that.

DEIANEIRA

Let her be. Let her go inside if she wishes.
I won't add to the pain she's been through.   410
She's had enough. Let's all go in—so you
can make an early start on your journey
while I see to some things in my house.

*LIKHAS and Captive Women start to go inside; the MESSENGER edges closer
to DEIANEIRA as she follows them inside.*

MESSENGER

(to DEIANEIRA)

Don't go inside just yet. Let all these folk
move out of earshot, so I can tell you
some things you haven't heard. Things I know.

DEIANEIRA

What things? Why are you keeping me here?

MESSENGER

Stay and hear me out. You valued what I told you
before. You'll value what I tell you now.

DEIANEIRA

Shall we call everyone back? Or do you want   420
to speak only to me and these women?

*LIKHAS pauses in the doorway as he notices that the MESSENGER has taken
DEIANEIRA aside.*

MESSENGER

I can speak freely to you—and these women.
Don't bother the others.

*DEIANEIRA waves for LIKHAS to go inside. He and the Captive Women
disappear into the house.*

DEIANEIRA

                    They're gone. Go ahead.

MESSENGER

None of what that man just told you is true.
Either he was lying to you here, or
lying to the rest of us a while back.

DEIANEIRA

What are you saying? Collect
your thoughts. Speak distinctly.
So far your words just puzzle me.

MESSENGER

I heard that man say—in front of witnesses—   430
that the girl was the real reason Herakles

crushed Eurytus and his city Oechalia.
It was Love, that god alone, who made him fight—
not his bondage to Omphale in Lydia.
It had nothing to do with Iphitus' death.
Likhas has pushed the true story aside
so he can tell you a much different one.

Now, when Herakles couldn't persuade
her father to let him bed this young girl
in secret, he blew up a minor insult   440
as a pretext to make war on her country—
then killed Eurytus and plundered his city.
Please try to see that it's no accident
he sends her to this house. She won't be a slave.
That's not likely to happen, when his heart's
burning for her.
                    I vowed, Queen, to tell you
everything I've heard from that man.
Many others heard him say it, along with me—
Trakhinian men gathered in the market—
who'll back me up and convict him.   450
If what I say hurts, I'm sorry.
But I've told you the straight truth.

DEIANEIRA

I'm in shock. What is happening to me?
Who is this secret rival I give houseroom?
I'm so stupid! She doesn't have a name,
as Likhas swore to me? No name? A girl
with such striking looks and royal bearing?

MESSENGER

She has a name. Her father is Eurytus
and her name is Iole. If Likhas
can't tell you her name or her family's,   460
it must be—as he says—because he never asked.

LEADER

(to DEIANEIRA)

Treachery to those who trust you
seems to me the worst kind of evil.

DEIANEIRA

What should I do, friends? That last piece
of news leaves me dumbfounded.

LEADER

Bring Likhas back. Question him. Maybe he'll
tell you the truth if you force him to talk.

DEIANEIRA

That's good advice. Exactly what I'll do.

MESSENGER

Should I stay? What would you like *me* to do?

DEIANEIRA

Wait here. Likhas is coming without my asking.   470

Enter LIKHAS.

LIKHAS

Lady, have you a message for Herakles?
If you do, instruct me. As you see, I'm off.

DEIANEIRA

You're leaving in a big hurry—for someone
who took so long getting here—and before
we've had time to finish our conversation.

LIKHAS

If there's something you want to ask, I'll oblige.

DEIANEIRA

Can I trust you to tell me the truth?

LIKHAS

You can—if I know it. Zeus will know if I lie.

DEIANEIRA

Who is that woman you've brought here?

LIKHAS

She's from Euboea. From what clan I can't say.   480

MESSENGER

You! Look at me. Who are you talking to?

LIKHAS

Who are *you*? Why ask *me* such a question?

MESSENGER

You understand me well enough to answer.

LIKHAS

I'm talking to Queen Deianeira—unless I'm blind.
Herakles' wife, Oeneus' daughter. My Queen.

MESSENGER

Your Queen. That's what I hoped you'd say.
So what does that make you?

LIKHAS

Her loyal servant.

MESSENGER

Right. What's the penalty for disloyalty?

LIKHAS

Disloyal how? What word game are you playing?   490

MESSENGER

If someone's playing games with words, you are.

LIKHAS

I'm a fool to put up with this. I'm gone.

MESSENGER

No! Not till you answer one brief question.

LIKHAS

Ask it. You don't seem bashful in the least.

MESSENGER

That girl slave you brought here—you know the one?

LIKHAS

I know the one. What about her?

MESSENGER

Didn't you tell us that this captive—the one
your eyes keep trying to avoid—
is Iole, Eurytus' daughter?

LIKHAS

Said that to whom? Where's the witness   500
who swears to have heard me say that?

MESSENGER

You said it to the whole town in the main square—
many Trakhinians heard you say it.

LIKHAS

Right. It's something I'd heard secondhand.
That's not the same as swearing it was true.

MESSENGER

Secondhand, eh? You swore on oath
you brought this girl to be Herakles' wife!

LIKHAS

Me? Bringing him a wife? For god's sake, Queen,
please tell me who this stranger is?

MESSENGER

I'm the man who heard you say that a city   510
was leveled out of lust for her—no Lydian woman
destroyed it—it was desire for that girl.

LIKHAS

Lady, get rid of him. It's undignified
for a sane person to conduct a ludicrous
quarrel with a man sick in the mind.

DEIANEIRA

By Zeus!—whose lightning scorches mountain glens,
don't cheat me of the truth! Tell it to me!
You won't find me a spiteful woman, or
one ignorant of what people are like.
I know the things that pleasure men can change.   520
Someone who picks a fight and trades blows
with Eros the love god is so foolish.
Eros rules even the gods, and he rules me
just as he rules any woman like me.
I would be mad if I blamed my husband
because he's lovesick—mad to blame that girl,
who has done nothing shameful, nor harmed me.
I can't think like that.

                                        But if you were taught

to lie by him, you learned a vulgar lesson.
If you're a self-taught liar, you'll always seem   530
treacherous when you're trying to be kind.
Tell me the truth, all of it. To be called a liar
is the worst reproach a free man can suffer.
Don't think I won't find it all out. Many men
heard you, and they'll tell me what you said.

DEIANEIRA pauses. LIKHAS says nothing.

You're worried you'll hurt me? You fear the wrong thing.
Not knowing the truth—*that* could damage me. What's
so terrible about finding out? Herakles
has been to bed with so many women—
more than any man living. Never once   540
has one of these women—ever—heard me speak
a harsh or jealous word. Nor will
she, even if she returns all
the affection he feels for her.
I pitied her as soon as I saw her
because her beauty has ruined her life.
And though she never willed it, her beauty
has looted and enslaved her fatherland.
But wind and water blow all this away.
Deceive somebody else. Tell me the truth.   550

LEADER
(to LIKHAS)
You're hearing good advice. Follow it. You'll
never have cause to complain of this woman.

And all of us will be grateful to you.

LIKHAS

So be it, Queen. Men are weak. You grasp that.
I see that you think like a sane woman.
I'll tell it to you plainly, hiding nothing.
That fellow has it right. The girl touched off
lust in Herakles that devoured his soul.
For her sake he drove his spear straight through
the desolate heart of her city, Oechalia.   560
And to be fair to the man, he never asked me
to hide these facts. I was afraid to wound you,
so the fault's mine—if it's truly a fault.
Now that you know the whole story—
for your own good as well as his—keep your promise
to treat her with kindness. For the man who has
proven himself stronger in every battle
has been beaten by his love for this girl.

DEIANEIRA

I haven't changed my mind. I'll keep my word.
Trust me, it would only make my sickness   570
worse—to wage hopeless war against the gods.
But we should both go inside. I'll give you
messages to take back, and fitting gifts.
The gifts we've just received should be repaid.
I don't want you to leave empty-handed,
since you came here with such precious goods.

DEIANEIRA, LIKHAS, and the MESSENGER enter the house.

CHORUS

Huge are the victories
the power of the love
goddess always wins!
I won't pause to tell   580
how she tamed gods,
beguiling Hades,
lord of the dark,
Zeus, son of Kronos,
and Poseidon
the earthshaker—
but when our lady's hand
was there for the winning,
who were the rivals
that met in battle,   590
trading blows in the dust?

One was a big Rivergod,
who took the monstrous
body of a spike-horned
four-legged bull—he
was Achelous, from Oeneus.
His rival from Thebes,
city Bakkhos adores,
came armed with a double
torsioned bow, spears,   600
and one huge club—he
was Herakles, son of Zeus.
Bride-hungry males,

they battered each other.
Aphrodite, the goddess
who brings joy to our beds,
was there as the sole referee.

Then came the thud
of pounding fists,
a bow twanging,   610
horn cracking bone!
Legs grappled torsos,
a forehead struck
murderous blows—
harsh groans of pain
bellowed from both,

while she in her fragile
beauty sat in plain view
on a hillside nearby,
soon to be claimed   620
by her husband-to-be.

So the battle roared on,
the bride, the dazzling prize,
helpless in her anguish,
till suddenly she's pulled
like a calf from its mother.

Enter DEIANEIRA.

DEIANEIRA

My friends, while our guest inside says good-bye
to the captives, I've stepped out here unseen
to tell you what my hands have done, and ask
your sympathy for my troubles.

      A virgin,   630
though I think she's been bedded by now,
has invaded my house like cargo stowed
on a ship—merchandise sure to drive
my own peace of mind on the rocks.
Now we both will sleep under one blanket
and share his lovemaking. That's my reward
from Herakles—the man I said was true
and loyal—my repayment for guarding
his home through all these grinding months.
Though I can't feel anger toward a man   640
so stricken by this sickness.

       But what woman
could live with *her*, inside the same marriage!
I see her youth bloom, while mine fades.
Men's eyes adore fresh young blossoms.
But they shun flowers turning dry.
That's my fear—that Herakles, whom I call
my husband, is now this young woman's *man*.

I've said anger is ugly in a woman of sense,
and I'll tell you, friends, my hope for its cure.
Years ago, a strange beast gave me something 650
that I've kept in a bronze urn. I got this gift,
when I was a girl, from that hairy-chested

creature Nessus—it was his own blood
that I scraped from the wound that killed him.
He was a centaur who took people over
the river Evenus, not rowing or sailing,
but swimming them across in his arms.
He carried me on his back when Father
sent me to marry Herakles. Out in midstream
he fondled me with his lewd hands. I yelled.   660
Herakles looked back and saw us. He whistled
an arrow through Nessus' chest into his lungs.
As Nessus' life dimmed, the centaur whispered,

"You listen to me, Oeneus' daughter!
Take at least this much profit from being
the last passenger I will ever carry.
If you scrape up some blood from my wound,
just where the arrow soaked in black bile hit—
bile leeched from the Hydra of Lerna—
you'll have something to charm Herakles' soul.   670
It will keep him from seeing and loving
any other woman but you."
                         I remembered
this charm, my friends, because after he died,
I hid it in my house—and now I've dampened
this robe with that gore, doing exactly
what the centaur told me to do. It's ready.

May I never know anything
about rash acts of malice. Keep me
from ever learning what they are.

I detest women guilty of such things.   680
But if I can defeat that girl by using
a love-spell that works only on Herakles,
I have the means. Unless you think
I'm being reckless. If so, I'll stop now.

LEADER

Don't! If you think this drug might work,
there is surely no harm in using it.

DEIANEIRA

I'm at least this much confident: there's a good
chance it will work, though it's untested.

LEADER

You test something in action. To test it
in your mind does no good at all.   690

DEIANEIRA

We won't have to wait long. I see him
coming out, eager to leave. You won't give
me away, will you? What's done out of sight,
even if it's shameful, won't expose me to shame.

Enter LIKHAS from the house.

LIKHAS

Your orders, lady? Is there more I can do,
daughter of Oeneus? I should be on my way.

DEIANEIRA

I was getting this ready, Likhas,
while you said good-bye to the slaves.

*DEIANEIRA (or a servant who has carried it onstage) hands LIKHAS a wooden
box holding the robe.*

Take this flowing handmade robe—my own
design—as a gift to my absent master.   700
When you hand it to him, make certain he,
nobody else, is the first to wear it. Be sure
to keep it in a dark place—no sunlight—
don't take it near grounds that are sacred,
or near an altar fire. Wait till he's standing
in plain sight before everyone. Give it to him
on a day he's killing bulls for the gods.

I made this vow: that on the day Herakles
came safely home, I'd wrap him in this robe,
and show him to the gods, radiant   710
at their altar in his bright new clothes.

So he'll have proof it's from me, take this ring.
He'll know my sign. It's carved into the seal.
It's time you left. Remember the first rule
of messengers—they shouldn't interfere.
Do this well, and you'll earn thanks from us both.

LIKHAS

Well, if I'm any good at Hermes' craft
there's no chance I'll ever fail you.
Count on my handing him this box intact,
adding only your words, to prove it's yours.   720

DEIANEIRA

You should be on your way, now that you've
found out how things stand in this house.

LIKHAS

I'll report all is going well here.

DEIANEIRA

You saw me greet the young stranger.
Will you tell him how I welcomed her?

LIKHAS

It was a gracious welcome. I was amazed.

DEIANEIRA

There's nothing more, then, for you to tell him,
is there? Don't tell him how much I want him
until we know whether he still wants me.

DEIANEIRA reenters the house as CHORUS sings.

CHORUS

All of you living   730
near the hot springs

between harbor and high rock
and on the heights of Oita—
all of you living
by the waters
of the landlocked
Malian Sea,
on shores sacred
to the Virgin Goddess
armed with arrows of gold—   740
shores where the Greeks met
in their storied conclave
at the grand shrine of Pylos.

Soon the vibrant-voiced
flute rises in your midst,
not resonant with grief,
but musical as a lyre
delighting the gods.
The son born to Zeus
and Alkmene   750
hurries to his home,
bearing all that his courage won.

We had lost Herakles
from our city
while he wandered the seas—
we heard nothing for twelve months
while the wife he treasures
waited in tears.
Now the Wargod,

enraged at last,   760
chases away
her days of hardship.

Let Herakles come home!
Let him come home!
Let there be no missed beat
in the pulse of the oars
of the ship sailing here
till it lands in our port,
leaving astern the island
where he built altars for the gods.   770

Let him come home fired by love,
melting with lust, feeling
the power which burns in the robe,
put there by the Goddess
of Yes—charming Persuasion.

DEIANEIRA returns from the house.

DEIANEIRA
Women, I'm scared. I think I've done
something extremely dangerous.

LEADER
Deianeira! Child of Oeneus! What's happened?

DEIANEIRA

I'm not sure. But I'm terrified
I'll be blamed for a savage crime—   780
while trying to do something lovely.

LEADER

It's not your gift to Herakles, is it?

DEIANEIRA

It is. Never act on impulse
if you can't see clearly what will happen!

LEADER

What makes you so upset? Please tell us.

DEIANEIRA

Something weird has just happened, sisters,
so strange you could never imagine it.
A ball of white fleece, with which I was rubbing
chrism into the ceremonial robe,
has disappeared. The wool ate itself up—   790
nothing in my house consumed it—it just
crumbled away to nothing on a stone slab.
But so you'll understand exactly
how it happened, I'll tell you step by step.

I followed the instructions given me
by the centaur, neglecting no detail.
What he told me writhing in pain, the arrow

still in his chest, I remember like words
hammered forever on a bronze tablet.
I did what he told me to do—no more: 800
keep the drug far from fire, hide it deep
in the house where the hot sun can't touch it—
keep it fresh till the moment it's smeared on.
That's what I did! Now, when the time came
to go into action, I rubbed it in secret
there in my dark house, using some wool tufts
that I pulled from one of our own sheep.
Then I folded the robe up and packed it
safely in a box. Sunlight never touched it.

But as I went back in, I saw something   810
strange beyond words—and human comprehension.
I happened to toss the damp tuft of wool
I was using into a patch of bright sunlight.
As it warmed up, it shriveled, dissolving
to powder fast as trees turn to sawdust
when men cut them down. So it lay there, right
where it fell. From the ground white gobs
foamed up, like the rich juice of Bakkhos' blue-
green grapes, poured—still fermenting—on the earth.

I'm stunned. I don't know what I should do now.   820
All I know is . . . I've done something awful.

Why should that dying monster have had
any possible motive for doing me

a kindness? I'm the one who got him killed!
No, he used *me* to kill the man who shot him.
I see this clearly, now that it's too late.
It's *me*, nobody else—unless I've lost
my mind—who's going to kill Herakles!
I know the arrow that hit Nessus maimed
even Chiron, who was a god—so its   830
poison kills every creature it touches.
The same black venom oozed from Nessus' wound.
Won't it kill my lord too? I know it will.
And if he dies, so will I, both of us
swept to our doom. What woman who values
her goodness could survive such disgrace?

LEADER

You're right to be alarmed by what's happened.
But don't assume the worst until it strikes.

DEIANEIRA

A person who's made a fatal mistake
has no use for that kind of wishful thinking.   840

LEADER

Men are forgiving when it's not your fault!
Their anger softens. So it will toward you.

DEIANEIRA

You can say that because it's not your life!
What if this menace pounded on your door?

LEADER

Better hold your tongue. Your son will hear you.
He's home from trying to find his father.

Enter HYLLOS.

HYLLOS

Mother! I wish any one of three things
had happened: that I'd found you dead;
or if you were living, you'd be somebody
else's mother. Or you'd somehow be changed,   850
so a kinder spirit lived in your body.

DEIANEIRA

Son, what did I do to make you hate me?

HYLLOS

Today you murdered your husband. My father!

DEIANEIRA

I'm stunned by what comes out of your mouth, child.

HYLLOS

The words I've spoken will be proven true.
Who can undo what's already been done?

DEIANEIRA

What did you say? On whose authority
do you charge me with this horrendous crime?

HYLLOS

I didn't hear it from anybody.
I've seen Father dying with my own eyes.   860

DEIANEIRA

Where did you find him? Were you with him?

HYLLOS

You listen while I tell you everything.
After he looted the famous city
of Eurytus, Herakles headed home,
loaded down with the spoils of victory.
At Cape Cenaeum, a headland off Euboea
where the sea crashes in, he dedicated altars
and a grove of trees to his father, Zeus.
When I saw him, I felt such love!

He'd just begun a great solemn sacrifice,   870
when his own herald, Likhas, arrived from home,
bringing your gift, the lethal robe, which he
put on, just as you planned he would. Then he
began slaughtering bulls, twelve flawless bulls,
the first he'd looted, but there must have been
a hundred animals herded toward the knife.

There he was, doomed already, serenely
praying, thrilled with his gorgeous attire.
But just as the blood-drenched fire blazed up
through the bulls and the resin-soaked pine logs,   880

sweat broke out on his body! The robe clung
to his ribs as if a craftsman glued it there.
Pain tore at his bones—and then the venom
sank its fangs into him, gorging on his flesh.

He yelled for doomed Likhas, who was in no
way guilty, demanding what treachery
inspired him to bring that robe. But Likhas,
totally ignorant, said he had the gift
from no one but you, that he delivered it
just as you sent it. Hearing that, his master—   890
a slashing pain clawing at his lungs—caught
Likhas by his ankle joint and launched him
at the sea-pounded rocks below. His brains
oozed white through his hair where the skull
broke open, then blood darkened it.
                                    The people
cried out in awestruck grief, seeing one man
gone mad, another dead—but no one dared
go near him. Pain wrestled him down, then forced him
to leap up, shrieking wild sounds that echoed
off the headlands of Locris and the capes of Euboea.   900

When he was worn out from throwing himself
so many times screaming on the ground,
cursing and cursing his catastrophic
marriage to you, miserable woman,
and his alliance with your father, Oeneus—
yelled that it ruined his life—at that instant,
half-hidden in swirling altar smoke, he looked up,

his fierce eyes rolling, and saw me weeping
in the crowd. "Come here, Son," he called to me.
"Don't turn your back on me now—even   910
if you must share the death I am dying.
Lift me up, take me somewhere men can't watch.
If you can pity me at all, take me away
so I'll die anywhere but in this place."

We did as he asked, carried him aboard,
and landed him—it wasn't easy—with him
suffering and groaning. You'll see him soon now,
still breathing, or just dead.
       Those, Mother, are
the plot and the acts of which you're guilty.
May Vengeance and the Furies destroy you.   920
And if they do crush you, I will rejoice.
And to exult is just. You've made it
just, killing the best man who ever lived.
You'll never see a man like him, ever.

DEIANEIRA turns and walks toward the house without a word.

LEADER
Why are you walking quietly away? Don't
you see? Your silence proves him right!

HYLLOS
Let her go.
Let a fair wind blow her away.
Why call her "Mother"

if there's no mother
left in the woman? Let her go—   930
good-bye and good luck to her.
Let the same joy
she gave Father
seize her.

HYLLOS *enters the house.*

CHORUS
O sisters—see how suddenly
the sacred promise of the oracle,
spoken so long ago, strikes home.
It promised us the twelfth year
would end the long harsh work
of Herakles, a true son of Zeus.   940
At last the oracle comes true.
For how can a dead man work,
once he has gone to the grave?

If death darkens his face
as the centaur's poison
pierces his sides, poison fathered
by Death and nourished
by the jewel-skinned
serpent, how can he live
to see tomorrow's sun?   950
Locked in the Hydra's
writhing grip, the black-

haired centaur's
treacherous words
erupt at last—lashing Herakles
with burning, surging pain.

Our Queen knew nothing of this,
but a marriage loomed
that threatened her home.
She saw it coming.   960
Her hand seized the cure.
But the virulent hatred
of a strange beast—spoken at their one
fatal encounter—now brings tears
pouring from her eyes.
And doom comes on,
doom comes on, making
ever more clear this huge
calamity caused by guile.

Our tears burn as this plague   970
invades him, a crueler blow
than any his enemies
ever brought down
on this glorious hero
Herakles.
      O dark
steel-tipped spear, keen
for battle, did you
capture that bride

from the heights
of Oechalia?   980
No! The love goddess,
Aphrodite, without
saying a word,
made it happen.

SERVANT

(offstage)

No! No!

SEMI-CHORUS 1

Do I imagine it?
Or is it the cry
of somebody grieving?

SEMI-CHORUS 2

No vague noise—
it's anguish inside.   990
More trouble
for this house.

LEADER

See how slowly, her face dark,
an old woman comes toward us,
bringing us news.

Enter SERVANT from the house.

SERVANT

Daughters, we are still harvesting evil
from the gift that she sent to Herakles.

LEADER

Old woman, do you bring worse news?

SERVANT

Deianeira has left on her last journey.
Gone without taking one step.   1000

LEADER

You mean death, don't you?

SERVANT

You heard me say it.

LEADER

Dead? That poor woman?

SERVANT

You've heard it twice.

LEADER

Wretched woman! How did she die?

SERVANT

The act itself was ruthless.

LEADER

Tell us what happened!

SERVANT

She stabbed herself.

LEADER

What rash fury,
what sick frenzy, made her do it? *How*
did she manage to make her death
follow his—and do it herself?

SERVANT

One thrust of a steel blade was enough.

LEADER

Then you saw *her* . . . kill *herself*? Poor woman!   1010

SERVANT

I saw it. I was there.

LEADER

What happened! How did it happen? Say it!

SERVANT

Her hand did what her mind chose.

LEADER

What are you saying?

SERVANT

        The simple truth.

LEADER

The first-born child
of that new bride
is an avenging Fury—
scourging this house!

SERVANT

Now you see it. If you had seen the act itself,
you would have pitied her even more.   1020

LEADER

(pausing a beat)
How could a *woman* dare . . . do such a thing?
With her own hand?

SERVANT

Yes. It stunned me.
You must know what she did.
So you can tell the others.

               When she came in alone,
and saw her son preparing a stretcher
in the courtyard—so he could go meet
his father—she hid, hoping no one could find her,
collapsing on the sacred altars, screaming
they'd be abandoned. When she touched
ordinary things that had been part of her life,

she wept. Aimlessly roaming, room to room,   1030
she saw the faces of servants she cherished.
This brought on more tears, more grief
at her own and her household's destruction.
Strangers, she said, would soon take over
her house. After she'd stopped all that,
I saw her burst into Herakles' bedroom.
Through an open doorway I watched.
She spread blankets on her lord's bed,
jumped onto it, huddled there, tears
welling from her eyes, and cried out: 1040
"Our room! Bed where we loved! Good-bye
forever! Since you will never again
feel me lie down." That's all she said.

She ripped her robe open, viciously, just
where a gold brooch was pinned over her breasts,
leaving her left arm and whole ribcage naked.
I ran—fast as I could—to find her son
and warn him what she meant to do. Before we
got back, she'd driven a sword through her heart.

When he saw her, her son roared, because   1050
he knew, *he knew*, that his own rage
had made her do it. He'd found out
too late from the servants that she hadn't
known what she was doing when she
followed the centaur's instructions.
Her young son, now so miserable,

mourned her passionately. Kneeling at her side,
he kissed and kissed her lips, then stretched out
sobbing on the ground next to her bed,
confessing he was wrong to attack her,   1060
weeping that he'd been orphaned for life,
his mother and his father, both of them, dead.
All this has just happened. He is rash
who makes plans for tomorrow, makes any
plans at all—tomorrow doesn't exist
until we have survived today.

LEADER

Who should I mourn first?
Whose death brings more grief?
I don't know.

CHORUS

There is one sorrow in this house,   1070
we wait for another to arrive—
anxiety and grief are blood brothers.

LEADER

May a blast of wind
blow through our house
to drive me out of this land,
so I won't die of terror
when I see him, the once
great son of Zeus.

CHORUS

He's coming home, they tell us,
a fire in his bones nothing can cure,   1080
an unspeakable miracle of pain.

LEADER

He isn't far away,
he's near, the man I grieve
in my ear-piercing
nightingale's voice.
Strangers are bearing him here,
but how do they carry him?
They seem to suffer his pain,
as they would for a friend.

*HERAKLES, unconscious, accompanied by the OLD MAN, is carried in by his
Soldiers on a stretcher.*

They walk on sad silent feet.   1090
Oh they bring him in silence!
Should I think he is dead?
Or think he is sleeping?

Enter HYLLOS from the house.

HYLLOS

Father, to see you like this
hurts me so much! Father,
what can I do?

OLD MAN

Don't talk. You'll only stir up spasms
that'll enrage him. He breathes, but he's still
unconscious. Keep your mouth shut.

HYLLOS

You're saying he's alive, old man?   1100

OLD MAN

Don't wake him! Don't start him
again on that crazed lashing out.

HYLLOS

I'm the one losing my mind
under the weight of his pain.

HERAKLES wakes.

HERAKLES

O Zeus, what country are we in?
Who are these men staring at me?
I'm worn out by this torture.
God it hurts! Like rats gorging on my flesh.

OLD MAN

You see, I was right. Better to keep still
than to chase sleep from his mind and eyes.   1110

HYLLOS

No! How can I stand here while he suffers?

HERAKLES

You—Cenaean Rock on the coast
where I built my altars—is *this* how
you thank me for those sacrifices?
O Zeus! To what weakness that Rock
brought me! What wretched weakness.
I wish I'd never seen that place—
the place that made these eyes
boil over with madness,
madness nothing can soothe.   1120
Where is the spellbinder, the shrewd doctor,
who can cure this disease? Only Zeus.
Will the healer visit my bed?

                     I'd be amazed if he did.

Aiiiie!
      Let me be. So unlucky! Let me die.
(to HYLLOS and the OLD MAN)
Don't touch me.
              Don't turn me over.
That will kill me! Kill me!
If any of my pains slept,
you woke them up.
It grinds me—
           O this plague
keeps coming back!   1130

Where are you now, you Greeks,
my coldhearted countrymen?
I wore myself out clearing
Greece of marauders—
sea monsters, forest brutes.
Now, when I'm struck down,
where is the man willing
to save me with the mercy
of fire and steel? Come—cut
this head from my neck—   1140
one solid blow will do it.
O Zeus, I am miserable.

OLD MAN

Help me with him—you are his son!
He's more than I can handle. Your strength
can lift him much better than mine.

HYLLOS

I'm holding him. But I don't know how—
does anyone know how?—
to deaden his flesh to this torture.
This is what Zeus wants him to feel.

HERAKLES

Where are you, Son?   1150
Lift me up. Hold me here,
under here. Here it comes—
this beast none of us can beat down,

lunging at me, sinking its teeth.
Goddess Athena, it hits me now, again.
Honor your father, Son. Take a sword,
no one will blame you, and drive it
through me—below my collarbone.
That will numb the screaming pain
your heartless mother tears from me.   1160

I want to see her quieted just like that—
screaming, the same way I'll go down.
Sweet Hades, Zeus' brother,
let me rest, take my life, take it
with one swift stroke of peace.

LEADER

Friends, I hear our lord suffer and I shiver.
Such a great man—and so much pain.

HERAKLES

I have done blazing work with my hands,
I've shouldered ugly burdens on this back,
but no task given me   1170
by Zeus' wife, or that hated
Eurystheus, equaled
what Oeneus' daughter—
Deianeira! Deianeira!
so lovely, so treacherous—
forced on me: this net
of the Furies

woven around my death!
It's plastered to my body, it
eats through to my guts.   1180

It's always in me—sucking
my lungs dry, leeching the fresh
blood from my veins—so my whole
body's wasted, crushed
by these flesh-eating shackles.

No fighting soldier,
no army of giants
sprung from the earth,
no shock of wild beasts,
hurt me like this—not my own Greece,   1190
not barbarous shores, no land
I came to save. No, a frail woman,
born with no male strength,
she beat me—only she.
And didn't even need a sword.

Son, prove you are my son in fact.
Show me you're my son, and not hers.
Bring her out here, the woman who bore you.
Take her in your hands and put her in mine.
When she suffers what she deserves,   1200
I'll know what causes you more pain—
my own broken body, or hers.

Go do it, Son. Don't cringe. Do it.
Show me some pity. Others will say
I have earned it. Look at me,
weeping and bawling like a girl. No man living
can say he saw me act like this, no!
I went wherever fortune sent me, without
a murmur. Now this hard man
finds out he's a woman.   1210

Come here, stand by your father,
look how Fate mauls me. I will
open my robe. Look, all of you,
on this sorry body. See how
disgusting and shocking my life is!

HERAKLES rips open the blood-soaked robe that's bonded to his chest.

Aiiiie!
That raw, flaming pain
is back, roaring through me,
forcing me to fight it again,
so hungry for my flesh.   1220

Hades, welcome me!
Zeus, drive your lightning
into my brain.
The beast is at me again,
it's famished and it's raging.

My hands, O you hands,
my shoulders, chest, arms—
how frail you are!
Once you did all that I asked.
You are the lethal weapons   1230
that strangled the lion prowling
the plains of Nemea—
no man could get near
that cattle-raiding cat—but you could!
You tamed the flailing Hydra of Lerna
and that monstrous herd, those centaurs—
men fused to horses, a breed
violent, lawless, brutally strong.
You mastered the wild boar
of Erymanthus, and the three-headed bitch   1240
Hades kept in his dark realm, a terror
that cowed all comers,
the whelp of Echidna the Dreaded.
You whipped the serpent who stood guard
over the golden apples at the ends of the earth.

These struggles—and a thousand more—
have tested me. No man can boast
he has beaten my strength.
But now, with my bones
unhinged and my flesh shredded,   1250
I lose to an invisible raider—
I, son of a mother so noble,
I, whose father they call Zeus,
god of the star-filled sky.

Be sure of this one thing—though I'm nothing,
though I can't walk a step—she, she who did this
will feel my stony hand, even now, even now.
Let her come here. She'll show the world
that in my death, as in my life, I punish evil.

LEADER

What a disaster. There's nothing
but mourning ahead for Greece   1260
if she must lose this man.

HYLLOS

Father, let me speak while you're quiet.
I know your pain's unbearable, but listen.
I ask for no more than you owe me.
Take my advice. Be calm. Cool your anger.
If you rage, you will never learn why
your hunger for vengeance is wrong.
Why your hatred has no cause.

HERAKLES

Say your piece, then be still. I'm in too
much pain to make sense of your riddles.   1270

HYLLOS

I want to tell you how my Mother is.
And that she never willed the wrong she did.

HERAKLES

You worthless son! You're brave to use
her name in my presence, the mother
who murdered—me—your father.

HYLLOS

There's something else about her you must know.

HERAKLES

Tell me her past crimes. Speak of them.

HYLLOS

Her acts today will speak to you.
When you've heard them, judge her.

HERAKLES

                                  Go on.
But don't disgrace yourself or betray me.   1280

HYLLOS

She is dead. Killed just now.

HERAKLES

Who killed her? Incredible! You couldn't
have given me more hateful news.

HYLLOS

She killed herself. With her own hand. No one else's.

HERAKLES

(raising his right arm)

It should have been *this* hand. She deserved this hand!

HYLLOS

You wouldn't hate her—if you knew.

HERAKLES

Wouldn't hate her? If I knew what?

HYLLOS

Her good intentions hurt you—that's the truth.

HERAKLES

Her "good intention" to kill me?

HYLLOS

When she saw the woman who's in our house,   1290
she used love medicine to keep you. It went wrong.

HERAKLES

And who in Trakhis has a drug so potent?

HYLLOS

Years back, the centaur Nessus
gave it to her—told her this drug
would make your passion burn again.

HERAKLES

O what a miserable creature I am!
I'm finished. Finished! For me
there will be no more sunlight.
This is my ruin. I know where I am.
Your father's life is over, Son.   1300
Gather all of my children here.
Bring unlucky Alkmene too—her coupling
with Zeus, *my* father, came to nothing—
so all of you can learn, from my
dying mouth, what oracles I possess.

HYLLOS

Your mother is not here. She's at Tiryns
on the seacoast, where she's been living.
She's taken some of your children, to raise
them there. Your other children are in Thebes.
Those of us left—we'll do what you ask.   1310
Tell me your wishes. I'll carry them out.

HERAKLES

Listen to my orders. Here is your chance
to show what you're made of.
To prove you're my son.
I learned long ago from my father
I would be killed by no creature who breathes—
but only by a dead beast from Hades. So
that centaur killed me—the dead kill the living—
just as the voice of Zeus had sworn to me.

Now hear how one old prophecy   1320
makes sense of an even older one,
the one I brought home from the grove
of the Selloi—mountain people who still
sleep on the ground—a prophecy
made by an oak tree of my father's,
an oak which spoke every language.
This oak whispered to me
that at the very hour
through which we now live,
I would be set free at last   1330
from my life of hard labor.
I thought that meant
good times would come,
but those words meant
no more than this:
that I would die now.
The dead do no work.

Son, since those old words are coming true,
you must help me. Don't obstruct me, don't
force me to use harsh words. Help me willingly— 1340
because you've learned the best law there is:
fathers must always be obeyed.

HYLLOS

Father, I am alarmed at where your talk
is taking us, but I'll do all you ask.

HERAKLES

First, put your right hand in mine.

HYLLOS

Why are you forcing me to pledge this way?

HERAKLES

Give me your hand—now! Don't refuse me.

HYLLOS

(reaching out to his father)

Here, take my hand. I can't refuse you.

HERAKLES

Swear by the head of Zeus, my father. Swear.

HYLLOS

Swear to do what? What am I promising to do?   1350

HERAKLES

You're promising *me* to do what I ask.

HYLLOS

I promise you. I swear this before Zeus.

HERAKLES

Ask Zeus to crush you if you break your word.

HYLLOS

I so pray. Zeus won't punish me. I'll keep my word.

HERAKLES

You know Mount Oita, whose peak is sacred to Zeus?

HYLLOS

Yes. I've gone there often to sacrifice.

HERAKLES

Carry me there, with your own hands,
helped by what friends you need.
Cut down a great oak, cut wild olive limbs.
Bed my body down on these branches.   1360
Then set them on fire with a flaming pine torch.

No tears. Don't sing hymns of mourning.
No, do not weep. Do it this way
because you are my son.
If you fail, I'll wait in Hades
to curse you through eternity.

HYLLOS

Father! What are you asking? You force me to do this?

HERAKLES

I ask you to do what must be done. If you can't
do it—go be some other man's son. You're not mine.

HYLLOS

Father, why this? You're asking me   1370
to be your killer, to curse myself with your blood.

HERAKLES

I don't ask that. I ask you to heal me,
to be the one healer who can cure my pain.

HYLLOS

How does setting fire to your body cure it?

HERAKLES

If burning me appalls you, do the rest.

HYLLOS

I'll take you there—I can at least do that.

HERAKLES

And will you build the pyre just as I asked?

HYLLOS

I will, but not with my own hands. Others will build it.
I'll do everything else. You can trust me.

HERAKLES

That will be more than enough.   1380
You do a great thing for me, Son.
But there's one small thing more I ask.

HYLLOS

Ask it. I'll do it. Nothing is too great.

HERAKLES

Do you know the girl whose father was Eurytus?

HYLLOS

You mean Iole.

HERAKLES

You know her. This is what I charge you
to do, my son. When I'm dead, if you would
honor the oath you swore to Zeus,
make her your wife. Do not disobey me.
No other man must marry this woman   1390
who shared my bed. No one but you, Son.
Marry her. Agree to it. You obeyed me
on the great things. If you fight me
on this minor one, you will lose
all the respect you have earned.

HYLLOS

How can I rage at a sick man? But who
could stand what this sickness does to his mind?

HERAKLES

You refuse to do what I ask.

HYLLOS

She caused my mother's death and your disease.
How could any man choose her—   1400
unless the Furies left him insane?

She's my worst enemy.
How could I live with her?
Better to die.

HERAKLES

I'm dying, and he scorns my prayer.
You can be sure, my son, that the gods' curse
will hound your defiance of my wishes.

HYLLOS

No, you are going to show us
how cursed you already are.

HERAKLES

You! You are waking up my rage!   1410

HYLLOS

There's nothing I can do. There's no way out.

HERAKLES

Because you've chosen not to hear your father.

HYLLOS

Should I listen, and learn blasphemy from you?

HERAKLES

It isn't blasphemy for a son
to make his dying father glad.

HYLLOS

Do you command me as your son?
Do you make it my duty to you?

HERAKLES

Son, I command you. May the gods judge me.

HYLLOS

Then I'll do it. Can the gods condemn me
if I do this out of loyalty to my father?   1420
The gods know—it is you who have willed this.

HERAKLES

In the end, Son, you do what's right.
Now make good on your words.
Put me on the pyre before the pain comes
searing back. Lift me up. The only cure
for Herakles' pain is Herakles' death.

HYLLOS

You'll have your wish.
Nothing stands in its way.
Your will prevails.

HERAKLES

Now you, my own hard-bitten soul—   1430
before my sickness attacks again—
clamp my mouth shut like a steel bit

so not one scream escapes your stony grip.
Do this harsh work as though it gives you joy.

The Soldiers lift the stretcher and carry it toward the mountain with the
CHORUS and then HYLLOS following in a cortege.

HYLLOS
Lift him up, friends. Forgive me
for what I am about to do.
But look at the cruelty of what
the ruthless gods have done
to us—the gods whom we call
our fathers, whose children we are—   1440
and yet how coolly they watch us suffer.
No one foresees the future,
but our present is awash with grief
that shames even the gods, and pain
beyond anything we can know
strikes this man who now meets his doom.
Women, don't cower in the house.
Come with us. You've just seen death
and devastating calamity, but
you've seen nothing that is not Zeus.   1450

HYLLOS and the Soldiers lift and carry the hero offstage toward the
mountain.

Philoktetes

INTRODUCTION
SOPHOCLES AT 87

Philoktetes. First performed in 409 BCE,
when Sophocles was 87 years old.

Philoktetes—with a festering, god-given wound in his foot—has been abandoned on the desolate island of Lemnos by the Greeks under Odysseus. They couldn't stand the stench, nor his screams of pain. That was ten years ago. Since then, they've learned they can't take Troy without Philoktetes and the bow given to him by Herakles—nor without Neoptolemos, son of the dead Achilles. Yet Philoktetes would rather kill Odysseus than return to Troy. It's up to Neoptolemos, inveigled by Odysseus, to trick Philoktetes into returning. Odysseus, an opportunistic character representing the Greek army, will use any means to carry out his mission. Philoktetes and Neoptolemos, however, are constantly at sea: shifting and re-shifting amidst mixed feelings, deceptions, suspicions, and qualms as they struggle with themselves and their obscurely evolving relationship.

There are many plays within this play. Philoktetes and Neoptolemos are driven not only by unbidden psychologies but by their through lines: the specific ends they want to achieve. With the scenario given him by Odysseus, Neoptolemos is caught between playing a character, a curtailed version of himself, and being his own person. He has a tenuous grip on his role. That, plus pressure from the nakedly visceral Philoktetes—by turns friendly, even fatherly, and bitterly hostile—will wear him down. Remarkably, there are no offstage events in this pressure cooker of a play. Everything happens in the moment, up close and personal. (The false Merchant and his tale are themselves an event, not the report of one.) Once Odysseus's hooks are set—in Neoptolemos and, through him, in Philoktetes—there's no let up.

Philoktetes is a discarded veteran of the Trojan War. He is as well a generic old man—sick, smelly, cantankerous, a burden abandoned in a seemingly blank space. Yet he isn't expendable. The Greeks can't win the war without him. Further, it seems elders in general are socially necessary. Curious about former comrades, Philoktetes asks if the "old and honest" Nestor is still alive—adding, with the hated sons of Atreus in mind: "He's the one / could baffle their schemes with wise advice" (471–472). He wonders what future may be envisioned without the 'good' people—the likes of Nestor, or the dead Achilles and Aias. "What's to be our outlook on life / when *they're* dead, and Odysseus, / who *should* be dead, isn't!" (478–480).

The novice Neoptolemos and the old hand, Philoktetes, occupy the opposite poles of a historical-*cum*-cultural continuum that is rediscovering itself over a dead space: the 'deadness' is not Lemnos, however, but the cynical, soulless present of Odysseus.[1] Objectively, Odysseus does have the right end in view. The goal to unite Neoptolemos, Philoketes, and Herakles' bow to capture Troy and so end the war is beyond question in this play. But Odysseus's crudely instrumentalist *means* lack the cultural and historical integrity, the broth of trust, needed to achieve that end.

Philoktetes' affliction is intolerable. His intransigence, exasperating. He wants to be cured but refuses to be cured—wants to leave Lemnos but refuses to leave—*if* that means returning to the Greek camp at Troy. On the face of it, his stubbornness doesn't make sense. Yet sense is also made extratextually. Brecht noted that production, unlike scripting, is risky. No one can predict how the 'acting out' will turn out. There are tones of voice, timings, silences. And bodies. Here there's extraordinary emphasis on the raw physicality of Philoktetes: from the crudity of his utensils to the stench haunting his every appeal for passage home to Oita. His eyeballs roll up into his head. His frequent outbursts, his screams, are not notational or formulaic but spontaneous and unbridled. Or, worse, gagged on themselves. These too make sense, but transmitted somatically rather than conceptually. It comes in shock waves of extratextual information. As these weigh in, his obstinacy, the most 'senseless' thing about him, accumulates yet another kind of sense. But to get it we need the kinesthetic, blow-by-blow feel of *being* Philoktetes, whose deepest wound is not in his body but in his spirit. What rationality or sensibleness is sufficient to cure that?

Given his awful solitude, not hearing another human voice, Philoktetes has vested the island, parts of his own body, and aspects of his affliction with vital existences of their own: his suppurating foot, his eyes, the intermittent fever: "this

wandering disease [that] comes to me / when it's tired wandering, / and having had enough / it goes away" (832–836). Birds,
cliffs, cave, breaking waves, nymphs of marshy meadows—all
these and more he grants the feeling life *of*. That is, he accepts
that they have their own conscious existence, independent of
him. This is sometimes taken as personification, yet is the an-
tithesis of that. It stems not from anthropomorphism but something akin to animism—a relation to the natural world that
respects the self-driven integrity of that world. Here it also testifies to the uncanny power emanating from the root *being* of this
ancient world and its Dionysian drama. Grasping that, we may
appreciate the generative power Philoktetes draws from a natural world that would otherwise, without the fuming *gravitas* of
his passion, lapse into the unredeemed desolation of Lemnos.
His immense will to live has vitalized what others, who have not
lived his life, see only as a dead land. Now, having made a life
on Lemnos—however poor and hard that life is—Philoktetes'
decision not to go back to Troy makes a counterintuitive, but
not incomprehensible, sense.[2]

Nevertheless, socially, and therefore humanly, his decision
not to return to Troy is the wrong one. Self-preoccupied after
so many years struggling to stay alive, utterly alone, he cannot come to the right, civically called-for decision: to rescue
the Greek forces that betrayed and abandoned him. It takes
Herakles to socialize (in the technical sense of 'civilize' or de-
individualize) the grounds Philoktetes stands on—and to give
those grounds staying power by historicizing them. Herakles'
bow testifies to their mutual history. It was Philoktetes who lit
the funeral pyre when Herakles, writhing in agony from the

poisoned shirt given him by Deianeira, could find no one else
willing to do it. If Herakles is a deus ex machina he is, as well,
an all-too-human hero out of Philoktetes' past, when Herakles
himself was desperate for help, and Philoktetes gave it.

Philoktetes was performed four years after the defeat of the
Greek fleet at Syracuse, and two years after the first oligarchic
coup in 411 BCE. Democracy was restored the following year,
but the ongoing stasis (i.e., a 'standing' apart or against, a state
of civil strife) portended the end of the Athenian empire. This
was five years before the absolute end, when the walls of Athens
were razed and an oligarchic constitution was installed under
the dunasteia—the 'collective tyranny' or junta—of the Thirty
Tyrants in 404–403 BCE. Given the protracted turmoil of the
times, it would seem Herakles speaks as much to the Athenian
audience as to Philoktetes. Reaching deeper than the factional-
ism that was surely rife in Athens, Herakles delivers the final
word on what is right, what is holy, what Zeus ordains. He
tells Philoktetes what is required of him, predicting his cure
and his success at Troy. Yet 'success' isn't everything. Just as significantly, Herakles goes on to demonstrate the proper attitude
Philoktetes must have in victory: "You will sack Troy and be
honored / with the choicest spoils. Bring these / home with you
to the Oitan highlands / to please your father, Poias. The other
/ spoils such as common soldiers get / lay on my funeral pyre: as
a tribute / to my bow" (1615–1621). Herakles, the most illustri-
ous of warriors, lines himself up with ordinary soldiers, setting aside his own aristocratic, heroic prerogative. How could
Philoktetes do less?

What then of Neoptolemos, whom we witness coming of

age—an ambitious, righteous, initially callow youth mellowed by Philoktetes and growing into a morally conscient, yet no less ambitious, maturity? Herakles has words for him as well. He doesn't name Neoptolemos—technically, he's still addressing Philoktetes—but the Greek audience would have known to whom the words referred: "Yet remember, when / you sack Troy show piety toward all things / relating to the gods. To Zeus, nothing / matters more. The sacred doesn't die / when men do. Whether they live or die, / holiness endures" (1631–36). Some values are sacralized: they transcend the moment, outlasting factions and parties. Yet even as Herakles makes this pronouncement, the audience knows that the youth we've watched growing fitfully into a decent, feeling man will become notorious for his savagery at the conquest of Troy—among other atrocities, killing old Priam, whom his own father Achilles had spared, at the altar of Zeus. Is nothing, then, to be sacred? Sophocles' vision toward the end of his long life, very nearly at the end of the Athenian empire, is not for the faint of heart.

—JS

NOTES

1. A view close to that of Sophocles—because its baseline is not one stratum of a stratified polity, but the whole of the polity, however internally stratified that whole may be—is articulated by Enzo Siciliano in remarks on the poet Pier Paolo Pasolini: "The [young] Pasolini already had clearly in mind the idea that *it is lethal in a collectivity to break, cast aside or forget historical continuity to the point of deny-*

ing it—and history is a synthesis of languages, customs and usages. The ideal of action, in such a poet, was directed, then, toward the defense of that 'continuity,' that 'historicity.' " In *Aias* as well as in *Philoktetes,* Sophocles assumes a comparably deep commitment to 'historicity.'

Given how "fragile and fractious" Athens became, especially from 461 BCE on, though plays "might be matchless in their honesty, with their forensic analysis of the extremes of the human condition, their investigation of human flaws . . . [they were also] where you came to process information, to learn to form an opinion of the world around you, and love your *polis.* . . . The experience of theater was meant to be one that reaffirmed Athens' [once] robust sense of *dêmos*-solidarity" (Hughes, 214–215, 262).

2. Philoktetes' refusal of salvation evokes depictions of a miserably risen Lazarus, or Donatello's rendering of Christ's Resurrection (in San Lorenzo, Florence). The comparison is not of individuals, certainly, but of their outlooks. The Resurrection is by definition a glorious event, yet Donatello shows the just-risen Christ drastically aged and stooped, clinging to his staff at the edge of his tomb as—melancholy beyond belief—he looks out onto the world: he had to come back to *this*? Not a rational response to his salvation, yet it does make sense. As does Philoktetes' tenacious refusal of an offer that, on the face of it, he should not be able to refuse. When Philoktetes does come round he does so spontaneously—not in the name of success, nor of a cure (he reasons nothing out), but responding instinctively to a vision and a 'call' of such scale and cultural depth it is irresistible.

Philoktetes

Translated by James Scully

CHARACTERS
    ODYSSEUS
    NEOPTOLEMOS
    CHORUS, sailors under the command of
        Neoptolemos
    LEADER of the Chorus
    PHILOKTETES
    MERCHANT, agent sent by Odysseus
    Sailors under the command of Odysseus
    HERAKLES

Cliff on the desolate island of Lemnos. Ocean below. Occasional glowing above Mosychlos, a distant volcano. ODYSSEUS appears, followed by NEOPTOLEMOS and one of his sailors (unseen). Sounds of the sea.

ODYSSEUS
    This is it!
Lemnos. A no-man's-land
in nowhere but ocean. No one
comes here, no one lives here.
Now, Neoptolemos, as you're truly the son
of Achilles, the noblest of all the Greeks,
listen to me.

      It's here years ago
I put Philoktetes the Malian, son of Poias,
ashore . . . *under orders from the chiefs*   10
of course . . . what with his foot all
runny with pus from a flesh-eating sore,
well, we couldn't get a moment's peace!
couldn't start the sacrifice, never mind
the wine offering, what with his
screaming, hollering, it was a bad sign,
it never let up! But that's . . . too much
to get into. This is no time for talk.
If he catches me here my scheme
to take him is wasted. From now on   20
it's your job to help me carry this out.
Look for a rock cave like a tunnel.
In cold weather, early or late in the day,
there's always a sunny spot to sit in.
In summer a cool breeze blows through
bringing sleep. Below, to the left,
there should be a bubbling spring
to drink from—if it's not dried up.

Easy now. Go see. Signal me if he's
still there, or should we look elsewhere,   30
then we'll know what to do. I'll tell you,
you'll listen. Together we can pull this off.

NEOPTOLEMOS cranes to look.

NEOPTOLEMOS

Odysseus, sir, what you're looking for is here.
That cave? I think I see it.

ODYSSEUS

Above you? Below? I can't see from here.

NEOPTOLEMOS

Above. No footsteps, far as I can hear.

ODYSSEUS

Watch out he's not sleeping in there.

NEOPTOLEMOS

Now I see. Empty, yes, nobody's there.

ODYSSEUS

No sign anyone lives there?

NEOPTOLEMOS

Yes. A bed of leaves pressed down   40
like it's been slept on.

ODYSSEUS

Nothing else in there? That's it?

NEOPTOLEMOS looks into the cave.

NEOPTOLEMOS

A wooden cup. Rough, poorly made.
And some kindling.

ODYSSEUS

Those would be his all right.

NEOPTOLEMOS

And rags drying in the sun. *Whew!*
Loaded with pus.

ODYSSEUS

That clinches it. He lives here. Can't be far off.
How far could he get with a rotting foot? No,
he's out scrounging for food, or some herb   50
to ease the pain. . . . Send your man to watch out
so he doesn't catch me off guard. Of all the Greeks
I'm the one he *really* wants to get his hands on.

NEOPTOLEMOS

(gestures off)
Say no more. He's going. Consider it done.

Sailor (unseen) leaves, as NEOPTOLEMOS stares after him.

He'll look out. But you were saying . . . ?

ODYSSEUS

As the son of Achilles you must carry out
your mission. But you can't just put

your *body* into it.
You may hear something *mmm* 'novel.'
Some plan you haven't heard yet. Well   60
you have to go along with it. That's what
you're here for.

NEOPTOLEMOS

What are your orders?

ODYSSEUS

As you're giving him your story
reach into his soul. Take it! He asks
who you are, where you're from, tell him
straight out: you're the son of Achilles.
Can't lie about that. Only you're headed home,
you've left the Greek fleet, you hate them. After
they'd begged you, prayed you, to leave your home   70
hey, you were their only hope of taking Troy
they didn't think you deserved Achilles' armor
or arms! wouldn't give them to you when you
claimed them; by rights they were yours! Instead
they handed them over to *Odysseus.* Say
anything you want about me, nothing's too nasty,
I couldn't care less—but if you don't do this
the whole Greek army will be demoralized. Just
get that bow. If you don't, you'll never take Troy.

It's you who will have to deal with him.   80
He'll trust you. Me, never. *You* didn't
come to Troy bound by an oath. You came

on your own, not forced to—unlike those
of us who came on that first expedition.
He sees me, and has that bow, I'm dead,
and you are too, my comrade in doom.
No, here's how we have to approach this:
as the bow is unbeatable, you have to be
clever enough to steal it.

        O . . . I know, it's not like you   90
my boy, to say or do anything out of line.
Yet to succeed is such a sweet thing,
go for it! We can be honest some other time.
Give yourself to me but one short, shameless
        stretch of day.
Then, forever after, you're free to be known
as the very soul of honor.

NEOPTOLEMOS

Son of Laertes, advice I can't stand to hear
I'd hate to act on. It's not in me
to scheme and lie. It wasn't in my father,   100
either. Everyone says so. I'd sooner
take him head on, not sneak around. He's got
one good foot! Can't get the best of us on *that*.
Of course I'm here to help you, do as you say.
I'd hate to be called a traitor. Yet I'd rather do
what's right, and fail, than succeed by deceit.

ODYSSEUS

You *are* your father's son. Brave man.
At your age, just like you, my hand

was quicker than my tongue.
But now I've learned it's words   110
that move people, not deeds.

NEOPTOLEMOS

Then you're ordering me to lie?

ODYSSEUS

I'm telling you: *disarm* Philoktetes.

NEOPTOLEMOS

By being 'disarming'? Why not
persuade him straight out?

ODYSSEUS

He won't listen. And then force *won't* work.

NEOPTOLEMOS

What is it makes him so sure of himself?

ODYSSEUS

Arrows definite as the death they deliver.

NEOPTOLEMOS

No one dares approach him then!

ODYSSEUS

No. Unless . . . you insinuate yourself.   120

NEOPTOLEMOS

You don't think it's shameful? To tell lies?

ODYSSEUS

Not if lying gets us through this
dragged-out war.

NEOPTOLEMOS

Won't the look on my face give me away?

ODYSSEUS

Look to what's in it for you! Can't be shy about it.

NEOPTOLEMOS

What good's it do *me* if he comes to Troy?

ODYSSEUS

Troy is taken . . . only with his arrows.

NEOPTOLEMOS

I'm not going to take Troy? Like you said?

ODYSSEUS

Not you without them. Nor them without you.

NEOPTOLEMOS

Well, if that's how it is, we'll have to go get them.   130

ODYSSEUS

You do that, you're coming away with *two* prizes.

NEOPTOLEMOS

Two? Tell me, and I won't hesitate.

ODYSSEUS

You'll be called both shrewd *and* brave.

NEOPTOLEMOS

Then no matter what, I'll do it. No shame.

ODYSSEUS

Remember what I told you then? Understood?

NEOPTOLEMOS

(irritated)

Yes! I'll do it. Now that I've said I would.

ODYSSEUS

Wait here. He'll show up. I'm leaving
so he doesn't see me here, with you.
I'll take the lookout back to your ship.
If you're running late I'll send him back   140
dressed like the skipper of a merchant ship.
The disguise will help. He'll spin a yarn,
you pay attention! he's feeding you leads,
go along with him. I'm going to the ship
now. But you know what you have to do.

May Hermes, who knows the way, lead us
on, and Victory, along with Athena
          Defender of Athens
who always watches over me!

*ODYSSEUS slips away. CHORUS of NEOPTOLEMOS's sailors (mostly
older than he) approach from the shore below. They cannot see
the cave.*

CHORUS
(severally)
          Sir: 150
what should we say, what
          not say?
we're strangers in a strange land,
this hermit will be suspicious!
Instruct us.

The cleverest
          of the clever,
the wisest advice, comes from
the one Zeus gave his godly scepter to.
          You, still in youth,   160
have had this passed down to you.

So tell us, how can we serve you?

NEOPTOLEMOS
For now, you might look at the sea-cliff cave
          he holes up in.

Don't worry, it's OK. But when this
dread figure works his way back
    be ready.
If I signal you, come running. Help
as best you can.

LEADER

We've been watching out for you   170
a long time now, sir. But at least
tell how he shelters himself. Where?
We need to know he can't sneak up on us.
Where does his foot touch the ground
    now? In there
or out here somewhere?

NEOPTOLEMOS

Well, you see where he lives up here.
Two openings. Rock . . .

LEADER

But the cursèd creature! *Where* is *he*?

NEOPTOLEMOS

I'm sure he's dragging his agony around   180
hereabouts, looking for food. Word is
that's how he lives: looking for game
    to kill
with his wingèd arrows.
Rotten miserable as he is,
no one comes to him with a cure.

CHORUS

(severally)

> I feel sorry for him: a man
> no one cares for
> with the face of a man
> no one lives with,   190
> alone always in pain.
> Each time he feels a new need
> bewildering him, his mind wanders.
> How does he go on?

> Dark are the doings of the gods. Unlucky
> the strains of men
> whose resources fall short of their doom.

> This man's as wellborn
> as anyone. Yet here
> stripped of all life gives,   200
> even human company,
> he lies alone
> among dappled or shaggy beasts—
> pitiful, tormented, hungering,
> his pain incurable
> the while the garbling Echo looms
> from afar
> crying back at him his own crying.

NEOPTOLEMOS

There's no mystery in it. From the beginning
the gods, I believe, were in on this,   210

working through the vicious Chrysē.
All his suffering all alone
    comes from a god—
to keep him from bending his almighty bow
    against Troy—
until the time comes
when the city *must* fall.

LEADER
Shsh!

NEOPTOLEMOS
What now?

CHORUS
(severally)
A sound came up!   220
Like what a man would make
excruciated by pain!

Over there!
    Or there! Listen,
listen! Such pain
      dragging this way!

The voice of a man, sure now, sounding
the anguish of his way.

LEADER
Time now sir . . .

NEOPTOLEMOS

> Why, what . . . ?   230

LEADER

Change of plans!

>   He's almost here!
That's no shepherd piping his way
home from pasture, no
>   it's *him*
stumbling, his moan carrying
a long way in pain seeing
nothing moored in the sea out there.

*PHILOKTETES—in rags, foot wrapped in filthy bandages, bow in hand—is
on them . . .*

PHILOKTETES

>   Strangers!
Who? From where? What brings you   240
rowing ashore
to this desolate island? And no harbor!?
What is your country? Who are your people?
Dressed like Greeks. I like that
>   more than anything.
Speak! It's OK, don't let the wild look of me
scare you off. Don't panic. Have pity
>   on a lonely miserable man,
say something if you really come as friends—
just answer!   250

It wouldn't be right,
us not exchanging words with one another.

NEOPTOLEMOS

Since you ask, sir, the first thing
you should know is: we're Greeks.

PHILOKTETES

O music to the ears! After so long
to hear Greek from such as you!
       Dear boy
what brought you to this place?
This very spot! What necessity? What urge?
      What most   260
merciful wind pushed you this way?
Tell me everything so I can know
who you are.

NEOPTOLEMOS

I'm sailing home to the island of Skyros.
I am Neoptolemos, son of Achilles.
Now you know everything.

PHILOKTETES

O my son of a beloved father,
      a beloved land,
brought up by your grandfather Lykomedes—
what's your mission here? Where are you coming from?   270

NEOPTOLEMOS

Right now I'm sailing from Troy.

PHILOKTETES

O? How so? For sure *you* weren't with us
when we first set sail for Troy.

NEOPTOLEMOS

You!? Were actually part of *that*!

PHILOKTETES

My boy, I'm standing here. You don't know me!?

NEOPTOLEMOS

Know you? How? I've never seen you before.

PHILOKTETES

Never heard my name? No word
of the miseries killing me to death?

NEOPTOLEMOS

Nothing. I don't know what you're talking about.

PHILOKTETES

I'm lost! The gods hate me!   280
Not one word of me abandoned here
has reached my home. No word
to Greeks anywhere out there!
The men who brought me here

in silence, in secret, make
mockery of me
while my disease
flourishes its worst, and spreads.

O my boy . . . Achilles' son . . .
I'm one you *must* have heard of!   290
the master of Herakles' bow!
      Philoktetes, son of Poias!
whom those two commanders and Odysseus
tricked and dumped
in this emptiness to waste away
with this vicious sickness,
venom-stricken by a vicious serpent.

Sickness I was left alone with.

The fleet had put in here
      having left sea-locked Chrysē.   300
They'd set me ashore. From rocking
on the stormy waters I'd fallen exhausted,
      they were glad to see,
asleep under an arch of rock. They left
some rags good enough for a beggar
and a little food. Me too they left
and may the gods give them the same.

Can you feel, son, how *I* felt, waking
to nobody here?

I burst into tears.   310
Can you feel how I felt cursing myself
seeing the very ships I'd sailed on
          gone! and on the island
nobody, not one human being
to give me a hand when I went down
          in pain? All I *saw*
was pain. Plenty of it.

Time passed me by. Season after season
cramped alone in my cave, I made do
myself. Had to. For something to eat   320
this bow knocked down fluttering doves.
The bowstring, as I released it, hummed!
          . . . then
whatever I'd hit I had to go after,
step & drag,
hauling this goddam foot.
Had to get water too. And winters
with frost, the water frozen,
step & drag, get
firewood to cut up.   330
No fire, none, but striking
stone on stone
I'd make the secret spark
leap up, out of darkness!
And this is what saved me.
A roof overhead, fire,
it's all I need—except
release from this disease.

Young man, I'll tell you something
about this place. No sailor   340
drops by on purpose—there's no harbor,
no port to trade in, no 'entertainment.'
No man in his right mind comes here.
Well, suppose some do. A lot happens
in the course of a lifetime. Then,
my boy, they feel sorry for me,
or so they say. And give me food
and clothing. But what they won't do,
when I can bring myself to mention it,
is take me home.   350

Ten miserable years now
I'm rotting away, feeding
this disease
it can't get enough of me!
This the sons of Atreus and ruthless Odysseus
            did to me.
May the Gods of Above give them what I got.

LEADER

I too feel for you, son of Poias,
much as those others did.

NEOPTOLEMOS

And I can testify to the truth of what you say.   360
I know, having been overridden
by the sons of Atreus—and the brutish Odysseus.

PHILOKTETES

You too? Have a grudge against those damned
sons of Atreus? On what grounds?

NEOPTOLEMOS

O if only my anger might find its hands!
Mycenaeans and Spartans alike would know
Skyros, too, raises great warriors.

PHILOKTETES

You said it, boy! But what *is* it
you in your anger go after them for?

NEOPTOLEMOS

Sir, I will tell you—*gods* it's hard   370
to talk about! but when I got to Troy
they humiliated me. Because when
fate gripped Achilles, and made him die . . .

PHILOKTETES

Wait! Enough! Let me get this straight.
He's dead? *Achilles!?*

NEOPTOLEMOS

Dead. Killed not by a man but a god.
An arrow from Apollo.

PHILOKTETES

No! . . . Noble killer, noble killed.
Where now should I begin? Ask how
they wronged you? Or mourn the dead?   380

NEOPTOLEMOS

You have enough to do mourning yourself,
poor man. No need to mourn others.

PHILOKTETES

True enough. Well go on then. Tell me
exactly how they insulted you.

NEOPTOLEMOS

They came for me in a ship, the prow
all decked out, colors flying—
the great Odysseus, and Phoinix
who'd raised my father from infancy—
saying (true or not, I don't know)
since my father was dead, it was fated   390
no one could capture Troy *but me.*
That was their story.

        It was all they needed to say.
I didn't wait to hear any more, but got myself
ready in a hurry. I wanted so to see my father
unburied. In all my life I'd never seen him
alive! Then too, they promised me that
when I got there, I alone could sack Troy.

Second day out, rowing along
    with a following wind   400
we landed at still painful Sigeion.

Soon as we hit shore, soldiers
crowded round, all swearing that
in me the dead Achilles lived again.
But he, he *was* dead. I wept for him, I felt
terrible. Then I went to the sons of Atreus,
figuring them as friends—to claim my father's arms
and whatever else he'd left. And, well . . .
they had the nerve to say: "Son of Achilles
take everything else of his, but those arms   410
belong to another man. The son of Laertes."

I choked up with rage and grief:
"You dared give away my arms
without so much as asking *me?*"

Then Odysseus—standing right there!—
he said: "That's right, boy. I saved them
and the remains of their owner."

I called him everything under the sun
    I was so mad I, I
didn'tleaveanythingout, no, what with   420
him thinking he could steal my arms!
And I *got* to him. He doesn't usually
get mad, but, you know, he did, he said:

"Your duty was here. But *you* weren't.
Now your mouth spits such insolence
you'll never take those arms back to Skyros."

Bawled out, disrespected, I sail home now—
robbed of what I had coming to me
by the sleaziest of a sleazy breed: Odysseus.
Even so, I don't blame him so much as the sons   430
of Atreus. An army, like a city, depends
completely on its leaders. When men trample on
others' rights, they get that from their leaders.
Anyway. That's my story. May the gods bless
any enemy of the sons of Atreus. *I* do.

CHORUS

Goddess of Mountains,
Bountiful Earth,
Mother of Zeus himself,
you through whom flows
Paktolos' great rush   440
of gold dust

Wondrous Mother
there too I called on you
that day the sons of Atreus
puffed up with arrogance
piled insults on this man,
giving his father's revered armor
to that son of Laertes

I prayed you then—now

hear me   450

Dread Mother who rides

lions that slaughter bulls

PHILOKTETES

Friends, the grief you've brought with you

rings true.

Your story tells my story. In it I see

the machinations of the sons of Atreus

and Odysseus. That one will talk up

any shady agenda—do *anything* for

any unconscionable end. Nothing new

in that. What's strange is how Aias   460

if he was there, could put up with this.

NEOPTOLEMOS

My friend . . . he wasn't! If he had been alive

they would never have robbed me like that.

PHILOKTETES

Him too!? Dead?

NEOPTOLEMOS

Think of him as gone . . . out, from the world of light.

PHILOKTETES

It can't be! And yet Diomedes and Odysseus,

the bastard Sisyphos begot then sold to Laertes—

the ones who should be dead—aren't!?

NEOPTOLEMOS

Those ones? Believe it, right now they're riding
high in the Greek army.   470

PHILOKTETES

What of my friend, the old and honest Nestor of Pylos?
        Alive still? He's the one
could baffle their schemes with wise advice.

NEOPTOLEMOS

It's no longer in him. He lost his son
Antilochos, who cared for him.

PHILOKTETES

Damn! Those two you mention, they're
the last ones I want to hear are dead.
What's to be our outlook on life
when *they're* dead, and Odysseus
who *should* be dead, isn't!   480

NEOPTOLEMOS

He's a cagey wrestler, Philoktetes, yet
even clever moves may be upended.

PHILOKTETES

Gods Above! where was Patroklos
        he didn't help you out?
He was your father's dearest friend.

NEOPTOLEMOS

Dead. Him too. The short of it
is: war doesn't single out evil men
but in general kills the good.

PHILOKTETES

I'll vouch for that. Speaking of which,
how goes the worthless one   490
with the quick, nasty tongue?

NEOPTOLEMOS

That would be Odysseus?

PHILOKTETES

Not *him*. Thersites, that one.
We had no way, ever, to shut him up
though everyone tried. He still alive?

NEOPTOLEMOS

I haven't seen him myself. I *heard* he is.

PHILOKTETES

He would be. Nothing evil ever dies.
The gods swaddle it up. They take
some kind of pleasure keeping
the slick smooth ones out of Hades,   500
yet send the just and the good away,
down there forever. What
can I make of this? How can I
go along with them when,

while praising all things divine,
I see the gods are evil?

NEOPTOLEMOS

As for me, O son of an Oitan father,
I'll be steering clear of Troy, keeping
my distance from the sons of Atreus.
Where the worst men overpower the best,   510
where the good die, while cowards rule,
I won't ever put up with such men.
From now on it's rockbound Skyros
for me. I will live my life
happily, at home . . .
(pause; then, abruptly . . .)
Well! Got to get back to the ship!
Good-bye son of Poias. Good luck
          with the gods!
Here's hoping they cure you
just as you wish!   520
(to sailors, all business)
Let's get going. We should be set to sail
the moment the heavens permit.

PHILOKTETES
          Already!? Going?

NEOPTOLEMOS
Yes. We need to be aboard
ready to sail when the wind shifts.

PHILOKTETES

My son, I beg you, in the name of
your father your mother your own
precious home—don't abandon me here
alone, helpless, living in the misery
you see, and more you've only heard of!   530
I won't be in your way!

          It puts you out
I know, a cargo like me, but put up with it
anyway. You're *noble*, you *despise* meanness,
to you decency is *honorable*. But leave me
here? your name will be covered with shame!
My son, the glory's all yours if you
return me alive to Oita. Do it, it won't take
hardly a day, stow me wherever—
in the hold, by the prow, the stern—   540
wherever's least noxious to the crew.

O say you will! My boy, by the grace of Zeus
look at me! on my knees, sick as I am, helpless,
a miserable cripple! Don't leave me outcast
here, where human footsteps are unheard-of.
Give me safe passage to your own homeland
or Chalkedon in Euboea. From there it's not
far to Oita, to rugged Trakhis, to the gorgeous
rolling Sperkheios—you can present me
to my most loving father. For a long time   550
now, I've been afraid he's passed on.
I kept sending messages with those

who happened through, begging him
come alone with a ship. Take me home!
But maybe he's dead. Or the messengers
thought no more of it, and hurried
their own way home.

You now, you're not just
a messenger, you're my escort—*you* take me.
Have mercy! Save me! You see how we all   560
live on the edge, with disaster a step away.
And the man who's doing well, he above all
should watch out for what *just like that*
will destroy his life.

CHORUS

(severally)

Sir, pity him.
He's told all
the sufferings he has struggled with,
not to be wished on any friend of mine.

Sir, if you hate the hateful sons of Atreus—
if it were me I'd turn   570
their evils to his advantage—
take him aboard your swift, well-rigged ship
to the home he's homesick for,
and escape the wrath of the gods.

NEOPTOLEMOS

     Careful.
It's easy to be easy-going . . . now. Yet
when you've lived awhile with his disease
you may disown your own words.

LEADER

Never. You will never, with justice,
accuse me of that.   580

NEOPTOLEMOS

I'd be ashamed if you seemed readier
than me to help him out. But if
that's what you want, let's sail. Quickly!
We should get a move on. The *ship*
won't turn him away. Just pray
the gods get us safely out of here,
wherever we're going.

PHILOKTETES

O glorious day! My dear friend! kind
sailors! if only I could *do* something
to prove how grateful I am to you!   590
Let's go, my boy—after we say good-bye
to the home that's not a home, inside.
You'll know then how I lived, and what
heart it took to survive. Just seeing it
anyone else would've given up. Out of
necessity, in time, I learned to live with it.

PHILOKTETES and NEOPTOLEMOS turn to enter the cave.

LEADER

      Wait! Hold on.

Two men coming—a shipmate with a stranger.

Before you go in, hear what they have to say.

MERCHANT (disguised Sailor) and another of Odysseus's Sailors appear.

MERCHANT

Son of Achilles? I asked this fellow here—   600

he with two others guarding your ship—

where I'd find you. Not that I expected

to come across you. I just . . . happened by!

Mine's the usual merchant ship, small crew,

returning home from Troy to the great vineyards

of Peparethos. On hearing these were *your* sailors

I decided not to sail away quietly—not without

giving you my news . . . and getting a reasonable

reward. I figured you know next to nothing

about your own affairs—new plots the Greeks   610

are mounting against you. Not idle talk

but actual doings already in the works.

NEOPTOLEMOS

Really, sir, that's thoughtful of you. If

I'm not unworthy of this, I'll remember you

with gratitude. But what 'doings'? What

exactly are the Greeks scheming against me?

MERCHANT

Old Phoinix and the sons of Theseus
are coming after you. In fully manned ships.

NEOPTOLEMOS

To force me back? Or talk me into it?

MERCHANT

I don't know. I'm just saying what I heard.   620

NEOPTOLEMOS

Are Phoinix and his crew so anxious
to get in good with the sons of Atreus?

MERCHANT

Believe it, they're on their way. Right now.

NEOPTOLEMOS

Odysseus couldn't sail himself, carrying
his own message? Is he afraid to?

MERCHANT

Just as I was weighing anchor
he and the son of Tydeus were setting out
after someone else.

NEOPTOLEMOS

Who? Odysseus himself after *what* someone?

MERCHANT

There was a man who, ah . . .   630
but first, who *is* that over there?
and keep your voice down.

NEOPTOLEMOS

Sir, you're looking at the famous Philoktetes.

MERCHANT

Then that's all you're getting from me.
Better haul yourself out of here. Now.

PHILOKTETES

What's he saying, boy? What's
your business, you two, haggling
in dark whispers over me?

NEOPTOLEMOS

I'm not sure yet. Whatever, he has to say it
openly, in the light, for everyone to hear.   640

MERCHANT

Son of Achilles, don't report me to the Greek army
for saying what I shouldn't! I'm a poor man, I get by
doing them favors. And getting a little something back.

NEOPTOLEMOS

The sons of Atreus hate me! And as *he* hates them,
that man is my best friend. Now you, coming here
with friendly intentions—you must tell us *everything*.

MERCHANT

Watch yourself. Young man.

NEOPTOLEMOS

I always have. And do so now.

MERCHANT

I'll hold you responsible.

NEOPTOLEMOS

Do that. Now talk.   650

MERCHANT raises his voice.

MERCHANT

OK. Right. . . . It's *this* man
those two are sailing after. The son of Tydeus
        and Lord Odysseus.
They swore they'd bring him in—by talking him into it
or by strong-arm arrest. All the Greeks heard Odysseus
say this, loud and clear. He was more sure of himself
than his partner was.

NEOPTOLEMOS

But why now? What moved the sons of Atreus
to think about this man? Years ago
        they threw him out!   660
What now has possessed them? The gods
demanding payback for their evil deeds?

MERCHANT

I'll tell you. Surely you haven't heard.
There was a seer, noble, a son of Priam
named Helenos. He was out and around
one night, alone, when wily Odysseus
(the creepy one none has a good word for)
caught him, chained him, and paraded him
before the Greeks. A prize catch.
Whatever they asked, Helenos had   670
a prophecy for. He said they'd never sack Troy
with its towers—unless they could persuade
this man to leave this island here and
bring him back. Right then Odysseus swore
he'd take him back and show him off
to the Greeks. He expected the man would come
willingly—if not, he'd be forced—and that if he,
Odysseus, failed, anyone who wanted his head
could have it. That's the whole story, young man.
You best get going now. You, and anyone   680
you care for.

PHILOKTETES

That bottomless pit of a man!
            He'd persuade *me*
back to the Greeks? That will be the day
I'm dead. He can persuade me to rise
out of Hades into the light of day,
like his own father did.

MERCHANT

I know nothing of all that, but . . .
good luck! Got to ship out now!
Gods be with you!   690

MERCHANT and Sailor leave.

PHILOKTETES

Horrifying, my boy, isn't it? The son of Laertes
dreams he'll sweet-talk me onto his ship,
lead me ashore, and show me off to the Greeks?
No way! I'd sooner listen to my deadliest enemy,
the snake that made my foot into a *thing*. Still
there's nothing *that* one wouldn't say or do,
and he'll be here soon!
    Come on, son,
let's get going—put a stretch of open sea
between his ship and us. Go let's go!   700
Making good speed at the right time means
we can rest when the work is over.

NEOPTOLEMOS

In time. The wind's against us.
When it lets up, we'll go.

PHILOKTETES

Escaping evil, it's always good sailing.

NEOPTOLEMOS

Sure, but the wind's against *them*, too.

PHILOKTETES

To pirates looking for plunder
no wind is an ill one.

NEOPTOLEMOS

Well, if you insist, let's go—soon as you get
whatever you need or want from in there.   710

PHILOKTETES

A few things I need. Out of so very little.

NEOPTOLEMOS

What do you need that's not already on board?

PHILOKTETES

A certain herb. To tame this vicious wound.

NEOPTOLEMOS

Then get it out here. What else?

PHILOKTETES

Stray arrows I maybe overlooked.
Wouldn't want anyone else to get
their hands on them.

NEOPTOLEMOS

      Is that really
the famous bow you have there?

PHILOKTETES

The one and only. This, in my hand.   720

NEOPTOLEMOS

May I take a closer look? Hold it?
Honor it as I would . . . a divine power?

PHILOKTETES

My boy, whatever's good for you,
anything I can give you, I will.

NEOPTOLEMOS

I'd love to touch it, but only—if the gods
think it right. Otherwise never mind.

PHILOKTETES

Son, as you're respectful, sure it's right.
It's you who put the gleam of sunlight
back into my eye—the hope of seeing
Oita again, my old father and friends—   730
you who, from under my enemies' feet,
have raised me up beyond their reach!
Take heart. The bow is yours to touch
before you hand it back. Then, for your
kindness to me, you'll be able to say
you alone of all mortal beings

touched it! As I myself did that day
I got it, by doing something kind.

NEOPTOLEMOS
I don't regret I happened on you—and found
a friend! Whoever knows how to pay back   740
kindness with kindness is worth more,
friend, than any possession. Go in, please.

PHILOKTETES
I'll show you in. My sickness wants you
to stand by, and support me.

PHILOKTETES and NEOPTOLEMOS go into the cave.

CHORUS
(severally)
> I've heard, but never seen,
> how the man who tried to slip into
> Zeus' wife's bed
> was caught, and bound on a whirling wheel
> by Zeus himself—

> but I'd never seen nor heard of   750
> a man with awfuller fate than this,
> who conned no one, harmed no one,
> who lived on good terms with everyone—
> yet was punished worse
> than anyone deserves.

I'm stunned at how
being so desolate here
hearing nothing ever but pounding surf
he yet
clung to his wretched life.   760

He himself was his only neighbor,
unable to walk,
with no one near to hear him suffer
screaming agony, nor feel with him
the disease eating his flesh, draining away his blood,

no one
to help gather healing herbs
from the good earth
—whenever a fit came over him—
to ease the burning pus from his ulcerous foot,   770

but went this way and that,
when the disease let up,
like a child with no nursemaid to steady it,
crawling around anywhere for anything
that might help somehow,

not for the food men work for
by seeding the blessed earth
but only, as happened,
with arrows shot from his quick-killing bow
he got food to eat.   780

A rotten life.

Ten years, and not one savoring taste of wine,

just

winding round toward any stagnant pool

he could find.

As PHILOKTETES and NEOPTOLEMOS are about to emerge from the cave . . .

LEADER

But now, after all that, he'll arrive at greatness

and a happy end. He's lucked out,

having met face to face the son of good people

who, in the fullness of so many moons, cutting across the sea

will bring him to his own   790

ancestral home

where Melian nymphs linger by the Sperkheios,

CHORUS

where bronze-shielded Herakles

rose in flames nearer the gods

amidst the lightning crashes of his father Zeus

high above Oita.

NEOPTOLEMOS and PHILOKTETES, with herbs and arrows, emerge.

NEOPTOLEMOS

Come on . . .

What's wrong? Why so awful still all of a sudden?

PHILOKTETES

(swallowing his agony)

Unh . . . Unh . . . Unh. . .

NEOPTOLEMOS

What's the matter?   800

PHILOKTETES

Nothing, nothing. Keep going, son.

NEOPTOLEMOS

You in pain? The usual?

PHILOKTETES

No, no. Think 's getting better . . .
                                 Good gods!!

NEOPTOLEMOS

Then why the groaning? Why call on the gods?

PHILOKTETES

So they'll come . . . make better.
Gd! gd!

NEOPTOLEMOS

What's got *into* you? Speak! say something!
I know something's wrong.

PHILOKTETES

Son I've had it. I can't hide the pain from you *o*   810
gods it runs right through me through me I'm
miserable *damn* done for! It's eating me alive!

    Son, I'm gone!

Buhh   Bbuhh   Buhhppuhpppuhppppuh

O for the gods you have a sword handy

      at hand?? USE IT!

Cut the heel OFF *now* now, no mind my life!

Quick son quick quick!

NEOPTOLEMOS

What? Why all of a sudden now?

what's new   820

all this screaming and hollering?

PHILOKTETES

You know.

NEOPTOLEMOS

What?

PHILOKTETES

My boy, you know.

NEOPTOLEMOS

Know what? What *is* the matter with you?

PHILOKTETES

You *have* to know! *Agaahh Agaaahhh*

NEOPTOLEMOS

Your disease. It's unbearable.

PHILOKTETES

Unbearable beyond words. *Pityme!*

NEOPTOLEMOS

What should I do?

PHILOKTETES

Don't let me down,   830
don't be afraid—
this wandering disease
comes to me
when it's tired wandering,
and having had enough
it goes away.

NEOPTOLEMOS

Luckless man. Every misery there is
shows through you.
          Should I hold you?
Give you a helping hand?   840

PHILOKTETES

No, don't touch! But take the bow, please,
like you asked to—watch it till the pain

goes away. Guard it. I'll pass out asleep
when the fit passes, have to, or the pain
won't leave. Yet let me sleep in peace.
And if those men come, by the gods above
I beg you, don't give them or anyone else
the bow, willingly or unwillingly, or you'll
destroy yourself and kill me. Begging you.

NEOPTOLEMOS

Don't worry. This passes into no hands but yours   850
and mine. Give it here. And with it, good luck!

PHILOKTETES

Here, son, take it. Pray the gods don't envy
you—so the bow won't destroy you the way
it did me, and him who owned it before me.

NEOPTOLEMOS

Gods, give us this! Make it so we sail
with a swift following wind wherever
the heavens send us and our mission ends.

PHILOKTETES

                    My boy, I'm afraid
you're praying for nothing. Look!
new dark blood oozing out   860
from somewhere deep,
dripping red again. I expect
a fresh worse attack. *Oooo*
          my foot

you excruciate me! The pain
slithers up, near, here! *Oooo*
          OoooOooo
NOW you know! Don't go! O
*Oooo*dysseus my friend if only this
          agony!   870
could stickstab through you
godgodgod
my generals general menelaos
general agamemnon if only
your flesh fed this sickness
as long as mine has
          AAHHHHZZ!
Death Death every day I beg you
what's keeping you
why don't you come?   880

My boy, you're a good boy
whyn't you
pick me up burn me in that fire out there,
          Lemnian fire,
I did the same for Herakles, son of Zeus,
for that I got the arms
you have there now. What say. What
          say, speak!
Why so quiet? Where are you?

NEOPTOLEMOS

Here, a long time here, heartsick   890
over your crushing pain.

PHILOKTETES

No, be brave *too*, my boy. The thing drops in
quickly yet goes quick too. Just please don't
leave me here alone.

NEOPTOLEMOS

Don't worry. We'll stay with you.

PHILOKTETES

You will?

NEOPTOLEMOS

Absolutely.

PHILOKTETES

Not that I'd ask you to swear to that, my boy.

NEOPTOLEMOS

Don't worry. It's not right to leave without you.

PHILOKTETES

Your hand on that! Give it.   900

NEOPTOLEMOS

I promise. We'll stay.

PHILOKTETES

Now. Up there. Take me.

NEOPTOLEMOS
What? Where there?

PHILOKTETES
(eyes rolling back into his head)
                    Up up . . .

NEOPTOLEMOS
(grabbing PHILOKTETES' arm)
Another fit? Why're you looking up . . . the *sky*?

PHILOKTETES
Let go me! Let go!

NEOPTOLEMOS
To go where?

PHILOKTETES
Let me go!

NEOPTOLEMOS
I won't.

PHILOKTETES
You'll kill me holding me like that.   910

NEOPTOLEMOS
(releases him)
OK OK. Now that you've calmed down.

PHILOKTETES

O Earth, take my dying body.
I can't stand up under this pain.

PHILOKTETES sinks to the earth.

NEOPTOLEMOS

I think . . . sleep will grip him soon. Look!
his head jerked back! His whole body's soaked
in sweat . . . the dark blood of a burst vein
trickling from his heel . . . Let's leave him
in peace, friends, so he can sleep.

CHORUS

Sweet sleep that feels no agony, no pain,
we pray you: kindly come   920
breathing your blessings, blessings
spread gently over him—
hold in his eyes this most serene glow
lowered on them now,
O lord of healing.
Come.

PHILOKTETES sleeps.

LEADER

Young man, you see the situation,
think where we're at.
What's the next move? Why don't we make it?

The Right Moment is everything!   930
When you see an opening you take it
quickly! That's the way to victory!

NEOPTOLEMOS
(raising his voice)
Sure, he doesn't hear a thing. But we've tracked him down
for what?—if we got the bow and sailed off, yet left him behind?
He's the victory trophy. It's him the gods want brought back.
We'd be shamed bragging of a job half done. Worse, done by lies!

CHORUS
(severally)
My boy, the gods will take care of that.
But when you speak next keep it down, *shsh*, down
to a whisper—
sick men sleep sleepless, they pick up on things.   940

So please, *whatever* you have to do
to achieve what you have in view
do it quietly
because if you keep on like this after this
—you know, doing what you're thinking—
a wise person can expect something real bad happening.

But now, my boy, the wind
the wind is right! The man lies

> blind, helpless, warmed into sleep
> as though under cover of night.   950
> He can't get a hand or foot to do anything!

Strengthless he is, like one laid at the edge of Hades.

LEADER

> Careful now. What are you thinking to do?
> Timing is all.
> As far as I can figure, it's safest to move
> quickly, without warning.

NEOPTOLEMOS

Shush! Watch it! His eyes
are open. He's raising his head.

PHILOKTETES

> Ah, sun,
taking up where sleep leaves off!   960
I never dreamed to hope these
strangers would keep watch for me.
I dared not even think it.
You're so patient, son, so feeling
to stand by me in my agonies
helping me. Those O so brave
commanders, the sons of Atreus,
didn't have it in them
to put up with this. But you, you're
naturally noble! It's your bloodline.   970

You weren't fazed by my screaming
pain, or the putrid smell.

          But now
the disease has left this little lull
of peace, easing off the pain—so
come, my boy, help me, get me
back on my feet.
When the wooziness goes
we'll head for the ship
and quick, get under way.   980

NEOPTOLEMOS

I would not have believed it. What
a relief! You're up, your eyes open
looking around, and no pain! It's more
than I'd hoped for. After all that agony
your sleep looked like death.

Come, get up now. If you want, these men
can carry you. They won't begrudge the job,
seeing you and I are in this together.

PHILOKTETES

Thank you, son. You help me up, will you,
like you said? Don't bother the men.   990
I wouldn't want them weighed down by this
awful stench *too* soon. When we're living aboard
the ship, they'll have enough to put up with.

NEOPTOLEMOS

Come, stand up. Grab hold of me.

PHILOKTETES

Don't worry. I'm well used to getting myself up.

NEOPTOLEMOS

(to himself, helping PHILOKTETES up)

Damn! What *now* am I to do!?

PHILOKTETES

What's up, my boy? Where're you getting at?

NEOPTOLEMOS

I'm running on. I don't know where I'm going.

PHILOKTETES

"Don't know where" why? Don't talk that way.

NEOPTOLEMOS

But it's where I feel I'm at. This impasse!   1000

PHILOKTETES

My disease disgusts you? You've had
second thoughts about having me on board!?

NEOPTOLEMOS

Everything's *disgust* when a man steps outside
his breeding. And does what's beneath him.

PHILOKTETES

Helping an honorable man you don't do
anything your own father wouldn't say or do.

NEOPTOLEMOS

I'll be seen as dishonorable. That's
what's been tearing me apart.

PHILOKTETES

Not for what you're *doing*!
It's your *words* that worry me.   1010

NEOPTOLEMOS

Zeus, what will I do? Expose myself
as a traitor, by saying nothing? And yet
again, for telling the shameful truth?

PHILOKTETES

(as though to himself)
Unless I've got it all wrong, this person here
will betray and abandon me. And sail away.

NEOPTOLEMOS

Abandon, no. But take you on a voyage
so bitter . . . it's been tearing me up inside.

PHILOKTETES

What are you saying, my boy? I don't follow you.

NEOPTOLEMOS

I'll hide nothing. You must sail with us
to Troy, to the Greek forces,   1020
and serve under the sons of Atreus.

PHILOKTETES

What! What are you saying!?

NEOPTOLEMOS

Don't go moaning yet! You don't know the rest of . . .

PHILOKTETES

       WHAT now?
What do you mean to do to me?

NEOPTOLEMOS

Save you from this misery—then, together
we'll lay waste the plains of Troy.

PHILOKTETES

That's your plan? Really?

NEOPTOLEMOS

       It's a matter of utmost . . .
necessity. Don't get mad hear me out.   1030

PHILOKTETES

I'm done for! Betrayed! You, stranger, why
do this to me? The bow! Give it *back* to me!

NEOPTOLEMOS

Can't. Have to do what's right. And for
my own good, obey commanders' orders.

NEOPTOLEMOS, face averted, stands holding the bow.

PHILOKTETES

You scorched earth you terror monster
you filthy piece of work! What
have you done to me? you played me!
Ashamed to look me in the face, me
kneeling at your feet, heartless bastard?
Taking my bow you took my life!   1040
Give it back, *please*, give it, I beg you, boy!
By the gods of your fathers, don't steal
this it's my life!

                    . . . Says
nothing. Looks away like
he'll never give it up.

                    O you bays, you headlands,
you sheer rockface, you wild animals roaming the hills
with me, it's *you* I speak to—who else is there?—to you
only I wail what the son of Achilles, this boy,   1050
has done to me. He swore he'd bring me home?
He hauls me to Troy. And with his right hand
having given his word, he grabs and holds
my sacred bow, the bow of Herakles, son of Zeus,
to show off to the Greeks like it's his own.

Me too he drags off, as if he'd brought down
a big powerful man. He can't see he's killing
a carcass, a shadow of ghosting smoke.
Had I my strength he wouldn't have taken me.
Even as is he wouldn't, if he hadn't tricked me.   1060
But he did. Now what can I do?
              HAND IT BACK!
It's not too late! You can still step back
inside your own true self!

What say? What's that? Silence?

That's it then. I'm nothing.

O rock tunnel, again I go back
into you. Disarmed, stripped
of the means to live, my life
will wither away in loneliness.   1070
No bird on the wing, no animal
browsing the hills will I kill
with that bow there. I'll be food
for those who fed me, hunted
by those I myself hunted.
              Aaaa . . .
then will I give my blood back
for the blood of those I've killed—
victim, me, of one who seemed
to know no evil. *Die you!* But   1080
(directly at NEOPTOLEMOS)
not yet. Not till I see if you change

your mind again. If not, may you
die a rotten death.

CHORUS

What will we do, lord? It's up to you.
Set sail? Or do as he says?

NEOPTOLEMOS

For him, I feel. Not this moment
only, but for some time now.

PHILOKTETES

Pity, my boy, for love of the gods! Don't
give men grounds to despise you
for deceiving me.   1090

NEOPTOLEMOS

What will I do? Better I'd never left Skyros
than come to so hard a place.

PHILOKTETES

It's not *your* shame! You learned this
from truly evil teachers. *They* sent you!
Let them do their own dirty work.
Sail away, but first—give me back my arms.

NEOPTOLEMOS

Men, what will we do?

ODYSSEUS jumps out from behind the rocks.

ODYSSEUS

      DO!?

Do what, traitor? You won't get back

     here and   1100

give me that bow?

Two Sailors emerge from behind ODYSSEUS.

PHILOKTETES

Who is that voice? Odysseus!?

ODYSSEUS

Odysseus for sure. It's me myself you see.

PHILOKTETES

I've been sold out! It's *him* trapped me,

he stole my arms.

ODYSSEUS

Me, yes, me alone. My word on it.

PHILOKTETES

(to NEOPTOLEMOS)

The bow, son, give it back. Give me.

ODYSSEUS

He won't, never, even if he wants to.

And you'll come with it—or *these*

—ODYSSEUS gestures toward the Sailors—

will force you to.   1110

PHILOKTETES

You, you're the worst of the worst.
Them? Force ME!?

ODYSSEUS

If . . . you don't come quietly.

Burst of light, fading. Distant rumbling.

PHILOKTETES   ⁚

O Lemnos—and you, O shooting flame
worked up by Hephestos—must I stand for this?
Let that man *drag* me off?

ODYSSEUS

Look here!
        it's ZEUS!
ZEUS rules here!
ZEUS decrees what happens!   1120
I carry out his orders.

PHILOKTETES

You're despicable. Hiding behind
your shield of lies and gods,
you make them liars, too.

ODYSSEUS

No, this is their truth.
This is the way we must go.

PHILOKTETES

No!

ODYSSEUS

Yes! You *must* submit.

PHILOKTETES

Then I'm damned! For sure my father
begot me not as a free man, but a slave.   1130

ODYSSEUS

No. You're the best among the best,
you're destined
to break Troy down into dust.

PHILOKTETES

Never! Whatever I suffer. Not while
I have these steep crags to stand on.

ODYSSEUS

And do what?

PHILOKTETES

Throw myself down, smash my head
on the rocks.

ODYSSEUS

(to Sailors)
Grab him! Both! Disable him!

Sailors hold PHILOKTETES.

PHILOKTETES

Poor bare hands, with no bow to draw,   1140
        hunted down now
together, held helpless under Odysseus . . .
(to ODYSSEUS)
As for you, you're the sort never has
a healthy or generous thought. Yet
sneaking up you've caught me out
again! hiding behind this boy stranger
who's too good for you, but for me
noble enough. All he'd thought to do
was what you wanted him to. Now he's
torn up over the terrible thing he did   1150
and the wrong done me. Your corrosive
soul, squinting out from some secret hole,
taught that boy what he didn't want to learn
—it wasn't in him—to be good at evil.

Now you want to tie me hand and foot,
take me from the same shore you cast me
up on—no friends, helpless, homeless—to live
my own death.
                Aie!
You should die! Out! I kept praying you would.   1160
But the gods leave nothing sweet for me. You,
you're happy to be alive. My pain is my life
lived among miseries, made a fool of
by the sons of Atreus you run errands for.

And yet, you sailed with them *only*
because you were tricked, and conscripted.
I, wretch, came on my own with seven ships
only to be dishonored, abandoned—for which
you blame them, and they blame you.

So why cart me off now? For what?   1170
I'm nothing. To you I'm a dead man.
Why's it now—for you, whom the gods
loathe—I'm not a stinking cripple?
How can you burn sacrifices to the gods
if I sail with you? How pour your offerings?
Wasn't that your excuse for dumping me here?

Die a rotten death, you! You'll have an awful end
if the gods love justice. And I'm sure they do—
because you wouldn't have sailed here
        looking for me   1180
if the gods hadn't driven you to it.

O gods of my fathers, O watchful ones,
when the time comes however late it comes
beat them all down, beat them, if you pity me.
My life is pathetic, but if I could see them
crushed, I could dream
I had been freed of my disease.

LEADER
A tough one, this stranger. Doesn't mince words,
Odysseus. He's not one to give in to misery.

ODYSSEUS

I'd have a lot to say back to him—if   1190
we had the time. For now all I'll say is
whatever the occasion, I'm the man for it.
If the times called for just and good, sure,
I could do that. As scrupulous as anyone.
But for me, in my very bones, victory is all.
Except now. With you.

                              For you, I'll back off.

(to the Sailors holding PHILOKTETES)
Yes! Let him go! Don't touch him. Let him
stay here. We've got your bow, we don't need you.
We have Teukros, an expert archer.   1200
And me. I can handle the bow as well as you
and damn well aim it, too. Who needs you?
        Good-bye!
Take a stroll around Lemnos. Enjoy yourself.

Sailors release PHILOKTETES.

                          Let's go.
Who knows? with this, your precious possession,
I may get the honors once meant for you.

PHILOKTETES

O gods, what will I do? You'll parade yourself
among the Greeks . . . showing off *my* bow?

ODYSSEUS

That's enough out of you! I'm going.   1210

PHILOKTETES

Son of Achilles! You, too? Without
a word for me, you'd leave?

ODYSSEUS

(to NEOPTOLEMOS)

Let's go! Don't even look. You being so
          noble and good
you'll spoil our good luck.

PHILOKTETES

(to CHORUS)

You too, strangers? You'd leave me all alone?
Have you no pity?

LEADER

The young man is our master. What he says, we say.

NEOPTOLEMOS

(to CHORUS)

The chief there will say I'm too soft, but you men
stay here, if that's what this one wants, for as long   1220
as it takes the sailors to set the rigging and get
everything shipshape. Until we've said our prayers
to the gods. By then maybe this one will think
better of us.

(to ODYSSEUS)

    All right let's go. The two of us.

(to CHORUS)

    You, when we call, come running.

ODYSSEUS *and* NEOPTOLEMOS *leave.*

PHILOKTETES

Then

O my deep hollow in the rock

—sun baked, icy cold—

I could never leave you after all!   1230

It's you will witness my death

o gods o gods

O forlorn space, all echoed up

reeking with my pain.

What now will befall my days?

Where will I find hope

—in my misery—of finding food?

You timid doves,

once so fearful,

fly freely in the whistling winds   1240

I can't stop you now!

LEADER

Your lot is hard, but *you*

you brought this damnation

down yourself *on* yourself,

unfortunate man. Know this.

Nothing outside you,
no overwhelming power
did—but you alone.
You had the chance
to choose a better way   1250
and chose a worse one.

PHILOKTETES

I'm miserable rotten miserable then—
abused in my misery
I have to live with this, with no human being
other! Ever! How will I
get food? when I can't,
with my strong hands, let
the feathered arrows fly.

Sly words of a swindling soul
unsuspected   1260
wormed into me.
May I see the one behind this scheme
suffer like me, and as long!

LEADER

It was the gods doomed
this on you, not me. I had
no hand in tricking you.
Aim your hate your curses
elsewhere. What I don't want
is you refusing my friendship.

PHILOKTETES

Aie me . . .   1270

somewhere, sitting on the shore

of the gray sea

he mocks me—showing off the weapon I lived by,

that none other ever handled.

Beloved bow

torn from hands that cared for you

if you have feelings feel for this

friend to Herakles.

He'll never use you again.

You're in the grasp of a new master,   1280

a crafty one: you will see

countless shameful deceptions rising in the face

of him, my enemy,

by whom a thousand awful things

O Zeus

were done to me.

LEADER

You're right to say what's right.
But once you've said it,
stop. Don't go on and on
needling and bitter.   1290
Odysseus was doing a job
the whole army wanted done,
doing what was best for all
them, in the long run.

PHILOKTETES

All you wingèd ones I've hunted,
all you tribes of glare-eyed beasts
feeding in the hills up here,
don't flee your nests or dens! Nor me!
I no longer hold the powerful bow
protecting me.   1300
Go where you want. I'm no threat now.
Get your own back, blood for blood,
glut yourselves much as you want
on my rotting flesh.

I'll die soon.
How will I find means to live?
Who lives on air without
all that life-giving earth gives?

PHILOKTETES heads back toward his cave.

LEADER

By the gods, if you respect anything
respect a stranger who entreats you.   1310
Meet him halfway! It's up to you
to help yourself out of this fate.
It's pitiful the way this sickening
doom keeps eating away at you.
All the time in the world cannot
teach your body to live with this.

PHILOKTETES

> AGAIN
> you bring old agony up!
> You, the kindest of all
> who've come ashore here.   1320
> Why have you killed me like this?
> *What* have you done to me?

CHORUS

(individual)

What do you mean?

PHILOKTETES

You planned to take me
back to Troy, which I hate.

CHORUS

(individual)

We think it's for the best.

PHILOKTETES

Then leave me. Now!

LEADER

Fine by us. More than glad to oblige.

(to the CHORUS)

Come on, let's take up
our stations on the ship.   1330

The CHORUS starts to leave.

PHILOKTETES

Please! As Zeus hears curses . . . Don't go.

LEADER

Get hold of yourself.

PHILOKTETES

Strangers! Wait! By the gods, I beg you!

LEADER

What is it?

PHILOKTETES

Doom! it's the doom got me.
Foot, damned foot, where ahead
can I *go* with you!?
Strangers! Come back!

Again the CHORUS has moved to leave.

LEADER

To do what *now* any different
from what you wanted before?   1340

PHILOKTETES

No sense getting angry at a man
so wild with pain he talks crazy.

CHORUS
(individual)
Unhappy man. Like we said, come with us.

PHILOKTETES
No! Never! Believe it. Not though
the lord of lightning bolts thunder
burn me up in his fire. Let Troy
die, die every man under its walls
who had the heart to cast out
this poor cripple of a foot.

But, strangers, one thing I pray you . . .   1350

CHORUS
(individual)
What thing?

PHILOKTETES
　　　A sword.
You have one at hand? Or ax?
Any weapon. Give it me.

CHORUS
(individual)
To do what?

PHILOKTETES
Hack this body limb from flesh

and *off* my head. Death is
death all I can think now.

CHORUS
(individual)
Why?

PHILOKTETES
So I can find my father.   1360

CHORUS
(individual)
Where?

PHILOKTETES
          In Hades.
No longer here, in the light.
O city of my fathers, if only
I could see you—fool as I was,
leaving your sacred streams
to help the Greeks, my enemies.
Only to come to . . . nothing

PHILOKTETES drags his foot back into the cave.

LEADER
I'd be gone back to the ship by now
if I hadn't seen Odysseus, and the son of Achilles,   1370
climbing this way.

NEOPTOLEMOS appears, dogged by ODYSSEUS.

ODYSSEUS

At least, would you be so *kind* as to say *why*
you're headed back here in such a hurry!

NEOPTOLEMOS

To undo the wrong I did. Back here.

ODYSSEUS

What kind of talk is that? What 'wrong'?

NEOPTOLEMOS

Obeying orders from you and the Greek army I . . .

ODYSSEUS

. . . did what? *What* that was beneath you?

NEOPTOLEMOS

I set a man up. Tricked him, and betrayed him.

ODYSSEUS

What man? You're not planning something *rash*, are you?

NEOPTOLEMOS

Rash? No. But to the son of Poias I'll . . .   1380

ODYSSEUS

         . . . what!? You'll what?
I feel strange uneasiness creeping up on me.

NEOPTOLEMOS

I'll . . . give him the bow back.

ODYSSEUS

By Zeus you can't mean that! Not *really* give it back?

NEOPTOLEMOS

Really. I got it by fraud. I have no right to it.

ODYSSEUS

Gods above! You're just giving me a hard time, right?

NEOPTOLEMOS

Only if truth gives you a hard time.

ODYSSEUS

What do you mean? Son of Achilles, what are you saying?

NEOPTOLEMOS

How many times do I have to go over this? Two? Three?

ODYSSEUS

Better you hadn't 'gone over' in the first place.   1390

NEOPTOLEMOS

Well relax. Now you've heard it all.

ODYSSEUS

There's someone will stop you from doing this.

NEOPTOLEMOS

Meaning what? Who's to stop me?

ODYSSEUS

The whole Greek army. Me with them.

NEOPTOLEMOS

Smart as *you* are, your words aren't.

ODYSSEUS

There's nothing smart in what you say *or* do.

NEOPTOLEMOS

Being *just* beats being 'smart.'

ODYSSEUS

How is it just to give up what you got
thanks to my . . . strategic advice?

NEOPTOLEMOS

I did something shameful. I have to undo it.   1400

ODYSSEUS

You're not afraid what the Greeks will do
to *you*, if you do that?

NEOPTOLEMOS

With justice by my side, I'm not afraid.

ODYSSEUS

You will be.

NEOPTOLEMOS

I won't back off. Even for you.

ODYSSEUS

We won't fight the Trojans then. But you.

NEOPTOLEMOS

If it comes to that, so be it.

ODYSSEUS

(reaching)

You see my right hand?

By my sword hilt?

NEOPTOLEMOS

(reaching)

Watch my own, it's   1410

quick as yours.

ODYSSEUS

(withdrawing his hand)

OK. I'm not bothering with you anymore.

I'll go tell the whole army about this.

They'll straighten you out.

ODYSSEUS leaves. Downhill, he hides behind rocks.

NEOPTOLEMOS

(partly to himself, as ODYSSEUS is hurrying off)

> Good thinking!

If you stay this sensible you might even
keep yourself out of trouble.

NEOPTOLEMOS turns to face the mouth of the cave.

NEOPTOLEMOS

But you, son of Poias, Philoktetes,
come out from your rocky enclosure!

PHILOKTETES

(from within)

What's all the racket out there? Strangers,   1420
why are you calling? What do you want from me?

PHILOKTETES emerges, surprised. He had expected only sailors.

O no. Not good. You here to announce
new bad news, on top of my other miseries?

NEOPTOLEMOS

Don't be afraid. Hear what I have to say.

PHILOKTETES

That scares me. Last time I believed
your reassuring words, I got taken.

NEOPTOLEMOS

But can't I change my mind? Again?

PHILOKTETES

Just how you talked when you stole my bow.
So trustworthy. Friendly. And treacherous.

NEOPTOLEMOS

Not now though. All I want to know is: 1430
you aim to hold on here, or sail with us?

PHILOKTETES

                    Stop! Enough!
Whatever you say, you're wasting your breath.

NEOPTOLEMOS

Your mind's made up?

PHILOKTETES

More than words can say. Yes.

NEOPTOLEMOS

I wish I could have brought you round on this,
but . . . if my words are getting nowhere, I quit.

PHILOKTETES

                    Right. You're getting nowhere.
I'll never feel friendly toward you. Now, after
stealing by deceit the bow that means my life,   1440

you come to give advice? The shameless son
of a noble father!? Die! the bunch of you,
sons of Atreus, Odysseus son of Laertes,
and you!

NEOPTOLEMOS

            Stop! Enough!
No more curses. Here. Take them.

NEOPTOLEMOS offers PHILOKTETES the bow and arrows.

PHILOKTETES

What *are* you saying! This another trick?

NEOPTOLEMOS

No, I swear. By the awesome majesty
of Zeus on high.

PHILOKTETES

Wonderful words! If true.   1450

NEOPTOLEMOS

The act speaks for itself. Hold out your right hand,
take these. They're yours.

NEOPTOLEMOS hands weapons to PHILOKTETES.

VOICE OF ODYSSEUS

The gods be my witness . . .

ODYSSEUS jumps out from behind rocks.

I FORBID THIS! By authority
of the sons of Atreus and the entire Greek army!

PHILOKTETES

My boy . . . whose voice . . . I hear *Odysseus?*

ODYSSEUS

Better believe it. Up close, too!
Me, see? The Odysseus who will
cart you off to the plains of Troy
by force, no matter what   1460
the son of Achilles wants.

PHILOKTETES

Not without paying for it . . .

—he has fitted an arrow to the bowstring and is drawing the bow back—

if this arrow flies true.

NEOPTOLEMOS

(grabbing PHILOKTETES' arm)
By the gods, no! Don't let it go!

PHILOKTETES

Let go let go my hand dear boy!

NEOPTOLEMOS

No. I will not.

PHILOKTETES

       Why did you stop me
killing my enemy *he hates me* with my bow?

NEOPTOLEMOS

This killing isn't worthy of you. Nor of me.

ODYSSEUS has run off.

PHILOKTETES

Well one thing's sure. Greek army chiefs   1470
who trumpet themselves with bold words
are cowards at backing them up.

NEOPTOLEMOS

So let that be. You have your bow now.
No reason to be mad, or hold anything
against me.

PHILOKTETES

No, son, there isn't. You've shown
the stock you come from. Not Sisyphos
but Achilles, the noblest man who lived, and now
no less so among the dead.

NEOPTOLEMOS

I'm pleased, hearing you speak so well   1480
of my father, and of me. But now listen.

I have something to put to you.
                              What fortunes
the gods give us, we have to live with.
But when, like you, we willfully *persist*
in being victims, there's no excuse for that.
No pardoning, no pity.
You're stubborn, like an animal. You won't
take advice. Someone says something helpful
you hate him. Like he's an enemy. Even so   1490
I'll speak up. May Zeus, god of oaths, witness.
Mark my words. Write them down in your heart.
Your sickness and pain are a doom from a god.
You came too close to the serpent you didn't see
guarding the open shrine of the god Chrysē.
You'll never find relief, not so long as this
sun rises in the east and sinks in the west,
till you come freely to the plains of Troy
and meet with the sons of Asklepios
who will cure you. With the bow then   1500
and with me, you will bring down Troy.

PHILOKTETES doesn't respond.

How do I know this will happen? I'll tell you.
We took a Trojan prisoner: Helenos, a prophet
as good as his word. He says straight out this
must happen. What's more, Troy must fall
this summer. If I lie, he says, then kill me.
                              Now you know.
So come with us, freely. The bonus is,

your glory will grow! You'll stand out among
the Greeks—find healing hands—and when   1510
you've reduced Troy *the source of so many*
tears to ruins, you'll be famous.

PHILOKTETES

(quietly, as if speaking into a void)
Hateful life! why do you hold me
still above ground, in the daylight
of here on earth?
Why haven't you let me go
down into darkest Hades?

What will I do? How can I not
hear this man's well-meant advice?
Should I give in then? But how,   1520
after that, show myself in public,
shunned as I am? Who will speak to me?
And O my eyes, you've seen all
they've done to me, how could you
bear to see me going along with
the sons of Atreus who, here,
have made me rot away?
Or that damned son of Laertes?

It's not bitterness over the past
that eats at me, but what I expect   1530
these men will make me suffer
in days to come. Men whose souls
have conceived, once, an evil know

ever after how to breed other evils.

(to NEOPTOLEMOS)

You too I wonder at, wondering . . .
you yourself shouldn't be going to Troy,
you should keep me from going too!
Those men humiliated you, stripped you
of your father's arms—now you want
to join them? And make me join too?   1540

No, my boy, no. Take me home, like
you promised. And you, stay in Skyros.
Let these evil men die their evil death.
My father and I, both, will thank you
twice over. By not helping these evil
ones, you won't seem to be one yourself.

NEOPTOLEMOS

Reasonable words. Even so I wish
you'd trust the gods, trust my word,
and as a friend
sail with me away from here.   1550

PHILOKTETES

To Troy!? To the despicable sons
of Atreus? With this putrid foot?

NEOPTOLEMOS

To those who'll save you *and* your pus-running foot
from the pain of rotting away.

PHILOKTETES

Meaning what? What's behind *that* advice?

NEOPTOLEMOS

What I see ahead, if we do this, will be best
for both of us.

PHILOKTETES

Aren't you ashamed? Saying such a thing
the gods can hear?

NEOPTOLEMOS

What shame? I'm helping out a friend.   1560

PHILOKTETES

Helping out the sons of Atreus? Or me?

NEOPTOLEMOS

You, I should imagine. Speaking as your friend.

PHILOKTETES

How's that? If you'd turn me over to my enemies?

NEOPTOLEMOS

Seeing as you're down, sir, you shouldn't be so difficult.

PHILOKTETES

You'll do me in, I just know it . . . talking that way.

NEOPTOLEMOS

I won't, I'm telling you. You don't understand.

PHILOKTETES

Don't I know the sons of Atreus exiled me here?

NEOPTOLEMOS

They did. But now know how
they would save you!

PHILOKTETES

Never happen. Not if it means   1570
agreeing I'll go back to Troy.

NEOPTOLEMOS

What will I do then, if I can't convince you
of anything? Easier for me to shut up, and you
can live on as you are, with no way out.

PHILOKTETES

Let *me* suffer what's mine. But you
with your hand in mine promised
you'd bring me home. Now, my boy,
you have to keep that promise.
No more talk of Troy. I've had enough
of cryings and sorrows.   1580

NEOPTOLEMOS

That's what you want? . . . Let's go then.

PHILOKTETES

    Nobly spoken!

NEOPTOLEMOS

(offering help)

Step by step, now. Careful.

PHILOKTETES

    What I can, I'll do.

NEOPTOLEMOS

But how can I keep from being
blamed by the Greeks?

PHILOKTETES

    Don't give that a thought.

NEOPTOLEMOS

I have to. Suppose they attack my country?

PHILOKTETES

    I'll be waiting for them.

NEOPTOLEMOS

How can you help?   1590

PHILOKTETES

    Herakles' bow. That's how.

HERAKLES appears on the rocks above them.

NEOPTOLEMOS

Meaning what?

PHILOKTETES

I'll make them keep their distance.

NEOPTOLEMOS

Then kiss this ground good-bye. We're going.

HERAKLES, still unnoticed by PHILOKTETES and NEOPTOLEMOS, steps nearer.

HERAKLES

Not yet! Not till you've heard
what *I* will say, son of Poias!

Startled, PHILOKTETES and NEOPTOLEMOS turn and look up.

The voice of Herakles, yes! and this
is his face. For you I've left
the heavens. To let you know
what Zeus plans—to keep you   1600
from going where you're going,
and get you to listen to me.

First, know my own story—how
after many ordeals I achieved
as you now see

the glory that is deathless.
It's certain your own sufferings
are destined to bring you, too,
to glory. Go with this man to Troy
where, first, you'll be cured of this   1610
horrible disease. The Greek army
will choose you as its foremost
warrior. With my bow you will
kill Paris, who began all this misery.
You will sack Troy and be honored
with the choicest spoils. Bring these
home with you to the Oitan highlands
to please your father, Poias. The other
spoils such as common soldiers get
lay on my funeral pyre: as a tribute   1620
to my bow.

(to NEOPTOLEMOS)
       This advice
goes for you, too, son of Achilles.
You're not strong enough to take Troy
without him. Nor he to take it without you.
You're like two lions prowling the same
grounds, each guarding the other.

(to PHILOKTETES)
       I'll send Asklepios
to Troy, to cure you of your disease,
for Troy is doomed to fall a second time   1630
beneath my bow. Yet remember, when
you sack Troy show piety toward all things

relating to the gods. To Zeus, nothing
matters more. The sacred doesn't die
when men do. Whether they live or die,
holiness endures.

PHILOKTETES

Voice bringing back so much
I've longed for! You showing yourself
after so many long years! *Your* words
I will not disobey.   1640

NEOPTOLEMOS

And I the same.

HERAKLES

Don't waste time then. Move.
The wind is fair and following.
The time to act is now.

HERAKLES vanishes.

PHILOKTETES

                Come then, just
let me pay my respects to the land
I'm leaving . . . . Good-bye, cave, you
that watched out with me. Good-bye
you nymphs of the marshy meadows,
and you, O low groaning ocean   1650
booming thunder spume

against the headland—where deep
within the cave, how often my head
was drizzled by gusts of southerly wind,
how often the Mount of Hermes broke
my own mournful echoes back,
storming me with my sorrows.

But now you springs, and you
Lycean well sacred to Apollo,
I'm leaving you, at long last   1660
leaving—

I had never dared hope
for this.

Good-bye, Lemnos, surrounded by sea:
set me free and uncomplaining
with smooth sailing where
a great destiny takes me
by the counsel of friends
and, above all, the god who
subduing everything   1670
has brought this to pass.

CHORUS
Let's all set off together
now, praying the nymphs of the sea
come take us safely home.

Elektra

INTRODUCTION
"HAVEN'T YOU REALIZED
THE DEAD . . . ARE ALIVE?"

Dawn is breaking. From a hilltop in Mycenae, three men—the Elder, Orestes, and Pylades—look down on a palace haunted by three generations of kin murder. The trio has traveled a distance: for two of them this is a long-delayed homecoming.

The Elder, a trusted, forthright slave, has been a mentor to Orestes, the son of Agamemnon, hero of the Trojan War. Orestes was just a young boy when his father returned from battle. That day, during a celebratory feast, Agamemnon's wife, Klytemnestra, and her lover, Aegisthus, murdered Agamemnon, splitting his skull with an ax. Orestes' sister Elektra, fearing for her brother's life, entrusted Orestes to the Elder, who spirited him away to a safe exile. He grew up in northern Greece, sheltered by Pylades' family. Elektra has since lived in misery, impatiently awaiting her brother's promised return to avenge their father, while Klytemnestra and Aegisthus, now married, nervously rule Mycenae.

The Elder now impresses on both younger men the magnitude and urgency of the job ahead. He, too, is impatient with his young master. Their plans must be in place before the palace awakes. Prompted to take charge, Orestes calmly lays out a strategy, aware that Klytemnestra and Aegisthus fear he might at any moment descend on them. He instructs the Elder to pose as a messenger with news that Orestes has died in a horrific chariot accident. Then, their victims' vigilance relaxed, Orestes and his accomplice Pylades, also in disguise, will carry out the killing. Despite Orestes' apparent command of the situation, he grows uneasy. Faking his own death could prove a danger-ous omen. What if *pretending* he's dead precipitates the real thing? Shaking off the thought, he reveals that his motive is not revenge per se, but taking back the power and wealth Aegisthus and his mother have stolen from him.

For fifth-century Greeks, to "help one's friends and harm one's enemies" was an unquestioned maxim governing personal, political, and international conflicts. But Sophocles suggests— at first almost subliminally via the unattractive nature of his main characters—that cycles of revenge ravage those trapped within them as well as their enemies. By portraying Orestes as icily efficient and materialistic, and his sister Elektra as brave but nearly deranged with hatred for her mother and Aegisthus, Sophocles discourages his audience from accepting the looming act of vengeance as a sacred obligation that will ennoble those who undertake it.

The acrimonious and legalistic debates in the first third of the play, between Klytemnestra and Elektra, reveal the insta-bility of the moral ground each invokes to justify homicide or revenge. Klytemnestra argues that killing Agamemnon was jus-tified. A decade earlier, he had sacrificed their daughter Iphi-genia to placate the goddess Artemis and thus gain a favorable wind for the Greek army anxious to sail for Troy. Klytemnestra

insists his blood relation to his daughter should have outweighed his obligation to prosecute a war. Elektra counters by
saying that the sacrifice of Iphigenia was not criminal: it was a
military necessity. Though both claim to argue from the *talio*,
the concept of justice as an "eye for an eye, a life for a life," each
manipulates and ignores evidence and principle. Their legalisms
cannot disguise the ferocity of their antipathies. Klytemnestra
wanted Agamemnon dead so she could marry Aegisthus. Elektra hates her mother for killing the father she mourns. Sophocles makes clear that it's impossible to sanction revenge, a gut
issue for those involved, simply through analysis and debate.
Revenge, the audience realizes, issues from hatred immune to
logic or morality.

When the Elder brings news of Orestes' 'death,' Elektra
is devastated and Klytemnestra elated. Orestes and Pylades
ratchet up the tension when they arrive with an urn they claim
holds Orestes' ashes and ask to present it to the queen. Moved
by his sister's despair and ravaged appearance, Orestes tells her,
with excruciating deliberation, who he really is. But when her
out-of-control joy threatens to alert their intended victims, Orestes tries to silence her. Elektra remains oblivious to danger.
As her grip on reality grows increasingly tenuous, she confuses
the Elder with her dead father and falls to her knees before him.
The Elder, untouched, flares up. It seems Orestes and Elektra
are too preoccupied with their reunion to realize they have to
kill Klytemnestra before her husband and his men return. The
Elder must keep them focused on the business at hand. For a
moment, it seems doubtful the conspirators fully grasp the seri-
ousness of what they're doing.

Athenian audiences in the last half of the fifth century BCE were familiar with previous dramatic versions of Orestes and Elektra, especially Aeschylus' *Oresteia* trilogy. Sophocles, departing from Aeschylus' version of the myth, allows Elektra's obsession with revenge to absorb and dissolve all other energies and desires. She is disturbed and disturbing. The Chorus of townswomen is by turns supportive and disapproving of her conduct, but to Elektra their sentiments are irrelevant. For her, revenge is an entrenched imperative, and she fully accepts that it has unbalanced her: "[H]ow could I be calm / and rational? Or god-fearing? / Sisters . . . I'm so immersed / in all this evil, how / could I *not* be evil too?" (343–347).

Sophocles' most imaginative departure from Aeschylus involves the seeming omission of the Furies, the ancient, ugly, and relentless divinities who haunt and punish kin murderers. In Aeschylus' version, they are grotesquely real, a terrifying swarm who appear as the eponymous chorus of his play *The Eumenides* (literally and ironically, "The Kindly Ones"). Aeschylus' Furies chase Orestes across Greece until Athena domesticates them by granting them a less violent but more acceptable role. Although Aeschylus shows Orestes suffering the guilt that the Furies inflict on him, he's eventually cleansed of pollution in Delphi and spared civil punishment by the Areopagus court. Sophocles, however, saw that while priests and jurors may absolve a murderer of public guilt, they cannot undo the mental damage that killing a relative inflicts on the killer.

R. P. Winnington-Ingram proposed that Sophocles intended his audience to perceive Elektra and Orestes—throughout the entire length of the action—as *proxy* Furies who pursue and take revenge on Klytemnestra and Aegisthus (1980, 236–247).

By taking this revenge, the siblings become first "agents" and then ultimately "victims" of the Furies now embedded in themselves. They suffer a warping of their decency as they pursue a vengeance that in time will be visited on *them* when a new generation of avengers seeks them or their children out.

At various moments Orestes elaborates on his foreboding that using his faked death as a ploy to exact revenge will backfire—or, in Winnington-Ingram's terms, that his role as an agent of revenge will make him its victim: first, he identifies with a soldier, mistakenly reported dead, who returns home alive to find himself revered; later, Elektra cherishes what she thinks are her brother's ashes and he savors the effect of his death on others; and finally, Aegisthus realizes Orestes did not die in a chariot wreck, but is alive and about to kill him, a living metaphor of how those murdered emerge from death to exact vengeance.

Aegisthus flinches as he uncovers Klytemnestra's body.

Orestes Scare you? An unfamiliar face?

Aegisthus These men! *Have got me*—I've stumbled
into a net with no exit. Who *are* they?

Orestes Haven't you realized by now "the dead"—
as you perversely called them—*are alive*? (1787–1791)

The last scene evokes an image of Orestes (and Elektra as well) as victims of the revenge just taken:

Aegisthus . . . why force me inside? If what
you plan is just, why do it in the dark?
What stops you killing me right here?

Orestes   Don't give *me* orders. We're going where
              you killed my father! You'll die there!

Aegisthus Must this house witness all the murders
              our family's suffered—and those still to come?

Orestes   This house will witness yours.
              That much I can predict.

Aegisthus Your father lacked the foresight you boast of.

[. . .]

Orestes   Justice dealt by the sword
              will keep evil in check.   (1812–1821, 1831–1832)

Orestes might have the last word, but Aegisthus' ominous prediction conveys an unwelcome truth: when it comes to Greek blood feuds, only the extinction of each and every antagonist ends them. Orestes believes killing Aegisthus and his mother will punish and discourage evil, but Aegisthus' assertion—that Orestes and Elektra will remain subject to an implacable curse on the house of Atreus—reasserts the self-perpetuating nature of revenge. Newer Furies, Aegisthus is confident, will sooner or later attack and destroy his killers. The abrupt end of the play, which gives no sense of elation at the "mission accomplished" shared by the conspirators, leaves the audience to ponder what indeed do this brother and sister have to celebrate?

—RB

Elektra

Translated by Robert Bagg

CHARACTERS

ELDER, long-serving slave, teacher, and adviser to
Orestes

ORESTES, son of Agamemnon and Klytemnestra

Pylades, noble companion of Orestes

ELEKTRA, daughter of Agamemnon and
Klytemnestra, ragged, unkempt, and bruised

CHORUS of Mycenaean women

LEADER of the Chorus

CHRYSÒTHEMIS, daughter of Agamemnon and
Klytemnestra

KLYTEMNESTRA, widow of Agamemnon, wife of
Aegisthus, co-murderer of Agamemnon

Maidservant to Klytemnestra

Aide to Orestes, male

AEGISTHUS, husband of Klytemnestra, co-killer of
Agamemnon

*The ELDER, ORESTES, and Pylades appear on a backstage hilltop, looking
out over the heads of the audience at the cityscape beyond. As the ELDER
recognizes familiar landmarks, he directs ORESTES' attention to them.*

ELDER

And now, son of the man who commanded
our armies at Troy! Son of Agamemnon!
Look! You can see with your own eyes
the sight you have craved for so long:
the storied Argos of your dreams.
Hallowed country, over which
the horsefly hounded Io, that daughter
of Înachos Hera made a cow.
Look *there*, Orestes. The outdoor market
named after Wolfkiller Apollo.   10
On the left is that famous temple of Hera's.
Believe it. What you see is Mycenae!
Gold city, with its house of Pelops
bloodied by all that death and mayhem.
Under orders from your sister,
I carried you away, even
as your father was being murdered.
I saved your life! Raised you to take
revenge—the strapping youth who gives
his dead father his honor back!   20
All right, Orestes—you too, Pylades,
our excellent new friend—our plan
of attack must be worked out quickly.
Nothing's left of the starry night.
Already you can hear the birds
singing up the dawn, loud and clear.
Before anyone leaves that house,
get it together. The moment's arrived.
No time to dither. Time to act.

ORESTES

My best friend,

my mentor! You've always come through   30

for our family! Like an old thoroughbred

who doesn't spook in a tight spot

you stick your ears out straight,

urging us on, charging

into the thick of it. You're

always right there beside us.

Here's what I think. Listen

closely. If anything I say

is off target, correct my aim.

I went to Delphi to ask Apollo—   40

through his Pythian oracle—

how best to avenge my father.

Kill his killers.

Apollo said: ALONE NO TROOPS

NO ARMOR BY STEALTH SLAUGHTER

WITH YOUR OWN RIGHTEOUS HAND.

That's what the god told me.

(to the ELDER)

So you must infiltrate the palace.

Seize the first chance you're given.

Find out what's going on, so you

can bring us hard information.   50

You're so old now. After all these years

they won't know you, they won't

suspect you, not with that gray hair.

Now here's your story. You're a stranger

from Phokis. Phantíus sent you.

He's their most powerful ally.
Tell them—and flesh it out—the good
news that Orestes had the horrible
luck to be killed in a chariot race.
He was thrown from his racing car   60
at the Pythian games in Delphi.
Make that the gist of your account.
Meantime we will honor Father
exactly as the god told us to do.
We'll pour milk mixed with honey
over his grave. Next we'll shear off
and leave him thick hanks of our hair.
Then we'll come back here, bearing
a bronze urn into the palace.
We've stashed it in the underbrush,   70
but I think you knew that.
We're sure to pick up their spirits
with the false news that this living
body of mine has been consumed
by fire. Now it's . . . nothing but ashes.

ORESTES *pauses, takes in the ominous implication of his own words.*

Why should this omen bother me—
by feigning my death I take back
my life! I make my name. I don't
think unlucky words can curse you—
if they work to your advantage.   80
Haven't I seen smart men
rumor themselves dead—

so when they do come home alive
the awe they inspire lasts a lifetime?
I'm counting on this bogus tale
to do the same for me. I'll rise
from death, flush with life—flaming
like a starburst over my enemies!

ORESTES *and his companions descend from their hilltop; as they do,*
the palace walls light up in the dawn. ORESTES *turns from the*
now-looming palace to face the city, the surrounding countryside,
and the audience. Over a small rise on stage right is a path leading
to the nearby tomb of Agamemnon. Outside the palace is a statue
of Apollo and smaller statues of the house of Pelops' domestic deities.
The palace façade has an oversize double door. A smaller entrance is
on the far stage left.

Land of my fathers! My people's gods! Welcome
me! And let my mission succeed.   90
And you, vast rooms my fathers built,
the gods have brought me home
to give you a righteous cleansing. Don't
drive me disgraced from my homeland.
Return our family's house to me.
Let me take power and rule what's mine.
Enough talk. Now it's up to you,
Graybeard. You do your job
and we'll do ours. Now *is* the time.
In whatever men do, timing's the key.   100

ELEKTRA

(within, in a low but resonant voice)

O what a rotten life!

ELDER

A servant? Behind that door.
Commiserating with herself.

ORESTES

Could that be Elektra? Shouldn't we wait?
Hear why she moans?

ELDER

(forcefully)

                         NO! Before anything else
we must obey Apollo. Begin
those libations for your father.
They'll bring victory within reach.
Make sure we control the situation.

*The ELDER exits stage left toward the palace's side entrance; ORESTES
and Pylades move to the right, toward Agamemnon's nearby tomb. Enter
ELEKTRA from the house gates.*

ELEKTRA

(singing)

Pure Sunlight! Air breathing   110
over the whole Earth!
How often have you heard
as darkness dies into day

me singing my sorrows,
pounding fists on my breasts
until blood breaks the skin?
And you, my rancid bed in that
palace of pain, you've heard
me, awake until dawn, crooning
mournful songs for my father, whom   120
Ares the bloodthirsty war god
never welcomed—when he fought
barbarians—to a brave death
and a hero's grave. So my mother
and her bedmate, Aegisthus,
laid open his skull like loggers
splitting oak with an ax.
No anguish broke from anyone's
lips but mine, Father, at your
repulsive, pitiful slaughter.   130
I won't stop mourning you—
not so long as I see stars
brilliant in the night sky,
not while I can see, still,
day breaking over the land.
I'm like the nightingale
who killed her children,
crying to everyone, outside
what used to be my father's door.
Hades! Persephone! Hermes!   140
And *you*, lethal Curses
I scream out loud!
You Curses who can kill!

And you Furies—
you daughters of Zeus,
who strike when you see
an innocent life taken,
or a cunning wife leading
a lover to her bed—
Furies, help me avenge   150
my father's death!
Give me back my brother!
I lack the strength to keep my grief
from dragging me under. I need help.

Enter CHORUS *of Mycenaean women from stage left, walking in small
groups from town center. The following lines through line 250 are sung or
acted as a duet.*

LEADER
Elektra, why do you
go on like this? *Why*, child?
Yes, your mother's atrocious. But
your grief never lets up—it goes
on and on, bemoaning Agamemnon.
It's been such a long time   160
since your ungodly mother
connived with that evil
bastard to cut him down.
May his killer be killed—
if I'm allowed such a prayer.

ELEKTRA

You're such considerate caring
women—coming here to coax me
out of my misery.
I know your concern, I feel it,
I'm not unaware—but   170
I can't let go, I can't
quit doing this until I'm done.
I can't stop mourning
my murdered father.
                              Friends,
you're always gracious, no matter
what mood I'm in. This time
let me be. Let me rage.

LEADER

Grief and prayer
can't bring your father
back from the swamp of Hades.   180
Someday we'll all sink into it.
But you're grieving yourself to death.
Yours is a grief that can't be quenched.
How will you ever satisfy it?
It will kill you! Tell me, *why*
do you love misery so much?

ELEKTRA

Only a callous child forgets
a parent who died horribly.

I'm like the nightingale, forever
mourning its child—*Littlewheel!*   190
Littlewheel!—that grief-crazed bird
Zeus sends to tell us it's spring.
And you too, Niobe, to me
you're the goddess of sorrow
in your tomb, tears running
forever down your stone face.

LEADER

You're not the only one who grieves . . . you just
take it much harder than your sisters inside,
Chrysòthemis and Iphianassa. They
go on living . . . as your young brother does.   200
He's restless in seclusion, ready
for Zeus to start him trekking—
proud of his heritage, awaiting the day
Mycenae welcomes Orestes home!

ELEKTRA

I'm waiting for him too.
I haven't given up,
getting through day after
daylong day, wishing he'd come,
doing all the chores a childless
unwed woman does, always   210
teary-eyed, hemmed in by my own
doom feeling, which never lets up.
My brother's forgotten everything.

All he went through, all he witnessed.
Has he sent me one message
that hasn't proven false?
Always aching to join me—but
for all the aching, never acts.

LEADER

Courage, child, and don't lose hope.
Zeus still watches us from the skies,   220
His power is huge—he controls
all that we do down here.
Let him handle your bitter quarrel.
Be vigilant—your foes hate you—
but don't let your own hatred
get ahead of itself. Time is a god
who eases us through the rough patches.
And Agamemnon's son, grazing
his oxen, is far from indifferent.
And nothing ever gets by   230
the god who rules Acheron
in the world under our own.

ELEKTRA

Hopeless frustration
devoured my youth.
My strength's gone. I dry up
in childless solitude
with no lover to protect me.
Like an immigrant

everyone scorns,
I slave in my father's house,   240
wear rags, eat on my feet.

LEADER

On the day he came home
we heard a heartbreaking
scream—when your father lay feasting
and the bronze blade arced
a quick unswerving blow.
Guile set it up, but lust
did the killing:
a monster was born
from that monstrous coupling—   250
whether humans
were behind it, or a god.

ELEKTRA

It was a day more acrid
than any in my life.
And that night! The terrors
of that unspeakable banquet—
the hacking, no mercy shown
by the slashing hands of that pair.
The same treacherous hands that took
me prisoner and fed me death.   260
May great Zeus on Olympus
punish them, may their glitter
give them no pleasure—
after what they did.

LEADER

You'd better stop talking.
Don't you see? How you stir
up trouble for yourself? Your spirit's
forever on the brink of war.
Don't force it. Don't provoke
fights you can't win.   270

ELEKTRA

I'm forced to be outrageous
by the outrage all around me!
I *know* how passionate I am.
How could I not know?
But what drives me
is so extreme . . .
I can't stop, not while I still
live and breathe. Let it go. Let me be!
Who in her right mind, dearhearts,
thinks *words* could console me?   280
There is no cure. I'll never quit
grieving, or stifle what I sing.

LEADER

But can't I *speak* as though I care,
like a mother! One you can trust?
Who tells you to stop reliving
old grievances time after time?

ELEKTRA

How do you measure misery?

Tell me this: how can it be right
for us to abandon our dead?
Is anyone ever born that cold-blooded?   290
I'll never go along with that—
and never, even if lucky enough
to live once more in comfort,
never would I cling to self-
centered ease, or dishonor
my father by clipping
the wings of my shrill grief.
If we let the dead rot in dirt
and disregard, while those killers
pay none of their own blood   300
for the blood of their victims, all
respect for human beings, all respect
for law, will vanish from this Earth.

LEADER

I'm here for your sake, daughter,
but also for my own. If what
I'm saying doesn't help, go your
own way. We're with you still.

ELEKTRA

Sister, I'm ashamed if you think
I grieve too often and too much.
But the compulsion is so strong—   310
I must. So forgive me.
What woman from a great family

could hold back, watching her father's
house suffer disaster? It's still
happening! All day, all night long.
It never withers, but blooms and blooms!

It begins with the mother
who bore me and hates me.
I live by the sufferance
of father's murderers.   320
They say if I eat. Or don't.
Think what my days are like.
Aegisthus sits, propped up
on father's throne in the great hall
—wearing my father's clothes—
pouring libations on the same
hearthstone where he killed him.
Worse than that, the killer
sleeps in my father's bed
with my mother, if that's   330
the right word. Mother? *Slut!*
So shameless she lives with,
lays herself under, that
piece of pollution. She's not
intimidated by the Furies—
she mocks her own depravity.
Now, waiting an eternity
for Orestes to come end this,
inside me I'm dying.
He's always *going* to do it   340

but never does—it's taken
all the hope out of me.
So how could I be calm
and rational? Or god-fearing?
Sisters . . . I'm so immersed
in all this evil, how
could I *not* be evil too?

LEADER

What about Aegisthus? Suppose
he hears you talking like this?
Or has he gone somewhere?   350

ELEKTRA

Of course he's gone.
If he were anywhere near here,
you think I could stroll out the door?
He's off in the fields someplace.

LEADER

If that's true, can we talk freely?

ELEKTRA

He's not around! Ask your question.
What's your pleasure?

LEADER

What about your brother?
You think he'll come? Or keep
putting it off? I'd like to know.   360

ELEKTRA

Says he'll come. Never does what he says.

LEADER

When a man's about to take on
something overwhelming—
won't he sometimes hold off a bit?

ELEKTRA

(coldly furious)

When I saved *him*, did I "hold off a bit"?

LEADER

Easy now. He's a good man.
He won't let his own people down.

ELEKTRA

Oh I trust him. I'd be
already dead if I didn't.

LEADER

(whispering)

Shhh! Don't talk.   370
I see Chrysòthemis—your real sister,
the one you share both parents with—
coming out of the house carrying
food and drink to offer the dead.

Enter CHRYSÒTHEMIS from the palace.

CHRYSÒTHEMIS

Making more trouble, sister?
Come out of the house on the street side,
have you, so you can rant in public?
What about?
Haven't you learned yet not
to indulge in pointless fury?   380
Listen, I too hate the way
we're made to live.
Had I the power, I'd let them know
I don't love them either. But
in waters rough as these
I'm going to reef sail,
not make threats, when I can't
possibly do them any harm.
I'd advise you to do the same.
Of course your rage is justified.   390
You do speak for justice. I don't.
But if I want to live my life freely,
I've got to do everything our rulers
tell me to do. No exceptions.

ELEKTRA

Strange, isn't it? That the daughter
of such a father should dishonor him
to humor a mother like ours.
She's taught you how to bawl me out.
Not one syllable is your own!
It's your choice: either act bravely—   400

or play it safe and betray
those you should love the most.
Weren't you just now telling me, *if
you only had the power*, you'd hate
them for the whole world to see!
Yet now when I'm doing all I can
to avenge Father, you back down.
You try to make *me* back down.
On top of everything . . . cowardice.
Tell me—no, let me tell *you*—what   410
do I gain if I stop grieving?
Now, I'm *alive*. Miserable,
for sure, but it's enough for me.
I give *them* grief—and that comforts our dead,
if they can feel pleasure in Hades.
But you, bragging about your hatred?
Your hate is *spoken*. When it comes to action,
you're in the camp of Father's killers.
I'll never surrender to them,
even if they tried to bribe me   420
with privileges they buy you with.
Keep your seat at their rich table.
Eat your fill. Enjoy your luxuries.
For me it's sustenance enough
that I don't starve my conscience.
I don't hunger for what you've got.
Nor would you, if you knew better.
But now, when you could be called
child of the best father ever, you

choose to be your mother's daughter.   430
People will call you a traitor to your
dead father and those who love him!

LEADER

No more angry talk! Please!
Elektra, Chrysòthemis, can't you
learn something from each other?

CHRYSÒTHEMIS

Learn what? I've heard all this before.
My friends, I wouldn't bring
this matter up, but I've heard
something truly evil will cut short
her incessant lamentations.

ELEKTRA

What kind of "evil"? Let's hear it!   440
If it *is* worse than my life now,
I *will* shut up for good.

CHRYSÒTHEMIS

All right, I'll tell you what I know.
They're going to shut you up
in a cave, in another country.
You won't see any sun down there,
but you can still feel sorry for yourself.
Face that prospect. Think about it.
Don't blame me when it's way too late.

ELEKTRA

That's what they plan to do to me?   450

CHRYSÒTHEMIS

Yes. When Aegisthus gets back.

ELEKTRA

That's it? Then I hope he comes soon.

CHRYSÒTHEMIS

You're crazy! What a sick wish!

ELEKTRA

Let him come, if that's what he intends.

CHRYSÒTHEMIS

So you can suffer? How insane is that?

ELEKTRA

It will put plenty of distance
between me and the likes of you.

CHRYSÒTHEMIS

You've no interest in the life you still have?

ELEKTRA

Oh what a lovely life I have.

CHRYSÒTHEMIS

It could improve. If you'd restrain yourself.   460

ELEKTRA

Don't give *me* any lessons in betrayal.

CHRYSÒTHEMIS

I don't teach that. Just . . . give in to power.

ELEKTRA

Give in to *them*? That's your way, not mine.

CHRYSÒTHEMIS

Better than suicidal folly.

ELEKTRA

If I'm killed, I'll do it fighting for my father.

CHRYSÒTHEMIS

I know Father forgives what I'm doing.

ELEKTRA

Cowards comfort themselves with pieties like that.

CHRYSÒTHEMIS

So you won't wake up? And take my advice?

ELEKTRA

Forget it. Be a while before I'm that desperate.

CHRYSÒTHEMIS

OK. I'll go finish my errand.   470

ELEKTRA

Go where? Who are those offerings for?

CHRYSÒTHEMIS

They're from our mother. For Father.

ELEKTRA

What are you saying? For her worst enemy?

CHRYSÒTHEMIS

                                        "The man
she killed with her own hands"—as you'd put it.

ELEKTRA

Who put her up to this? Who wanted it done?

CHRYSÒTHEMIS

She was reacting, I think, to a nightmare.

ELEKTRA

Oh you family gods! At last you're with me!

CHRYSÒTHEMIS

What terrifies her, inspires you?

ELEKTRA

First tell me her dream. Then I'll explain.

CHRYSÒTHEMIS

I know very little of it.   480

ELEKTRA

Then let's hear that. One little word
has often made men or broken them.

CHRYSÒTHEMIS

Word has it she saw our father in sunlight,
come back to sleep with her again.
He took hold of the scepter—his own, once,
though now Aegisthus carries it around—
and planted it by his hearth. Instantly
a fruit-laden bough shot up from it,
casting darkness all over Mycenae.
I heard this from someone who was there—
when she was telling her dream to the Sungod.   490
That's all I know—except . . . because of that
alarming dream, she sent me on this errand.

ELEKTRA

Don't, my dear sister, do this.
Don't let any of these offerings
touch his tomb. They're from a wife he hates!
Neither custom nor devotion allows food
or drink to be passed on to our father from *her*.

No. Let the wind blow them away.
Or bury them deep, at a distance.
Leave Father's tomb undisturbed. Then,   500
when she's dead, *she* can dig them up.
If she weren't the most unfeeling of women,
she'd never try to pour remorse
offerings over the grave mound
of the husband she murdered.
Think now. Is it likely he'd take
these honors kindly—from the same hands
that hacked off his extremities?
As if he were an enemy soldier?
Then wiped the blood off on his hair?   510
How could she think what's in your hands
would absolve her of that murder?
It can't. Just throw these things away.
Take him some of your own hair instead,
then something from me—though I'm such a mess.
I've nothing to offer but my unwashed hair.
And this sash—no baubles stitched into *it*.

ELEKTRA *unties her plain cloth belt and, using the knife hanging from it, cuts
off a lock of her hair and hands both to* CHRYSÒTHEMIS.

Then fall face down and pray for him
to rise up from Hades and help us
attack his enemies. Pray that his son   520
Orestes lives—powerful enough to crush
Father's enemies underfoot. So ever after

we may decorate Father's tomb with hands
richer than ours are now. I'm thinking that . . .
Father had something to do . . . with sending
her these terrifying dreams. Go, sister,
honor him. You will do yourself some good—and me—
and him, the most belovèd man ever,
who lives now with Hades. Your father. Mine.

LEADER

Devout advice you'd be wise to take, friend.   530

CHRYSÒTHEMIS

I agree. And I'm duty bound.
There's no reason to weigh
any alternatives.
I'll do it now. And while
I do it, tell no one.
If mother hears what I'm up to,
I think I'll regret it.

CHRYSÒTHEMIS exits.

CHORUS
(singing)
If I'm not some deluded prophet,
Justice, who sent us this signal,
will strike the righteous blow   540
herself, and strike soon, child.
I'm breathing in the sweetness
of that reassuring dream.

The lord of Hellas, who
begot you, hasn't forgotten.
That keen, bronze, twin-bladed ax
hasn't forgotten either—forced to strike
the savage blow that killed him.
The Fury whose legs never tire,
who waits in her deadly ambush,   550
will destroy with an army's might
the wicked—still blazing with the lust
that flung them on a stolen bed, then
into a guilt-cursed, blood-drenched
adulterous marriage.
We'll see, I don't doubt,
this nightmare omen
punish the criminal pair.
And if it fails to happen
we mortals are hopeless   560
at reading the future
from oracles or dreams.
Curse the chariot race
Pelops ran generations ago!
It doomed your family forever,
scattered disaster in its wake—
when dazed Myrtilos sank
to his rest on the sea bottom
after a murdering hand shoved him
deathward off that golden racing car.   570
Since then, this house has never
been free from savagery and grief.

Enter KLYTEMNESTRA.

KLYTEMNESTRA

I see you're running around loose—
because my husband isn't here
to stop you sneaking out the gates—
where you embarrass the family.
And with him gone you couldn't care
less about me. Forever telling people
I'm a tyrannical bitch who puts
down you and all you care about.   580
But don't charge *me* with insolence.
You lash out at me, I lash back!
Your father—now *this* always sets
you off—was killed by me. True.
I'm sure he was. Without a doubt.
But it was Justice herself, *not
just me*, who killed him. And Justice
is a goddess you should respect,
if you had any sense whatever,
knowing that this father of yours,   590
the one you can't stop crying over,
was the only Greek generous
enough to please the gods by killing
his own daughter—he, who never felt
what a mother feels giving birth.
So tell me this: why, or to please
whom, did he sacrifice her life?
Dare you say: to please the Argives?

No. They had no right to kill her.

Or if he was obliging his brother   600

Menelaus when he killed my daughter,

shouldn't he owe me his death—for that!

Menelaus had two children, *they*

should have been sacrificed before

my child was—*their* parents caused that war!

Or did Hades have some perverse

craving to feast on *my* children,

not Helen's? Or had this heartless father

stopped loving children born from my womb,

loving instead those from that whore?   610

What sort of sick, selfish parent

would do that? Oh, you disagree?

But wouldn't your dead sister

side with me, *if* she had a voice?

I regret nothing I have done,

and if you think I'm cold-blooded,

ask how impartial your judgment is

before you condemn someone else's.

ELEKTRA

You can't say, this time, that something

I did provoked what you've just said.   620

But if you'll permit me, I'll tell you

the truth about my father and sister.

KLYTEMNESTRA

Go ahead. Permission granted.

If you always spoke in a tone
this calm, it wouldn't be so painful.

ELEKTRA

All right, I'll talk to you. You said you killed
my father. Could you say anything
more damning? Whether you killed him
justly or not? But killing him
wasn't just. No. You were seduced   630
to murder him by the criminal
lowlife who is now your husband.
Ask Artemis, who looks after hunters,
what crime she punished when she stilled
the sea breeze at Aulis to a dead calm.
No! Let *me* tell you. She never would.
Here's what I know. My father once
was tracking game, when his footsteps
startled a stag with a giant rack.
He shot it down, recklessly   640
whooping a boast about his kill.
Outraged, Artemis then becalmed
the Greek fleet, demanding *this*
price for killing her forest creature:
that he sacrifice *his own daughter*!
That's how it happened. How she died.
Otherwise the fleet was marooned.
Couldn't sail to Troy *or* sail home.
That was Father's predicament—he
was forced to make the choice he did.   650

He was bitterly reluctant,
but he did finally kill her.
And not for Menelaus' sake!
But let's suppose you're right. That he
did do it to help out his brother.
Would that justify killing him?
With your own hands? What law was that?
Take care. If you invent a law
and apply it to all humankind, won't it
inflict guilt and grief back on you?   660
For if it's going to be blood for blood,
you'll be the next to die,
you'll get the justice you deserve.
Take a hard look at your own life.
Living openly with a killer
who helped you slaughter my father?
You started a family with *him*—
cutting off your legitimate children
who have done nothing wrong. You have!
Who could approve the things you've done?   670
You married Aegisthus to avenge your
daughter? What a coarse claim: marry
an enemy for your daughter's sake?
Why am I even giving you advice?
You shout that I disparage my mother.
Well, I think you're much less
a mother than my slavemistress,
so rotten is the life I lead,
kicked around by you and your mate.

Then there's the one who got away,   680
who slipped through your fingers, pathetic
Orestes, bored stiff, rotting in exile.
You accuse me of raising him
to make you both pay for your crimes;
I would have done that—if I could.
You better believe it. Go ahead,
tell everyone I'm treacherous
if you like. Tell them I'm strident,
that I'm brazen—because if I
possessed all those traits   690
I'd be a daughter worthy of you.

LEADER

(to KLYTEMNESTRA)

Lady, I can tell you're seething.
But ask yourself. Could she be right?

KLYTEMNESTRA

(to CHORUS)

Should I care how I treat her—a grown
woman abusing her mother! Is there
one thing she'd be ashamed to do?

ELEKTRA

I'll tell you one! I *am* ashamed
of my rage, though you won't see why.
I know my conduct's unbecoming

for a woman my age.   700
It's utterly unlike who I was.
But your hostility, your actions—
they have made me do things
that aren't in my nature.
I'm so given to disgusting
displays because they're all around me.

KLYTEMNESTRA

Aren't you a piece of work. Obsessed
with *Who I am, what I say, what I do!*
I give that mouth of yours
way too much grist to grind.   710

ELEKTRA

You said it! I didn't! Right.
What you *do* provokes what I *say*.

KLYTEMNESTRA

Artemis will make you
pay for your insolence
when Aegithus gets back.

ELEKTRA

Look at yourself—fuming mad,
out of control! You want me
to speak—then you don't listen.

KLYTEMNESTRA

Then won't you just shut up
and allow me to sacrifice?
Now that you've had your say?   720

ELEKTRA

Go ahead, sacrifice.
I won't get in your way.

KLYTEMNESTRA

(to a Maidservant carrying a basket)
Girl! You. Lift those fruits up high,
so I may start praying to our god.
And quiet the anxiety I feel.

KLYTEMNESTRA looks up at the statue of Apollo.

You have protected us a long time,
Apollo, my lord. Do listen
attentively to me now. My language
may be somewhat oblique, because
I'm not among friends here.   730
It wouldn't be wise to speak
plainly, since she can hear.
Her loud spiteful mouth will spew out
exaggerated versions all over town.
No, listen the same way I speak:
aware of what I'm implying.

Promise me, Wolfkiller, if signs I saw
in my perplexing dreams last night

seem harmless, make sure they come true.
But if they seem to you dangerous,   740
turn them against those who hate me!
If anyone plots to throw me
out of this house, and steal my wealth,
stop them! Allow me to go on
living in the house of Atreus,
ruling this kingdom, enjoying
the company of those living with me now.
Spare the offspring who don't hate me.
Lose those who blame their pain on me.
Hear me, Wolfkiller Apollo.   750
Grant me all that I pray for.
Other matters that concern me,
must, since you are a god,
be on your mind, even if I
don't mention them at all.
Surely a son of Zeus
sees everything there is.

The ELDER enters from stage left where he has quietly waited.

ELDER

Ladies, please help a stranger
who'd like to know if this palace
belongs to your ruler, Aegisthus.   760

KLYTEMNESTRA

It does, stranger. You've guessed right.

ELDER

And I imagine this lady is . . .
his wife? She looks like a queen.

LEADER

That she does. You're in the presence.

ELDER

Greetings, my lady. I have sweet news
for you and Aegisthus. From a friend.

KLYTEMNESTRA

I'll take that as a good omen.
But first, tell me who sent you.

ELDER

Phantíus the Phokaian.
On a vital matter.   770

KLYTEMNESTRA

How vital, sir? Let's hear it. Since
it comes from a man we admire
I'm sure we'll like his news.

ELDER

Orestes is dead. That's my news.

ELEKTRA

I'm devastated. Today I die!

KLYTEMNESTRA

What, stranger? What!!
Don't listen to that one.

ELDER

I'll repeat what I said. Your son's dead.

ELEKTRA

Then I am. I don't exist.

KLYTEMNESTRA

(to ELEKTRA)

Then go bury yourself! Stranger,   780
tell me exactly how he died.

ELDER

That's why I'm here. To tell it all.
Orestes had just come into the stadium—
intent on competing in the most high-stakes
athletic games in Greece, those at Delphi—
when he heard a man bellowing
that the sprint was about to start.
It's always the games' first event.
So Orestes steps to the starting line
on fire, impressing the onlookers.   790
He led the pack from start to finish,
walking off with the laurel crown.
I'll skip most of it, there's so much
to tell: nobody matched this man

in what he did and what he won.
In each event the marshals staged
he took the laurels every time—
sprints, middle distances, pentathlon.
People assumed he had uncanny luck.
Time after time the herald boomed out: 800
"Orestes the Argive, born
to Agamemnon, who marshaled
once the armed might of Greece!"
So far, so good. But when a god
takes you down, not even a great
strong man escapes. There came the day
for chariots to race at dawn.
He joined a crack field of drivers.
First on the track was an Achaean,
then a Spartan. Two expert drivers   810
up from Libya. Next Orestes
with mares from Thessaly,
the fifth team to join the parade.
The sixth entry, an Aetolian,
drove chestnut colts. A Magnesian
was seventh, and eighth to appear
came four white Aenian stallions.
The ninth team was from the godbuilt
city, Athens, and one last entry,
the tenth, was out of Boeotia.   820

All teams were settled into lanes
the race stewards had drawn by lot,

the trumpet blared, and they took off,
urging their horses on, shaking
their reins in their fists, the stadium
resounding with chariot racket,
each trailing a plume of dust, cutting
each other off in mass confusion,
slashing their horses' backs without
mercy, each driver determined   830
to overtake the wheels, the snorting
horses of his competitors—
wet gusts of the horses' foaming breath
drenching their backs and churning wheels.
Orestes cut the pillars close
at both ends of the race course—
as his wheels grazed by the posts
he slackened the outside horse's reins,
pulling back hard on the inside left-
hand horse. Till now all chariots   840
had managed to avoid over-
turning, but the Aenian's stiff-
mouthed three-year-olds bolted sideways,
swerving into the seventh team's path,
butting heads with the Barkarian's
stallions. Other sideswipes followed,
smashup on smashup, crash after
crash, clotting the entire track
with tangled wreckage of race cars.
Reacting quickly, the skittish   850
Athenian pulled his horses off

to one side and slowed, allowing
the surge of chariots to pass him.
Orestes too laid off the pace,
in last place, trusting his stretch run.
But when he saw the Athenian,
his only rival, still upright, he whistled
shrilly in the ears of his fast fillies
to give chase. The teams drew even,
first one man's head edging in front,   860
then the other's, as they raced on.
Till now Orestes had gone clean
through every circuit of the track,
rock solid in his well-built car,
but then, as he loosened the right rein
going into a turn, his left wheel
caught the post, breaking the axle
box open, throwing him over
the chariot rail, snared in the reins,
smashing the ground as his mares spooked   870
across the infield of the racetrack.
When the crowd saw that he'd been thrown
it gasped in pity for the brave lad
so suddenly, hideously doomed,
gouging earth, feet kicking at sky,
till the other charioteers,
fighting their runaway horses
to a standstill, cut him loose, so
soaked in blood no friend who knew him
whole would know his disfigured corpse.   880

They burned him on a pyre right there,
right then. Picked men from Phokis
are transporting what's left of him
in a small urn—the sorry dust
and ashes of that mighty
physique. So that his home country
can see to his worthy burial.

CHORUS
(with emotional murmuring)
Our ancient rulers are wiped out—
their roots, their limbs, wiped out.

KLYTEMNESTRA
O Zeus! What has happened?   890
Can I say—it's good news?
Or horrible—yet a blessing?
It's so harsh—that a calamity
makes my life safe.

ELDER
Why does my news depress you, woman?

KLYTEMNESTRA
It is so very strange, birthing a child.
Even when a child betrays you,
you can't make yourself hate him.

ELDER

Then it seems I've come here for nothing.

KLYTEMNESTRA

Not for nothing. How can you say that   900
when you've brought proof he's dead—
the boy who got his life from my
life, sucked my milk, yet he deserted me,
went into exile! He's a stranger now.
Having left his homeland, he never
saw me again, but kept on blaming me
for killing his father. He swore
he'd do something terrible to me.
Those threats keep me awake, night
and day. Sleep never shuts my eyes.   1000
I've been forced to live out my life
thinking any moment I could die.
But now it's gone, my fear of him,
and of this girl who's worse—living
inside my house, leeching my lifeblood.
Now that her threats are dead, I'm at peace.

ELEKTRA

Yes, I'm finished. But free to grieve
the crash that killed you, Brother,
while your mother condemns you.
Orestes—aren't I better off?   1010

KLYTEMNESTRA

No, you're not. Yet. He's better off.

ELEKTRA

Listen, Nemesis! How she respects the dead!

KLYTEMNESTRA

Nemesis heard both of us out!
She came to the right conclusion.

ELEKTRA

Go ahead, sneer. Your great moment.

KLYTEMNESTRA

Won't you and Orestes shut me up?

ELEKTRA

We're the ones shut up! How can we silence *you*?

KLYTEMNESTRA

(turning to ELDER)
We'd owe you a great deal, my man,
if you've finally put a stop
to that jarring clamor of hers.   1020

ELDER

Then may I leave? If all is well?

KLYTEMNESTRA

Certainly not! We haven't shown
proper appreciation, to either you
or to our good friend who sent you.
Come inside. We'll leave her out here
crying for herself and her dear departed.

KLYTEMNESTRA and the ELDER enter the palace.

ELEKTRA

What do you think of that? What a mother!
Heartbroken, grief-stricken—an
awesome display of maternal
feeling for a son's ghastly death.
She tosses off a snide slur   1030
as she takes her leave. Makes me sick.
Orestes, your death kills me too.
You've stolen my last hope—
that you'd come back, avenge
your father and what's left of me.
Now I have nobody. I'm alone.
As bereft of you as of Father.
I'll go back to being enslaved
by people I despise. His murderers.
Aren't things fine with me now?   1040
(stares at the great doors to the palace)
I won't cross that threshold ever—
to live with them. I'll rough it here
next to the gate. A dried-up crone,

I'll have no friends. I won't care
how I look. And if those
inside don't like it, they can do me
a favor and kill me. Life now
will be torture. I don't want it.

LEADER

Why no lightning from Zeus?
Where is the Sun, if he can look at *this*—   1050
and pretend it's not happening?

ELEKTRA

(whispering, then quietly sobbing)
Yes! Where are *They*? Where?

LEADER

Daughter? Why the tears?

ELEKTRA

(now raises her hands at the heavens and screams)
Curse you!

LEADER

Don't scream at *Them*!

ELEKTRA

You'll kill me.

LEADER

For doing what?

ELEKTRA

If you tell me to keep on
hoping the dead in Hades
can still help me, you'll crush
me further—when I'm   1060
already heartbroken.

LEADER

I was thinking of Amphiaraos—whose wife,
bribed with a golden necklace,
convinced him to start the war
that got him killed—yet now
in the world below . . .

ELEKTRA

No! Don't do this.

LEADER

. . . he still lords it there,
his mind robust as ever.

ELEKTRA

(lifting her fists and glaring again at the skies)
Aaagggh!   1070

LEADER

(also looking at the sky)

Aaagggh indeed. For that murderess—at least they killed . . .

ELEKTRA

. . . the killer!

LEADER

Her. Yes.

ELEKTRA

I know! I know that! Those bereaved
people had an avenger!
But who will my avenger be?
The only one I ever had
is dead, and lost to me.

LEADER

You. Your life. Defenseless.

ELEKTRA

I know that. Only too well.   1080
Month after month my life's
a raging flood that keeps
churning up horror after horror.

LEADER

We watched while it happened.

ELEKTRA

Then stop trying to distract me,
when I . . .

LEADER

When you what?

ELEKTRA

. . . no longer have the slightest hope
my royal brother can save me.

LEADER

Everyone alive has a death date.   1090

ELEKTRA

To die like my doomed brother? Tangled in leather,
dragged under the bone-crushing hooves of horses?

LEADER

So cruel it's beyond comprehension.

ELEKTRA

Beyond mine. So far from
my loving hands I couldn't . . .

LEADER

But who could?

ELEKTRA

. . . ready his body for the fire,
bury him, cry over him.

Enter CHRYSÒTHEMIS, *out of breath, from Agamemnon's tomb.*

CHRYSÒTHEMIS

I'm so elated, sister—my feet flew—   1100
it isn't ladylike, I know,
to race here so fast. But I've got
great news. Your past troubles,
your grieving? Over. Done with!

ELEKTRA

How could *you* have found a cure
for *my* suffering? I can't imagine.

CHRYSÒTHEMIS

(still speaking in bursts)
Orestes! *Here.* He's alive.
As I am. Here. *Now!*

ELEKTRA

Are you out of your mind, girl?
Making fun of my pain? *And* yours?   1110

CHRYSÒTHEMIS

I swear by our father's hearthstone.
I'm not joking. I'm telling you he's *here.*

ELEKTRA

Oh my. You innocent. Where did you
get such a story? You believed it?

CHRYSÒTHEMIS

I believe it because my eyes saw it!
I didn't *get it* from anyone.

ELEKTRA

You're so naïve! Where's your proof?
What did you *see* that has you red-faced,
as if you'd caught some deadly fever?

CHRYSÒTHEMIS

For god's sake, listen, please.   1120
Hear me out. Then decide
how "naïve" I am, or not.

ELEKTRA

Go ahead. Talk. If it makes you happy.

CHRYSÒTHEMIS

All right, I'll tell you everything I saw.
As I walked toward Father's ancient
grave site, on top of the mound I saw
fresh milk running down it, his urn
decorated with all kinds of blossoms.
I was stunned. I looked to see
if anybody was around anywhere,   1130

but no. It was very quiet.
I got closer to the tomb. So help me,
there, on its edge, was a swatch of hair.
That instant my breath caught,
I flashed on the face I most loved—
I knew it was his hair,
a signal from Orestes that he's back!
I cupped it in my hands, careful
not to say anything unlucky.
Right away my joystruck eyes   1140
teared up. I'm sure now, just as I
was then: that hair was *his* hair.
Who else would have, could have
left it? Except us. It wasn't me.
How could it be you? You can't leave
the house, not even for prayers,
without great risk. As for Mother,
she wouldn't do such a thing.
She *couldn't* have done it. We'd've known.
No, the hair left in tribute at the tomb   1150
could only be Orestes' doing.
Look up, sister, show some spirit!
Nobody's luck is always rotten.
Ours was horrific once. Maybe today
will show us it's getting better.

ELEKTRA

While you spoke, all I could
feel was pity for you.

CHRYSÒTHEMIS

What's wrong? Why didn't my news thrill you?

ELEKTRA

You've wandered clear out of this world.

CHRYSÒTHEMIS

How could I mistake what I just saw?

ELEKTRA

Our brother's dead. There's no chance
he'll come save us. Don't hope he will.   1160

CHRYSÒTHEMIS

Ohhh! Whoever told you that?

ELEKTRA

The man who saw him die.

CHRYSÒTHEMIS

Where is this person? My mind's reeling.

ELEKTRA

Inside. Mother's giving him a warm welcome.

CHRYSOTHEMIS

Then who put all those tributes on the tomb?

ELEKTRA

Someone who wanted to honor
Orestes, now that he's dead.

CHRYSÒTHEMIS

Stupid! Here I'm rushing
to you with good news—
ignorant of the mess we're in.   1170
Now that I'm here, I find
worse grief waiting to crush me.

ELEKTRA

So you have. But trust me.
You can lift this weight off.

CHRYSÒTHEMIS

By raising the dead back to life?

ELEKTRA

I didn't mean that. I'm not a fool.

CHRYSÒTHEMIS

What would you have me do?
Something I really *can* do?

ELEKTRA

Yes. If you've got the nerve to join me.

CHRYSÒTHEMIS

If it will help us, how can I refuse?   1180

ELEKTRA

Anything worthwhile . . . has risks.

CHRYSÒTHEMIS

I'm with you, as far as I can be.

ELEKTRA

Then listen. Here's my plan. Nobody
here will help us. You must know that.
We're alone. Our men are in Hades.
I had hoped, while my brother lived,
he'd come back to avenge his father.
Now that he's dead, I'm turning to
you—to help me kill father's killer.
Aegisthus. I won't keep   1190
anything from you. From now on.
How long are you willing to wait
doing nothing? Who else will do it?
Sure you can bitch you've been robbed
of Father's wealth—that you're too old
now for a wedding, for married love.
So don't keep hoping you'll enjoy
its benefits. Aegisthus isn't
so thickheaded he'd let us have
sons who would be sure to kill him.   1200
But if you act on my plan, our dead
father in Hades will approve,

so will our brother. What's more,
you'll be a free woman, you'll make
a good marriage, for true courage
is something everyone values.
And as for men talking about us,
don't you see the fame we'll win
if you will just listen to me?
Can you imagine any citizen,   1210
any *stranger*, who wouldn't be
impressed? "Look at those two sisters,
they saved their father's house—
brought down their dug-in enemies,
without a thought for their own lives!"
That's what they'll say about us.
Dead or alive, we'll be famous.
Do it, sister. Work with your father,
help your brother and me, free us all
from any further suffering.   1220
A shameful life shames anyone
born to a family as noble as ours.

LEADER

In situations like this,
foresight's a friend, of both
speaker and spoken to.

CHRYSÒTHEMIS
(to CHORUS)
Right, and before she said a word,
women, if she had any sense,

she'd have remembered plots like hers
often go wrong. But she forgot about that.

(to ELEKTRA)

What are you trying to accomplish,   1230
making recklessness your weapon,
and calling on me to do the same?
Don't you get it? You're a woman,
not a man. You don't have
the strength our enemies command.
Their power grows, ours wastes away.
Who could plot to kill such a man
without being themselves cut down?
You'll make the trouble we're in worse
should anybody overhear us.   1240
If we win fame then get killed, what
possible good does that do us?
I'm begging you, before we die,
forever wiping out our family,
control yourself. I guarantee
no one will know what you just said,
nobody's going to get hurt.
You should learn to respect power
when you have none of it yourself.

LEADER

(sharply, to ELEKTRA)

Listen to her. Nothing's more vital   1250
than thinking clearly—and thinking ahead.

ELEKTRA

(to CHRYSÒTHEMIS)

You're so predictable. I knew
you'd hate what I have in mind.
I'll act alone. I'm not quitting.

CHRYSÒTHEMIS

Too late! I wish you'd shown
this much spunk the day Father died.
Then you could have brought it all off.

ELEKTRA

I had the impulse, not the brains.

CHRYSÒTHEMIS

Then work on that.   1260

ELEKTRA

Is that why you won't help me *do* something—
because you think that *I'm* naïve?

CHRYSÒTHEMIS

You are. Any attempt to kill him will fail.

ELEKTRA

I envy your cool self-control.
I hate your spinelessness.

CHRYSÒTHEMIS

I'll listen as coolly to your
praise as I do to your insults.

ELEKTRA

Don't worry. You'll hear no praise from me.

CHRYSÒTHEMIS

The future lasts a long time. It will decide.

ELEKTRA

Go away. You're no help at all.   1270

CHRYSÒTHEMIS

I could help. You're incapable
of understanding how I could.

ELEKTRA

Go. Tell all this to your mother.

CHRYSÒTHEMIS

No. I may hate you. But not like that.

ELEKTRA

Then admit your lack of respect!

CHRYSÒTHEMIS

Lack of respect? I am
trying to save your life.

ELEKTRA
Do you expect me to follow
your idea of what's just?

CHRYSÒTHEMIS
Yes! When you get your sanity back,   1280
then you might show us the way.

ELEKTRA
It's depressing when someone so
well-spoken can go so wildly wrong.

CHRYSÒTHEMIS
That's a perfect description of you.

ELEKTRA
How so? You think I'm being *unjust?*

CHRYSÒTHEMIS
Justice itself can sometimes wreak havoc.

ELEKTRA
I'm not willing to live by laws like that.

CHRYSÒTHEMIS
If you're dead set on doing this, you'll
end up admitting I was right.

ELEKTRA

My mind's made up. You don't scare me.   1290

CHRYSÒTHEMIS

Better think it through one more time.

ELEKTRA

There's nothing more to think about.

CHRYSÒTHEMIS

You haven't understood a thing I've said.

ELEKTRA

I worked this out long ago. Not just now.

CHRYSÒTHEMIS

Well, if you call that sense,
keep on thinking like that.
When you find out how much trouble
you're in, you'll think better of what I said.

Exit CHRYSÒTHEMIS abruptly into the palace.

CHORUS
(singing)
When we see airborne birds
instinctively cherish the parents   1300
who fed them and raised them,
why don't we ask why

we don't treasure *our* parents,
our children, the same way?
When the lightning of Zeus
strikes targets chosen by Themis,
the goddess of Justice,
agony's on them in an instant.
You voices of the dead
who burrow under the earth,   1310
carry your heart-wrenching summons
to Agamemnon in Hades.
Tell him that he's dishonored here,
that discord ravages his house,
that sisters, battling each other,
tear asunder the caring web
of their life together,

how Elektra, abandoned,
braves fierce seas of sorrow
mourning her father's doom   1320
tirelessly, like a nightingale
scornful of death, prepared
to leave sunlight forever
if she could purge the twin
Furies—like the loyal daughter
she is—from her father's palace.
No decent person
prefers to live a life
of squalor, blacken
her decency, amass   1330

a legacy of shame.
So you, my girl,
make grief a weapon!
You scorn disgrace,
fighting for, and winning,
two kinds of glory,
for wisdom, and for being
the best daughter alive.

In power and wealth may you
tower over your enemies   1340
as they now lord it over you.
Fate has beaten you down,
that I see. Yet here you are
winning fame where it counts,
driven by the great laws of our nature,
inspired by your reverence for Zeus.

Enter ORESTES and Pylades stage right with an Aide carrying a bronze urn.

ORESTES
Ladies—the directions we were given—
have they brought us to the right place?

LEADER
What place? What are you looking for?

ORESTES
I'm looking for where Aegisthus lives.   1350

LEADER

Well whoever told you to come here
told you right. That's his house.

ORESTES

They've been expecting us. For some time.
Will someone tell those inside we've arrived?

LEADER

(indicating ELEKTRA)
This young woman. *If* it's right
for close kin to announce you.

ORESTES

Go right in, girl, tell them men
from Phokis are looking for Aegisthus.

ELEKTRA

(reacting to the urn the Aide carries)
No! No! You're not bringing us proof
the rumor that we've heard is true?   1360

ORESTES

I know nothing of any rumor.
Old Strophios sent me with news of Orestes.

ELEKTRA

What news? I'm afraid what I'll hear!

ORESTES

(gestures to the urn carried by his Aide)

He's dead. Look how small an urn he's in.
There wasn't much left to bring home.

ELEKTRA

(crying gently)

I'm heartsick to see, at last, my misery.
Which you hold there in your hands.

ORESTES

If you weep for Orestes' suffering—
what there is of him is right here.   1370

ELEKTRA

Let me hold it in my hands, sir, please.
If this urn really holds him, I'll weep
and keen for myself, our whole family.
Not only for these few ashes.

ORESTES

(to his Aide)

Come over here. Give it to her,
whoever she may be.
If she wants it that badly.
She's not someone who hated him
but a friend, most likely blood kin.

ELEKTRA

(taking and holding the urn)

Dearest remains of you I loved   1380
best on Earth, Orestes, nothing
is left of you but *this*. So different
from what I hoped you'd become
when I sent you away. And this
is how you come home. My own hands
lift you like you're nothing. Yet how
radiant was the boy I sent off!
I should have died before these hands
picked you up and packed you off
to a strange land, to keep you   1390
from being murdered. Better
you were killed the same day
your father was, and buried beside him.
Now, remote from your homeland
and your sister, you've died a grim death.
My grieving hands didn't, as was my duty,
wash and dress your body, or scrape
the sad remnant from the ravenous fire.
No. Hands of strangers did this
for you, long gone brother, and now   1400
as ashes in an urn they bring you home.

My loving care, my bathing you
so long ago—seems a waste now.
You were never your mother's child,
you were mine! No one in our house

nursed you but me, the one you called sister.
Now in one day that's gone—
like a whirlwind you've sucked up
everything, taken it with you.
Father's gone. You've killed me.   1410
Our enemies gloat. That unmothering
mother is mad with joy, the one
so many times in secret letters
you promised me you'd punish.
But your bad luck and mine
has sent you home to me
as this!

ELEKTRA sifts the ashes through her fingers.

     Not the shape
of one I loved. The ashes of a ghost.

Dear lifeless dust!
When you raced on that terrible circuit,   1420
dear brother, see how you've killed me.
I was wrecked by your side. Now,
take me with you. To your new home.
I'll join my nothingness to yours.
We'll be there forever, together, below.
Up here, we share even our doom.
I'd like to die now. Don't leave me
behind. The dead, I can see, feel no pain.

LEADER

Elektra! Think! Your father was mortal.
So was your brother. You shouldn't   1430
grieve too much. We're all going to die.

ORESTES

(breathes in and out a huge sigh)
What should I say?
When the right words won't come?
I can't use my own tongue.

ELEKTRA

What's wrong with you? Why did you say that?

ORESTES

Are you the famous Elektra? *The* Elektra?

ELEKTRA

I am myself. In the pit of misery.

ORESTES

I'm sorry, truly, for this horrible misfortune.

ELEKTRA

Surely, stranger, you can't be sorrowing for me.

ORESTES

Someone was abused. Atrociously.   1440

ELEKTRA

Nobody fits your grim words like me. Stranger.

ORESTES

What kind of life is this?
Unmarried. Despondent.

ELEKTRA

Why are you staring at me like that?
Why this concern at what you see?

ORESTES

I didn't know I had so much to grieve for.

ELEKTRA

What's been said to make that apparent?

ORESTES

I *see* your miseries. They ravage you.

ELEKTRA

You see very little of my misery.

ORESTES

What could be worse, that I don't see?   1450

ELEKTRA

I live in the same house with murderers.

ORESTES

Whose murderers? What are you getting at?

ELEKTRA

My father's. They made me their slave. By force.

ORESTES

Who forces you to be a slave?

ELEKTRA

She's called my mother. Doesn't act like one.

ORESTES

How so? She beats you? Demeans you?

ELEKTRA

Beats, starves, demeans, everything.

ORESTES

No one has ever come to help you? Or stop her?

ELEKTRA

One would have. You gave me his ashes.

ORESTES

Poor woman. I've pitied you a long while.   1460

ELEKTRA

You are one of a kind. No one else has.

ORESTES

The only one who's come. Who shares your pain.

ELEKTRA

You aren't some distant relative?

ORESTES

I'd answer that, if I could trust these ladies.

ELEKTRA

They're friends. You words are safe with them.

ORESTES

Give me the urn. I'll tell you everything.

ELEKTRA

Don't ask me to do that! For gods' sake!

ORESTES

Do as I say. You won't ever go wrong.

ELEKTRA

(clinging to the urn and gripping ORESTES' chin with her free hand)
Do you love this? Then don't steal him I love!

ORESTES

(placing a hand on the urn)
You can't keep this.   1470

ELEKTRA

(speaking to the urn)

If I can't bury you, Orestes,
I'll be devastated.

ORESTES

Don't talk like that. You tempt fate!
You have no right to grieve.

ELEKTRA

(outraged)

No right to grieve for my own brother?

ORESTES

It's not a good thing for you to mourn him.

ELEKTRA

My dead brother thinks I'm not good enough!

ORESTES

(his hand is still on the urn)

He feels no disrespect for you. This isn't yours.

ELEKTRA

It is, if these are his ashes.

ORESTES

They're not. That's just a story.   1480

ORESTES gently takes the urn from ELEKTRA and hands it to his Aide.

ELEKTRA
Then where *is* my dead brother buried?

ORESTES
Nowhere. The living don't inhabit tombs.

ELEKTRA
Young man, what are you saying?

ORESTES
Nothing . . . that isn't true.

ELEKTRA
He's alive?

ORESTES
If I am. Alive.

ELEKTRA
He . . . is *you?*

ORESTES
(removes and hands ELEKTRA his signet ring)
Look at this signet. Our father's.
Tell me if I speak true.

ELEKTRA

O day . . . of light!   1490

ORESTES

Mine too.

ELEKTRA

Your voice! It's you. You're here!

ORESTES

I'll never be anywhere else.

ELEKTRA throws her arms around ORESTES, embracing him for a while, then stands close to him, looking into his eyes until he turns away at line 1538.

ELEKTRA

It's you I'm clinging to.

ORESTES

Don't ever not . . . hold me.

ELEKTRA

(turning to address CHORUS)
Dearest friends, dear citizens,
look! It's Orestes! Who deceived us
into thinking him dead, yet by that
deception, he lives again!

LEADER

We see him, daughter.   1500
After so much has happened to you both
your happiness has us crying with joy.

ELEKTRA

Son of the father I loved,
you're here at last! Come
to find those you love!

ORESTES

I'm here. But say nothing. Yet.

ELEKTRA

Why not?

ORESTES

We'd better keep it quiet.
Someone inside might hear us.

ELEKTRA

Artemis knows, eternal virgin that she is,
those housebound women don't scare me.   1510
They're worthless—dead weight on the Earth.

ORESTES

Women are warlike too.
I believe you've experienced that.

ELEKTRA

Yes I have. And you bring me back
to a bitterness nothing can hide.
One I can't outlive or forget.

ORESTES

That I know just as well as you.
So when the trouble starts
remember all they did.

ELEKTRA

Every moment of the future,   1520
as we live it, will be the right
moment for my fury—only
now are my lips free to speak.

ORESTES

So they are. Keep them free.

ELEKTRA

How? What should I do now?

ORESTES

Don't talk too much. It's not the time.

ELEKTRA

But how could I by *silence*—show
how glad I am you're back?
I never hoped, never believed
I'd see your face again.   1530

ORESTES

You see my face . . . because . . .
the gods inspired me to come.

ELEKTRA

Then it's a greater miracle
than if you'd come on your own—
a god sent you! It had to be:
the gods are in on this.

ORESTES

I'm reluctant to curb your joy,
but it's so *intense* it scares me.

ORESTES, agitated, turns away from ELEKTRA, who loses her grip on him.

ELEKTRA

After all these years, after
coming here, meaning   1540
everything to me . . .
Oh don't, not *now*, seeing me
in all my misery . . .

ORESTES

(turning back toward ELEKTRA)
Don't what?

ELEKTRA

(reaching to take his face in her hands)

Don't take away the joy I feel
just looking at your face.

ORESTES

I would be angry . . . if
someone else tried to stop you.

ELEKTRA

Then you agree?

ORESTES

How could I not?   1550

ELEKTRA

Brother, your voice was one
I never thought I'd hear again.
I suppressed what I felt,
kept quiet, didn't shout
when I first heard its sound.
Now that I'm holding you,
I see your face light up, the face
that in the depths of my grief
I could never forget.

ORESTES

(abruptly, refocused on his task)
Let go of it. No excess words.   1560
Don't explain how evil
our mother is, or how Aegisthus

siphons off Father's wealth,
wasting it on pointless
opulence—don't, because
you won't know when to stop.
Just tell me what I need to know *now*—
when the coast will be clear
or where we can ambush
our enemies—so our   1570
arrival freezes their laughter.
Make sure your mother doesn't
guess your intentions.
Don't let your face glow
when you enter the palace.
Stick to your grief,
pretend my false death
really happened.
When we're victorious,
then we can laugh, breathe   1580
easy, and celebrate freely.

ELEKTRA

Brother, what pleases you pleases me.
You brought me joy when I had none
And I'll accept nothing for myself,
no matter how much it might mean,
if it would inconvenience you.
Doing so would put me in the way
of the god who's befriending us.
You know how things stand here.

Aegisthus is somewhere outside.   1590
Mother's inside. But don't worry.
She'll never see my face light up.
My hatred for her runs too deep.
Since you've come home, I feel
so much joy it makes me cry.
How could I not? One moment
you're dead, the next, you're not!
You've made me believe *anything*
can happen. If Father reappeared
alive I wouldn't think I'd gone   1600
crazy, I'd believe what I saw.
Now you've come so amazingly back
home, tell me what you'd have me do.
If you'd never come, one of two
things would have happened. I'd have
killed my way to freedom, or died trying.

ORESTES

Quiet! I hear someone coming out.

ELEKTRA

Go inside, friends. No one will stand
in your way—considering what you carry—
though there's no joy in it for them.   1610

Enter the ELDER, furious, through the great doors.

ELDER

Fools! Are you children bored with life?
Born with no sense in your head?
Can't you see? You're not *near* danger,
you're *in* it. If I hadn't watched
at the door, word of your plans would
have wafted in ahead of your bodies.
I've taken care to spare you that.
But now stop jabbering, stop
your giddy racket. Get in there!
Hanging back *now* means disaster.   1620
Come on, get on with it.

ORESTES

What are my chances in there?

ELDER

Excellent. No one will know you.

ORESTES

You *have* reported my death, right?

ELDER

To them, you're a shade among shadows.

ORESTES

Are they in high spirits? What are they saying?

ELDER

Save that for later. When we're done.
As things now stand, everything's fine.
Even things that might not seem fine at all.

ELEKTRA

Who is this person? For gods' sake, tell me!   1630

ORESTES

You don't see?

ELEKTRA

See? What.

ORESTES

You don't recognize the man
whose hands you gave me to?

ELEKTRA

Man? What man?

ORESTES

The man who took me to Phokis,
thanks to your own quick thinking.

ELEKTRA

One of the few we could trust,
after Father was murdered?

ORESTES

Yes! Stop questioning me!   1640

ELEKTRA

(kneeling at the ELDER's feet)

Dear light! You, you alone
saved Agamemnon's house.
How did you get here? Are you *really*
the one who saved my brother and me
from unending sorrow?

ELEKTRA seizes the ELDER's hands.

Dear hands! Dear faithful servant
whose feet so kindly walked you here,
how *could you* be near me so long—
unrecognized? You gave no hint
who you were. I didn't know you!   1650
You misled me with fictions—yet
they held a sweet reality.
O blessings, Father—for in you
I see my father! Know that in one day
I've hated and loved you more
than any man in the world.

ELDER

(abruptly, yet kindly)

That's enough! As for the story
of what went on while I was gone,

our days and nights to come
will make all of it clear.   1660

(turning to ORESTES and Pylades)
But I'm telling you two, *still*
standing here, you *must act*. Now.
Klytemnestra's alone. No men
are inside. But, if you hang back,
think how many you'll have to fight—
not just servants, but trained killers.

ORESTES

He's right, Pylades, no more talk.
Let's go—once we've paid our respects
to my father's gods on our porch.

ORESTES, Pylades, and the ELDER pause to pray briefly to Apollo's statue,
then enter the palace. ELEKTRA addresses the statue and kneels.

ELEKTRA

Apollo, lord, please honor their prayers   1670
and mine, too. Often I have come
to offer you what little I possessed.
But now, Wolfkiller Apollo, I come
with all I have, on my knees. Help us.
I beg you. Take an active part
in our plans. Show how gods
break those who break your laws.

ELEKTRA enters the palace.

CHORUS

(singing)

See how Ares comes on:
his breath . . . breathing . . . bloody
vengeance no one outruns.
Already into the rooms, his   1680
relentless hounds tracking evil—
what my soul dreamed
soon will be done.

He who stands up for the dead
moves soundless through
the power and wealth
of his father's ancient home—
the edge of his vengeance
newly honed ahead of him,
while Hermes, Maia's son, keeps   1690
his guile dark, till the finish line's
crossed, and all delay dies.

ELEKTRA comes out of the palace but pauses in the doorway to look back at what's happening inside.

ELEKTRA

Dear women, the men are
about to finish it.
Yet wait. Be quiet.

LEADER

Finish it? What do you mean?

ELEKTRA

She's getting the urn ready
for burial. They stand next to her.

LEADER

Then why are you out here?

ELEKTRA

I'm watching for Aegisthus.   1700

KLYTEMNESTRA sends a bloodcurdling shriek from deep in the house.

KLYTEMNESTRA
(screaming within)
NOOOOO! No guards!
Assassins in the house!

ELEKTRA

Someone's screaming in there! Hear it?

LEADER

I can't bear to! I'm still shaking.

KLYTEMNESTRA
(from within)
Aaaagggh! Aegisthus!! *Where are you Where are you?*

ELEKTRA

Again! Someone screaming.

KLYTEMNESTRA

(from within)

My child, my own son, pity your mother!

ELEKTRA

(shouting back)

You had none for him! *Or* his father!

LEADER

Doomed kingdom. Doomed family.
The destiny that shadowed you   1710
day after day is done now.

KLYTEMNESTRA

(from within)

My god I'm stabbed!

ELEKTRA

(shouting)

Stab her again—
if you have the strength.

KLYTEMNESTRA

(from within)

*Aaaaah*gain!

ELEKTRA

I wish it struck Aegisthus too.

CHORUS

(singing)

The Curses work!

The buried live!

Blood for blood flows

from veins opened   1720

by those murdered

so long ago.

           And here they are!—

—enter ORESTES and Pylades, bloody—

hands smeared with blood

sacrificed to the war god.

I can find nothing to blame

in what they've done.

ELEKTRA

Orestes . . . how did it go?

ORESTES

It went well. If

Apollo oracled well.

ELEKTRA

Is that wretch dead?

ORESTES

      Nothing to fear.   1730

She'll never demean you again.

LEADER

(looking offstage right)

Quiet! Here's Aegisthus.

ELEKTRA

Boys, back inside!

ORESTES

Which way is he coming?

ELEKTRA

From the fields. Smiling. He's ours.

LEADER

(to Pylades and ORESTES)

Go in! Quick! Wait in the entryway.

You've done the first job well,

but there's one more to do.

ORESTES

Don't worry, we'll do it.

ELEKTRA

Hurry! Get going.   1740

ORESTES

We're gone.

ELEKTRA

I'll see to things here.

ORESTES and Pylades go inside.

LEADER

(to ELEKTRA)

Speak gently to him. So he'll walk
blind into combat with Justice.

Enter AEGISTHUS.

AEGISTHUS

Who can tell me where those Phokaians are—
I hear they're telling us Orestes
was killed in a chariot wreck.
(addressing ELEKTRA)
You! Yes you! You're always outspoken.
I think you've a lot at stake here.   1750
You must know what's happened. Tell me.

ELEKTRA

Of course I know. If I didn't,
I'd be ignorant of what's
befallen my nearest kinfolk.

AEGISTHUS

Then tell me where the strangers are.

ELEKTRA

Inside. They've found a way
into the heart of their hostess.

AEGISTHUS

Did they really report him dead?

ELEKTRA

Even better. They've shown us a body.

AEGISTHUS

I'd like to see this corpse with my own eyes.

ELEKTRA

You can, but it won't be an agreeable sight.

AEGISTHUS

But you've just given me agreeable   1760
news. And that's not like you at all.

ELEKTRA

If you can take pleasure in it,
go ahead, celebrate.

AEGISTHUS

(shouting as if to servants inside the palace)
Enough. Open the doors, let all
Mycenaeans—and all Argives—
observe. Whoever put hopes in this man,
seeing his body, will now take my bit
in his mouth, quite willingly—without
waiting for my lash to break his spirit.

ELEKTRA

*(starts swinging the heavy doors open; ORESTES and Pylades help from
inside)*
Oh I've learned *my* lesson. Time has taught   1770
me to join forces with those stronger than me.

*The doors open fully, revealing a covered bier with ORESTES and Pylades
standing beside it.*

AEGISTHUS

O Zeus. Only avenging gods
could permit this unpleasant sight.
But if I have offended Nemesis,
whose reprisals are always just,
I'll take back what I've just said.

Uncover his face. Since he was
blood kin, I should mourn him.

ORESTES

Lift it yourself. It's not for me
to do, it's for you—to look at   1780
these remains, and speak well of them.

AEGISTHUS

You're right. Of course. Good advice, well taken.
(to ELEKTRA)
Will you call Klytemnestra? If she's near?

ORESTES

She's close by. No need to look far.

AEGISTHUS lifts the cloth.

AEGISTHUS

My god. What *is* this?

AEGISTHUS flinches as he reveals KLYTEMNESTRA's body.

ORESTES

Scare you? An unfamiliar face?

AEGISTHUS

These men! *Have got me*—I've stumbled
into a net with no way out. Who *are* they?

ORESTES

Haven't you realized by now "the dead"—   1790
as you perversely called them—*are alive*?

AEGISTHUS

(pauses a beat)
Oh yes. That's a puzzle I've solved.
This must be Orestes I'm talking to.

ORESTES

How come, though you're a discerning
prophet, we deceived you so long?

AEGISTHUS

We're done. Ruined. But
give me just one brief word . . .

ELEKTRA

For gods' sake, brother,
don't let him talk!
You'll get a *speech*!   1800
He's going to die.
What good does it do
to drag this out?
Kill him now. Throw his corpse
somewhere way out of sight—
scavengers will give him
the burial he deserves.
Nothing else will free me
from all I've been through.

ORESTES

(to AEGISTHUS*)*

Get inside! Now! Move! This isn't   1810
a debate, it's an execution.

AEGISTHUS

Then why force me inside? If what
you plan is just, why do it in the dark?
What stops you killing me right here?

ORESTES

Don't give *me* orders. We're going where
you killed my father! You'll die there!

AEGISTHUS

Must this house witness all the murders
our family's suffered—and those still to come?

ORESTES

This house will witness yours.
That much I can predict.   1820

AEGISTHUS

Your father lacked the foresight you boast of.

ORESTES

More words. You're stalling. Go.

AEGISTHUS

After you.

ORESTES

Go in first.

AEGISTHUS

Afraid I'll escape?

ORESTES

(to AEGISTHUS in a calm, confiding tone)
No. To keep you from dying
where you choose. I want your death
to be bitter and without mercy.
Justice should always be instant—
for anyone who breaks the law.   1830
Justice dealt by the sword
will keep evil in check.

CHORUS

(facing the palace façade)
House of Atreus, you've survived
so much grief, but what's been
accomplished today sets you free.

*ALL leave, except ELEKTRA, who remains, standing alone, until the lights
dim or the curtain falls.*

*Oedipus
the King*

INTRODUCTION
"SOMETHING . . . I REMEMBER . . . WAKES UP TERRIFIED"

The story of a man named Oedipus who unknowingly kills his father and marries his mother goes back at least to Homer.[1] Epic poets and Athenian playwrights in classical times found the story irresistible, and scores tried their hands at it, including Sophocles' contemporaries Aeschylus and Euripides, whose versions survive only in scattered lines or lists of plays produced. Aristotle was fascinated by Sophocles' version. He referred to it often, analyzed its craft astutely, and cited it as the finest example of the playwright's art. Its centrality continues. Because so much of our cultural tradition radiates from it, and because the nerves it touches are so sensitive and its issues so immense, *Oedipus the King* still provokes passionate debate. Is Oedipus, prophesied by Apollo to commit patricide and father children with his mother, truly innocent or in some sense guilty? What does the play imply about the nature of divinity, the family, and the human psyche? If this is the ultimate tragedy, how should we define *tragedy*? Answers to these questions fill many splendid books that discuss the qualities underlying the play's greatness. Such scholarship has been indispensable to me in making this translation, particularly Richard Jebb's and Thomas Gould's translations with commentary.

In Sophocles' time, most Greeks believed the fate of an individual was bound up with a *daimon*, a divinity that presided over every person's life. The Greek word for happiness, *eudaimonia*, meaning "well-daimoned," implies that a person so blessed might be permanently protected. But a *daimon* could quickly and just as often devastate an individual or an entire family. One abiding question *Oedipus the King* asks is whether Oedipus controls his own destiny or whether Apollo and/or a personal divinity, or *daimon*, does.

Sophocles deploys two metaphors to establish his own implicit answer. The first is a common Greek metaphor for a king, general, or statesman—he's a helmsman facing trouble in a storm. This image supports our confidence that a resourceful leader can handle threats from gods or mortals. Oedipus and (initially) all the characters, except the seer Tiresias, view Oedipus as a courageous sailor who can weather problems churned up in his stormy life. But Oedipus' superior intelligence proves of no use in riding out the diabolical dangers he confronts.

The second metaphor appears in a succession of images that show the *daimon* as a dynamic force: it leaps, strikes, or plunges directly at its target. As Oedipus commits each act of violence throughout the play, the *daimon* destroying him would be seen by a Greek audience as present in each blow Oedipus delivers or receives. This audience would also understand that each blow Oedipus struck would, as his life played out, be seen as a blow he struck against himself. Thus Oedipus' consultation with the Delphic oracle, his fatal attack on his father, the

sexual mounting of his mother/wife, and his self-blinding near
the play's end (when he plunges the pins of Jokasta's brooch
into his eyes), as well as the search he undertakes for his true
father and for Laios' killer, are all physical aspects of one divine
intent: they are blows Apollo struck through Oedipus' own actions that guilefully manipulate Oedipus' proactive nature until
it destroys him. Apollo has made Oedipus both his weapon and
his victim. Throughout the play, the presence of his *daimon*
looms continually in echoes, double meanings, and ironies.

The play opens with Oedipus well established as the king of
Thebes. Some fifteen years have passed since Apollo revealed
his terrifying prediction to Oedipus, who then refused to return to his home in Korinth. Heading toward Thebes, Oedipus
struck and killed a man who attacked him at a three-way inter-
section, leaving as well the rest of the man's traveling companions for dead. That man, King Laios of Thebes, will prove to
be Oedipus' father. When Oedipus, shortly after the violence at
the crossroads, risked his life and used his wits to rid Thebes of
the Sphinx that tortured the city, grateful Thebans asked him to
assume the kingship. He accepted and married Jokasta, Laios'
widow, who eventually bore Oedipus' four children.

Now an epidemic has struck Thebes, and the cure requires
solving the mystery of Laios' murder. As the investigator, Oedipus naturally refers to himself as the hunter. As he comes closer
to discovering his own responsibility, we realize Oedipus is the
one being hunted. The audience (who will be familiar with the
Oedipus myth) feels the *daimon*'s effect in the first scene, when
Oedipus tells his people that though each of them is sick, none is
so sick as he, and again when Jokasta's brother Kreon describes

Laios' disappearance: "He told us his journey would take him /
into god's presence. He never came back" (129–130). The word
expanded and translated with the phrase "take him into god's
presence" is *theoros*, which normally refers to a pilgrim or dev-
otee who sees or takes part in a holy event or rite. By using
that word, Kreon implies that Laios' destination was Delphi.
But by not naming Delphi, Sophocles can use the inclusiveness
of the word *theoros* to suggest that "god's presence" might be
manifest in a consultation with Apollo at Delphi or in an out-
of-control encounter on a road.

In the middle of a speech in which Jokasta intends to prove
Oedipus' innocence, she supplies the detail that informs Oedipus of his almost certain guilt. Long ago, a prophecy warned
"that Laios was destined to die / at the hands of a son born
to him and me. / Yet, as rumor had it, foreign bandits / killed
Laios at a place where three roads meet" (829–832). Hearing
those last words strikes Oedipus a physical blow, as Jokasta
instantly notices. (An actor portraying Oedipus should react
to her speech: perhaps start, stare, freeze, or shudder.) Jokasta
asks him about his reaction. He replies, "Just now, something
you said made my heart race. / Something . . . I remember . . .
wakes up terrified" (844–845). He proceeds to tell his wife in
detail how he left Korinth, visited Apollo at Delphi, and killed
a man on his way to Thebes.

The play's spare, ingenious, and suspenseful plot, its bravura
characterizations, unflagging eloquence, and terrifying subject
set it apart. But *how* this artistry intensifies the terror is worth
pursuing. We learn, well into the play, that Apollo's priests at
Delphi communicated an existential threat to Oedipus' parents:

their newborn would kill his father. Jokasta and Laios took an immediate preventive measure by giving the infant to a shepherd with instructions to expose him far from Thebes on the mountain where Laios' flocks grazed. But the shepherd, moved by compassion, disobeyed and gave the infant to a fellow shepherd from Korinth. Clearly Oedipus' parents did not take into account how human kindness might upset their plans—and Apollo was perfectly willing to use such kindness to outwit his victims.

Meanwhile, Oedipus conceptualizes the task of finding Laios' killers: "unless I can mesh some clue I hold / with something known of the killer, I will / be tracking him alone, on a cold trail" (265–267). *Symbolon*, the word translated as "clue," was a physical object, part of a larger whole, typically a jagged potsherd (*ostrakon*) that would fit with another potsherd to authenticate a message brought by a stranger, for instance, or to reunite long-lost kin. By simply using the word *symbolon*, Sophocles invokes the context of a child finding its lost parents. As the action unfolds, Oedipus will "mesh" many clues, but the decisive fit occurs when two men meet onstage after many years: the compassionate Theban herdsman and his friend, the Korinthian shepherd who took Oedipus from him and then saw to it that the child would be raised by King Polybos of Korinth.

This same Korinthian now brings news that seems to prove Apollo's prophecy wrong. Polybos, the 'father' whom Oedipus believed Apollo had predicted he would kill, has died, and Oedipus is his designated heir. But the reunion of the Korinthian and the herdsman, who both admit to their earlier actions, irretrievably links Oedipus' Korinthian life to his birth in Thebes as the son of Jokasta and Laios.

The two shepherds are, in the flesh, halves of the *symbolon* Oedipus believed from the start he must find; their coming together onstage becomes the living symbol whose destructive effect extends beyond prediction or intuition. Now that he has meshed this last final clue with its other half, Oedipus sees his killing and incest as parts of a monstrous, divinely ordained whole—and we see it as a series of events that could not have happened had not a man taken pity on a child left to die. While such compassion is never universal, it thrives within a healthy culture or a loving family. Unforgivable violations of familial love, in fact, drive the plots of all the Athenian theater's dynastic plays.

Oedipus, who refuses to forgive himself for killing his father and defiling his mother, his children, and himself, sees no escape from the unbreakable embrace of his family, be it loving or crushing. This conviction leads Oedipus to one of his finest and most shocking imaginative leaps. In his misery he names what creates all families, the sexual act in marriage, and declares *it* the source of humankind's self-immolation: "O marriages! You marriages! You created us, / we sprang to life, then from the same seed / you burst fathers, brothers, sons, / kinsmen shedding kinsmen's blood, / brides and mothers and wives—the most loathsome / atrocities that strike mankind" (1591–1596).

Where the bonds of love are most intense, the danger is greatest. Oedipus knows he has suffered more of this potential misery than any other man, but he also immediately declares that all humankind is equally vulnerable. He realizes that love itself, which causes such pain, is the irresistible weapon Apollo has used against him. He is the victim of his loyalties—loyalties through which the god controls his responses and his choices.

In his grief, Oedipus foresees a barren and lonely future for his daughters, whom no man will marry because they carry the family's curse. He takes his daughters in his arms as he speaks to them. We see the tangible result of incest here; the father's arms are the brother's. Sophocles focuses our attention on what remains of this family, not on the gods. Oedipus' love is as palpable to us at the end of the play as his wrath, his intelligence, his energy, and his special relation with divinity. This side of his character is uppermost in our minds as we leave the theater. It reminds us of a truth that might be lost in the fury of the drama, that the intensity of his love for his family and his city underlies the intensity of his misery, and is as full, if unwitting, a partner in his destruction as divinity itself.

—RB

NOTE

1. *Odyssey* (11. 211ff.), "And I saw the mother of Oedipus, beautiful Epicaste. / What a monstrous thing she did, in all innocence— / she married her own son . . . / who'd killed his own father, then he married *her*! / But the gods soon made it known to all mankind. / So he in growing pain ruled on in beloved Thebes, / lording Cadmus' people— thanks to the gods' brutal plan— / while she went down to Death who guards the massive gates. / Lashing a noose to a steep rafter, there she hanged aloft, / strangling in all her anguish, leaving her son to bear / a world of horrors a mother's Furies bring to life."

Oedipus the King

Translated by Robert Bagg

CHARACTERS
Delegation of Thebans, young, middle-aged, elderly
OEDIPUS, king of Thebes
PRIEST of Zeus
KREON, Jokasta's brother
CHORUS of older Theban men
LEADER of the Chorus
TIRESIAS, blind prophet of Apollo
Boy to lead Tiresias
JOKASTA, Oedipus' wife
MESSENGER from Korinth
Attendants and maids
HERDSMAN, formerly of Laios' house
SERVANT from Oedipus' house
Antigone and Ismene, Oedipus' daughters

The play opens in front of the royal palace in Thebes. The palace has an imposing central double door flanked by two altars: one to Apollo, one to household gods. The Delegation of Thebans enters carrying olive branches wound with wool strips. They gather by the palace stairs. The light and atmosphere are oppressive. OEDIPUS enters through the great doors.

OEDIPUS

My children—*you* are the fresh green life
old Kadmos nurtures and protects.
Why do you surge at *me* like this—
with your wool-strung boughs? While
the city is swollen with howls of pain,
reeking incense, and prayers sung
to the Healing God? To have others
tell me these things would not be right,
my sons. So I've come out myself.
My name is Oedipus—the famous—   10
as everyone calls me.

            Tell me, old man,
yours is the natural voice for the rest,
what troubles you? You're terrified?
Looking for reassurance? Be certain
I'll give you all the help I can.
I'd be a hard man if an approach
like yours failed to rouse my pity.

PRIEST

You rule our land, Oedipus! You can see
who comes to your altars, how varied
we are in years: children too weak-winged   20
to fly far, others hunched with age,
a few priests—I am a priest of Zeus—
joined by the best of our young lads.
More of us wait with wool-strung boughs
in the markets, and at Athena's two temples.
Some, at Ismenos' shrine, are watching

ashes for the glow of prophecy.
You can see our city going under,
too feeble to lift its head clear
of the angry murderous waves.   30
Plague blackens our flowering farmland,
sickens our cattle where they graze.
Our women in labor give birth to nothing.
A burning god rakes his fire through our town.
He hates us with fever, he empties
the House of Kadmos, enriching
black Hades with our groans and tears.
We haven't come to beg at your hearth
because we think you're the gods' equal.
We've come because you are the best man   40
at handling trouble or confronting gods.
You came to Thebes, you freed us
from the tax we paid with our lives
to that rasping Singer. You did it with no
help from us. We had nothing to teach you.

People say—they believe!—you had a god's
help when you restored life to our city.
Oedipus, we need *now* the great power
men everywhere know you possess.
Find some way to protect us—learn it   50
from a god's intimation, or a man's.
This much I know: guidance
from men proven right in the past
will meet a crisis with the surest force.
Act as our greatest man! Act

as you did when you first seized fame!
We believe your nerve saved us then.
Don't let us look back on your rule and say,
He lifted us once, but then let us down.
Put us firmly back on our feet,   60
so Thebes will never fall again.

You were a bird from god, you brought good luck
the day you rescued us. Be that man now!
If you want to rule us, it's better
to rule the living than a barren waste.
Walled cities and ships are worthless—
when they've been emptied of people.

OEDIPUS

I do pity you, children. Don't think I'm unaware.
I know what need brings you: this sickness
ravages all of you. Yet, sick as you are,   70
not one of you suffers a sickness like mine.
Yours is a private grief, you feel
only what touches you. But my heart grieves
for you, for myself, and for our city.
You've come to wake me to all this.
There was no need. I haven't been sleeping.
I have wept tears enough, for long enough.
My mind has raced down every twisting path.
And after careful thought, I've set in motion
the only cure I could find: I've sent Kreon,   80
my wife's brother, to Phoibos at Delphi,
to hear what action or what word of mine

will save this town. Already, counting the days,
I'm worried: what is Kreon doing?
He takes too long, more time than he needs.
But when he comes, I'll be the guilty one—
if I don't do all the gods show me to do.

PRIEST

Well timed! The moment you spoke,
your men gave the sign: Kreon's arriving.

OEDIPUS

O Lord Apollo   90
may the luck he brings save us! Luck so bright
we can see it—just as we see him now.

*KREON enters from the countryside, wearing a laurel crown speckled
with red.*

PRIEST

He must bring pleasing news. If not, why would
he wear laurel dense with berries?

OEDIPUS

We'll know very soon. He's within earshot.
Prince! Brother kinsman, son of Menoikeos!
What kind of answer have you brought from god?

KREON

A good one. No matter how dire, if troubles
turn out well, everything will be fine.

OEDIPUS

What did the god say? Nothing you've said   100
so far alarms or reassures me.

KREON

Do you want me to speak in front of these men?
If so, I will. If not, let's go inside.

OEDIPUS

Speak here, to all of us. I suffer
more for them than for my own life.

KREON

Then I'll report what I heard from Apollo.
He made his meaning very clear.
He commands we drive out what corrupts us,
what sickens our city. We now harbor
something incurable. He says: purge it.   110

OEDIPUS

Tell me the source of our trouble.
How do we cleanse ourselves?

KREON

By banishing a man or killing him. It's blood—
kin murder—that brings this storm on our city.

OEDIPUS

Who is the man god wants us to punish?

KREON

As you know, King, our city was ruled once
by Laios, before you came to take the helm.

OEDIPUS

I've heard as much. Though I never saw him.

KREON

Well, Laios was murdered. Now god tells you
plainly: with your own hands punish   120
the very men whose hands killed Laios.

OEDIPUS

Where do I find these men? How do I track
vague footprints from a bygone crime?

KREON

The god said: here, in our own land.
What we look for we can capture.
What we ignore goes free.

OEDIPUS

Was Laios killed at home? Or in the fields?
Or did they murder him on foreign ground?

KREON

He told us his journey would take him
into god's presence. He never came back.   130

OEDIPUS

Did none of his troop see and report
what happened? Isn't there anyone
to question whose answers might help?

KREON

All killed but a single terrified
survivor, able to tell us but one fact.

OEDIPUS

What was it? One fact might lead to many,
if we had one small clue to give us hope.

KREON

They had the bad luck, he said, to meet bandits
who struck them with a force many hands strong.
This wasn't the violence of one man only.   140

OEDIPUS

What bandit would dare commit such a crime . . .
unless somebody here had hired him?

KREON

That was our thought, but after Laios
died, we were mired in new troubles—
and no avenger came.

OEDIPUS

But here was your kingship murdered!
What kind of trouble could have blocked your search?

KREON

The Sphinx's song. So wily, so baffling!
She forced us to forget the dark past,
to confront what lay at our feet.   150

OEDIPUS

Then I'll go back, start fresh,
and light up that darkness.
Apollo was exactly right, and so were you,
to turn our minds back to the murdered man.
It's time I joined your search for vengeance.
Our country and the god deserve no less.

This won't be on behalf of distant kin—
I'll banish this plague for my own sake.
Laios' killer might one day come for me,
exacting vengeance with that same hand.   160
Defending the dead man serves *my* interest.
Rise, children, quick, up from the altar,
pick up those branches that appeal to god.
Someone go call the people of Kadmos—
tell them I'm ready to do anything.
With god's help our good luck
is assured. Without it we're doomed.

Exit OEDIPUS, into the palace.

PRIEST

Stand up, children. He has proclaimed
himself the cure we came to find.

May god Apollo, who sent the oracle,   170
be our savior and end this plague!

The Delegation of Thebans leaves; the CHORUS enters.

CHORUS
What will you say to Thebes,
Voice from Zeus? What sweet sounds
convey your will from golden Delphi
to our bright city?
We're at the breaking point,
our minds are wracked with dread.
Our wild cries reach out to you,
Healing God from Delos—
in holy fear we ask: does your will   180
bring a new threat, or has an old doom
come round again as the years wheel by?
Say it, Great Voice,
you who answer us always,
speak as Hope's golden child.

Athena, immortal daughter of Zeus,
your help is the first we ask—
then Artemis, your sister
who guards our land, throned
in the heart of our city.   190
And Apollo, whose arrows
strike from far off! Our three
defenders against death: come now!

Once before, when ruin threatened,
you drove the flames of fever from our city.
Come to us now!

The troubles I suffer are endless.
The plague attacks our troops.
I can think of no weapon
that will keep a man safe.   200
Our rich earth shrivels what it grows.
Women in labor scream, but no
children are born to ease their pain.
One life after another flies—
you see them pass—
like birds driving their strong wings
faster than flash-fire
to the Deathgod's western shore.

Our city dies as its people die
these countless deaths, her children   210
rot in the streets, unmourned,
spreading more death.
Young wives and gray mothers
wash to our altars, their cries
carry from all sides, sobbing
for help, each lost in her pain.
A hymn rings out to the Healer—
an oboe answers,
keening in a courtyard.
Against all this, Goddess,   220

golden child of Zeus,
send us the bright shining
face of courage.

Force that raging killer, the god Ares,
to turn his back and run from our land.
He wields no weapons of war to kill us,
but burning with his fever,
we shout in the hot blast of his charge.
Blow Ares to the vast sea-room
of Amphitritê, banish him   230
under a booming wind
to jagged harbors in the roiling
seas off Thrace. If night
doesn't finish the god's black work,
the day will finish it.
Lightning lurks
in your fiery will,
O Zeus, our Father. Blast it
into the god who kills us.
Apollo, lord of the morning light,   240
draw back your taut, gold-twined
bowstring, fire the sure arrows
that rake our attackers and keep them at bay.

Artemis, bring your radiance
into battle on bright quick feet
down through the morning hills.
I call on the god whose hair

is bound with gold,
the god who gave us our name,
Bakkhos!—the wine-flushed—who answers   250
the maenads' cries, running
beside them! Bakkhos,
come here on fire,
pine-torch flaring.
Face with us the one god
all the gods hate: Ares!

OEDIPUS *has entered while the* CHORUS *was singing.*

OEDIPUS
I heard your prayer. It will be answered
if you trust and obey my words:
pull hard with me, bear down on the one cure
that will stop this plague. Help   260
will come, the evils will be gone.
I hereby outlaw the killer
myself, by my own words, though I'm a stranger
both to the crime and to accounts of it.

But unless I can mesh some clue I hold
with something known of the killer, I will
be tracking him alone, on a cold trail.
Since I've come late to your ranks, Thebans,
and the crime is past history,
there are some things that you,   270
the sons of Kadmos, must tell me.

If any one of you knows how Laios,
son of Labdakos, died, he must
tell me all that he knows.
He should not be afraid to name
himself the guilty one: I swear
he'll suffer nothing worse than exile.
Or if you know of someone else—
a foreigner—who struck the blow, speak up.
I will reward you now. I will thank you always.   280
But if you know the killer and don't speak—
out of fear—to shield kin or yourself,
listen to what that silence will cost you.
I order everyone in my land,
where I hold power and sit as king:

don't let that man under your roof,
don't speak with him, no matter who he is.
Don't pray or sacrifice with him,
don't pour purifying water for him.
I say this to all my people: 290
drive him from your houses.
He is our sickness. He poisons us.
This the Pythian god has shown me.
This knowledge makes me an ally—
of both the god and the dead king.
I pray god that the unseen killer,
whoever he is, and whether he killed
alone or had help, be cursed with a life
as evil as he is, a life
of utter human deprivation.   300

OEDIPUS

But I've seen to this already.
At Kreon's urging I've sent for him—twice now.
I find it strange that he still hasn't come.

LEADER

There were rumors—too faint and old to be much help.   350

OEDIPUS

What were they? I'll examine every word.

LEADER

They say Laios was killed by some travelers.

OEDIPUS

That's something even I have heard.
But the man who did it—no one sees him.

LEADER

If fear has any hold on him
he won't linger in Thebes, not after
he hears threats of the kind you made.

OEDIPUS

If murder didn't scare him, my words won't.

LEADER

There's the man who will convict him:
god's own prophet, led here at last.   360

God gave to him what he gave no one else:
the truth—it's living in his mind.

Enter TIRESIAS, led by a Boy.

OEDIPUS

Tiresias, you are master of the hidden world.
You can read earth and sky. You know
what knowledge to reveal and what to hide.
Though your eyes can't see it,
your mind is well aware of the plague
that afflicts us. Against it, we have no
savior or defense but you, my Lord.
If you haven't heard it from messengers,   370
we now have Apollo's answer: to end
this plague we must root out Laios' killers.
Find them, then kill or banish them.
Help us do this. Don't begrudge us
what you divine from bird cries, show us
everything prophecy has shown you.
Save Thebes! Save yourself ! Save me!
Wipe out what defiles us, keep
the poison of our king's murder
from poisoning the rest of us.   380
We're in your hands. The best use a man
makes of his powers is to help others.

TIRESIAS

The most terrible knowledge is the kind
it pays no wise man to possess.

I knew this, but I forgot it.
I should never have come here.

OEDIPUS

What? You've come, but with no stomach for this?

TIRESIAS

Let me go home. Your life will then
be easier to bear—and so will mine.

OEDIPUS

It's neither lawful nor humane   390
to hold back god's crucial guidance
from the city that raised you.

TIRESIAS

What you've said has made matters worse.
I won't let that happen to me.

OEDIPUS

For god's sake, if you know something,
don't turn your back on us! We're on our knees.

TIRESIAS

You don't understand! If I spoke
of my grief, then it would be yours.

OEDIPUS

What did you say? You know and won't help?
You would betray us all and destroy Thebes?   400

TIRESIAS

I'll cause no grief to you or me. Why ask
futile questions? You'll learn nothing.

OEDIPUS

So the traitor won't answer.
You would enrage a rock.

                        Still won't speak?
Are you so thick-skinned nothing touches you?

TIRESIAS

You blame your rage on *me*? When you
don't see how she embraces you, this fury
you live with? No, so you blame me.

OEDIPUS

Who wouldn't be enraged? Your refusal
to speak dishonors the city.   410

TIRESIAS

It will happen. My silence can't stop it.

OEDIPUS

If it must happen, you should tell me now.

TIRESIAS

I'd rather not. Rage at that, if you like,
with all the savage fury in your heart.

OEDIPUS

That's right. I *am* angry enough to speak
my mind. I think you helped plot the murder.
Did everything but kill him with your own hands.
Had you eyes, though, I would have said
you alone were the killer.

TIRESIAS

That's your truth? Now hear mine: 420
honor the curse your own mouth spoke.
From this day on, don't speak to me
or to your people here. You are the plague.
You poison your own land.

OEDIPUS

So. The appalling charge has been at last
flushed out, into the open. What makes you
think you'll escape?

TIRESIAS

                              I have escaped.
I nurture truth, so truth guards me.

OEDIPUS

Who taught you this *truth*? Not your prophet's trade.

TIRESIAS

You did. By forcing me to speak.   430

OEDIPUS

Speak what? Repeat it so I understand.

TIRESIAS

You missed what I said the first time?
Are you provoking me to make it worse?

OEDIPUS

I heard you. But you made no sense. Try again.

TIRESIAS

You killed the man whose killer you now hunt.

OEDIPUS

The second time is even more outrageous.
You'll wish you'd never said a word.

TIRESIAS

Shall I feed your fury with more words?

OEDIPUS

Use any words you like. They'll be wasted.

TIRESIAS

I say: you have been living unaware   440
in the most hideous intimacy
with your nearest and most loving kin,
immersed in evil that you cannot see.

OEDIPUS

You think you can blithely go on like this?

TIRESIAS

I can, if truth has any strength.

OEDIPUS

Oh, truth has strength, but you have none.
You have blind eyes, blind ears, and a blind brain.

TIRESIAS

And you're a desperate fool—throwing taunts at me
that these men, very soon, will throw at you.

OEDIPUS

You're living in the grip of black   450
unbroken night! You can't harm me
or any man who can see the sunlight.

TIRESIAS

I'm not the one who will bring you down.
Apollo will do that. You're his concern.

OEDIPUS

Did you make up these lies? Or was it Kreon?

TIRESIAS

Kreon isn't your enemy. You are.

OEDIPUS

Wealth and a king's power,
the skill that wins every time—
how much envy, what malice they provoke!
To rob me of power—power I didn't ask for,   460
but which this city thrust into my hands—
my oldest friend here, loyal Kreon, worked
quietly against me, aching to steal my throne.
He hired for the purpose this fortune-teller—
conniving bogus beggar-priest!—a man
who knows what he wants but cannot seize it,
being but a blind groper in his art.
Tell us now, when or where did you ever
prove you had the power of a seer?
Why—when the Sphinx who barked black songs   470
was hounding us—why didn't you speak up
and free the city? Her riddle wasn't the sort
just anyone who happened by could solve:
prophetic skill was needed. But the kind
you learned from birds or gods failed you. It took
Oedipus, the know-nothing, to silence her.
I needed no help from the birds.
I used my wits to find the answer.
I solved it—the same man for whom you plot
disgrace and exile, so you can   480
maneuver close to Kreon's throne.
But your scheme to rid Thebes of its plague
will destroy both you and the man who planned it.
Were you not so frail, I'd make you
suffer exactly what you planned for me.

LEADER

He spoke in anger, Oedipus—but so
did you, if you'll hear what we think.
We don't need angry words. We need insight—
how best to carry out the god's commands.

TIRESIAS

You may be king, but my right   490
to answer makes me your equal.
In this respect, I am as much
my own master as you are.
You do not own my life.
Apollo does. Nor am I
Kreon's man. Hear me out.
Since you have thrown my blindness at me
I will tell you what your eyes don't see:
what evil you are steeped in.
                              You don't see
where you live or who shares your house.   500
Do you know your parents?
                              You are their enemy
in this life and down there with the dead.
And soon their double curse—
your father's and your mother's—
will lash you out of Thebes
on terror-stricken feet.
Your eyes, which now see life,
will then see darkness.
Soon your shriek will burrow
in every cave, bellow   510

from every mountain outcrop on Kithairon,
when what your marriage means strikes home,
when it shows you the house
that took you in. You sailed
a fair wind to a most foul harbor.
Evils you cannot guess
will bring you down to what you are.
To what your children are.
Go on, throw muck at Kreon,
and at the warning spoken through my mouth.   520
No man will ever be
ground into wretchedness as you will be.

OEDIPUS

Should I wait for him to attack me more?
May you be damned. Go. Leave my house
now! Turn your back and go.

TIRESIAS

I'm here only because you sent for me.

OEDIPUS

Had I known you would talk nonsense,
I wouldn't have hurried to bring you here.

TIRESIAS

I seem a fool to you, but the parents
who gave you birth thought I was wise.   530

OEDIPUS

What parents? Hold on. Who was my father?

TIRESIAS

Today you will be born. Into ruin.

OEDIPUS

You've always got a murky riddle in your mouth.

TIRESIAS

Don't you surpass us all at solving riddles?

OEDIPUS

Go ahead, mock what made me great.

TIRESIAS

Your very luck is what destroyed you.

OEDIPUS

If I could save the city, I wouldn't care.

TIRESIAS

Then I'll leave you to that. Boy, guide me out.

OEDIPUS

Yes, let him lead you home. Here, underfoot,
you're in the way. But when you're gone,   540
you'll give us no more grief.

TIRESIAS

I'll go. But first I must finish
what you brought me to do—
your scowl can't frighten me.
The man you have been looking for,
the one your curses threaten, the man
you have condemned for Laios' death:
I say that man is here.

                  You think he's an immigrant,
but he will prove himself a Theban native,
though he'll find no joy in that news.   550
A blind man who still has eyes,
a beggar who's now rich, he'll jab
his stick, feeling the road to foreign lands.

OEDIPUS enters the palace.

He'll soon be shown father and brother
to his own children, son and husband
to the mother who bore him—she took
his father's seed and his seed,
and he took his own father's life.
You go inside. Think through
everything I have said.   560
If I have lied, say of me, then—
I have failed as a prophet.

Exit TIRESIAS.

CHORUS

What man provokes
the speaking rock of Delphi?
This crime that sickens speech
is the work of *his* bloody hands.
Now his feet will need to outrace
a storm of wild horses, for
Apollo is running him down,
armed with bolts of fire.   570
He and the Fates close in,
dread gods who never miss.

From snowfields
high on Parnassos
the word blazes out to us all:
track down the man no one can see.
He takes cover in thick brush.
He charges up the mountain
bull-like to its rocks and caves,
going his bleak, hunted way,   580
struggling to escape the doom
Earth spoke from her sacred mouth.
But that doom buzzes low,
never far from his ear.

Fear is what the man who reads birds
makes us feel, fear we can't fight.
We can't accept what he says
but have no power to challenge him.

We thrash in doubt, we can't see
even the present clearly,   590
much less the future.
And we've heard of no feud
embittering the House
of Oedipus in Korinth
against the House of Laios here,
no past trouble and none now,
no proof that would make us blacken
our king's fame as he seeks
to avenge our royal house
for this murder not yet solved.   600

Zeus and Apollo make no mistakes
when they predict what people do.
But there is no way to tell
whether an earthbound prophet sees
more of the future than we can—
though in knowledge and skill
one person may surpass another.
But never, not till I see the charges
proved against him,
will I give credence   610
to a man who blames Oedipus.
All of us saw his brilliance
prevail when the wingèd virgin
Sphinx came at him: he passed the test
that won the people's love.
My heart can't find him guilty.

KREON

Citizens, I hear that King Oedipus
has made a fearful charge against me.
I'm here to prove it false.
If he thinks anything I've said or done   620
has made this crisis worse, or injured him,
then I have no more wish to live.
This is no minor charge.
It's the most deadly I could suffer,
if my city, my own people—you!—
believe I'm a traitor.

LEADER

He could have spoken in a flash
of ill-considered anger.

KREON

Did he say *I* persuaded the prophet to lie?

LEADER

That's what he said. What he meant wasn't clear.   630

KREON

When he announced my guilt—tell me,
how did his eyes look? Did he seem sane?

LEADER

I can't say. I don't question what my rulers do.
Here he comes, now, out of the palace.

OEDIPUS enters.

OEDIPUS

So? You come here? You have the nerve
to face me in my own house? When you're exposed
as its master's murderer?
Caught trying to steal my kingship?
In god's name, what weakness did you see
in me that led you to plot this?   640
Am I a coward or a fool?
Did you suppose I wouldn't notice
your subtle moves? Or not fight back?
Aren't you attempting something
downright stupid—to win absolute power
without partisans or even friends?
For that you'll need money—and a mob.

KREON

Now you listen to me.
You've had your say, now hear mine.
Don't judge until you've heard me out.   650

OEDIPUS

You speak shrewdly, but I'm a poor learner
from someone I know is my enemy.

KREON

I'll prove you are mistaken to think that.

OEDIPUS

How can you prove you're not a traitor?

KREON

If you think mindless presumption
is a virtue, then you're not thinking straight.

OEDIPUS

If you think attacking a kinsman
will bring you no harm, you must be mad.

KREON

I'll grant that. Now, how have I attacked you?

OEDIPUS

Did you, or did you not, urge me   660
to send for that venerated prophet?

KREON

And I would still give you the same advice.

OEDIPUS

How long ago did King Laios . . .

KREON

Laios? Did what? Why speak of him?

OEDIPUS

. . . die in that murderous attack?

KREON

That was far back in the past.

OEDIPUS

Did this seer practice his craft here then?

KREON

With the same skill and respect he has now.

OEDIPUS

Back then, did he ever mention my name?

KREON

Not in my hearing.   670

OEDIPUS

Didn't you try to hunt down the killer?

KREON

Of course we did. We found out nothing.

OEDIPUS

Why didn't your expert seer accuse me then?

KREON

I don't know. So I'd rather not say.

OEDIPUS

There is one thing you can explain.

KREON

What's that? I'm holding nothing back.

OEDIPUS

Just this. If that seer hadn't conspired with you,
he would never have called me Laios' killer.

KREON

If he said that, *you heard him*, I didn't.
I think you owe me some answers.   680

OEDIPUS

Question me. I have no blood on my hands.

KREON

Did you marry my sister?

OEDIPUS

Do you expect me to deny that?

KREON

You both have equal power in this country?

OEDIPUS

I give her all she asks.

KREON

Do I share power with you both as an equal?

OEDIPUS

You shared our power and betrayed us with it.

KREON

You're wrong. Think it through rationally, as I have.
Who would prefer the anxiety-filled
life of a king to one that lets him sleep at night—   690
if his share of power still equaled a king's?
Nothing in my nature hungers for power—
for me it's enough to enjoy a king's rights,
enough for any prudent man. All I want,
you give me—and it comes with no fear.
To be king would rob my life of its ease.
How could my share of power be more pleasant
than this painless preeminence, this ready
influence I have? I'm not so misguided
that I would crave honors that are burdens.   700
But as things stand, I'm greeted and wished well
on all sides. Those who want something from you
come to me, their best hope of gaining it.
Should I quit this good life for a worse one?
Treason never corrupts a healthy mind.
I have no love for such exploits.
Nor would I join someone who did.
Test me. Go to Delphi yourself.
Find out whether I brought back
the oracle's exact words. If you find   710

I plotted with that omen-reader, seize me
and kill me—not on your authority
alone, but on mine, for I'd vote my own death.
But don't convict me because of a wild thought
you can't prove, one that only you believe.
There's no justice in your reckless confusion
of bad men with good men, traitors with friends.
To cast off a true friend is like suicide—
killing what you love as much as your life.
Time will instruct you in these truths, for time   720
alone is the sure test of a just man—
but you can know a bad man in a day.

LEADER

That's good advice, my lord—
for someone anxious not to fall.
Quick thinkers can stumble.

OEDIPUS

When a conspirator moves
abruptly and in secret against me,
I must outplot him and strike first.
If I pause and do nothing, he
will take charge, and I will have lost.   730

KREON

What do you want? My banishment?

OEDIPUS

No. It's your death I want.

KREON

Then start by defining "betrayal"...

OEDIPUS

You talk as though you don't believe me.

KREON

How can I if you won't use reason?

OEDIPUS

I reason in my own interest.

KREON

You should reason in mine as well.

OEDIPUS

In a traitor's interest?

KREON

What if you're wrong?

OEDIPUS

I still must rule. 740

KREON

Not when you rule badly.

OEDIPUS

Did you hear him, Thebes!

KREON

Thebes isn't yours alone. It's mine as well!

LEADER

My Lords, stop this. Here's Jokasta
leaving the palace—just in time
to calm you both. With her help, end your feud.

Enter JOKASTA from the palace.

JOKASTA

Wretched men! Why are you out here
so reckless, yelling at each other?
Aren't you ashamed? With Thebes sick and dying
you two fight out some personal grievance?   750
Oedipus. Go inside. Kreon, go home.
Don't make us all miserable over nothing.

KREON

Sister, it's worse than that. Oedipus,
your husband, threatens either to drive me
from my own country or to have me killed.

OEDIPUS

That's right. I caught him plotting to kill me,
Lady. False prophecy was his weapon.

KREON

I ask the gods to sicken and destroy me
if I did anything you charge me with.

JOKASTA

Believe what he says, Oedipus.   760
Accept the oath he just made to the gods.
Do it for my sake too, and for these men.

LEADER

Give in to him, Lord, we beg you.
With all your mind and will.

OEDIPUS

What do you want me to do?

LEADER

Believe him. This man was never a fool.
Now he backs himself up with a great oath.

OEDIPUS

You realize what you're asking?

LEADER

I do.

OEDIPUS

Then say it to me outright.   770

LEADER

Groundless rumor shouldn't be used by you
to scorn a friend who swears his innocence.

OEDIPUS

You know, when you ask this of me
you ask for my exile—or my death.

LEADER

No! We ask neither. By the god
outshining all others, the Sun—
may I die the worst death possible, die
godless and friendless, if I want those things.
This dying land grinds pain into my soul—
grinds it the more if the bitterness   780
you two stir up adds to our misery.

OEDIPUS

Then let him go, though it means my death
or my exile from here in disgrace.
What moves my pity are your words, not his.
He will be hated wherever he goes.

KREON

You are as bitter when you yield
as you are savage in your rage.
But natures like your own
punish themselves the most—
which is the way it should be.   790

OEDIPUS

Leave me alone. Go.

KREON

I'll go. You can see nothing clearly.
But these men see that I'm right.

KREON goes off.

LEADER

Lady, why the delay? Take him inside.

JOKASTA

I will, when you tell me what happened.

LEADER

They had words. One drew a false
conclusion. The other took offense.

JOKASTA

Both sides were at fault?

LEADER

Both sides.

JOKASTA

What did they say?   800

LEADER

Don't ask that. Our land needs no more trouble.
No more trouble! Let it go.

OEDIPUS

I know you mean well when you try to calm me,
but do you realize where it will lead?

LEADER

King, I have said this more than once.
I would be mad, I would lose my good sense,
if I lost faith in you—you
who put our dear country
back on course when you found her
wandering, crazed with suffering.   810
Steer us straight, once again,
with all your inspired luck.

JOKASTA

In god's name, King, tell me, too.
What makes your rage so relentless?

OEDIPUS

I'll tell you, for it's you I respect, not the men.
Kreon brought on my rage by plotting against me.

JOKASTA

Go on. Explain what provoked the quarrel.

OEDIPUS

He says I murdered Laios.

JOKASTA

Does he know this himself? Or did someone tell him?

OEDIPUS

Neither. He sent that crooked seer to make the charge   820
so he could keep his own mouth innocent.

JOKASTA

Then you can clear yourself of all his charges.
Listen to me, for I can make you believe
no man, ever, has mastered prophecy.
This one incident will prove it.
A long time back, an oracle reached Laios—
I don't say Apollo himself sent it,
but the priests who interpret him did.
It said that Laios was destined to die
at the hands of a son born to him and me.   830
Yet, as rumor had it, foreign bandits
killed Laios at a place where three roads meet.

OEDIPUS *reacts with sudden intensity to her words.*

But the child was barely three days old
when Laios pinned its ankle joints together,
then had it left, by someone else's hands,
high up a mountain far from any roads.
That time Apollo failed to make Laios die
the way he feared—at the hands of his own son.
Doesn't that tell you how much sense

prophetic voices make of our lives?   840
You can forget them. When god wants
something to happen, he makes it happen.
And has no trouble showing what he's done.

OEDIPUS

Just now, something you said made my heart race.
Something . . . I remember . . . wakes up terrified.

JOKASTA

What fear made you turn toward me and say that?

OEDIPUS

I thought you said Laios was struck down
where three roads meet.

JOKASTA

That's the story they told. It hasn't changed.

OEDIPUS

Tell me, where did it happen?   850

JOKASTA

In a place called Phokis, at the junction
where roads come in from Delphi and from Daulis.

OEDIPUS

How long ago was it? When it happened?

JOKASTA

We heard the news just before you came to power.

OEDIPUS

O Zeus! What did you will me to do?

JOKASTA

Oedipus, you look heartsick. What is it?

OEDIPUS

Don't ask me yet. Describe Laios to me.
Was he a young man, almost in his prime?

JOKASTA

He was tall, with some gray salting his hair.
He looked then not very different from you now.   860

OEDIPUS

Like me? I'm finished! It was aimed at me,
that savage curse I hurled in ignorance.

JOKASTA

What did you say, my Lord? Your face scares me.

OEDIPUS

I'm desperately afraid the prophet sees.
Tell me one more thing. Then I'll be sure.

JOKASTA

I'm so frightened I can hardly answer.

OEDIPUS

Did Laios go with just a few armed men,
or the large troop one expects of a prince?

JOKASTA

There were five only, one was a herald.
And there was a wagon, to carry Laios.   870

OEDIPUS

Ah! I see it now. Who told you this, Lady?

JOKASTA

Our slave. The one man who survived and came home.

OEDIPUS

Is he by chance on call here, in our house?

JOKASTA

No. When he returned and saw
that you had all dead Laios' power,
he touched my hand and begged me to send him
out to our farmlands and sheepfolds,
so he'd be far away and out of sight.
I sent him. He was deserving—though a slave—
of a much larger favor than he asked.   880

OEDIPUS

Can you send for him right away?

JOKASTA

Of course. But why do you need him?

OEDIPUS

I'm afraid, Lady, I've said too much.
That's why I want to see him now.

JOKASTA

I'll have him come. But don't I have the right
to know what so deeply disturbs you, Lord?

OEDIPUS

So much of what I dreaded has come true.
I'll tell you everything I fear.
No one has more right than you do
to know the risks to which I'm now exposed.   890
Polybos of Korinth was my father.
My mother was Merope, a Dorian.
I was the leading citizen, when Chance
struck me a sudden blow.
Alarming as it was, I took it
much too hard. At a banquet,
a man who had drunk too much wine
claimed I was not my father's son.
Seething, I said nothing. All that day
I barely held it in. But next morning   900
I questioned Mother and Father. Furious,
they took their anger out on the man
who shot the insult. They reassured me.
But the rumor still rankled; it hounded me.

So with no word to my parents,
I traveled to the Pythian oracle.
But the god would not honor me
with the knowledge I craved.

                            Instead,
his words flashed other things—
horrible, wretched things—at me: 910
I would be my mother's lover.
I would show the world children
no one could bear to look at. I
would murder the father whose seed I am.
When I heard that, and ever after,
I traced the road back to Korinth
only by looking at the stars. I fled
to somewhere I'd never see outrages,
like those the god promised, happen to me.
But my flight carried me to just the place   920
where, you tell me, the king was killed.
Oh, woman, here is the truth. As I approached
the place where three roads joined,
a herald, a colt-drawn wagon, and a man
like the one you describe, met me head-on.
The man out front and the old man himself
began to crowd me off the road.
The driver, who's forcing me aside,
I smash in anger.

                    The old man watches me,
he measures my approach, then leans out   930
lunging with his two-spiked goad
dead at my skull. He's more than repaid:

I hit him so fast with the staff
this hand holds, he's knocked back
rolling off the cart. Where he lies, face up.
Then I kill them all.

But if this stranger and Laios . . . were the same blood,
whose triumph could be worse than mine?
Is there a man alive the gods hate more?
Nobody, no Theban, no foreigner,   940
can take me to his home.
No one can speak with me.
They all must drive me out.
I am the man—no one else—
who laid this curse on myself.
I make love to his wife with hands
repulsive from her husband's blood.
Can't you see that I'm evil?
My whole nature, utter filth?
Look, I must be banished. I must   950
never set eyes on my people, never
set foot in my homeland, because . . .
I'll marry my own mother,
kill Polybos, my father,
who brought me up and gave me birth.
If someone said things like these
must be the work of a savage god,
he'd be speaking the truth. O you
pure and majestic gods! Never,
never, let the day such things happen   960
arrive for me. Let me never see it.

Let me vanish from men's eyes
before that doom comes down on me.

JOKASTA

What you say terrifies us, Lord. But don't lose hope
until you hear from the eyewitness.

OEDIPUS

That is the one hope I have left—to wait
for this man to come in from the fields.

JOKASTA

When he comes, what do you hope to hear?

OEDIPUS

This: if his story matches yours,
I will have escaped disaster.   970

JOKASTA

What did I say that would make such a difference?

OEDIPUS

He told you Laios was killed by bandits.
If he still claims there were several,
then I cannot be the killer. One man
cannot be many. But if he says: one man,
braving the road alone, did it,
there's no more doubt.
The evidence will drag me down.

JOKASTA

You can be sure that was the way
he first told it. How can he take it back?   980
The entire city heard him, not just me.
Even if now he changes his story,
Lord, he could never prove that Laios'
murder happened as the god predicted.

                                   Apollo

said plainly: my son would kill Laios.
That poor doomed child had no chance
to kill his father, for he was killed first.
After that, no oracle ever
made me look right, then left, in fear.

OEDIPUS

You've thought this out well. Still, you must   990
send for that herdsman. Don't neglect this.

JOKASTA

I'll send for him now. But come inside.
Would I do anything to displease you?

OEDIPUS and JOKASTA enter the palace.

CHORUS

Let it be my good luck
to win praise all my life
for respecting the sky-walking laws,
born to stride

through the light-filled heavens.
Olympos
alone was their father.   1000
No human mind could conceive them.
Those laws
neither sleep nor forget—
a mighty god lives on in them
who does not age.

A violent will
fathers the tyrant,
and violence, drunk
on wealth and power,
does him no good.   1010
He scales the heights—
until he's thrown
down to his doom,
where quick feet are no use.
But there's another fighting spirit
I ask god never to destroy—
the kind that makes our city thrive.
That god will protect us
I will never cease to believe.

But if a man   1020
speaks and acts with contempt—
flouts the law, sneers
at the stone gods in their shrines—
let a harsh death punish

his doomed indulgence.
Even as he wins he cheats—
he denies himself nothing—
his hand reaches for things
too sacred to be touched.
When crimes like these, which god hates,   1030
are not punished—but *honored*—
what good man will think his own life
safe from god's arrows piercing his soul?
Why should I dance to *this* holy song?

Here the CHORUS *stops dancing and speaks the next strophe motionless.*

If prophecies don't show the way
to events all men can see,
I will no longer honor
the holy place untouchable:
Earth's navel at Delphi.
I will not go to Olympia   1040
nor the temple at Abai.
You, Zeus who hold power, if Zeus
lord of all is really who you are,
look at what's happening here:
prophecies made to Laios fade;
men ignore them;
Apollo is nowhere
glorified with praise.
The gods lose force.

JOKASTA enters from the palace carrying a suppliant's branch and some
smoldering incense. She approaches the altar of Apollo near the palace
door.

JOKASTA

Lords of my country, this thought   1050
came to me: to visit the gods' shrines
with incense and a bough in my hands.
Oedipus lets alarms of every kind
inflame his mind. He won't let past
experience calm his present fears,
as a man of sense would.
He's at the mercy of everybody's
terrifying words. Since he won't listen to me,
Apollo—you're the nearest god—

Enter MESSENGER from the countryside.

I come praying for your good will. Look,   1060
here is my branch. Cleanse us, cure our sickness.
When we see Oedipus distraught, we all shake,
as though sailing with a fearful helmsman.

MESSENGER

Can you point out to me, strangers,
the house where King Oedipus lives? Better
yet, tell me if you know where he is now.

LEADER

That's the house where he lives, stranger. He's inside.
This woman is his wife and mother . . . of his children.

MESSENGER

I wish her joy, and the family joy
that comes when a marriage bears fruit.   1070

JOKASTA

And joy to you, stranger, for those kind words.
What have you to tell us? Or to ask?

MESSENGER

Great news, Lady, for you and your mate.

JOKASTA

What news? Who sent you to us?

MESSENGER

I come from Korinth.
You'll rejoice at my news, I'm sure—
but it may also make you grieve.

JOKASTA

What? How can it possibly do both?

MESSENGER

They're going to make him king. So say
the people who live on the isthmus.   1080

JOKASTA

Isn't old Polybos still in power?

MESSENGER

No longer. Death has laid him in the tomb.

JOKASTA

You're saying, old man, Polybos has died?

MESSENGER

Kill me if that's not the truth.

JOKASTA speaks to a maid, who then runs inside.

JOKASTA

Girl, run to your master with the news.
You oracles of the gods! Where are you now?
The man Oedipus feared he would kill,
the man he ran from, that man's dead.
Chance killed him. Not Oedipus. Chance!

OEDIPUS enters quickly from the palace.

OEDIPUS

Darling Jokasta, my loving wife,   1090
why did you ask me to come out?

JOKASTA

Listen to what this man has to say.
See what it does to god's proud oracle.

OEDIPUS

Where's he from? What's his news?

JOKASTA

From Korinth. Your father isn't . . .
Polybos . . . is no more . . . he's dead.

OEDIPUS

Say it, old man. I want to hear it from your mouth.

MESSENGER

If plain fact is what you want first,
have no doubt he is dead and gone.

OEDIPUS

Was it treason, or did disease bring him down?   1100

MESSENGER

A slight push tips an old man into stillness.

OEDIPUS

Then some sickness killed him?

MESSENGER

That, and the long years he had lived.

OEDIPUS

Oh, yes, wife! Why should we scour Pythian smoke
or fear birds shrieking overhead?

If signs like these had been telling the truth,
I would have killed my father. But he's dead.
He's safely in the ground. And here I am,
who didn't lift a spear. Or did he
die of longing for me? That might   1110
have been what my killing him meant.
Polybos' death has dragged all those
worthless oracles with him to Hades.

JOKASTA

Didn't I tell you that before?

OEDIPUS

You did. But I was still driven by fear.

JOKASTA

Don't let these things worry you anymore.

OEDIPUS

Not worry that I'll share my mother's bed?

JOKASTA

Why should a human being live in fear?
Chance rules our lives!
Who has any sure knowledge of the future?   1120
It's best to take life as it comes.
This marriage with your mother—don't fear it.
In their dreams, before now, many men
have slept with their mothers.

Those who believe such things mean nothing
will have an easier time in life.

OEDIPUS

A brave speech! I would like to believe it.
But how can I if my mother's still living?
While she lives, I will live in fear,
no matter how persuasive you are.   1130

JOKASTA

Your father's tomb shines a great light.

OEDIPUS

On him, yes! But I fear her. She's alive.

MESSENGER

What woman do you fear?

OEDIPUS

I dread that oracle from the god, stranger.

MESSENGER

Would it be wrong for someone else to know it?

OEDIPUS

No, you may hear it. Apollo told me
I would become my mother's lover, that I
would have my father's blood on these hands.
Because of that, I haven't gone near Korinth.

So far, I've been very lucky—and yet,   1140
there's no greater pleasure than to
look our own parents in the eyes!

MESSENGER

Did this oracle drive you into exile?

OEDIPUS

I didn't want to kill my father, old man.

MESSENGER

Then why haven't I put your fears to rest,
King? I came here hoping to be useful.

OEDIPUS

I would give anything to be free of fear.

MESSENGER

I confess I came partly for that reason—
to be rewarded when you've come back home.

OEDIPUS

I will never live where my parents live.   1150

MESSENGER

My son, you can't possibly know what you're doing.

OEDIPUS

Why is that, old man? In god's name, tell me.

MESSENGER

Is it because of them you won't go home?

OEDIPUS

I am afraid Apollo spoke the truth.

MESSENGER

Afraid you'd do your parents unforgivable harm?

OEDIPUS

Exactly that, old man. I am in constant fear.

MESSENGER

Your fear is groundless. Do you understand?

OEDIPUS

How can it be groundless if I'm their son?

MESSENGER

But Polybos was no relation to you.

OEDIPUS

What? Polybos was not my father?   1160

MESSENGER

No more than I am. Exactly the same.

OEDIPUS

How the same? He fathered me and you didn't.

MESSENGER

He didn't father you any more than I did.

OEDIPUS

Why did he say, then, that I was his son?

MESSENGER

He took you from my hands as a gift.

OEDIPUS

He loved me so much—knowing I came from you?

MESSENGER

He had no children of his own to love.

OEDIPUS

And you? Did you buy me? Or find me somewhere?

MESSENGER

I found you in the wooded hollows of Kithairon.

OEDIPUS

Why were you wandering way out there?   1170

MESSENGER

I had charge of the sheep grazing those slopes.

OEDIPUS

A migrant hired to work our flocks?

MESSENGER

I saved your life that day, my son.

OEDIPUS

When you picked me up, what was wrong with me?

MESSENGER

Your ankles know. Let them tell you.

OEDIPUS

Ahh! Why do you bring up that ancient wound?

MESSENGER

Your ankles had been pinned. I set you free.

OEDIPUS

From birth I've carried the shame of those scars.

MESSENGER

That was the luck that named you, Oedipus.

OEDIPUS

Did my mother or my father do this to me?   1180
Speak the truth for god's sake.

MESSENGER

I don't know. The man who gave you to me
will know.

OEDIPUS

You took me from someone?
You didn't chance on me yourself?

MESSENGER

I took you from another shepherd.

OEDIPUS

Who was he? Tell me plainly as you can.

MESSENGER

He was known as someone who worked for Laios.

OEDIPUS

The same Laios who was once king *here*?

MESSENGER

The same. This man worked as his shepherd.

OEDIPUS

Is he alive? Can I see him?   1190

MESSENGER

Someone from here could answer that better.

OEDIPUS

Does anyone here know what has become
of this shepherd? Has anyone seen him
in town or in the fields? Speak up now.
The time has come to make everything known.

LEADER

I believe he means that same herdsman
you've already sent for. Your wife
would be the best one to ask.

OEDIPUS

                              Lady, do you
recall the man we sent for?
Is that the man he means?   1200

JOKASTA

Why ask about him? Don't listen to him.
Ignore his words. Forget he said them.

OEDIPUS

With clues like these in my hands, how can I
fail to solve the mystery of my birth?

JOKASTA

For god's sake, if you care about your life,
give up your search. Let my pain be enough!

OEDIPUS

You'll be fine! What if my mother was born
from slaves—from three generations of slaves—
how could that make you lowborn?

JOKASTA

Listen to me: I beg you. Don't do this.   1210

OEDIPUS

I cannot listen. I must have the truth.

JOKASTA

I'm thinking only of what's best for you.

OEDIPUS

What's best for me exasperates me now.

JOKASTA

You poor child! Never find out who you are.

OEDIPUS

Someone, bring me the herdsman. Let
that woman glory in her precious birth.

JOKASTA

Oh you poor doomed child! That is the only name
I can call you now. None other, forever!

JOKASTA runs into the palace.

LEADER

Why has she left like that, Oedipus,
driven off by a savage grief? I'm afraid   1220
something horrendous will break this silence.

OEDIPUS

Let it burst! My seed may well *be* common!
Even so, I still must know who I am.

The meanness of my birth may shame
her womanly pride. But since, in my
own eyes, I am the child of Luck—
she is the source of my well-being—
never will I be dishonored.
Luck is the mother who raised me. The months
are my brothers, who've seen me through   1230
the low times in my life and the high ones.
Those are the powers that made me.
I could never betray them *now*—
by calling off the search
for the secret of my birth!

CHORUS

By the gods of Olympos, if I have
a prophet's range of eye and mind—
tomorrow's moonlight
will shine on you, Kithairon.
Oedipus will honor you—   1240
his native mountain,
his nurse, his mother. Nothing
will keep us from dancing
then, mountain joyful to our king!
We call out to Phoibos Apollo:
be the cause of our joy!

CHORUS *turns toward* OEDIPUS.

My son, who was your mother?
Which nymph bore you to Pan,

the mountain rover?
Was it Apollo's bride   1250
to whom you were born
in the grassy highlands?
Or did Hermes, Lord of Kyllene,
or Bakkhos of the mountain peaks,
take you—a sudden joy—
from nymphs of Helikon,
whose games he often shares?

OEDIPUS

Old men, if it's possible
to recognize a man I've never met,
I think I see the herdsman we've been waiting for.   1260
Our fellow would be old, like the stranger approaching.
Those leading him are my own men.
But I expect you'll know him better.
Some of you will know him by sight.

Enter HERDSMAN, led by OEDIPUS' Attendants.

LEADER

I do know him. He is from Laios' house,
a trustworthy shepherd if he ever had one.

OEDIPUS

Korinthian, I'll ask you to speak first:
is this the man you mean?

MESSENGER

You're looking at him.

OEDIPUS

~~Now you, old man. Look at me.~~   1270
Answer every question I ask you.
Did you once come from Laios' house?

HERDSMAN

I did. I wasn't a bought slave.
I was born and raised in their house.

OEDIPUS

What was your job? How did you spend your time?

HERDSMAN

My life I have spent tending sheep.

OEDIPUS

In what region did you normally work?

HERDSMAN

Mainly Kithairon, and the country thereabouts.

OEDIPUS gestures toward the MESSENGER.

OEDIPUS

That man. Do you recall ever seeing him?

HERDSMAN

Recall how? Doing what? Which man?   1280

OEDIPUS goes to the MESSENGER and puts his hand on him.

OEDIPUS

This man right here. Have you ever seen him before?

HERDSMAN

Not that I recognize—not right away.

MESSENGER

It's no wonder, master. His memory's faded,
but I'll revive it for him. I'm sure he knows me.
We worked the pastures on Kithairon together—
he with his two flocks, me with one—
for three whole grazing seasons, from early spring
until Arcturos rose. When the weather turned cold
I'd drive my flocks home to their winter pens.
He'd drive his away to Laios' sheepfolds.   1290
Do I describe what happened, old friend? Or don't I?

HERDSMAN

That's the truth, but it was so long ago.

MESSENGER

Do you remember giving me a boy
I was to raise as my own son?

HERDSMAN

What? Why ask me that?

MESSENGER

There, my friend, is the man who was that boy.

The MESSENGER nods toward OEDIPUS.

HERDSMAN

Damn you! Shut up and say nothing.

OEDIPUS

Don't attack him for speaking, old man.
Your words beg to be punished more than his.

HERDSMAN

Tell me, royal master, what've I done wrong?   1300

OEDIPUS

You didn't answer him about the boy.

HERDSMAN

He's trying to make something out of nothing.

OEDIPUS

Speak of your own free will. Or under torture.

HERDSMAN

Dear god! I'm an old man. Don't hurt me.

OEDIPUS

One of you, bind his arms behind his back.

Attendants approach the HERDSMAN and start to seize his arms.

HERDSMAN

Why this, you doomed man? What else must you know?

OEDIPUS

Did you give him the child, as he claims you did?

HERDSMAN

I did. I wish that day I had died.

OEDIPUS

You will die if you don't speak the truth.

HERDSMAN

Answering you is what will get me killed.   1310

OEDIPUS

I think this man is deliberately stalling.

HERDSMAN

No! I've said it once. I gave him the boy.

OEDIPUS

Was the boy from your house? Or someone else's?

HERDSMAN

Not from my house. Someone gave him to me.

OEDIPUS

The person! Name him! From what house?

HERDSMAN

Don't ask me that, master. For god's sake, don't.

OEDIPUS

If I have to ask one more time, you'll die.

HERDSMAN

He was a child from the house of Laios.

OEDIPUS

A slave? Or a child born of Laios' blood?

HERDSMAN

Help me! I am about to speak terrible words.   1320

OEDIPUS

And I to hear them. But hear them I must!

HERDSMAN

The child was said to be Laios' own son.
Your lady in the house would know that best.

OEDIPUS

She gave the child to you?

HERDSMAN

She gave him, King.

OEDIPUS

To do what?

HERDSMAN

I was to let it die.

OEDIPUS

Kill her own child?

HERDSMAN

She feared prophecies.

OEDIPUS

What prophecies?

HERDSMAN

That this child would kill his father.

OEDIPUS

Why, then, did you give him to this old man?

HERDSMAN

Out of pity, master. I hoped this man   1330
would take him back to his own land.
But that man saved him for this—
the worst grief of all. If the child
he speaks of is you, master, now you
know: your birth has doomed you.

OEDIPUS

All! All! It has all happened!
It was all true. O light! Let this
be the last time I look on you.
You see now who I am—
the child who must not be born!   1340
I loved where I must not love!
I killed where I must not kill!

OEDIPUS runs into the palace.

CHORUS

Men and women who live and die,
I set no value on your lives.
Which one of you ever, reaching
for blessedness that lasts,
finds more than what *seems* blest?
You live in that seeming
a while, then it vanishes.
Your fate teaches me this, Oedipus,   1350
yours, you suffering man, the story

god spoke through you: never
call any man fortunate.

O Zeus, no man drew a bow like this man!
He shot his arrow home,
winning power, pleasure, wealth.
He killed the virgin Sphinx,
who sang the god's dark oracles;
her claws were hooked and sharp.
He fought off death in our land;   1360
he towered against its threat.
Since those times I've called you my king,
honoring you mightily, my Oedipus,
who wielded the great might of Thebes.

But now—nobody's story
has the sorrow of yours.
O my so famous Oedipus—
the same great harbor
welcomed you
first as child, then as father   1370
tumbling upon your bridal bed.
How could the furrows your father plowed, doomed
man, how could they suffer so long in silence?

Time, who sees all, caught you
living a life you never willed.
Time damns this marriage that is
no marriage, where the fathered child

fathered children himself.
O son of Laios, I wish
I'd never seen you! I fill my lungs,   1380
I sing with all my power
the plain truth in my heart.
Once you gave me new breath,
O my Oedipus!—but now
you close my eyes in darkness.

Enter SERVANT from the palace.

SERVANT

You've always been our land's most honored men.
If you still have a born Theban's love
for the House of Labdakos, you'll be crushed
by what you're about to see and hear.
No rivers could wash this house clean—   1390
not the Danube, not the Rion—
it hides so much evil that now
is coming to light. What happened here
was not involuntary evil. It was willed.
The griefs that punish us the most
are those we've chosen for ourselves.

LEADER

We already knew more than enough
to make us grieve. Do you have more to tell?

SERVANT

It is the briefest news to say or hear.

Our royal lady Jokasta is dead.   1400

LEADER

That pitiable woman. How did she die?

SERVANT

She killed herself. You will be spared the worst—

since you weren't there to see it.

But you will hear, exactly as I can

recall it, what that wretched woman suffered.

She came raging through the courtyard

straight for her marriage bed, the fists

of both her hands clenched in her hair.

Once in, she slammed the doors shut and called out

to Laios, so long dead. She remembered   1410

his living sperm of long ago, who killed Laios,

while she lived on to breed with her son

more ruined children.

                        She grieved for the bed

she had loved in, giving birth

to all those doubled lives—

husband fathered by husband,

children sired by her child.

From this point on I don't know how she died—

Oedipus burst in shouting,

distracting us from her misery.   1420

We looked on, stunned, as he plowed through us,

raging, asking us for a spear,
asking for the wife who was no wife
but the same furrowed twice-mothering Earth
from whom he and his children sprang.
He was frantic, yet some god's hand
drove him toward his wife—none of us near him did.
As though someone were guiding him, he lunged,
with a savage yell, at the double doors,
wrenching the bolts from their sockets.   1430
He burst into the room. We saw her there:
the woman above us, hanging by the neck,
swaying there in a noose of tangled cords.
He saw. And bellowing in anguish
he reached up, loosening the noose that held her.
With the poor lifeless woman laid out on the ground
this, then, was the terror we saw: he pulled
the long pins of hammered gold clasping her gown,
held them up, and punched them into his eyes,
back through the sockets. He was screaming: 1440
"Eyes, now you will not, no, never
see the evil I suffered, the evil I caused.
You will see blackness—where once
were lives you should never have lived to see,
yearned-for faces you so long failed to know."
While he howled out these tortured words—
not once, but many times—his raised hands
kept beating his eyes. The blood kept coming,
drenching his beard and cheeks. Not a few wet drops,
but a black storm of bloody hail lashing his face.   1450

What this man and this woman did
broke so much evil loose! That evil joins
the whole of both their lives in grief.
The happiness they once knew was real,
but now that happiness is in ruins—
wailing, death, disgrace. Whatever misery
we have a name for, is here.

LEADER

Has his grief eased at all?

SERVANT

He shouts for someone to open the door bolts:

"Show this city its father-killer," he cries,   1460
"Show it its mother . . ." He said the word. I can't.
He wants to banish himself from the land,
not doom this house any longer
by living here, under his own curse.
He's so weak, though, he needs to be helped.
No one could stand up under a sickness like his.
Look! The door bolts are sliding open.
You will witness a vision of such suffering
even those it revolts will pity.

*OEDIPUS emerges from the slowly opening palace doors. He is blinded, with
blood on his face and clothes, but the effect should arouse more awe and
pity than shock. He moves with the aid of an Attendant.*

LEADER

Your pain is terrible to see,   1470
pure, helpless anguish,
more moving than anything
my eyes have ever touched.

                  O man of pain,
where did your madness come from?
What god would go
to such inhuman lengths
to savage your defenseless life?
(moans)
I cannot look at you—
though there's so much
to ask you, so much to learn,   1480
so much that holds my eyes—
so strong are the shivers of awe
you send through me.

OEDIPUS

Ahhh! My life
screams in pain.
Where is my misery
taking me?
How far does my voice fly,
fluttering out there
on the wind?   1490
O god, how far have you thrown me?

LEADER

To a hard place. Hard to watch, hard to hear.

OEDIPUS

Darkness buries me in her hate, takes me
in her black hold.
Unspeakable blackness.
It can't be fought off,
it keeps coming,
wafting evil all over me.
Ahhh!
Those goads piercing my eyes,   1500
those crimes stabbing my mind,
strike through me—one deep wound.

LEADER

It is no wonder you feel
nothing but pain now,
both in your mind and in your flesh.

OEDIPUS

Ah, friend, you're still here,
faithful to the blind man.
I know you are near me. Even
in my darkness I know your voice.

LEADER

You terrify us. How could you   1510
put out your eyes? What god drove you to it?

OEDIPUS

It was Apollo who did this.
He made evil, consummate evil,
out of my life.
But the hand
that struck these eyes
was my hand.
I in my wretchedness
struck me, no one else did.
What good was left for my eyes to see?   1520
Nothing in this world could I see now
with a glad heart.

LEADER

That is so.

OEDIPUS

Whom could I look at? Or love?
Whose greeting could I answer
with fondness, friends?
Take me quickly from this place.
I am the most ruined, the most cursed,
the most god-hated man who ever lived.

LEADER

You're broken by what happened, broken   1530
by what's happening in your own mind.
I wish I had never even known you.

OEDIPUS

May he die, the man
who found me in the pasture,
who unshackled my feet,
who saved me from that death for a worse life,
a life I cannot thank him for.
Had I died then, I would have caused
no great grief to my people and myself.

LEADER

I wish he had let you die.   1540

OEDIPUS

I wouldn't have come home to kill my father,
no one could call me lover
of her from whose body I came.
I have no god now.
I'm son to a fouled mother.
I fathered children in the bed
where my father once gave me
deadly life. If ever an evil
rules all other evils
it is my evil, the life   1550
god gave to Oedipus.

LEADER

I wish I could say you acted wisely.
You would have been better off dead than blind.

OEDIPUS

There was no better way than mine.
No more advice! If I had eyes, how could
they bear to look at my father in Hades?
Or at my devastated mother? Not even
hanging could right the wrongs I did them both.
You think I'd find the sight of my children
delightful, born to the life they must live?   1560
Never, ever, delightful to my eyes!
Nor this town, its wall, gates, and towers—
nor the sacred images of our gods.
I severed myself from these joys when I
banished the vile killer—myself!—
totally wretched now, though I was raised
more splendidly than any Theban.
But now the gods have proven me
defiled, and of Laios' own blood.
And once I've brought such disgrace on myself,   1570
how could I look calmly on my people?
I could not! If I could deafen my ears
I would. I'd deaden my whole body,
go blind and deaf to shut those evils out.
The silence in my mind would be sweet.
O Kithairon, why did you take me in?
Or once you had seized me, why didn't you
kill me then, leaving no trace of my birth?
O Polybos and Korinth, and that palace
they called the ancient home of my fathers!   1580
I was their glorious boy growing up,
but under that fair skin

festered a hideous disease.
My vile self now shows its vile birth.

You,

three roads, and you, darkest ravine,
you, grove of oaks, you, narrow place
where three paths drank blood from my hands,
my fathering blood pouring into you:
Do you remember what I did while you watched?
And when I came here, what I did then?   1590
O marriages! You marriages! You created us,
we sprang to life, then from that same seed
you burst fathers, brothers, sons,
kinsmen shedding kinsmen's blood,
brides and mothers and wives—the most loathsome
atrocities that strike mankind.
I must not name what should not be.
If you love the gods, hide me out there,
kill me, heave me into the sea,
anywhere you can't see me.   1600
Come, take me. Don't shy away. Touch
this human derelict. Don't fear me, trust me.
No other man, only myself,
can be afflicted with my sorrows.

LEADER
Here's Kreon. He's come when you need him,
to take action or to give you advice.
He is the only ruler we have left
to guard Thebes in your place.

OEDIPUS

Can I say anything he'll listen to?
Why would he believe me?   1610
I wronged him so deeply.
I proved myself so false to him.

KREON enters.

KREON

I haven't come to mock you, Oedipus.
I won't dwell on the wrongs you did me.

KREON speaks to the Attendants.

Men, even if you've no respect
for a fellow human being, show some
for the life-giving flame of the Sun god:
don't leave this stark defilement out here.
The Earth, the holy rain, the light, can't bear it.

Quickly, take him back to the palace.   1620
If these sorrows are shared
only among the family,
that will spare us further impiety.

OEDIPUS

Thank god! I feared much worse from you.
Since you've shown me, a most vile man,
such noble kindness, I have one request.
For your sake, not for mine.

KREON

What is it? Why do you ask me like that?

OEDIPUS

Expel me quickly to some place
where no living person will find me.　　　1630

KREON

I would surely have done that. But first
I need to know what the god wants me to do.

OEDIPUS

He's given his command already.
I killed my father. I am unholy. I must die.

KREON

So the god said. But given
the crisis we're in, we had better
be absolutely sure before we act.

OEDIPUS

You'd ask about a broken man like me?

KREON

Surely, by now, you're willing to trust god.

OEDIPUS

I am. But now I must ask for something　　　1640
within your power. I beg you! Bury her—
she's lying inside—as you think proper.

Give her the rites due your kinswoman.
As for me, don't condemn my father's city
to house me while I'm still alive.
Let me live out my life on Kithairon,
the very mountain—
the one I've made famous—
that my father and mother chose for my tomb.
Let me die there, as my parents decreed.   1650
And yet, I know this much:
no sickness can kill me. Nothing can.
I was saved from that death
to face an extraordinary evil.
Let my fate take me now, where it will.

My children, Kreon. My sons.
They're grown now. They won't need your help.

They'll find a way to live anywhere.
But my poor wretched girls, who never
ate anywhere but at my table,   1660
they've never lived apart from me.
I fed them with my own hands.
                              Care for them.
If you're willing, let me touch them now,
let me give in to my grief.
Grant it, Kreon, from your great heart.
If I could touch them, I would
imagine them as my eyes once saw them.

The gentle sobbing of OEDIPUS' two daughters is heard offstage. Soon two small girls enter.

What's this?
O gods, are these my children sobbing?
Has Kreon pitied me?   1670
Given me my own dear children?
Has he?

KREON

I have. I brought them to you
because I knew how much joy,
as always, you would take in them.

OEDIPUS

Bless this kindness of yours. Bless your luck.
May the gods guard you better than they did me.
Children, where are you? Come to me.
These are your brother's hands, hands
of the man who created you, hands that caused   1680
my once bright eyes to go dark.
He, children, saw nothing, knew nothing.
He fathered you where his own life began,
where his own seed grew. Though I can't
see you, I can weep for you . . .

—OEDIPUS takes his daughters in his arms—

when I think how bitter your lives will be.
I know the life that men will make you live.
What public gatherings, what festivals
could you attend? None! You would be sent home
in tears, without your share of holy joy.   1690
When the time comes to marry, my daughters,
what man will risk the revulsion—
the infamy!—that will wound you
just as it wounded your parents?
What evil is missing? Your father killed
his father. He had children with the mother
who bore him, fathered you
at the source of his own life.

                Those are the insults
you will face. Who will marry you?
No one, my children. You will grow old   1700
unmarried, living a dried-up childless life.
Kreon, you're all the father they have now.
The parents who conceived them are both lost.
Keep these two girls from rootless wandering—
unmarried and helpless. They are your kin.
Don't bring them down to what I am.
Pity them. They are so young, and but for you,
alone. Touch my hand, kind man,
make that touch your promise.

KREON touches him.

Children, had you been old enough   1710
to comprehend, I would have taught you more.

Now, all I can do is ask you to pray
that you live only where you're welcomed,
that your lives be happier than mine was—
the father from whose seed you were born.

KREON

Enough grief. Go inside now.

OEDIPUS

Bitter words that I must obey.

KREON

Time runs out on all things.

OEDIPUS

Grant my request before I go.

KREON

Speak.   1720

OEDIPUS

Banish me from my homeland.

KREON

Ask god to do that, not me.

OEDIPUS

I am the man the gods hate most.

KREON

Then you will have your wish.

OEDIPUS

You consent?

KREON

I never promise if I can't be sure.

OEDIPUS

Then lead me inside.

KREON

Come. Let go of your children now.

OEDIPUS

Don't take them from me.

KREON

Give up your power, too.   1730
You won the power once, but you couldn't
keep it to the end of your life.

KREON leads OEDIPUS into the palace.

LEADER

Thebans, that man is the same Oedipus
whose great mind solved the famous riddle.
He was a most powerful man.

Which of us seeing his glory, his prestige,
did not wish his luck could be ours?
Now look at what wreckage the seas
of savage trouble have made of his life.
To know the truth of a man, wait   1740
till you see his life end.
On that day, look at him.
Don't claim any man is god's friend
until he has passed through life
and crossed the border into death—
never having been god's victim.

ALL leave.

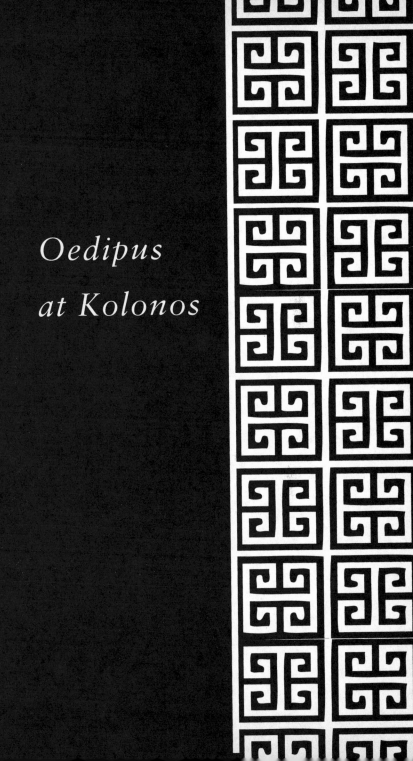

Oedipus

at Kolonos

INTRODUCTION
"HIS DEATH WAS A CAUSE FOR WONDER"

The Oedipus we meet in Kolonos, a lush country village a mile north of Athens, where Sophocles was raised, has suffered through years of blindness, poverty, and exile. He is old and frail, but still recognizable as the fearless, vengeful, and quick-witted hero of *Oedipus the King*. Traits that characterized his youth (and contributed to his downfall) still energize the aged Oedipus as he repeatedly recalls, and forcefully defends, his earlier conduct. Only at the end of his journey, as he approaches the afterlife that Apollo promised would somehow distinguish him, does Oedipus become a gentler and more loving man.

The Greek word for the grace or favor extended by men and gods to the worthy, the needy, the damaged, and the miserable is *charis*. By setting *Oedipus at Kolonos* on the edge of a sacred grove blessed with flowers, grape vines, nightingales, shade trees, and clearings suitable for dancing, Sophocles creates a physical setting where men and gods converge, one that makes manifest the metaphysical space where the human and divine pay their respects and offer *charis* to each other. *Charis* becomes a palpable presence onstage, its promise growing more significant as the drama unfolds.

In the sacred grove of the Eumenides, Oedipus will find the mercy, and in a sense the rebirth, Apollo promised him at Delphi—almost as an afterthought—when as a troubled young man he received the worst news any Greek ever heard from a god: he was doomed to kill his father and his mother would bear his children. Now, within the grove's precincts, the weakened Oedipus will be transformed from a reviled exile into a revered hero. As the classicist John Gould put it, "Nowhere else in Greek tragedy does the primitively mysterious power of boundaries and thresholds, the 'extraterritoriality' of the sacred, make itself felt with the fierce precision that Sophocles achieves" in the song the Old Men sing as they arrive on the scene (1973, 90). We sense immediately the primitive dread aroused by the grove's divine inhabitants. Oedipus, guided by Antigone, hides in the trees as the chorus sweeps angrily onstage. The Old Men denounce the hidden intruder. They scour the grove for signs of him and sing their terror of the all-seeing Furies, whom they refer to circumspectly as the Kindly Ones. To escape the goddesses' withering glances, the old men walk with their eyes lowered. As even the uttering of the Furies' names is forbidden, the prayers they mouth are silent.

Oedipus responds to the Old Men's warnings by emerging from his hiding place in the grove. He gives himself up to them. He won't reenter the grove until a god's voice calls to him in the play's climactic moments. Meanwhile, by dramatizing Oedipus' claims to deserve the gods' *charis*, Sophocles explores a subject that fascinated him—heroes and their deaths as paradigms for the fully empowered human spirit.

Thus the final surviving work by Sophocles, the second of his two dramas about Oedipus, brings his hero's story to a tantalizing but still satisfying conclusion, one we could not have predicted for the broken and abandoned man we saw at the end of *Oedipus the King*. In addition to chronicling Oedipus' reversal of fortune, the *Kolonos* also conveys the wise old citizen-playwright's last reflections on themes keenly important to him: the damage that lives wrecked in one generation inflict on the next; the difference between moral guilt and religious defilement; the responsibilities of parents and children to each other; the miseries of old age; and the greatness of Athens.

The *Kolonos*, which was produced posthumously at the Theater of Dionysos in 401 BCE by Sophocles the Younger, coincides with Athens' darker endgame—the final defeat by Sparta that closed Athens' century-long era of political innovation, military hegemony, and theatrical genius. Sophocles celebrates Athens' past and timeless moral and mythical glory throughout the play—most brilliantly in a song of gratitude to the "mother city, / for the great gifts the gods have given her" (775–776). A few incidents in the plot might also allude to Athens' decline: Polyneikes' reckless and self-obsessed campaign against Thebes recalls Athens' own military failures stretching back to the invasion of Sicily in 415. Theseus' unsentimental appreciation of Oedipus, as well as his swift dispatch of troops that foil Kreon's attempt to abduct Oedipus' daughters, reminds us that skilled and gracious men, like Perikles and Themistokles, once led Athens.

The commanding presence with which Oedipus engages his benefactor Theseus (and his enemies—his own son Polyneikes and his old nemesis Kreon) revives Oedipus' dormant greatness.

Cumulative scenes of accusation and defense test and confirm
Oedipus' strengths and his sangfroid: his stubbornness, his
quick analytic intelligence, his love for his caring daughters, his
rhetorical flair, his sense of his own value to others, his un-
flinching moral fury. The play's unusual length affords Sophocles the scope to develop and nuance his vision of an eternally
embattled hero.

Modern readers will relate to most of Oedipus' convictions
and obsessions—belief that he's innocent of willful murder and
incest; confidence that he'll achieve the good death the gods
have promised—but will find others puzzling. A look at ancient
Greek religious and social practices will bring these less familiar and ambiguous issues into focus.

We use the word "fate," often casually, to describe the mysterious and invincible (but possibly nonexistent) force that may
or may not govern our lives. Fate, to the Greeks, was a potent
reality. Their word for it is *tyche* (pronounced too-KAY). Both
the English and the Greek words point to life-altering events
that happen outside a person's control. But to possess the ancient context of *tyche*—which may also be translated as "luck"
or "destiny"—we should imagine it as a force that puts constant
pressure on a person's mind, a reality beyond comprehension or
appeal. No wonder then, considering how ordinary Greeks believed *tyche* governed the events of their lives, that plots which
precipitate disaster, as do those of *Oedipus the King* and Euripides' *Medea*, and plots with upbeat outcomes, such as Euripides' *Alkestis* or Aeschylus' *Eumenides*, were equally popular
with Athenian audiences and playwrights. A theatrical plot was
no more likely to be censured for its credulity-straining twists

than a man's action-packed life would have been interpreted as meaningless happenstance. Both a play's and a life's plot revealed the gods at work and therefore implicitly conveyed to observers the gods' moral encouragement or their warning.

Just as the concept of the *daimon* helps explain why Oedipus' seemingly rational choices turn out so badly in *Oedipus the King*, the *charis* finally granted him by the gods illuminates the significance of Oedipus' death in the *Kolonos*. *Oedipus the King* shows the gods—through their proxy, the personal *daimon* who acts on behalf of Apollo to govern the events of Oedipus' life—using cruel duplicity to destroy him. The *Kolonos*, on the other hand, reveals the gods' change of heart, their ultimate, if long withheld, concern and grace. Both dramas thus share the goal of understanding and radically reinterpreting past events in the hero's life that were predicted and, apparently, ordained by the gods. The earlier Oedipus' intellect was helpless against the malevolence of his *daimon*. But in the *Kolonos*, Oedipus' justifications, conscious choices, and cogent analyses are reinterpreted, rewarded, and finally blessed.

The secondary prophecy Apollo made to the young Oedipus—that at the point of death, safe haven would await him in a grove of the Eumenides near Athens—parallels the transformation in Aeschylus' *Orestia* in which Orestes' Furies, once the hounding tormentors of all kin murderers, are transformed by the gods at Orestes' trial in Athens into benign protectors of the family. Both Oedipus and Orestes live through crises wherein their traumatic actions change who they are for the better. Fury has driven Oedipus to commit the acts that fulfilled Apollo's original prophecy. His once self-destructive

fury now attacks only his outward enemies—and will endur-
ingly protect what Oedipus now values, his adopted city Athens. He achieves an inner peacefulness during his final hour
that precedes his entry into Hades and his promised emer-
gence into the afterlife as a hero.

Oedipus' sexual violation of his mother and the killing of
his father are both forgiven and perhaps evoked during the
miraculous vanishing into the Earth that Sophocles lets us
imagine through the Messenger, a witness who does not have
a close-up view—only Theseus has that privilege—but who
tries to imagine what he partially sees. Here the Messenger
recounts the death of Oedipus:

> But the exact nature
> of the death Oedipus died, no man
> but Theseus could tell you. Zeus didn't
> incinerate him with a lightning blast,
> no sudden squall blew inland from the sea.
> So it was either a god spiriting
> him away, or else the Earth's lower world—
> her deep foundations—opening to him,
> for he felt nothing but welcoming kindness.
>
> When this man vanished, there was no sorrow.
> He suffered no sickness. His death, like no
> other man's, was a cause for wonder.   (1812–1823)

The Messenger takes it upon himself to note what Oedipus' death was not—no sudden skyward abduction by Zeus, no

lightning blast, no hurricane blowing him out to sea. Sorrow, suffering, sickness—none is present. It was indeed a death that suggested forgiveness, a death administered in all its gentleness by the Earth Mother, Gaia. She opened to him, with no suggestion of violation, "for he felt nothing but welcoming kindness" (1820). After all the horrific violations he committed unaware, such a death was indeed "a cause for wonder."

—RB

Oedipus at Kolonos

Translated by Robert Bagg

CHARACTERS

OEDIPUS, exiled king of Thebes
ANTIGONE, Oedipus' daughter
STRANGER from Kolonos
OLD MEN of Kolonos (Chorus)
LEADER of the Chorus
ISMENE, Oedipus' daughter
Ismene's Servant
THESEUS, king of Athens
Theseus' Men
KREON, Oedipus' brother-in-law
Kreon's Soldiers
POLYNEIKES, Oedipus' son, deposed king of
   Thebes
MESSENGER

The play opens in the countryside a mile and a quarter northwest of the Acropolis in Athens. A sacred grove is at stage rear. Olives, grape vines, crocus, and narcissus bloom within it; birds sing and fountains splash. A path leads over the gentle rise down into the grove's depths. A natural stone bench sits upstage just inside the grove. A rock ledge running across the slope has a flat sitting place at its lower downstage end; near it is a statue of the hero Kolonos. Entering from the road to Thebes, on the spectators' left,

*ANTIGONE guides her father, the aged OEDIPUS, onstage. Both are dusty
and weary. OEDIPUS carries a staff and a traveler's pouch.*

OEDIPUS

Daughter, I'm old and blind. Where are we now,
Antigone? Have we come to a town?
(calling out)
Who will indulge Wandering Oedipus
today—with some food and a place to sleep?

I ask little, I'm given less, but it's
enough. The blows I've suffered
have taught me acquiescence. So has Time,
my enduring companion.
So has my noble birth.

Daughter, if you see somewhere   10
to rest—on public land, or in a grove
set aside for the gods—
guide me to it, sit me down there.
Then we'll determine where we are.
We're strangers here. We must listen
to the locals and do what they say.

ANTIGONE

My poor exhausted father!
Oedipus, the towers guarding the city
seem far off. I have the feeling
we're in some holy place—   20

there's so much olive and laurel and grape vine
running wild. Listen. Deep inside, it's packed
with nightingales! Rest on this ledge.
For an old man, this has been a long trek.

OEDIPUS

Ease the blind man down. Be my lookout.

ANTIGONE

No need to tell me! I've been doing this awhile.

OEDIPUS sits on a stone outcrop just inside the grove.

OEDIPUS

Now, can you tell me where we are?

ANTIGONE

Athens, but I don't know which part.

OEDIPUS

Travelers on the road told us that much.

ANTIGONE

Shouldn't I go ask what this place is called?   30

OEDIPUS

Do that, child. If this place can support life.

ANTIGONE

But people *do* live here. No need to search.
I see a man nearby. Right over there.

OEDIPUS

Is he headed in our direction?

Enter STRANGER, who strides toward them.

ANTIGONE

(whispering)
No. He's already close. Whatever seems
called for, say it to him now. He's here.

OEDIPUS

Stranger, this girl—whose eyes see for us both—
tells me that you've arrived opportunely,
to help us resolve our quandary . . .

STRANGER

                     Hold it.
Before you start asking *me* questions,   40
get off that rock! You're on forbidden ground.

ANTIGONE helps OEDIPUS rise slowly to his feet.

OEDIPUS

What kind of ground? Belonging to which gods?

STRANGER

It's off-limits. No one's allowed to live here.
It's sacred to some fearsome goddesses—
daughters of Darkness and the Earth.

OEDIPUS

By what respectful name do you call them—
since I'm about to offer them a prayer?

STRANGER

People here call them the Kindly Ones—
the goddesses who see everything.
Other places might give them harsher names.   50

OEDIPUS

Then let them be kind to *this* suppliant!
I'll never leave this sacred ground.

STRANGER

Why do you say that?

OEDIPUS

It all fits: *here* is where I meet my fate.

STRANGER

Well, then, I won't presume to drive you out.
Not till I get permission from the city.

STRANGER starts to leave.

OEDIPUS

For god's sake, man! Don't scorn me because I
look like a tramp. I need to know something.

STRANGER

Then say what you need. I won't hold back.

OEDIPUS

This place we've entered—what do they call it?   60

STRANGER

I'll say only what I know *personally*.
This entire grove is holy and belongs
to grim Poseidon. Prometheus the firegod
also has a shrine here. That rock ledge
you're on is our country's brass-footed threshold.
It anchors Athens. The horseman over there—

—STRANGER gestures toward an equestrian statue—

is Kolonos, who settled the farmland
hereabouts. We've all taken his name. That's
the story, stranger. Kolonos isn't
so much a legend as a presence we feel.   70

OEDIPUS

Then people do live around here?

STRANGER

Of course! They're named after that hero there.

STRANGER nods toward the statue of Kolonos.

OEDIPUS

You have a king? Or do the people rule?

STRANGER

We have a king who governs from Athens.

OEDIPUS

Whose eloquence and strength brought him to power?

STRANGER

Theseus. Old King Aigeus' son.

OEDIPUS

I wonder . . . could someone from here go find him?

STRANGER

To take a message? Bring him back? What for?

OEDIPUS

So he may be hugely repaid for a small kindness.

STRANGER

Tell me, how can a blind man be of use?   80

OEDIPUS

My words, every one of them, can see.

STRANGER

Look, friend, don't do anything reckless.
Your bearing tells me you're from noble stock,
but it's clear you're down on your luck.
Stay put, right where I found you, while I go
let the men in town know what's happened.
Never mind Athens—*we* will decide
whether you stay here or move on.

Exit STRANGER.

OEDIPUS

Has the stranger left, child?

ANTIGONE

He's gone, Father. You can speak freely.   90
It's quiet now. I'm the only one here.

OEDIPUS assumes a posture of prayer.

OEDIPUS

Ladies whose eyes we dread, since your grove
is the first in this land where I've come to pray,
don't be unkind
either to me or to Apollo.
When the god condemned me to such grief,
he assured me my long life would end here—
that I'd find a haven, and be taken in
by vengeful goddesses, to be a source

of strength to those who welcomed me, and a curse   100
to those who drove me out. The god promised
he'd show a sign—an earthquake, some thunder,
or lightning flamed from Zeus' own hand.

It must have been, Ladies, a trustworthy
omen from you that led me to this place.
Why else would you be the first deities
I've met on my travels? I—a sober man—
find my way to you, who spurn wine. What else
could have brought me to this rough stone bench?

Please, Goddesses, do as Apollo bids: 110
grant me a clear path to my life's end—unless
I seem in some way beneath your concern,
profaned as I am by the worst evils
a man may endure. Respond to me,
delightful daughters of primeval darkness!
And help me Athens, most
honored city in Greece,
homeland of Pallas Athena! Pity
this feeble ghost of the man Oedipus.
My body hasn't always looked like this.   120

ANTIGONE
Shhh, be quiet now. Some old men—they look
ancient!—have come searching for you.

OEDIPUS

I'll be quiet. Get me to the trees,
off the road, so I can hear what they say.
What we learn will help us
decide our best course of action.

*ANTIGONE guides OEDIPUS up the slope and into the grove. Chorus of OLD
MEN enters. Gracefully, they probe along the grove's edge in a coordinated
dancing movement while singing their entry song.*

OLD MEN

Look for him,
though we don't know
who he is, or where
he's hiding now.   130
He's bolted for cover,
totally brazen!
Search the whole grove.
Look sharp, look everywhere.
The old fellow's
a foreigner, an intruder.
No native would invade
prohibited grounds
of virgins so violent,
so uncontrollable—   140
their very names
we fear to say out loud.
We walk in their midst,
eyes lowered, not breathing

a word, though our lips
mouth silent prayers.

LEADER

We've heard the report:
Someone with no respect
for the goddesses has arrived.
But looking across the sacred glen 150
I don't see him or his hiding place.

OEDIPUS steps forward from the foliage.

OEDIPUS

I'm here. The man you're looking for. I see
with my ears, as people say of the blind.

LEADER

Aggghh! Aggghh!
The sight of you, the sound of your voice, appalls us.

OEDIPUS

Don't look at me as though I'm some outlaw.

LEADER

Spare us, Zeus! Who is this haughty old man?

OEDIPUS

Not someone whose life you might envy—
you men charged with guarding your country!

Isn't that obvious? Why else   160
would I walk as I do, dependent
on other people's eyes, and tethered,
large as I am, to this frail creature?

LEADER

Ah! Then you were born blind?
You must have led a long,
bleak life. Take our advice:
Don't add one more curse
to your miseries. You've gone
too far! Please step back!
Don't go stumbling   170
through that green glade
where speech is forbidden,
where we pour
clear water from a bowl,
blending it
with honey-sweet libations.

Watch yourself,
stranger with such
horrendous luck—
stand back, walk away!   180
Move further back!
Do you hear me? If you
have something to tell us,
get off that sacred ground!
Speak only

where talk is allowed.
Until then, keep quiet.

OEDIPUS

Daughter, what should we do?

ANTIGONE

(conferring quietly with OEDIPUS)
Respect their customs, Father.
Do as they ask. Be deferential.   190

OEDIPUS

Give me your hand, then.

ANTIGONE

                              Here, feel mine.

OEDIPUS, with ANTIGONE supporting him, very cautiously approaches the OLD MEN.

OEDIPUS

I'm going to trust you, strangers. Don't
betray me when I leave this holy ground.

LEADER

Nobody will force you to leave
this resting place against your will.

OEDIPUS pauses in his progress.

OEDIPUS

Further?

LEADER

Keep going.

OEDIPUS

More?

LEADER

Keep him moving, girl, you can see the path.

ANTIGONE

Come on, Father.   200
Keep stepping
into the dark
as I lead you.

LEADER

You are, old man, a stranger
in a strange land.
Accustom yourself
to hating what our city
despises and revering
what it loves.

OEDIPUS

Guide me, child, to some spot   210
where I can speak and listen

without offending the gods.
Let's not fight the inevitable.

LEADER

Stop right there. Don't move
beyond that rock ledge.

OEDIPUS

Stop here?

LEADER

That's far enough, I'm telling you!

OEDIPUS

May I sit down?

LEADER

Yes. Edge sideways and squat down on that rock.

ANTIGONE holds OEDIPUS and guides his steps.

ANTIGONE

Father, let me do this. Take one   220
easy step after another . . .

OEDIPUS

                 Oh, my.

ANTIGONE

. . . leaning your tired body
on my loving arm.

OEDIPUS

I'm sorry for my weakness.

ANTIGONE sits him on the rock ledge downstage.

LEADER

Poor fellow, now that you're at ease,
tell us who you are in the world.
Who would want to be moved about
in such excruciating pain?
Tell us where you live.

OEDIPUS

Strangers, I have no home! But please don't . . .   230

LEADER

What don't you want us to ask, old man?

OEDIPUS

Don't! Just don't ask who I am.
No questions, no more probing.

LEADER

Is there a reason?

OEDIPUS

The horror I was born to.

LEADER

Go on.

OEDIPUS

(whispering)

Child, what should I tell them?

LEADER

Speak up, stranger: tell us
your bloodlines. Start with your father.

OEDIPUS

What's going to happen to me, child?

ANTIGONE

You've been pushed to the brink. Better tell them.

OEDIPUS

All right, I'll say it. There's no way to hide it.   240

LEADER

You both take too much time. Go on, speak.

OEDIPUS

You've heard of Laios' son . . .

OLD MEN

Aaaaah!

OEDIPUS

. . . and the house of Labdakos . . .

OLD MEN

O Zeus!

OEDIPUS

      . . . and doomed Oedipus?

LEADER

That's who you are?

OEDIPUS

Don't fear my words . . .

OLD MEN

Aaagghhh! Aaagghhh!

As their cries of apprehension overwhelm OEDIPUS' *previous words, the* OLD MEN *en bloc turn away from him.*

OEDIPUS

      . . . because I am a broken man.

OLD MEN

Aaagghhh! Aaagghhh!

OEDIPUS

What's going to happen, child?

LEADER

Get out of here! Leave our country!   250

OEDIPUS

And the promise you made me?
How do you plan to honor that?

LEADER

When someone who's been wronged
defends himself by striking back,
Fate doesn't punish him. And when
deception is used to counter
deceit, it should cause pain, not gratitude.
Stand up! Now! Get off that seat! Leave this land
as fast as you can walk, so you won't burden
our city with your deadly contagion.   260

ANTIGONE

Strangers, so full of holy sentiments!
You can't abide my agèd father's presence,
can you? Because you've heard the rumors
about those actions he took in ignorance.
Think how unhappy it makes me
to plead with you on my father's behalf.
Strangers, I am looking at you with eyes
that aren't blind, and I beg *you* to see *me*

as though I were your family—and to feel
responsible for this afflicted person.   270
Our miserable lives depend on you
as if you all were gods. Give us the help
that we've stopped hoping for!

I'm begging you, in the name
of whatever you hold dear—
whether it's your child or your wife,
your fortune or your god!

               However hard
you look, you'll never find a man who can
escape his own fate-driven actions.

LEADER

We pity both of you, daughter—   280
you and your father, Oedipus.
You've led unfortunate lives.
But we fear the gods, we fear their anger,
if we say more than we've already said.

OEDIPUS

What good are fame and glory, if they just
trickle away and accomplish nothing?
Men call Athens the most god-fearing city,
a safe haven for persecuted strangers,
their best hope when they need a helping hand.
But how do these virtues benefit me   290
when you force me to climb down these ledges

and depart from your country? Does my *name*
frighten you? My appearance? Or my past deeds?
I performed every one of those actions,
you should know, but I willed none. You want me
to speak of my relations with my father
and mother—is that the source of your fear?

I have no doubt it is exactly that.
Yet, tell me: how is my *nature* evil—
if all I did was to return a blow?   300
How could I have been guilty, even if
I'd known where my actions would take me
while I was living them? But those who tried
to murder me—*they knew* what they were doing.

My friends, the gods inspired you to drive
me off that ledge. So respect these same gods—
and grant me the refuge that you've offered.
Don't act *now* as though gods don't exist.
They protect those who fear them,
but they also destroy those who don't.   310
And no godless mortal ever escapes.

Let the gods show you the way: don't blacken
Athens' reputation by taking part
in crimes of irreverence! I am
a suppliant to whom you promised
safety. Don't break that promise. And don't
shun me because of my disfigured face.

I've come here a devout and sacred man,
and I'll prove myself useful to your people.
When the man who holds power arrives,   320
whoever that may be, I will tell him
everything. Until then, do me no harm.

LEADER

We're impressed by the way you think, old man.
How could we not be? You speak with force.
We don't take you lightly, but we'd prefer
to have our rulers deal with this problem.

OEDIPUS

Where then, my friends, is this leader of yours?

LEADER

He's now in Athens, his home city. The same
person who sent us went on to find him.

OEDIPUS

Do you think he'll have sufficient   330
concern and regard for a blind old man
to travel all the way out here himself?

LEADER

He will come as soon as he hears your name.

OEDIPUS

And how will he hear my name?

LEADER

It's a long road,
but it's busy with foot traffic. News spreads
quickly. Don't worry. He'll recognize your name,
then come immediately to this place.
Your story's widely known, old man. Even
if he's asleep and wakes slowly,
word you're here will bring him in a hurry.   340

OEDIPUS

His coming will help Athens, and help me.
A good man is always his own best friend.

ANTIGONE looks offstage, brightens, and then calls out loudly.

ANTIGONE

O Zeus! What do I say now, Father? Or even think?

OEDIPUS

What do you see, Antigone?

ANTIGONE

(raising her voice)

A woman riding
a young Sicilian horse. Wearing a hat
from Thessaly to keep sun off her face.
What can I say? Is she, or isn't she?
Am I hallucinating? Yes? No?
I can't tell yet. Yes! YES!

There's no one else it could be.   350
As she comes closer, I can see her
smiling at me. It's my sister, Ismene!

OEDIPUS

What's that you're shouting, girl?

ANTIGONE

(still shouting)
That I see your daughter and my sister!
You'll recognize her as soon as she speaks.

*Enter ISMENE, having just dismounted from a small horse. She is
accompanied by her Servant.*

ISMENE

Father! Sister! It's wonderful to say those names!
It was so hard to find you. Now that I have,
I can hardly see you through my tears.

OEDIPUS

You've come, child?

ISMENE

                                I hate to see you like this, Father.

OEDIPUS

But you've joined us.

ISMENE

> Not without some trouble.   360

OEDIPUS

Touch me, daughter.

ISMENE

> Each of you take a hand.

OEDIPUS, ANTIGONE, and ISMENE join hands and hold them a while.

OEDIPUS

My daughters. Sisters.

ISMENE

> Two wretched lives!

OEDIPUS

Hers and mine?

ISMENE

> Yes. And my life as well.

OEDIPUS

Why did you come, child?

ISMENE

> I care about you, Father.

OEDIPUS

Then you missed me?

ISMENE

                              I did. And I bring news
I wanted you to hear from me.
I also brought our last faithful servant.

OEDIPUS

Our family's menfolk, your brothers—
where are they when we need them?

ISMENE

They are . . . wherever they are. Grim times for them.   370

OEDIPUS

Those two boys imitate the Egyptians
in how they think and how they run their lives.
Egyptian men stay in their houses weaving,
while their women are out earning a living.
Your brothers, who should be here helping me,
are back home keeping house like little girls,
while you two shoulder your father's hardships.
Antigone has been traveling with me
since she outgrew the care a child needs.
She gained enough strength to be an old man's   380
guide, picking her way barefoot through forests,
hungry, rain-drenched, sun-scorched.
                              Home comforts

took second place to caring for her father.
And you, Ismene, slipped out of Thebes
undetected so many times—to bring
the latest oracles to your father.
You were my eyes inside Thebes after I
was banished. Ismene, what's the news
you've brought? Why have you come?
I'm sure you haven't traveled here empty-   390
handed. Is there something I should fear?

ISMENE

Father, I'd rather not describe
the trouble I had trying to find you.
Just let it be! Retelling it
would only revive all the misery.

It's the real trouble your miserable sons are in—
it's their wrath I've come to tell you about.
They were keen, at first, to let Kreon rule,
so as not to pollute the city, well
aware the curse we inherit from way back   400
still holds your house in a death grip.
But spurred on by a god, and by their own
disturbed minds, my brothers—three times cursed!—
began battling each other for dominance
and the king's throne in Thebes.
                                    Now that hothead,
Eteokles, your youngest, has stripped
Polyneikes, your firstborn, of all power

and driven him out of the country.
Polyneikes was, from the reports I hear,
exiled to Argos. There he married power,   410
gaining friends willing to fight his battles—
determined to make Argos glorious
if it can conquer Thebes,
or to lift Thebes' reputation
sky-high should Argos lose.
It isn't just loose talk, father,
it has become horrible fact.
When will the gods lighten
your troubles? I wish I knew.

OEDIPUS

Do you hold out some hope that the gods   420
might take notice and end my suffering?

ISMENE

I do, Father. I have new oracles.

OEDIPUS

What are they? What do they say, daughter?

ISMENE

That your own people will someday need you,
living—and dead—to ensure their survival.

OEDIPUS

How could a man like me save anyone?

ISMENE

They say: you will hold Thebes' life in your hands.

OEDIPUS

When I'm nothing . . . how can I still be a man?

ISMENE

The gods who ruined you will now restore you.

OEDIPUS

Does little good to restore an old man   430
after they have laid waste to his youth.

ISMENE

Listen! The gods *will* transform you, and Kreon
will come here earlier than you might think.

OEDIPUS

Has he a plan, child? Tell me.

ISMENE

To station you at the Theban frontier,
but prevent you from crossing over.

OEDIPUS

What help am I if I'm outside their borders?

ISMENE

It's your tomb. If it's not paid proper respect,
that could cause them serious trouble.

OEDIPUS

They shouldn't need a god to tell them that.   440

ISMENE

It's still the reason they want you nearby,
not off someplace where you'd be in charge.

OEDIPUS

Then will they bury me in Theban earth?

ISMENE

Father, that's not allowed. You killed your father.

OEDIPUS

Then they must never have me in their power!

ISMENE

If they don't, things will go badly for Thebes.

OEDIPUS

What will cause things to go badly, daughter?

ISMENE

Your rage, when they're deployed around your tomb.

OEDIPUS

Who told you, child, what you have just told me?

ISMENE

Sacred envoys sent to the Delphic hearth.   450

OEDIPUS

Did the god truly say this about me?

ISMENE

All the returning envoys swore he did.

OEDIPUS

Did either of my sons hear them say it?

ISMENE

They heard it and they both knew what it meant.

OEDIPUS

With this knowledge, did those scoundrels
put the kingship ahead of helping me?

ISMENE

It hurts me to say this, Father. Yes, they did.

OEDIPUS

Gods, don't interfere with this brawl you've ordained!
But give me the right to decide how it ends—
this battle toward which my sons lift up spears   460
and on which they're now dead set. May my son
in power, who wields the scepter, lose it.
May my exiled son never make it home.
When I was driven shamefully from Thebes,
they made no move to stop it or help me.
They were spectators to my banishment.
They heard me proclaimed a homeless outcast!

You might think that Thebes acted properly,
that it gave me what I once craved. That's wrong.
On the far-off day when my fury seethed,   470
a death by stoning was my heartfelt wish.
But there was no one willing to grant it.
Later, when my suffering diminished,
I realized my rage had gone too far
in punishing my mistakes. Only then
did the city decide to force me out—
after all those years. And my own two sons,
who could have saved their father, did nothing.
It would have taken just one word. But I
wandered off into permanent exile.   480
My two unmarried girls fed me as best
they could. They sheltered and protected me,
my only family. But my sons traded
their father for power and a kingdom.

You can be certain I'll give them no help
in fighting their battles, and they will gain
nothing from having been rulers of Thebes.
I know that because, when I heard the oracles
this girl brought, I recalled some prophecies—
ones Phoibos Apollo has now fulfilled.   490

I'm ready. Let them send Kreon to find me—
or anyone who's powerful in Thebes.
If you strangers, together with those
intimidating goddesses who live

among you, are willing to enlist me,
you'll get a champion in the bargain,
someone who will defend your country
against its enemies, and damage his own.

LEADER

You've earned our pity, Oedipus,
both you and your daughters here.   500
And because you've offered to defend us,
I'm going to give you some advice.

OEDIPUS

Whatever my host wants done, I'll do.

LEADER

Ask atonement from the goddesses you first
met here, and whose ground you've invaded.

OEDIPUS

By what means? Tell me what I must do, friends.

LEADER

Dip water from a stream that flows year round,
wash your hands in it, then bring some here.

OEDIPUS

And when I've brought this pure water, what then?

LEADER

You'll find bowls made by a skilled craftsman.   510
Adorn their handles and their rims.

OEDIPUS

With branches or wool cloths—and then what?

LEADER

Gather fresh-cut fleece from a she-lamb.

OEDIPUS

How shall I end the ritual?

LEADER

Face the sunrise and pour an offering.

OEDIPUS

From the bowls you've just described?

LEADER

Spill some from each bowl, then empty the last.

OEDIPUS

Tell me what to put in the bowls.

LEADER

No wine. Just pure water sweetened with honey.

OEDIPUS

After I've drenched the ground under the trees?   520

LEADER

Using both hands, set out three bundles of nine
olive twigs each, while you recite a prayer.

OEDIPUS

That's it—get to the heart of the matter.

LEADER

Pray that the goddesses called the Gracious Ones
protect the suppliant, in their kindness,
and grant him a safe refuge. That's your prayer,
or someone else's who will pray for you.
Don't raise your voice, pray quietly,
and, without looking back, leave.
Do as I've said, and I'm sure you'll succeed.   530
If you don't, stranger, I'm afraid for you.

OEDIPUS

Daughters, have you heard what our friend here said?

ANTIGONE

We heard. What would you like us to do?

OEDIPUS

I lack the eyes—and the strength—to go myself.
My double loss. One of you must do it.

It is possible for one living soul
to pay a debt that's owed by ten thousand,
provided it's done with conviction.
One of you go—but don't leave me alone.
My body's too weak to move without help.   540

ISMENE

I'll carry out the ritual, but someone
must show me the right place to perform it.

LEADER

Go around to the far side of the grove.
If you need anything else, there's a man
living nearby who will point you the way.

ISMENE

I'll go now, Sister. You stay with Father.
Helping a parent who can't help himself
should never seem a burden.

Exit ISMENE and her Servant.

LEADER

Unpleasant it may be, stranger, to stir up
a long dormant grief. Yet there is something   550
I would like to hear straight from you.

OEDIPUS

                                What's your concern?

LEADER

That bitter, incurable anguish—
the kind you had to wrestle with.

OEDIPUS

Out of consideration for a guest,
don't dwell on my unfortunate past.

LEADER

Your story's widely told, my friend.
I'd like to hear the truth of it.

OEDIPUS

(pronouncing with a brusque hissing sound)
Ssstop!

LEADER

Hear me out, let me speak!

OEDIPUS

(aspirated vowel; spoken querulously)
Whhhy?   560

LEADER

You owe me this. I've granted all you've asked.

OEDIPUS

I suffered anguish, friends,
suffered what my own

blind actions caused.
But let the gods testify:
I chose to do none.

LEADER

Then how did this happen?

OEDIPUS

Thebes married me, who suspected nothing,
to a woman who would destroy me.

LEADER

Was she your mother, as I've heard,   570
who shared your infamous marriage bed?

OEDIPUS

She was. Your words feel
harsh as death in my ears.
And those daughters I fathered . . .

LEADER

What are you saying now?

OEDIPUS

                    —twin scourges—

LEADER

O Zeus!

OEDIPUS

. . . were born from the birth pangs
of the mother we shared.

LEADER

They're your daughters, and . . .

OEDIPUS

                              Yes! They're my sisters.

OLD MEN
(low whispering)
How horrible.

OEDIPUS

Oh yes! A thousand evils   580
surge back, all through me.

LEADER

                              Then you suffered . . .

OEDIPUS

I suffered an indelible torment.

LEADER

                              Then you've sinned . . .

OEDIPUS

There was no sin.

LEADER

How did you not?

OEDIPUS

I was presented with a gift—
one that would break my heart—
to repay me for all the help
I gave Thebes. It was a gift
I should never have accepted.   590

LEADER

Horrible. And then? You killed . . . ?

OEDIPUS

Why this? What are you asking me?

LEADER

                          . . . your father?

OEDIPUS

You open one old wound after another.

LEADER

Then you killed him.

OEDIPUS

                  Yes, I killed him. But I have . . .

LEADER

You have what?

OEDIPUS

        Justice on my side.

LEADER

                     How could that be?

OEDIPUS

Let me tell you. The men
I fought and killed
would have killed me.
Before the law
my hands are clean.   600
My actions were driven
not by malice,
but by ignorance.

One of Theseus' Men enters, whispers to the LEADER, and then exits.

LEADER

Aigeus' son, our king, has arrived, willing
to do all you have asked of him.

Enter THESEUS, who walks up and examines OEDIPUS.

THESEUS

For years I've heard that you had done
bloody damage to your eyes—so I
recognize you, son of Laios. What I learned
on my way here made me almost certain.
And to see you now at your journey's end   610

removes all doubt. Your clothes, your ravaged face,
tell me your name. Oedipus, I
truly pity you. And I will help you.
You and this poor girl have come here
suddenly—why? To request a favor
from Athens and from me? If so, ask it.
You would need to tell me an appalling
story indeed before I'd turn you down.
Remember, I was also raised in exile,
combating threats to my life of a kind   620
no other man has ever had to face.
I would never refuse a homeless man—
which you are—my help. I'm also mortal,
like you, with no greater assurance
than you have that I'll be alive tomorrow.

OEDIPUS

There's little I need add, Theseus.
With a few gracious words
you've said exactly who I am, and who
my father was, and what country I'm from—
so nothing remains. Except to tell you   630
what most concerns me. Then I'll be silent.

THESEUS

Go on. Say what you mean. I must know.

OEDIPUS

I came to offer you my disfigured
body as a gift. Though not pleasant

to look at, it will generate benefits
beauty could not.

THESEUS

                    This advantage
you claim to have brought us—what is it?

OEDIPUS

In time you will know. But not for a while.

THESEUS

Your . . . enhancement—when will it be revealed?

OEDIPUS

After I'm dead and you have buried me.   640

THESEUS

You ask me to oversee your last rites,
but say nothing of your life before then.

OEDIPUS

Grant my wish. Everything else will follow.

THESEUS

This favor you're asking seems a small one.

OEDIPUS

Take care. This is no trivial matter.

THESEUS

Then you anticipate trouble. From your sons?

OEDIPUS

King, my sons want to return me to Thebes.

THESEUS

If that's your desire, why would you refuse?

OEDIPUS

(loudly and with fury)

Because, when I wished to stay, *they* refused!

THESEUS

Fool! When you're in trouble, rage never helps.   650

OEDIPUS

Wait till you've heard me out. Then chastise me.

THESEUS

Go on. I shouldn't speak without the facts.

OEDIPUS

Theseus, I have suffered terribly.

THESEUS

You mean the ancient curse on your family.

OEDIPUS

No. Not that story every Greek has heard.

THESEUS

Then what superhuman pain *do* you suffer?

OEDIPUS

Here's what my two sons did to me.
They banished me from my homeland. I can't
return because I killed my own father.

THESEUS

If that's the case, why would Thebes want you back?   660

OEDIPUS

God's voice will *compel* them to take me back.

THESEUS

Oracles must have frightened them. Of what?

OEDIPUS

That Fate will strike them down in your country.

THESEUS

And what could cause such hatred between us?

OEDIPUS

Gentle son of Aigeus, only the gods
never grow old and die. All-powerful
Time ravages the rest. Just as the Earth
decays, so does the body's strength. When trust
between people dies, betrayal begins.
A spirit of respect can never last   670

between two friends, or between two cities,
because sooner or later resentment
kills all friendships. Though sometimes they revive.

The weather now is sunny between Thebes
and Athens, but Time in due course will bring
on a war sparked by a minor grievance—
endless days and nights in which Theban spears
shatter the peace they had promised to keep.

Then my dead body, slumbering, buried,
deathly cold, will drink their hot blood—if Zeus   680
is still Zeus, if Apollo spoke the truth.
But since there's no pleasure in pronouncing
words that should never be said, I will stop.
Keep *your* word and you'll never be sorry
you welcomed Oedipus to your city—unless
the gods abort their promises to me.

LEADER

From the beginning, King, this man has shown
he has the nerve to keep every promise
he's made to our country—and he'll keep more.

THESEUS

Who would refuse the kindness of a man   690
like this? We welcome him to our home fires.
As our wartime ally he's earned the right.
Now he comes asking our gods to help him,

an act with no small implication
for Athens and myself. I value
what he brings. Reject his offers?
Never! I'll settle him in our land
with the rights of a citizen.
If it's the stranger's desire to live *here*,
(*turning toward the LEADER*)
I will charge *you* with his protection.   700
Or he may wish to join me.
                                    Oedipus,
it's your decision. I'll respect your choice.

OEDIPUS

O Zeus, do your utmost for this man.

THESEUS

What is your pleasure? To live in my house?

OEDIPUS

If that were allowed. But *here* is the place . . .

THESEUS

Here? What will you do here? I'm not opposed . . .

OEDIPUS

. . . where I will punish those who drove me out.

THESEUS

Then the great gift you meant—is your presence?

OEDIPUS

Yes. If you keep the pledges you gave me.

THESEUS

Don't doubt me. I will never betray you.   710

OEDIPUS

I won't demand an oath from you—as though
you were a man who couldn't be trusted.

THESEUS

But that's all I can offer you: my word.

OEDIPUS

How then will you act . . .

THESEUS

What is your worst fear?

OEDIPUS

That troops will come.

THESEUS

My men will deal with them.

OEDIPUS

Take care that when you leave me . . .

THESEUS

Please. Don't tell me what to do.

OEDIPUS

How can I *not* be afraid?

THESEUS

My heart isn't pounding.

OEDIPUS

You don't know what they threaten . . .

THESEUS

I know this:

no men will seize you unless I allow it.   720
And if they brag how simple it will be
to kidnap you, I think the sea they're crossing
will prove too vast and too rough for their skills.
For now, take courage. Aside from any
assurance *I've* given, it was *Apollo*
who sent you. While I'm gone,
my word will protect you.

Exit THESEUS.

OLD MEN

You've come, stranger, to shining Kolonos
abounding with horses
and Earth's loveliest farms.   730
Here the Nightingale
sings her long clear trills
under green forest trees
laden with apples and berries.

In the wine-dark ivy she sings,
in the forbidden
thickets of goddesses
untroubled by hot sun
or the chill blast of winter.

She sings in the clearings   740
where Dionysos dances
among the everloving
maenads who raised him.
Here, drinking dew from the sky
morning after morning,
narcissi flourish.
Their heavenly blossoms
crown two immortals,
Persephone and Demeter—sunlight
illumines the golden crocus.   750

Bountiful fountains send Kephisos
cascading down the mountain.
He never stops flowing, greening
all that grows, pouring daily
his pure waters
through the valley's nurturing hills.
Nor do the Muses,
singing in harmony, or the Goddess of Love
with golden reins in her hands,
stay away long.   760

A tree not found in Asia,
or on the Dorian Island of Pelops,
lives here, a tree born from itself,
a tree no one plants.
A terror to enemy spears,
the gray-green olive
grows freely on our land,
nourishing our children.
Neither the young men nor the old
will shatter and destroy it,   770
for Zeus of the Olive Groves,
and Athena with seagreen eyes,
guard it with tireless glare.

And now with all our strength we sing
our gratitude to our mother city,
for the great gifts the gods have given her:
that peerless glory of our land,
the strength of stallions, the speed of colts—
and the rolling power of the sea.
It was you, son of Kronos,   780
who gave Kolonos our throne,
and you, Lord Poseidon,
who taught us to harness, out on these roads,
the fury of horses, taught us to drive
the long-limbed oar that pulses us
over salt seas, in pursuit
of fifty Nereids' skittering feet.

ANTIGONE's attention is drawn offstage left.

ANTIGONE

You've praised your land beyond all others—
prove now you can act on those glowing words.

OEDIPUS

What makes you say that to them, daughter?   790

ANTIGONE

Kreon's arriving, Father, backed by troops.

OEDIPUS

Can I trust these kind old men to protect me?

LEADER

Don't worry, you're in good hands. I may have aged,
but this country has lost none of its strength.

Enter KREON, escorted by his armed Soldiers.

KREON

You men must be the local nobility.
I detect some fear showing in your eyes
at my arrival. Don't be alarmed.
There's no need for hostile murmuring.
I haven't come intending to use force.
I'm an old man. Yours is a powerful city,   800
if ever there was one in Greece. So yes—

I was sent here, on account of my age,
to reason with that man, and bring him home.
No single person sent me—all Thebes did.
Kinship demands I show greater concern
for his troubles than do my countrymen.
(turning to face OEDIPUS)
You've suffered for too long, Oedipus.
Please hear me out, then we can both go home.
It's high time your fellow Kadmeans
took you back. More than anyone else, I   810
share your sorrows, old man, now that I see
how you live in your miserable exile—
drifting in constant want, with only this girl
as your servant.

              I never thought her life
would sink to such gross squalor, but it has:
tending to you, to your personal needs,
living in poverty. And at her age,
with no experience of men, she's ripe
for the first vulgar lout who comes along.
Those are harsh judgments, aren't they, alas,   820
on you and on me? On our whole family.

Since there's no way to hide your obvious
degradation, Oedipus, please agree
to placate our family gods by coming
home to the house and city of your fathers.
Thank Athens for her kindness as you leave,
for she deserves it. But your birthplace must,

if you would do the right thing, have the final
claim on you. Long ago, she nurtured you.

OEDIPUS

You! You'll try anything! You have based your   830
insidious arguments on the most
ethical grounds. But why make the attempt?
Why try to slide a noose around my neck?
That would cause me unendurable pain.

Some time ago, when I was tormented
by self-inflicted agony and wanted
with all my heart to be banished from Thebes,
you refused me. Later, when my grief eased
and I wished to remain home, you drove me
from my house, off the land, into exile,   840
without one thought of this kinship you claim.

Now this time, seeing the friendly welcome
Athens and her people have given me,
you try to abduct me—your harsh purpose
sheathed in amiable words. What joy is there
in kindness that's imposed against our will?
Suppose someone refuses to help you—
though you've begged him for help. But once
you possess what your heart craves—then he
offers to give what you no longer want.   850
Would that be kindness? Fulfillment like that
is worthless—as are your offers to me.
They sound good, but in fact they're evil.

Let me explain your motives to these men,
so they'll see just how treacherous you are.

You have sought me out—not to take me home—
but to plant me outside your borders,
so that your city will emerge unscathed
from any invasion launched against it.
You won't get *that*, but you'll get something else: 860
this part of me—my *spirit*—ravaging
your country. And it will rage there always:
my sons will inherit from their father
only enough of my homeland to die in!

Don't you see? I know the future of Thebes
better than you do. A great deal better,
because my sources are better: Apollo,
for instance, and his father, Zeus himself.
Your lying mouth has come here spitting out
all those words—your tongue's keener than a blade.   870
But your guile hurts you far more than it helps.

I don't think I've persuaded you. So leave!
Let me live here! Poor as I am, I won't
live in want if I'm at peace with myself.

KREON

In our exchange, who do you think suffers
more, *me* by your views, or *you* by your own?

OEDIPUS

All that matters to me is that you've failed
to change my mind, or the minds of these men.

KREON

Growing old hasn't improved your judgment,
friend. It's perpetuated your disgrace.   880

OEDIPUS

Your tongue's extremely quick. But a good man
never pleads a dishonorable cause.

KREON

Making noise doesn't prove you're making sense.

OEDIPUS

As if *you* spoke briefly, and to the point?

KREON

Not pointedly enough to pierce your mind.

OEDIPUS

Go! I speak for these men and for myself.
Don't keep me under hostile surveillance
in a land that's destined to be my home.

KREON gestures toward the OLD MEN and his Soldiers.

KREON

I ask *these* men—not you—and I ask my . . .
comrades here, to note the tone you're taking   890
with a kinsman. If I ever seize you . . .

OEDIPUS

Who could seize me against my friends' will?

KREON

I swear you'll suffer even if we don't.

OEDIPUS

How do you plan to back up your bluster?

KREON

I've already seized one of your daughters
and removed her. I'll take the other soon.

OEDIPUS

My god.

KREON

Soon you'll have greater cause to say, "My god."

OEDIPUS

You took Ismene?

KREON

                    And I'll soon take this one.

KREON indicates ANTIGONE.

OEDIPUS

What will *you* do, my hosts—my friends?   900
Fail me by not banishing
this blaspheming thug?

LEADER

(to KREON)
Stranger, go. There's no way to justify
what you're attempting, or what you've just done.

KREON

(to his Soldiers)
It's time we take this girl away, by force
if she puts up the slightest resistance.

ANTIGONE

I don't know where to run. Are there men
or gods willing to help me?

LEADER

                    What are you doing, stranger?

KREON

I'll leave him, but I will take *her.* She's mine.

OEDIPUS

You men in power here!

LEADER

                              Stranger, there's no   910
justification for what you're doing.

KREON

I can justify it.

LEADER

                 How can you do that?

KREON

I'm taking what belongs to me.

KREON grabs ANTIGONE.

OEDIPUS

                   Stop him, Athens!

LEADER

What is this, stranger? Let the daughter go—
or you'll discover who holds power here.

KREON

Stand back!

LEADER

            Not from you! Not while you do this!

KREON

Touch me, and you're at war with Thebes.

OEDIPUS

All of this I foresaw.

LEADER

Release the girl.

KREON

Don't issue orders when you have no power.

LEADER

I warn you, let her go.

KREON

And I warn you: leave!   920

LEADER

(yelling offstage)

Over here, citizens! Join our fight! My city,
our city, is attacked! Come help us!

ANTIGONE

They're dragging me away! Friends! FRIENDS!

OEDIPUS

Where are you, child?

ANTIGONE

. . . I . . . can't . . . get . . . free!

OEDIPUS

Reach out to me, daughter.

ANTIGONE

They are too strong.

KREON

(to his Soldiers)

Take her away from here.

ANTIGONE

                 I'm so weak! So weak! I can't stop them.

KREON's Soldiers drag ANTIGONE offstage.

KREON

Now you won't have two daughters for crutches.
But since you want to lay waste your country
and its people—who've ordered me to do this,
though I remain their king—go right ahead,   930
fight for victory! You will find that nothing
you're doing now, nothing you've ever done,
has done you any good—you've turned your back
on those who love you, while they've tried
to stop your self-destructive fury.

LEADER

Stop where you are, stranger.

LEADER grabs hold of KREON.

KREON

Keep your hands off me.

LEADER

When you've brought back his daughters!

KREON

That will cost Thebes a much steeper ransom.
I'll take something worth more than these two girls.   940

LEADER

What are you threatening?

LEADER lifts his hands from KREON.

KREON

                    To seize that man there.

LEADER

Those are shocking words.

KREON

                    But ones I'll make good.

LEADER

You might—unless our king stops you.

OEDIPUS

That is outrageous! So you would seize me?

KREON

Shut up!

OEDIPUS

    NO!

        Goddesses, don't gag
the curse rising in my throat—on you, scum,
who have stolen my dear defenseless eyes,
gone like the sight I once possessed.
Let the Sun, who sees all there is, give you,
and every member of your family,   950
an old age as miserable as my own.

KREON

You people who live here, do you see that?

OEDIPUS

They see us both. They know you have caused me
real harm, while I've struck back with mere breath.

KREON

I will not curb my rage! Though I'm alone,
though age enfeebles me, I will take him.

KREON takes hold of OEDIPUS.

OEDIPUS

He's done it.

LEADER

Stranger, what arrogance possessed you?
You think you can accomplish this?

KREON

I *will* accomplish it.   960

LEADER

Then I'll cease to believe Athens is a city.

KREON

The weak overcome the powerful
if they have justice on their side.

OEDIPUS

                              Did you hear him?

LEADER

Zeus, back me up! He can't enforce his boast.

KREON

But Zeus knows that I can. And you don't know.

LEADER

That's an outrage!

KREON

An outrage you can't stop.

LEADER

You men who govern us! Come here! Be quick!
These men are heading for the border.

Enter THESEUS and his Men. KREON releases OEDIPUS and steps back.

THESEUS

What makes you shout? What's wrong?
Are you so panicked that you'll disrupt   970
my sacrifice to the seagod of Kolonos?
Speak up! Tell me the whole story, so I'll
know why I've run here so fast my legs ache.

OEDIPUS

I recognize your voice, friend. That man
over there has done me serious harm.

THESEUS

What harm? Which man?

OEDIPUS

Kreon. He's right there, you see him. He's taken
two of my children—the two I have left.

THESEUS

What are you saying?

OEDIPUS

I've told you what he did.

THESEUS

Someone run to my people at the altars.   980
Order every man there to leave the sacrifice
and converge at the crossroads. Go on foot,
or loosen your horses' reins and make them
gallop. Stop those girls from leaving town,
so I won't look useless to this stranger,
caught off guard by a desperate act. Go now!
And as for that man standing over there—
if I could punish him for what he's done
there is no way he would ever go free.
As things stand, he's protected by the laws   990
that authorized his visit to Athens.

(to KREON)

But we won't turn you loose until you bring
the girls here, where I can see them. Your actions
shame me, your family, and your country.

You've come to a city that loves justice.
We will do nothing contrary to law,
even though you flout our laws—invading
our territory, grabbing what you please,
keeping it by force. Do you think no men,
only slaves, live here? That I don't matter?   1000
It's not your breeding that makes you
a vile man. Thebes does not breed criminals.

She wouldn't support you, not if she knew
you were plundering what belongs to me—
and to the gods—using force to abduct
helpless suppliants.
                 If I had crossed
your borders, no matter how just my cause,
I would first ask your ruler's agreement,
whoever he might be, before I dragged
anybody off. I'd know how a stranger   1010
should deal with your country's citizens.
But you've given your city a bad name
it doesn't deserve. And as you've grown old
the years have blighted your intelligence.

I said before, and I say now: Someone
must bring the girls back. Unless you'd like
to take up permanent residence here.
These aren't just words. They speak my mind.

LEADER

Do you see what's become of you, stranger?
We thought at first that you were honest—like   1020
your people. Now we see the harm you cause.

KREON

I didn't take these actions assuming,
as you would have it, that this city lacked
brave or intelligent men. I took them
because I assumed that its people

were not so taken with my relatives
as to feed and house them against my will.
I was sure you people wouldn't shelter
a morally toxic father-killer,
a man whose wife bore children to her son.   1030

I knew that the Council of Mount Ares
convenes in your city, and believed it
much too wise to let vagrants enter Athens.
I trusted my conviction when I seized him.
Nor would I have abducted him
if he hadn't laid curses on my kinfolk.
I am a man maligned! I have a right
to strike back. Anger doesn't diminish
as we age. It consumes us till we die.
Only the dead are immune from anguish.   1040

Do what you want with me.
Though I'm nothing, mine is a just cause.
I may be old, but I'll attempt
to pay you back blow for blow.

OEDIPUS

You have no shame! Tell me, does your nonsense
about a weak old man best fit you? Or me?
You charge me with murder, incest, disgrace—
misfortunes I suffered, but none of which
I chose. Perhaps it pleased the gods to hate
my ancestors. Examine my whole life.   1050

You can accuse me of no personal
wrongdoing, no crime whose expiation
impelled me to harm myself and my kin.

Tell me this. If the oracle of god
had decreed my father must die
at the hands of his own son, how
could you possibly think it just
to blame me? I wasn't even born!
No father had begotten me,
no mother had conceived me.   1060

And if, born to this miserable fate
as I most surely was, I traded blows
with my father in combat, and killed him,
not knowing what I was doing, or to whom—
how could you condemn that ignorant act?
As for my mother—you disgrace yourself
when you force me to speak of her marriage.
She was your sister, and our marriage
happened in just the way I'll now describe.
Given what's come from your vulgar mouth,   107/
there is no reason to shut mine.

Yes!—she bore me. And that wrecked both our lives.
I didn't know the truth, neither did she.
She give birth to me, and then she give birth
to children I fathered—to her shame.

I'm certain of one thing: it is your own
free choice to condemn us. But was my will
free when I married her? No! Nor do I
have any choice but to speak of it now.
Neither my marriage, nor the killing   1080
of my father—actions you keep on
throwing in my face—can be called crimes.

Of all my questions, answer just this one:
if, right now, a man standing beside you—
righteous you—tried to kill you, would you ask
whether or not the would-be murderer
was your father, or would you strike him down?
If your life mattered to you, I believe
you'd fight your assassin before you asked
yourself whether you were doing the right thing.   1090

Into such cataclysms the gods led me.
If my father's spirit came back to life,
I don't think he would disagree.

But you! Because you're not a moral man,
because you're willing to say anything,
because to you it's all the same—
speech that's vulgar and specch that's not—
you slander and defame me
in the presence of these good men.

You're quite happy to flatter Theseus—   1100
nd Athens, for being such a well-run state.

Yet, in the midst of your adulation,
you have forgotten that if any city
knows the best way to venerate the gods,
it is Athens above all. So you try
to snatch me from this country, abuse me,
an old man, a suppliant! And worst of all
you seize my daughters! For all these reasons
I ask the goddesses living over there
for their help—provide me with friends!—so you   1110
may learn what kind of men defend this city.

LEADER

He's a good man, King. His destiny
may horrify us, but he's earned our help.

THESEUS

Enough discussion! The abductors
and their captives are on the move, while we,
the injured parties, just stand here.

KREON

What will you force a weak old man to do?

THESEUS

You can show me their route. I'll go with you.
If you're holding the girls we're searching for
nearby, you'll take me there yourself—but if   1120
your men have galloped off with their prizes,
that will save us some trouble, for my horsemen
will ride them down. Your men, thank god,

could never outrun mine to the frontier.
Let's go! Listen to me: the snake's defanged.
Fate's caught the marauder in her trap.
Whatever you win by cunning, you will lose.
You'll also lose your partners in this outrage.
I doubt you would have dared to attack us
unless you had some armed accomplices—   1130
perhaps you were counting on some traitor.
I'd better look to it—or else one lone
man could overthrow the whole city.
Are you hearing me? Or will you
ignore my words like the warnings you had
while you were planning this atrocity?

KREON

You're on home ground, so nothing you can say
disturbs me. Back in Thebes I'll know what to do.

THESEUS

Threaten me all you like—but start walking.
Oedipus, stay here. I'm sure you'll be safe.   1140
And I promise you this: unless I'm killed
I'll bring both of your daughters back alive.

OEDIPUS

May the gods bless your kindness, Theseus.
Bless your devotion to our welfare.

Exit THESEUS and his Men, escorting KREON.

OLD MEN

Oh let us be there,
to see the enemy
turn and fight! Bronze banging
bronze on the Pythian shore
or on torch-lit beaches
where two great queens—lips sworn   1150
to unbreakable silence
by the priests of Eumolpos—
nurture and watch over
funeral rites for the dead.
Out where Theseus,
the battle-igniter, and two
young girls, captive sisters,
converge at our borders,
surrounded by shouting
soldiers sure they have won.   1160
Or will the thieves be run down
in pastures west of the snowy
rock in the town of Oea,
as they flee on fast horses
or chariots driven at speed?
Kreon is beaten!
Men from Kolonos
make powerful warriors!
The steel of every bridle
flashes, the mounted troop   1170
charges ahead at full gallop.
They worship Athena;

they worship Poseidon,
the ocean-embracing
son of the goddess Rhea.

Are they in action yet,
or do they hold back?
My heart gives me
hope that the girls,
harshly tested,   1180
brutally abused
at the hands of their uncle,
will soon see us, face to face.

Today! Today is the day that Zeus
will conclude a great work,
the victory in battle I foresee!
Were I a dove right now, the storm's
thrust lifting my strong wings,
I might soar through a cloud,
the battle raging below me.   1190

Hear it, Zeus, who rules
all other gods, who sees
all that there is to see!
Let our country's defenders
strike the decisive blow
that will bring the prize home.
Help us, fearsome Athena!
Come, huntsman Apollo,

bring Artemis, your sister!
Come all you trackers   1200
of the dappled fast-moving deer—
help this land and our people!
You won't find me a false prophet,
wandering friend. I'm looking now
at the girls and their escort coming home.

OEDIPUS
Where? Can you tell me? What are you saying?

Enter ANTIGONE and ISMENE with THESEUS and his Men.

ANTIGONE
(from a distance)
Father!—if only some god would show you
this princely man who's brought us back to you!

OEDIPUS
Daughter? Is it you?

ANTIGONE
                            Yes! All these strong arms—
the king and his loyal men—set us free.   1210

OEDIPUS
Come toward me, child. Returned to me,
after I had lost hope. Come to my arms.

ANTIGONE

You ask for what I want to give.

OEDIPUS

Where are you, child?

ANTIGONE

We're both coming to you.

OEDIPUS *embraces his daughters.*

OEDIPUS

My darling children!

ANTIGONE

You love us all.

OEDIPUS

You strengthen my old frame.

ANTIGONE

And share your grief.

OEDIPUS

I hold all my dear ones. If I die now,
I won't die totally wretched, so long
as you two hold me like this. Cling so hard
you graft yourselves to your father, so tight   1220
I'll feel released at last from the wanderings
that have left me bone-tired and miserable.

Now tell me quickly what happened out there.
A girl your size should keep it short.

ANTIGONE

The man who saved us is right here.
It was all his doing. Let him tell it.
That's as brief as I can make it.

OEDIPUS

Don't be surprised, my friend, that I've spoken
so long and so intently to my daughters.
I was quite sure they were lost forever.   1230
I owe the joy I'm feeling now
to you. You freed them, no one else.

May the gods grant all that I wish for you—
both you and your city—for I've found you
the most god-fearing, evenhanded
people on Earth. And your tongues never lie.
I know your virtues. Let me honor them:
you—and no other—gave me what I have.

Please reach your right hand out to me, King,
so I may hold it and then kiss your face,   1240
if that's allowed.
                    What am I asking for?
Ill-omened creature that I've been since birth—
why should I want you to touch someone
like me—steeped in every evil?

No, I can't let you do it, not even
if you wished it. Those who have lived through
misery the same as my own, only they
may touch me. Take my salute where you stand.
As for the future, treat me justly.
Just as you've done so far.   1250

THESEUS

I'm not surprised you've spoken at such length,
elated as you are at your daughters' return,
or that you wanted to speak first with them.
Nothing like that would ever annoy me.
I want my life to shine through my actions,
not through my words. The proof, old man, is this:
I've kept my promises to you—brought back
unharmed both your stolen daughters.
How did we win the skirmish? Why should I
bother with that? Your daughters will tell you.   1260

But something happened just as I returned.
Perhaps you could advise me about it.
A small matter, but a surprising one,
and even small things shouldn't be ignored.

OEDIPUS

Son of Aigeus, what is this small thing?
Please tell me. I don't know why you're asking.

THESEUS

They tell me a man—your kinsman, but not
one from your city—lies on his stomach,
a suppliant at Poseidon's altar,
where I sacrificed before I set out.   1270

OEDIPUS

What country is he from? What does he want?

THESEUS

They tell me he wishes to speak briefly
with you. Nothing very consequential.

OEDIPUS

Speak of what? No one asks a god's help lightly.

THESEUS

He prayed, I'm told, for a meeting with you—
from which he'd be allowed to leave unharmed.

OEDIPUS

Who'd make an appeal like that to the god?

THESEUS

Do you recall having a kinsman in Argos—
someone who might ask you for help?

OEDIPUS

Friend, don't say any more.

THESEUS

What's wrong with you?   1280

OEDIPUS

Don't question me.

THESEUS

Not ask you what? Say it!

OEDIPUS

From what you've said, I know this suppliant.

THESEUS

But why should he offend me? Who is he?

OEDIPUS

King, he's my son. I hate him. His voice would
give me more pain than any other man's.

THESEUS

How so? Can't you listen, but do nothing
you don't wish to? Is it harmful to listen?

OEDIPUS

His voice itself is loathsome to me, King.
Don't compel me to do what you're asking.

THESEUS

You had better consider this: 1290
aren't you compelled by his

suppliant status? Haven't you
a solemn duty to honor the god?

ANTIGONE
Father, please hear me, even though I'm young
to give advice. Respect the king's conscience—
let him honor his god the way he must!
And for your daughters' sake, let our brother
come here. No matter how he maligns you,
he can't force you to change your mind, can he?
Hear what he has to say. What's wrong with that?   1300

You are his father, and you know that even
if he blames you in the most ungodly
vicious way, to do him wrong can't be right.
Show him compassion! Other fathers
afflicted with bad children, and just as short-
tempered as you, have softened in response
to the calming influence of their loved ones.
Look at your own past, and remember how
your parents' misery became your own.
And when you consider how theirs happened,   1310
I think you'll see that the surest outcome
of any evil you inflict—is more evil.

Please change your mind. It's not right for someone
pleading a just cause to plead it forever!
Or for a man who has been given help
to hesitate when asked to repay it.

OEDIPUS

Your arguments are winning me over,
daughter. Though what makes you happy
devastates me, I'll do what you ask.

(turning to THESEUS)

But if you let that man come here,   1320
my friend, no one, at any time,
must be given power over my life.

THESEUS

I wouldn't want to hear you repeat that,
old man. I never boast, but believe me,
as long as the gods let me live, you're safe.

Exit THESEUS and his Men.

OLD MEN

Anyone who craves
all the years he can have,
expecting to enjoy
a lifespan longer
than normal, makes,   1330
we promise you,
a foolish choice.

For the days that stretch out ahead
hold more sorrow than joy,
and the body whose limbs
once gave you pleasure

will soon give you none,
when you've lived past your prime.
And when the Caregiver comes,
he ends all lives the same way.   1340
Hades is suddenly real—
no lyre, no dancing, no marriage-song.
There is nothing but Death.

By any measure, it is best
never to have been born.
But once a man is born,
the next best thing, by far,
is for him to return,
as soon as he can,
to the place he came from.   1350
For once youth—with its mindless
indulgence—goes by, is there a single
punishing blow that won't find him?
Any misfortune that doesn't
attack his life? Envy, feuding,
revolt, battle, and murder!
And finally, old age: despised,
decrepit, lonely, friendless old age
takes him in—there he keeps house
with the worst of all evils.   1360

(looking toward OEDIPUS)

He too has arrived at those years,
that ruin of a man—we're not alone.
He's like some headland facing north,

lashed by the huge waves of winter.
He too is battered by the troubles
breaking over him, billows pounding in
from both the rising and the setting sun—
from the south, where it's noon all day long,
and from the black northern mountains.

ANTIGONE

I think a stranger's about to arrive.   1370
Just one lone man, Father. And he's in tears.

OEDIPUS

Who is he?

Enter a distraught, weeping POLYNEIKES.

ANTIGONE

The one we've been discussing:
Polyneikes. He's here.

POLYNEIKES

What should I do? Feel sorry for myself?
Or for the frail father I'm looking at?
I find him banished to a foreign country—
along with you two—living in rancid
rags for so long they've bonded to his flesh
like some disease. And his unruly hair   1380
snarls in the wind over his blinded face.
Just as miserable are the rations
he carries to feed his aching belly.

POLYNEIKES walks over to address OEDIPUS.

It shames me to have learned this so late.
I'll admit it: in all that touches
your welfare I've been wholly
irresponsible. But you're hearing this
from my mouth, not from anyone else's.
Father, you know that the goddess Respect
joins every action that Zeus takes. May she   1390
inspire you! I can atone for my sins;
I can't possibly make them any worse.

POLYNEIKES pauses for a response; OEDIPUS is silent.

You're quiet, father. Why? Please speak to me.
Don't turn your back. You won't respond at all?
Will you deny me with silent contempt?
You'll give no explanation for your rage?
My sisters! His daughters! Please make him talk.
Break through his sullen, stony silence.
Stop him from disdaining me like this.
I have the god's protection, yet this man   1400
turns me away without a single word.

ANTIGONE
Then tell him what you came for! You coward!
If you speak freely you might give him pleasure.
Try glowing with anger or affection.
Maybe then this mute man will find a voice.

POLYNEIKES

That was harsh but just. I *will* speak
plainly. But first I must ask help—of the god
from whose altar the king of this country
pulled me up, so I could come make my case,
hear yours, and be granted safe conduct   1410
to go my way. I hope I can trust you—
Father, Sisters—to honor those assurances.

I want to tell you why I'm here, Father.
I've been forced to flee my own country, exiled
after I claimed, as the elder son, my right
to inherit your throne and your power.
Eteokles, although my junior, expelled me.
He hadn't beaten me in court or tested
his strength against mine in battle, but he
somehow persuaded Thebes to back him.   1420

It's likely that the Fury who stalks you
strengthened his case. At least, that's what I'm told
by the omen-readers.

                       Soon after I arrived
in Argos I married King Adrastos'
daughter. That won me the support,
by a sworn oath, of the most battle-proven
warriors on the Peloponnesus, men
who would help me raise seven companies
of spearmen to fight Thebes, ready to die
for my cause—or drive out the vile rebels   1430
from our land.

Why do I come here now?
I bring prayers, Father, my own, and those
of my allies—seven columns, seven
poised spears surrounding Thebes on all sides.
Quick-thrusting Amphiaraos joins me,
unmatched in battle or in prophecy,
then Oineus' son, Tydeus,
from Aitolia. The third, Eteoklos,
comes from Argos. Fourth is Hippomedon,
sent by his father, Talaos. The fifth one,   1440
Kapaneus, promises he'll use fire
to burn down Thebes. Parthenopaios,
named after his mother, the aging virgin
Atalanta, whose late marriage produced him,
hurries to war from Arcadia.

And I, your son—or if I'm not really
your son, but the spawn of an evil fate,
at least I'm yours according to my name—
I lead Argos' brave army against Thebes.

All of us, father—for your children's sake,   1450
for the sake of your own life—beg you now
to give up your anger at me,
now that I'm ready to punish the brother
who banished me and robbed me of my country.

If what the oracles predict holds true,
victory will go to the side you join.
Now, in the name of the fountains of home,

in the name of our tribal gods, I ask you
to listen and relent. I'm a beggar,
an exile, but so are you. The kindness   1460
of others supports us both, and we share
a common fate—while he, that arrogant
dictator back in our homeland, mocks us
equally. But if you support me now,
I'll crush him soon and without much trouble.
When I've expelled him by force, I'll put you
back in your house, and myself back in power.
If you join me, I'll make good on that boast.
But if you don't help me, I'm a dead man.

LEADER

(sotto voce)

Respect the person who sent him to us,   1470
Oedipus. Say something expedient
to him—before you send him on his way.

OEDIPUS

No, my friends, you who oversee this grove:
if Theseus hadn't ordered him here,
believing me obliged to answer him,
he would never have heard me raise my voice.
But now, before he goes, he'll feel that blessing.
And he will hear from me some things
that won't make him happy:
(suddenly turning on POLYNEIKES)
There are no worse men than you!   1480

When you held the power your brother now holds
you made me an outcast with no city,
forced to wear the rags that bring tears to your eyes—
now that you're facing the same ordeal.
I've put tears behind me. As long as I live
I'll bear the burden of knowing that you
would have killed me. You made me swallow filth,
you drove me out, and you made me a foul
tramp who begs his daily bread from strangers!
Had I not begotten caring daughters   1490
I'd be dead—for all the help you gave me.

These two girls keep me alive. They nurse me.
When the work's hard, they're men, not women.
You're not my sons, you're someone else's sons,
alien to me.
        Right now, Fate watches you,
but not as it soon will, when your soldiers
march on Thebes. You won't destroy Thebes. You'll die.
The blood you shed will defile you, just as
your blood defiles your brother as he dies.

I cursed you both from my heart long ago.   1500
I summon those same curses to help me
fight you now, to impress you with the need
to respect your parents and not to treat
your father with contempt—a sightless man
who begot the kind of men you became.
Your sisters never disgraced me!

My curses
will overpower your prayers and your thrones—
if Justice still sits there, alongside Zeus,
enforcing the laws of our ancestors.

As for you now, clear out! I spit on you!   1510
I'm not your father, you despicable
bastard! And don't forget to take with you
the curses I have called down on your head—
you'll never win this war on your homeland.
You won't survive to skulk back to the plains
of Argos. By your brother's hand you will
die—as you'll kill the man who threw you out.
That is my curse: and I ask the blackest
paternal darkness of the underworld
to become your new home in Tartaros.   1520
I summon the spirits native to this place.
I summon Ares the Destroyer, who has
inflamed your minds with murderous hatred!

Now that you've heard this, go tell Thebes, go
tell all your staunch allies, what a great favor
Oedipus has done for his own two sons.

LEADER
Polyneikes, this account of your life
gives me no pleasure. And now, you should go.

POLYNEIKES

So much for my journey and my wrecked hopes.

So much for my fellow soldiers. What a way   1530

to end our march from Argos! I'm finished!

There is no way I can tell my army

what happened here. Retreat? Out of the question.

I must face my destiny in silence.

My sisters, his daughters, since you've heard

my father's savage curse, promise me this:

if that curse does come true and you manage

to make your way home, don't dishonor me,

but bury me. Perform the rituals.

You've already won praise for the loyal   1540

care you've given this man, but you will earn

equal praise for the honor you show me.

ANTIGONE

Polyneikes, I've got to change your mind.

POLYNEIKES

About what, dear Sister? Tell me, Antigone.

ANTIGONE

Turn your army around. Go back to Argos.

Do it now. Don't destroy yourself and Thebes.

POLYNEIKES

That's something I can't do. How could I lead

my troops out here again, once I'd shown fear?

ANTIGONE

Why would you renew your anger, Brother?
And what do you gain, razing your homeland?   1550

POLYNEIKES

Because I was disgraced, banished,
ridiculed, by my younger brother.

ANTIGONE

Don't you see, if you attack you'll fulfill
your father's prophecies—that you will both
kill each other?

POLYNEIKES

                 Isn't that what he wants?
Why shouldn't I obey him?

ANTIGONE

Listen to your wretched sister: who will
obey you, once they've heard his prophecies?

POLYNEIKES

Why should I tell them bad news? Skillful
generals report good news and censor bad.   1560

ANTIGONE

Oh my brother! You're absolutely determined?

POLYNEIKES

That's right. Please don't get in my way. My job
is to take that road, no matter what deadly
consequences Father predicts for me—
he and his Furies. But you two—I hope
Zeus will protect your future, so you can
carry out my wishes after I'm killed.
Let me leave—say goodbye. For you'll
never again see me alive.

POLYNEIKES pulls away from her arms.

ANTIGONE

                    This breaks my heart.

POLYNEIKES

                              Don't let it.

ANTIGONE

Who wouldn't feel grief for a brother   1570
when he's headed toward certain death?

POLYNEIKES

If that's my fate, then I must die.

ANTIGONE

Don't die. Please listen to me!

POLYNEIKES

You must stop this. My mind's made up.

ANTIGONE

And I am truly devastated.
Now that I'm sure I'll lose you.

POLYNEIKES

No, Fate will determine how my life goes.
I pray that you two never come to harm.
All men know that you don't deserve it.

Exit POLYNEIKES.

OLD MEN

We've just seen   1580
the blind stranger
start a new round
of deadly violence—
unless Fate working
its will is the true cause.
You'll never hear us declare
that a god wills something in vain:
for Time always keeps watch
over the gods' decrees—
ruining somebody's chances,   1590
then rescuing somebody else
the very next morning
when his turn comes.

A crash of thunder.

That was thunder! O Zeus!

OEDIPUS
Children! Children!
Is there someone nearby
who could bring Theseus?
There is no better man.

ANTIGONE
Father, why do we need Theseus here?

OEDIPUS
Because Zeus sends that thunder, and its great wings   1600
will carry me to Hades. Find him now.

More and louder thunder.

OLD MEN
Look, Zeus throws down
a great unspeakable
blast of fire!
Terror races
to the tips of my hair,
my spirit cowers,
the lightning strikes again—
crackles down the sky—
forcing what? To be born.   1610

I am afraid. Lightning never
erupts to no purpose, it always
portends something horrendous.
O mighty sky! O Zeus!

OEDIPUS

Daughters, the death promised to your father
is at hand. Nothing can stop it now.

ANTIGONE

How do you know? What warnings have you had?

OEDIPUS

It's beyond doubt. Quickly now, someone go
find the king and bring him back to me.

Another blast of thunder.

OLD MEN

Yes! Yes! Hear it! That voice of raging thunder   1620
is yet again all around us!
Be gentle with us, god, gentle—
if you are about to darken
our motherland.
Forgive us, if we've sheltered
a man you despise.
Don't punish our compassion!
I ask that of you, Zeus!

OEDIPUS

Is he nearby? Will he find me alive,
children, when he comes? Will my mind be clear?   1630

ANTIGONE

Why do you worry that your mind's unsound?

OEDIPUS

I promised I'd repay Theseus
for his kindness. Now I must give him
everything he has earned.

LEADER

(calling offstage)
You there, my son, we need you! Come!
Break off the sacrifice to seagod Poseidon,
leave the crevice among the high rocks
and come back! The stranger is moved
to provide you, your city, your friends,
with the fruits of your kindness to him.   1640
Move quickly, King.

Enter THESEUS and his Men.

THESEUS

What's all this noise,
this frantic summons—from both
my people and our guest?
Did Zeus' lightning upset you? Did

a hailstorm raise a sudden uproar?
A storm like that, when a god sends it,
inspires every kind of fear.

OEDIPUS

We're reassured, King, now that you've come.
A god's behind this good timing.   1650

THESEUS

What's happened, son of Laios?

OEDIPUS

My life is weighted to sink down.
I must not die without fulfilling
my guarantees to you and Athens.

THESEUS

What makes you think your death is imminent?

OEDIPUS

The gods themselves told me. Every sign
I was promised has now been given me.

THESEUS

Which sign made it entirely clear?

OEDIPUS

A great crash of thunder and bolts of lightning
flashing from the All-Powerful's hand.   1660

THESEUS

I believe you. You've made some prophecies,
not one of them false. What should I do now?

OEDIPUS

I will describe, son of Aigeus,
how the future of Athens will become
impervious to the ravages of time.
Soon, I myself, with no hand guiding me,
will lead you to the place where I must die.
Never reveal that place to anyone—
not how it's hidden, nor its whereabouts.
It will endure, an ever-present defense,   1670
more powerful than a rampart of shields,
or allies with spears racing to save you.

As for those mysteries speech would profane,
you will see what they are, once you are there,
alone. I will not reveal them now, not
to these people, not even to the children
I love. No, you must keep all those secrets.
When you're near death, tell them to your successor.
Let him teach his heir, and so on forever.

In this way, your own city will survive   1680
unscathed any attack launched by the Thebans.
Many cities, even well-governed cities,
slide smoothly into violence.
Though the gods act slowly, they see clearly

men who cease to believe and go mad.
Keep this from happening to you, son of Aigeus.

But you don't need such tutoring from me.
Now we must move toward that place,
for god's power drives me on.
Don't linger, follow where I lead.   1690
Daughters, in some uncanny way
I have become your guide, as you
once guided your father. Come with me, but
don't touch me with your hands, let me find
the sacred tomb with no help, and the ground
where it's my destiny to be buried.
This way. That's right. Through here. Down this path
my guide Hermes escorts me, he and the dark goddess.

*OEDIPUS, with uncanny ease, leads his daughters and THESEUS toward the
grove, his voice still heard after he vanishes offstage. THESEUS, ANTIGONE,
and ISMENE, one by one, follow OEDIPUS out of sight.*

O light—dark to me now,
though once you were mine—I feel   1700
your warmth on my body one last time.
I'm going down, to hide my death
in Hades. Come, dearest stranger:
bless you, bless this land, bless your people.
And in your prosperous state,
remember me when I am dead,
the source of your boundless well-being.

OLD MEN

If she, the unseen goddess,
accepts my solemn prayer,
and if you, god of the night people,   1710
will hear me out, Aidoneus, Aidoneus!
I pray you let this stranger go
untortured and undamned
down to the dark fields of the dead,
down to the house of Styx.
Troubles beyond reason
besieged him. In return
a just god shall pull him clear.

Earth Goddesses! And you,
invincible apparition!   1720
Savage guard-dog! Rumor
has told us for ages that you
kennel at Hades' gate, snarling

from cavernous jaws at every
stranger who walks past.
Hear me, Death!
Son of Earth and Tartaros!
Let the hound clear a path
for this stranger who craves
the sunken fields of the dead.   1730
Grant him eternal rest.

Enter MESSENGER.

MESSENGER

Townsmen, I could shorten my news to this:
Oedipus is gone. But the full story
of what happened out there cannot be cut short,
nor did the things themselves happen quickly.

LEADER

Is he dead—that tormented man?

MESSENGER

                                    You can be sure
this man has left our common life behind.

LEADER

How? Did the gods take him? Did he feel pain?

MESSENGER

How it happened will take your breath away.
How he left, you saw. None of his loved ones   1740
knew the way, but he knew where to lead us.
As soon as he neared the gateway where you climb
down those steep brass steps rooted in the earth,
he paused—within a maze of crossing paths—
where a bowl had been hollowed from a rock shelf.
There the immortal pact that Theseus
made with Peirithoüs is written in stone.

He stood between that basin and the rock
of Thoricos, easing himself to the ground

beside a hollow pear trunk and a stone tomb.   1750
He peeled off all his filthy clothes, then called
to his daughters, asking them to bring water
from the stream nearby, so he could bathe
and then pour out some libations.
The green hill of Demeter rose close by
in plain sight. They climbed it, and soon
carried out these duties for their father.
First they washed him and then they dressed him
in white clothes customary for the dying.

When he was content with what had been done,   1760
every last one of his orders obeyed,
Zeus of the Underworld thundered, and the girls
shuddered when they heard it. Then, clinging
to their father's knees, they cried out and kept
pounding their breasts and weeping and shouting.
When he heard them crying, he wrapped his arms
around both their bodies and told them,
"Children, this day will end your father's life.
All the acts I lived for have come to pass.
No longer will you need to care for me—   1770
a burden, I know, that has not been easy.
But let one word relieve you of this hardship:
for no man loves you more than I love you.
Now you must live out your lives without me."

Holding each other close, all of them sobbed,
and when they had finished their lamenting,

as the sounds died away, there was stillness.
Suddenly an enormous voice called him,
making everyone's hair rise in terror.
For the god called many times and his voice   1780
echoed from all sides: "You there, Oedipus!
You! Oedipus! Why do we hesitate?
You've waited far too long. Far too long!"

Now that he knew it was the god calling,
he asked King Theseus to stand by him.
And when the king approached, Oedipus said,
"Dear friend, will you promise, by giving your
right hand to my daughters, while they give you
their hands, that you will never willingly
forsake them, and that you will always act   1790
as their friend, providing what they will need?"
And like a prince, with no hesitation,
Theseus swore to the stranger that he would.
And after this promise, Oedipus at once
embraced his children with enfeebled hands,
and said, "Daughters, you must have the courage
to leave this place now. Don't look back
at things you must not see, and must not hear.
Leave quickly as you can. Let Theseus,
who is entitled to do so, remain   1800
to witness all that will happen here."

That's what he said, we all heard him, and followed
his daughters as they left, tears blurring

our own eyes. When we had walked on awhile,
we looked back and saw he was gone, and saw
our king, his hand screening his eyes, reacting
to the shock of a terrifying sight, something
he could not bear to look at, something still
happening. A moment later, we saw him
silently saluting the Earth, then the sky   1810
where the Olympian gods live, his arms
opened in prayer.
                    But the exact nature
of the death Oedipus died, no man
but Theseus could tell you. Zeus didn't
incinerate him with a lightning blast,
no sudden squall blew inland from the sea.
So it was either a god spiriting
him away, or else the Earth's lower world—
her deep foundations—opening to him,
for he felt nothing but welcoming kindness.   1820

When this man vanished, there was no sorrow.
He suffered no sickness. His death, like no
other man's, was a cause for wonder.
If anyone listening doesn't believe me,
I have no interest in persuading him
that I am not some credulous fool.

LEADER
Where are the girls and their escort now?

MESSENGER

Not far away. The sounds of their grief
growing louder tells you they're almost here.

ANTIGONE

(anguished cries)
No reason now   1830
for we two woeful sisters
to hold back the full
wretchedness that we feel—
the doomed blood of our father
flowed at birth into our blood.
As long as our father lived
we suffered its relentless agony.
Even from his last moments,
we take with us things seen and things
suffered that defy understanding.   1840

LEADER

What did you see?

ANTIGONE

Friends, we can only guess.

LEADER

Then he's gone?

ANTIGONE

In the very way you'd wish—
because it wasn't the war god or the waves,

it was the endless marsh of death that drew
him away, in a weird, sudden vanishing.
And now, Sister, there's a deathly darkness
clouding our vision—for how can we stand
our harsh life to come, drifting across some
remote back country, or over breaking seas?   1850

ISMENE

I don't know. I'd rather murderous Hades
forced me to share my agèd father's death.
I'm shaking. I can't face the life ahead.

LEADER

You two sisters,
loving daughters,
accept what the god brings.
Do not inflame yourselves
with so much grieving.
You should not regret
the path your life took.   1860

ANTIGONE

Yes, there was something
to treasure in our pain.
What gave me no comfort then
did, in the end, console me.
Yes it did—while I held him
lovingly in my arms.
Dear Father, loved one, you
will wear Earth's darkness

forever, but even down there
you won't be denied   1870
my love and her love.

LEADER
Then what took place . . .

ANTIGONE
                              . . . was what he desired.

LEADER
How so?

ANTIGONE
To die on foreign earth
was his wish. He will sleep
in that dark grave forever.
And the mourners he left
behind are not dry-eyed.
With my own eyes pouring
I grieve for you, Father.   1880
I don't know how to stop,
my ache is so huge.
I know your wish was to die
in a distant country.
But now you have died
bereft of my care.

ISMENE

Poor desolate Sister,
what will come of us both,
now that Father is gone?

LEADER

Since the way he met death   1890
was a blessing, children,
stop grieving. Not one of us
escapes misfortune.

ANTIGONE

Sister, we must go back there.

ISMENE

To do what?

ANTIGONE

I'm filled with . . .

ISMENE

With what?

ANTIGONE

. . . longing. To see the earthly resting place . . .

ISMENE

Whose?

ANTIGONE

Our father's!   1900

ISMENE

Such a thing can't possibly
be right. Can't you see that?

ANTIGONE

Why are you judging me?

ISMENE

There's one more thing that you don't know . . .

ANTIGONE

What will you tell me next?

ISMENE

No one saw him die! There's no tomb!

ANTIGONE

Take me out there, and kill me too.

ISMENE

That would kill *me*! With no friends and no strength,
where would I live out my deserted life?

LEADER

Children, you have nothing to fear.   1910

ANTIGONE

Then where can we go?

LEADER

We know of a refuge . . .

ANTIGONE

What do you mean?

LEADER

. . . where you'll be safe.

ANTIGONE

I think I know it . . .

LEADER

What are you thinking?

ANTIGONE

I don't see how we can go home.

LEADER

Then I don't think you should try.

ANTIGONE

Trouble pursues us.

LEADER

It has from the start.   1920

ANTIGONE

It was horrible. Now it's worse.

LEADER

Your life has been a huge sea of hardship.

ANTIGONE

So it has.

Enter THESEUS with his Men.

THESEUS

Stop weeping, children. When the Earth Powers
have shown all of us so much grace,
grief is uncalled for. Don't anger them.

ANTIGONE

Son of Aigeus, please help us.

THESEUS

What do you want me to do, children?

ANTIGONE

Let us see Father's tomb with our own eyes.

THESEUS

That would violate divine law.   1930

ANTIGONE

What do you mean, my lord?

THESEUS

Daughters, his orders were to let no one
approach that place, to let no one
speak to the sacred tomb where he's sleeping.
If I keep my word, this land
will never be harmed. Horkos,
the servant of Zeus
who hears all oaths,
heard mine. He misses nothing.

ANTIGONE

I'm content, if my father's wishes   1940
are fulfilled. Now send us home
to prevent, if we can, the slaughter
that threatens our brothers.

THESEUS

I will do that. I'll give you all the help
you may need: anything the dead man,
now gone under the earth, would approve.

LEADER

Stop mourning now. Let it be. In all
that's happened, there's nothing you can change.

ALL leave.

Antigone

INTRODUCTION
"FROM WHAT KIND OF PARENTS WAS I BORN?"

*A*ntigone opens just before dawn in Thebes, on the day after the city's defenders have repelled a massive assault by fighters from seven Argive cities. The Argive objective had been to return the Theban throne to Polyneikes, elder son of Oedipus. But Polyneikes and his younger brother, Eteokles, Thebes' reigning king, killed each other with simultaneous spear-thrusts during the failed assault.[1] Antigone, the sister of the slain men, returns fierce and agitated from the battlefield with news for their sister Ismene: Kreon has just become Thebes' ruler following the deaths of his two nephews. He has apparently already honored and buried the loyal Eteokles, but has vilified Polyneikes for attacking his own city and now forbids his burial. Antigone declares she will bury her brother, no matter what it costs her.

Antigone thrived throughout the twentieth century as the perfect ancient play to dramatize rebellion against tyrants. Kreon could be costumed and directed to represent any number of oppressors, and Antigone's fearless eloquence inflected to expose their evil and banality. Productions have reimagined her as a martyred fighter in various righteous causes: she's been a member of the French resistance, the sister of an IRA terrorist or an Argentinean *desaparacido*, and a Vietnam War resister. Antigone will undoubtedly be drafted to face down tyrants yet unborn.

There's a downside, however, to interpreting *Antigone* solely through its capacity for embodying contemporary political battles. None of the play's clashes is as clear-cut, or its characters as consistent, as they first seem. (Thebes' resident prophet—Tiresias, who appears in a single scene as the play's most commanding figure and who delivers an unambiguous condemnation of Kreon—is the sole exception.) Kreon, for instance, addressing his aristocratic peers hours after assuming power, reassuringly articulates his democratic principles and policies. He promises to accept good advice, act on it, avoid and denounce policies that would lead Thebes to destruction, and punish any citizen who betrays Thebes, including his traitorous and deceased nephew. But Kreon will fail to follow every one of his precepts. In the end, the consequences of his own actions will even force him to order a proper burial for Polyneikes. A look into Kreon's soul to locate his core beliefs—opening him up like a wax writing tablet in its case, to paraphrase Kreon's son Haimon—would reveal his moral emptiness. As Kreon puts his crowd-pleasing but insincere inaugural speech behind him, he acts on intense and ugly prejudices, not principles.

Antigone, who possesses both character and principle in abundance, also has suppressed something of her nature in order to steel herself against Kreon's power and arrogance. She will accept nothing less than giving Polyneikes his full burial rights and will welcome her own death, if that's what it takes.

But as she elaborates her view of the world, she reveals the life-suppressing extremity of her allegiances. The deaths of her parents and brothers have made her passionate to rejoin them in Hades. But when actually facing death, Antigone suddenly yearns for the marriage and childbearing she has denied herself. The number and decisiveness of his characters' reversals suggest that Sophocles views human nature as often unsure or unaware of its own deepest desires. As the pressure of catastrophic events increases, sudden surges of desire reveal the major characters' contradictions, their second thoughts, and their consequent desperation. The conflicted Guard, who debates whether it's safe or suicidal to bring Kreon the bad news that Polyneikes' body has been illegally buried, comically prefigures Sophocles' encompassing vision: events can overpower the persons mortals think they are. Staging *Antigone* exclusively to unsettle contemporary political orthodoxies risks turning a blazing but nuanced play into propaganda.

Greek dramatists in the fifth century BCE, and certainly Sophocles, did in fact reflect the impact of political issues in their plays, though they did so invariably by shaping an ancient myth to illuminate their audience's present-day concerns. This strategy both aroused and distanced emotional response. *Antigone* itself, for instance, has at its core a bitter and sometimes deadly public issue in Athenian life: the burial of war casualties. Athens' pro-war ruling party had tried to suppress the resentment of the bereaved and limit mourning of fallen soldiers to a once-a-year ceremony at which a chosen orator gave a patriotic speech. The women of Athens resented both the wars and the deprivation of their chance to give their dead proper burials.

Aristophanes, who was, like most of his fellow aristocrats, anti-war, turns their resentment into a full-scale comic rebellion in *Lysistrata*.

Though Sophocles is wholly sympathetic to Antigone's rebellion and her contempt for Kreon, he shows us she still possesses desires and emotions normal to a woman. As she faces death, she feels these intensely and expresses them in her farewell speeches. *Antigone*, as it unfolds, has become less about dictatorship and honoring the dead than about love's destructive powers.

In the play's opening scene, Antigone explains to Ismene how and why she must bury her brother:

> I'll bury Polyneikes myself. I'll do
> what's honorable, and then I'll die.
> I who love him will lie down
> next to him who loves me—
> my criminal conduct blameless!—
> for I owe more to the dead, with whom
> I will spend a much longer time,
> than I will ever owe to the living. (85–92)

The Greek verb Antigone uses for "lie down," *keisomai*, is equally appropriate to describe lying down in death (either before burial or in Hades) or having sexual relations with a lover. The English phrase, of course, has a similar range. The words she uses to describe their kinship, *philê* with *philou* (translated here as "I who love him" next to "him who loves me"), accentuate both the emotional bond and the comforting physical proximity of siblings.[2] The Greek words translated as "my criminal conduct blameless," *hosia panourgesas* (literally, "sacred transgressions"), refer primarily to the outlawed act of burying her "traitor" brother, but as some scholars have argued, they could also suggest, given the way they are embedded in the sentence, incestuous love. They may convey simply a sister's need to embrace her brother. Her family's incestuous history does haunt Antigone, as she says at lines 946–949. If Sophocles did intend the erotic implication, it allows him to heighten Antigone's passionate feelings for her dead brother beyond any conventional intrafamilial love. Antigone ends this conversation with her sister Ismene by permanently disowning her cautious sister for refusing to help and then heads to the battlefield alone.

When, after performing the forbidden rituals, Antigone is caught, she admits and then fiercely defends her crime, citing immutable laws of *philia* that require a family to bury and honor its dead. Unmoved, Kreon condemns her to die, confident that only those who support Thebes may claim true *philia*. The Greek conception of *philia*, which involves the loyalty and affection binding friends and loved ones in one community, and the city and its citizens in another, will become a central battleground in the play. In the following lines Kreon and Antigone each invoke *philia* to justify their position:

Kreon   The brave deserve better than the vile.
Antigone Who knows what matters to the dead?
Kreon   Not even death reconciles enemies.
Antigone I made no enemies by being born!

	I made my lifelong friends at birth.
Kreon	Then go down to them! Love your dead brothers!

(564–569)

Shared birth parents and nothing else, Antigone declares, determines her *philoi* (friends and loved ones) for life. Audiences (and Kreon, of course) know Antigone and her siblings were born of incestuous sexual intercourse, and that the pollution incurred is sure to pass from one generation to the next. Kreon's taunt, that she should "go down to" her dead brothers, resonates with disgust—not only for her lack of shame but because it infuriates Kreon that his son Haimon plans to marry this distasteful rebel. When Haimon arrives to defend Antigone, Kreon denounces her as both a traitor and an unsuitable wife, warning Haimon that she will be spiteful in the house and frigid in bed. Love now takes center stage. A choral hymn to the power of Eros and Aphrodite immediately follows the father-son conflict. Addressing Eros directly, they sing:

And those you seize go mad.

You wrench even good men's minds
so far off course they crash in ruins.
Now you ignite hatred in men
of the same blood—but allure flashing
from the keen eyes of the bride
always wins, for Desire wields
all the power of ancient law:
Aphrodite the implacable
plays cruel games with our lives.   (871–880)

Antigone's outward expression of erotic feeling remains limited to her fleeting wish, in the first scene, to embrace the dead Polyneikes. She never acknowledges that she is betrothed to Haimon, or so much as mentions his name. She pursues a different commitment: "Long ago / I dedicated [my life] to the dead" (604–605). Although she never abandons this dedication, she soon dramatizes both its costs and its ironies. Just before she's led away to be entombed in a cave, Antigone (who might have changed her costume and returned to the stage wearing a bridal gown) reaches up to lift her veil, uncovering her whole head and addressing the Chorus: "Look at me, princely citizens of Thebes" (1032). This gesture echoes the climactic moment of a traditional Greek marriage celebration: after the bride exposes her face to all in attendance, the groom lifts her onto a mule cart (or chariot) that carries them to his family home and the nuptial bed. Antigone, however, announces she will consummate an anti-marriage, one she achingly describes:

> Hades, who chills each one of us to sleep,
> will guide me down to Acheron's shore.
> I'll go hearing no wedding hymn
> to carry me to my bridal chamber, or songs
> girls sing when flowers crown a bride's hair;
> I'm going to marry the River of Pain.   (890–895)

Her perplexed outburst "From what kind of parents was I born?" (950) recalls Oedipus' sweeping denunciation of marriage in *Oedipus the King* (1591–1596). She has always known that her parents' incestuous marriage will have an evil impact on her. Since in ancient Greek culture only the women were blamed for incestuous sexual relationships, even if men or gods initiated them, she attributes her family's curse solely to her mother's "horrendous . . . coupling" with her father (948–949).

Kreon, an extended member of this family, seems cursed as well. Not until Tiresias appears does Kreon understand how wrong he was to oppose Antigone. Thebes' perennial prophet denounces Kreon in both secular and religious terms:

> You have thrown children from the sunlight
> down to the shades of Hades, ruthlessly
> housing a living person in a tomb,
> while you detain here, among us, something
> that belongs to the gods who live below
> our world—the naked unwept corpse you've robbed
> of the solemn grieving we owe our dead.
> None of this should have been any concern
> of yours—or of the Olympian gods—
> but you have involved them in your outrage!
> Therefore, avengers wait to ambush you—
> the Furies sent by Hades and its gods
> will punish you for the crimes I have named.
>
> (1180–1192)

Kreon himself rushes to release Antigone. But it's too late. Haimon, next to Antigone's corpse, lunges to kill his father, misses, and then falls on his own sword. Hearing the news, Kreon's wife runs into the palace and kills herself, thrusting a blade into her side. The play continues to its swift conclusion with Kreon's belated self-castigation. Antigone, as she predicted, receives no mourning from what's left of her Theban royal family. Her absence, during the play's final scene, from Kreon's and the Elders' remorse, is a masterstroke. The damage that their denial of her passion has inflicted on the Theban community is bitter testimony enough to her courage and its cost.

—RB

NOTES

1. Eteokles is never named as the king whom Kreon succeeds, but it is implicit in 203–206.

2. Winnington-Ingram (92–116) has explored erotic passion's decisive impact on the characters' actions as well as its powerful presence in several choral odes.

Antigone

Translated by Robert Bagg

CHARACTERS
   ANTIGONE, daughter of Oedipus
   ISMENE, daughter of Oedipus
   ELDERS of Thebes (Chorus)
   LEADER of the Chorus
   KREON, king of Thebes, uncle of Antigone,
      Polyneikes, and Eteokles
   GUARD
   Kreon's Men
   HAIMON, son of Kreon
   TIRESIAS, prophet of Thebes
   Lad
   MESSENGER
   EURYDIKE, wife of Kreon

It is dawn in front of KREON's palace in Thebes, the day after the battle in which the Theban defenders repelled an attack on the city by an Argive coalition that included the rebel Polyneikes, elder son of Oedipus. Polyneikes and his younger brother, Eteokles, who has remained loyal to Thebes, have killed each other simultaneously in face-to-face combat at one of Thebes' seven gates. KREON has suddenly seized the throne. In dim, streaky light, ANTIGONE runs from offstage and calls out ISMENE's name. ISMENE enters through the central doors.

ANTIGONE

Ismene, love! My own kind! Born
like me from that same womb!
Can you think of one evil—
of all those Oedipus started—
that Zeus hasn't used *our own lives*
to finish? There's nothing—no pain,
no shame, no terror, no humiliation!—
you and I haven't seen and shared.
Now there's this new command
our commander in chief   10
imposes on the whole city—
do you know about it?
Have you heard? *You don't know,*
do you? It threatens our loved ones
as if they were our enemies!

*ANTIGONE is out of breath. ISMENE is startled but slow to comprehend the
reason for her sister's agitation.*

ISMENE

Not a word about our family has reached *me,*
Antigone—encouraging or horrible.
Not since we sisters lost our brothers
on the day their hands struck
the double blow that killed them both.   20
And since the Argive army fled last night
I've not heard anything that could improve
our luck—or make it any worse.

ANTIGONE

That's what I thought.

And why I've brought you out past the gates—
where no one else can hear what I say.

ISMENE

What's wrong?

It's plain something *you've heard* makes you livid.

ANTIGONE

It's Kreon. The way he's treated our brothers.
Hasn't he buried one with honor?
But he's shamed the other. Disgraced him!
Eteokles, they say, was laid to rest   30
according to law and custom.
The dead will respect him in Hades.
But Polyneikes' sorry body can't be touched.

The city is forbidden to mourn him or bury him
—no tomb, no tears. Convenient forage
for cruising birds to feast their fill.
That's the clear order our good general
gives you and me—yes, I said me!
They say he's coming here to proclaim it
in person to those who haven't heard it.   40

This is not something he takes lightly.
Violate any provision—the sentence is
you're stoned to death in your own city.

Now you know.

And soon you'll prove
how nobly born you really are.
Or did our family breed a coward?

ISMENE

If that's the bind we're in, you poor thing,
what good can *I* do by yanking the knot
tighter—*or* by trying to pry it loose?

ANTIGONE

Make up your mind. Will you join me?   50
Share the burden?

ISMENE

At what risk? What are you asking?

ANTIGONE

(raising up her hands)
Will you help these hands lift his body?

ISMENE

You want to bury him? Break the law?

ANTIGONE

I'm going to bury my brother—your brother!—
with or without your help. I won't betray him.

ISMENE

You scare me, Sister. Kreon's forbidden this.

ANTIGONE

He's got *no right* to keep me from what's mine!

ISMENE

(raising her voice)

He's mine too!

              Just think what our father's

destruction meant for us both.

Because of those horrible deeds—   60

all self-inflicted, all self-detected—

he died hated and notorious,

his eyes battered into blindness

by his own hands. And then

his wife and mother—two roles

for one woman—disposed

of her life with a noose

of twisted rope. And now

our poor brothers die the same day

in a mutual act of kin murder!   70

Think how much worse

our own deaths will be—abandoned

as we are—if we defy the king's

proclamation and his power.

Remember, we're women. How

can we fight men? They're stronger.

We must accept these things—and worse to come.

I want the Spirits of the Dead

to understand this: I'm not free.

I must obey whoever's in charge.   80

It's crazy to attempt the impossible!

ANTIGONE

Then I'll stop asking you! And if you change
your mind, I won't accept your help.
Go be the person you've chosen to be.
I'll bury Polyneikes myself. I'll do
what's honorable, and then I'll die.
I who love him will lie down
next to him who loves me—
my criminal conduct blameless!—
for I owe more to the dead, with whom   90
I will spend a much longer time,
than I will ever owe to the living.
Go ahead, please yourself—defy
laws the gods expect us to honor.

ISMENE

I'm not insulting them! But how can I
defy the city? I don't have the strength.

ANTIGONE

Then make that your excuse. I'll heal
with earth the body of the brother I love.

ISMENE

I feel so sorry for you. And afraid.

ANTIGONE

Don't waste your fear. Straighten out your own life.   100

ISMENE

At least tell nobody what you're planning!
Say nothing about it. And neither will I.

ANTIGONE

No! Go on, tell them all!
I will hate you much more for your silence—
if you don't shout it everywhere.

ISMENE

You're burning to do what should stop you cold.

ANTIGONE

One thing I do know: I'll please those who matter.

ISMENE

As if you could! You love fights you can't win.

ANTIGONE

When my strength is exhausted, I'll quit.

ISMENE

Hopeless passion is wrong from the start.   110

ANTIGONE

Say that again and I'll despise you.
So will the dead—and they'll hate you
far longer. But go! Let me and my
recklessness deal with this alone.

No matter what I suffer
I won't die dishonored.

Exit ANTIGONE *toward open country;* ISMENE *calls out her next lines as her
sister leaves, then she enters the palace through the great central doors.*

ISMENE

If you're determined, go ahead.
And know this much: you are a fool
to attempt this, but you're loved all
the more by the family you love.   120

Chorus of Theban ELDERS *enters singing.*

ELDERS

Morning sunlight, loveliest ever
to shine on seven-gated Thebes!
Day's golden eye, risen at last
over Dirke's glittering waters!
You stampede the Argive!
Invading in full battle gear,
his white shield flashing, he's wrenched
by your sharp piercing bit
headlong into retreat!
This attacker who championed   130
quarrelsome Polyneikes
skimmed through our farmland—
a white-feathered Eagle
screeching, horsehair

flaring from the helmets
of well-armed troops.

He had circled our houses, threatening
all seven gates, his spearpoints
out for blood, but he was thrown back
before his jaws could swell   140
with our gore, before the Firegod's
incendiary pine tar
engulfed the towers ringing our walls.
He cannot withstand the harsh blare
of battle that roars up
around him—as our Dragon
wrestles him down.

How Zeus hates a proud tongue!
And when this river of men
surged forward, with arrogance   150
loud as its flash of gold,
he struck—with his own lightning—
that firebrand shouting in triumph
from the battlements!
Free-falling from the mad
fury of his charge, torch
still in his hand,
he crashed to earth, the man
who'd turned on us the raving
blast of his loathsome words.   160
But threats stuck in his throat:

to each enemy soldier
Ares the brute wargod,
our surging wheelhorse,
assigned a separate doom,
shattering every attack.

Now seven captains guarding seven gates—
our captains facing theirs—
throw down their arms as trophies
for Zeus—all but the doomed pair   170
born to one father, one mother,
who share even their death—
when their twin spears drive home.

Victory is now ours!
Her name is pure glory,
her joy resounds
through Thebes' own joy—Thebes
swarming with chariots!
Let us now banish
this war from our minds   180
and visit each god's temple,
singing all night long! May
Bakkhos, the god whose dancing
rocks Thebes, be there to lead us!

Enter KREON.

LEADER

(sotto voce to his fellow ELDERS)

Enter our new king,
Kreon, the son of Menoikeus,
who came to power
abruptly, when the gods changed our luck.
What plans does he turn over
in his mind—what will he ponder   190
with this Council of the Wise
summoned in his new role?

KREON

Men, we have just survived some rough weather.
Monstrous waves have battered our city,
but now the gods have steadied the waters.
I sent my servants to gather you here
because, of all my people, I know
your veneration for Laios' royal
power has never wavered. When Oedipus
ruled our city, and then was struck down, you   200
stood by his sons. Now both have fallen
together, killed in one lethal exchange.

Because each struck the other's deathblow, each
was defiled by his own brother's blood.
As nearest kin to the men killed,
I've taken power and assumed the throne.

You cannot measure a man's character,
policies, or his common sense—until
you see him at work enforcing old laws
and making new ones. To me, there's nothing   210

worse than a man, while he's running a city,
who fails to act on sound advice—but fears
something so much his mouth clamps shut.
Nor have I any use for a man whose friend
means more to him than his country.
Believe me, Zeus, for you miss nothing,
I'll always speak out when I see Thebes choose
destruction rather than deliverance.
I'll never think our country's enemy
can be my friend. Keep this in mind: 220
our *country* is the ship that must keep us safe.
It's only on board her, among the men
who sail her upright, that we make true friends.

Such are the principles I will follow
to preserve Thebes' greatness. Akin to these
are my explicit orders concerning
Oedipus' sons: Eteokles, who died
fighting for our city, and who excelled
in combat, will be given the rituals
and burial proper to the noble dead.   230

But his brother—I mean Polyneikes, who
returned from exile utterly determined
to burn down his own city, incinerate
the gods we worship, revel in kinsmen's blood,
enslave everyone left alive—
as for him, it is now a crime for Thebans
to bury him or mourn him. Dogs and birds
will savage and outrage his corpse—

an ugly and a visible disgrace.
That is my thinking. And I will never   240
tolerate giving a bad man more respect
than a good one. Only those faithful to Thebes
will I honor—in this life and after death.

LEADER

That is your pleasure, Kreon: punish Thebes'
betrayers and reward her defenders.
You have all the authority you need
to discipline the living and the dead.

KREON

Are you willing to help enforce this law?

LEADER

Ask someone younger to shoulder that burden.

KREON

But I've already posted men at the corpse.   250

LEADER

Then what instructions do you have for me?

KREON

Don't join the cause of those who break this law.

LEADER

Who but a fool would want to die?

KREON

Exactly. He'd be killed. But easy money
frequently kills those it deludes.

Enter GUARD. He tends to mime the actions he describes.

GUARD

I didn't run here at such a breakneck
pace, King, that I'm winded. Pausing to think
stopped me, wheeled me around, headed me back
more than once. My mind kept yelling at me:
"Reckless fool—why go where you'll be punished?"   260
Then: "Lazy clod! Dawdling, are you? What if
Kreon hears this news from somebody else?—
you'll pay for it."
            I made myself dizzy,
hurrying slowly, stretching out a short road.
I finally realized I had to come.
If I'm talking annihilation here,
I'll still say it, since I'm of the opinion
nothing but my own fate can cause me harm.

KREON

What's making you so agitated?

GUARD

The need to explain my role in this matter.   270
I didn't do it, I didn't see who did.
So it wouldn't be right to punish me.

KREON

You're obsessed with protecting yourself.
That's a nice fortified wall you've thrown up
around your news—which must be odd indeed.

GUARD

You bet. And bad news must be broken slowly.

KREON

Why not just tell it? Then you can vanish.

GUARD

But I *am* telling you! That corpse—someone's
buried it and run off. They sprinkled thirsty
dust on it. Then did all the rituals.   280

KREON

What are you saying? What man would dare do this?

GUARD

I've no idea. No marks from a pickax,
no dirt thrown up by a shovel. The ground's
all hard and dry, unbroken—no wheel ruts.
Whoever did this left no trace.
When the man on dawn-watch showed it to us,
we all got a nasty surprise. The dead man
had dropped out of sight. He wasn't buried,
but dusted over, as though someone had tried
to stave off defilement. There was no sign   290
dogs or wild animals had chewed the corpse.

Then we all started yelling rough words, threats,
blaming each other, every guard ready
to throw punches—nobody to stop us.
All of us under suspicion—but none
of us convicted. We all denied it—
swearing to god we'd handle red-hot iron
or walk through fire to back up our oaths.

After interrogation got us nowhere,
one man spoke up and made us hang our heads   300
toward the ground in terror. We couldn't do
what he said—or avoid trouble if we did.
He advised us to tell you what happened,
not try to hide it. That seemed our best move.
So we drew lots to choose the messenger.
I lost. I'm no happier to be here
than you are to see me. Don't I know that.
Nobody loves the man who brings bad news.

LEADER

King, something has been bothering me: suppose
this business was inspired by the gods?   310

KREON

Stop! Before your words fill me with rage.
Now, besides sounding old, you sound senile.
How could anyone possibly believe
the gods protect this corpse? Did *they* cover
his nakedness to reward him for loyal

service—this man who came here to burn
their colonnaded temples and treasuries,
to wipe out their country and tear up its laws?
Do you think that the gods honor rebels?
They don't. But for a good while now   320
men who despise me have been muttering
under their breaths. My edict bruised their necks.
They were rebelling against a just yoke—
unlike you good citizens who support me.
I'm sure these malcontents bribed my sentries
to do what they did.

                Mankind's most deadly
invention is money. It plunders cities,
encourages men to abandon their homes,
tempts honest people to do shameful things.
It instructs them in criminal practice,   330
drives them to act on every godless impulse.
By doing this for silver, these men have
guaranteed that, sooner or later,
they'll pay the price.

(addressing the GUARD)

              But you who worship Zeus—
since Zeus enforces his own will through mine—
be sure of this, it is my solemn oath:
if you don't find the man who carried out
this burial and drag him before me,
a quick trip to Hades won't be your fate.
All of you will be strung up—and you'll hang   340
for a while, your insolence on display.

From then on, you may calculate exactly
how much profit to expect from your crimes.
More men are destroyed by ill-gotten wealth
than such "wealth" ever saved from destruction.

GUARD

May I speak further? Or shall I just leave?

KREON

Don't you realize that your words pain me?

GUARD

Do your ears ache, or does the pain go deeper?

KREON

Why does the source of my pain interest you?

GUARD

I only sting your ears. The man   350
who did this stabs your gut.

KREON

You've run off at the mouth since you were born.

GUARD

Maybe so. But I had no part in this crime.

KREON

I think you did. Sold your life for some coins.

GUARD

It's a sad thing when a judge gets it wrong.

KREON

You'll soon be on the wrong end of a judgment
yourself.
        If you don't find the guilty one,
you'll find your greed buys you nothing but grief.

GUARD

I hope he's caught, but Fate will decide that.
And you'll never see me coming back here.   360
Now that I have been spared—when everything
seemed so desperate—all I can think about
is how much gratitude I owe the gods.

Exit GUARD to open country; KREON enters his palace.

ELDERS

Wonders abound, but none
more astounding than man!
He crosses to the far side
of white seas, blown
by winter gales, sailing
below huge waves.
He wears Earth down—   370
our primal, eternal,
inexhaustible god,
his stallion-sired mules

plowing her soil
back and forth
year after year.

All breeds of carefree
bird, savage beast,
and deep-sea creature,
ingenious man   380
snares in his woven nets.
He drives the mountain herds
from wild lairs down to his folds.
He coaxes rough-maned horses
to thrust their necks through his yoke.
He tames the tireless mountain bull.

He has taught himself speech,
wind-quick thought,
and all the talents
that govern a city—   390
how to take shelter
from cold skies or pelting rain.
Never baffled,
always resourceful,
he accepts every challenge.
But from Hades alone
has he found no way out—
though from hopeless disease
he has found a defense.

Exceeding all expectation,   400
his robust power to create
sometimes brings evil,
at other times, excellence.
When he follows the laws
Earth teaches him—
and Justice, which he's sworn
the gods he will enforce—
he soars with his city.
But reckless and corrupt,
a man will be driven   410
from his nation disgraced.

Let no man guilty of such things
share my hearth or invade my thoughts.

Enter GUARD, from countryside, leading ANTIGONE.

LEADER
I'm stunned—what's this? A warning from the gods?
I know this girl. She is Antigone.
Don't we all recognize her?
Unlucky Oedipus was her father.
And now her own luck runs out.
What's happening? You—under guard?
Are you a prisoner? Did you break   420
the king's law? Commit some thoughtless act?

GUARD

There's your perpetrator. We caught her
burying the corpse. Where's Kreon?

Enter KREON.

LEADER

Here he comes. Just in time.

KREON

What makes my arrival so timely?

GUARD

Sir, never promise something won't happen.
Second thoughts can make your first one a lie.
I vowed I'd never come back here,
after you tongue-lashed me with those threats.
Then came a pleasure like no other,   430
because it's a total surprise, something
we hope for but can't believe will happen.
So I came back—though I swore I wouldn't—
to bring you the girl we caught sprinkling dust
on the dead body. No need to throw dice.
This time the good fortune was all mine.
Now she's all yours. Question and convict her.
Do as you see fit. But I have the right
to go free of trouble once and for all.

KREON

Your prisoner—where was she when captured?   440

GUARD

Covering up the dead body. There you have it.

KREON

Do you know what you just said? No mistake?

GUARD

I saw her bury the man you said no one
could bury. How can I say it plainer?

KREON

How did you see her? Was she caught in the act?

GUARD

Here's what happened. We went back there
after those ugly threats of yours, to brush
the dirt off the body and strip it down
to its rotting flesh. Afterwards, we hunkered
upwind under some hills to spare us any stench   450
the body might have sent our way. Each man
kept alert, and kept his neighbor alert,
by raking him with outbursts of abuse
if he seemed to neglect his watch.
We kept at it until the round sun had climbed
the heavens and baked us in the noon heat.
Then, rising from the earth, a whirlwind

whipped up the dust, and terror filled the sky,
choking the grasslands, tearing leaves off trees,
churning up grit all around us.

                              Our eyes squeezed shut,   460
we waited out this god-sent pestilence.
After a bit the dust cleared, and we saw her
cry out in anguish, a piercing scream
like a bird homing to find her nest robbed.
When she saw the body stripped naked,
she wailed one more time, then yelled a string
of curses at those who'd done it. She scooped up
powdery dust and, from a graceful bronze
urn, poured out three cool swallows for the dead.
Soon as we saw this, we moved in to stop her.   470
She wasn't a bit shocked when we charged her
with the earlier crime, and now this one.
Didn't deny a thing. That pleased,
but also troubled me. Escaping blame
oneself is always a relief. Still, it hurts
to cause your own people grief. But all that
matters much less to me than my own safety.

KREON

(to ANTIGONE)

You! Don't stand there nodding your head.
Out with it! Admit this or deny it.

ANTIGONE

I swear I did. And I don't deny it.   480

KREON

(to GUARD)

You are excused from this grim business.
You're now free to go anywhere you please.

Exit GUARD. KREON turns to ANTIGONE.

Explain something to me without elaborating.
Were you aware of my decree forbidding this?

ANTIGONE

Of course I knew. We all knew.

KREON

And still you dared to violate the law?

ANTIGONE

I did. It wasn't *Zeus* who issued me
this order. And Justice—who lives below—
was not involved. They'd never condone it!
I deny that your edicts—since *you*, a mere man,   490
imposed them—have the force to trample on
the gods' unwritten and infallible laws.
Their laws are not ephemeral—they weren't
made yesterday. They will rule forever.
No man knows how far back in time they go.
I'd never let any man's arrogance
bully me into breaking the gods' laws.
I'll die someday—how could I not know that?
I knew it without your proclamation.

If I do die young, that's an advantage,   500
for doesn't a person like me, who lives
besieged by trouble, escape by dying?
My own death isn't going to bother me,
but I would be devastated to see
my mother's son die and rot unburied.
I've no regrets for what I've done. And if you
consider my acts foolhardy, I say:
look at the fool charging me with folly.

LEADER

It's apparent this girl's nature is savage
like her father's. She hasn't got the sense   510
to back off when she gets into trouble.

KREON

Stubborn spirits are the first to crack.
It's always the iron tool hardened by fire
that snaps and shatters. And headstrong horses
can be tamed by a little iron bit.
There's no excuse for a slave
to preen when her master's home.
This girl learned insolence long before
she broke this law. What's more, she keeps on
insulting us, and then gloats about it.   520
There is no doubt that if she emerges
victorious, and is never punished,
I am no man. *She* will be the man here.

I don't care if she is my sister's child,
a blood relative, closer than all those
who worship Zeus in my household,
she—and her sister—still must die.
I charge her sister too with conspiring
to bury Polyneikes. Bring her out.
I observed her inside just now,   530
screaming, hysterical, deranged.
Someone who intends to commit a crime
can lose control of a guilty conscience.
Her furtive treason gives itself away.

Two of Kreon's Men enter the palace. KREON *turns back to* ANTIGONE.

But I also hate it when someone caught
red-handed tries to glorify her crime.

ANTIGONE

Take me and kill me—is that your whole plan?

KREON

That's it. When that's done I'll be satisfied.

ANTIGONE

Then what stops you? Are you waiting for me
to accept what you've said? I never will.   540
And nothing I say will ever please you.
Yet, since you did mention glory, how
could I do anything more glorious

than build my own brother a tomb?
These men here would approve my actions—
if fear didn't seal their lips.

                    Tyranny
is fortunate in many ways: it can,
for instance, say and do anything it wants.

KREON

These Thebans don't see it your way.

ANTIGONE

But they do. To please you they bite their tongues.   550

KREON

Aren't you ashamed not to follow their lead?

ANTIGONE

Since when is it shameful to honor a brother?

KREON

You had another brother who died fighting him?

ANTIGONE

That's right. Born to the same mother and father.

KREON

Then why do you honor Polyneikes
when doing so desecrates Eteokles?

ANTIGONE

Eteokles wouldn't agree with you.

KREON

Oh, but he would. Because you've honored
treason as though it were patriotism.

ANTIGONE

It was his *brother* who died, not his *slave*!   560

KREON

That brother died ravaging our country!
Eteokles fell fighting to protect it.

ANTIGONE

Hades will still expect his rituals!

KREON

The brave deserve better than the vile.

ANTIGONE

Who knows what matters to the dead?

KREON

Not even death reconciles enemies.

ANTIGONE

I made no enemies by being born!
I made my lifelong friends at birth.

KREON

Then go down to them! Love your dead brothers!
While I'm alive, no woman governs me.   570

Enter ISMENE, led in by Kreon's Men.

LEADER

Ismene's coming from the palace.
She cries the loving tears of a sister.
Her eyes fill up, her flushed face darkens.
Tears pour down her cheeks.

KREON

                              Now you—a viper
who slithered through my house, quietly
drinking my blood! I never knew
I nurtured *two* insurrections,
both attacking my throne.

                              Go ahead,
confess your role in this burial
party. Or do you claim ignorance?   580

ISMENE

I confess it—if she'll let me.
I accept my full share of the blame.

ANTIGONE

Justice won't let you make that claim, Sister!
You refused to help me. You took no part.

ISMENE

You're leaving on a grim voyage. I'm not
ashamed to suffer with you the whole way.

ANTIGONE

The dead in Hades know who buried him.
I don't want love that just shows up in words.

ISMENE

You'll disgrace me, Sister! Don't keep me
from honoring our dead! Take me with you!   590

ANTIGONE

Don't try to share my death! Don't try to claim
you helped me bury him! My death's enough.

ISMENE

With you dead, why would I want to live?

ANTIGONE

Ask Kreon that! You sprang to his defense.

ISMENE

Why do you wound me? It does you no good.

ANTIGONE

I'm sorry if my scorn for him hurts you.

ISMENE

I can still help you. Tell me what to do.

ANTIGONE

Go on living. I'd rather you survived.

ISMENE

Then you want to exclude me from your fate?

ANTIGONE

You made the choice to live. I chose to die.   600

ISMENE

And I've told you how much I hate that choice.

ANTIGONE

Some think you're right. *Others* will think I am.

ISMENE

Then aren't we both equally wrong?

ANTIGONE

Gather your strength. Your life goes on. Long ago
I dedicated my own to the dead.

KREON

One woman only now shows her madness—
the other's been out of her mind since birth.

ISMENE

King, when you are shattered by grief
your native wit vanishes. It just goes.

KREON

You surely lost your wits when you teamed up   610
with a criminal engaged in a crime.

ISMENE

What would my life be like without her?

KREON

You're living that life now. Hers is over.

ISMENE

Then you're willing to kill your own son's bride?

KREON

Oh yes. He'll find other fields to plow.

ISMENE

No other woman would suit him so well.

KREON

I want no pernicious wives for my son.

ISMENE

Dearest Haimon! How your father hates you!

KREON

Enough! No more talk about this marriage.

ISMENE

You're going to rob your son of his bride?   620

KREON

Hades will cancel their marriage for me.

ISMENE

Then you've made up your mind she will die?

KREON

Both *my* mind and *your* mind. No more delay,
men, take them in. Make sure they behave
like women. Don't let either slip away.
Even the brave will try to run
when they see death coming at them.

Kreon's Men take ANTIGONE *and* ISMENE *inside.*

ELDERS

Lucky are those
whose lives
never taste evil!   630
For once the gods
attack a family,
their curse never relents.
It sickens life after life,
rising like a deep

sea swell, a darkness
boiling from below, driven
by the wild stormwinds
of Thrace that churn up
black sand from the seafloor—   640
the battered headlands
moan as the storm pounds in.

I see sorrows that struck
the dead Labdakids long ago
break over their children,
wave on wave of sorrows!
Each generation fails
to protect its own youth—
because a god always hacks
at their roots, draining   650
strength that could set them free.
Now the hope that brightened
over the last rootstock
alive in the house
of Oedipus, in its turn
is struck down—
by the blood-drenched dust
the death gods demand,
by reckless talk,
by Furies in the mind.   660

O Zeus,
what human arrogance
can rival your power?

Neither Sleep,
who beguiles us all,
nor the tireless, god-driven months
overcome it.

O Monarch
whom time cannot age—
you live in the magical
sunrays of Olympos!   670
One law of yours rules
our own and future time,
just as it ruled the past:
nothing momentous man
achieves will go unpunished.

For Hope is a wanderer
who profits multitudes
but tempts just as many
with light-headed longings—
and a man's failure   680
dawns on him only
when blazing coals
scald his feet.

The man was wise
who said these words:
"Evil seems noble—
early and late—to minds
unbalanced by the gods,
but only for a moment

will such men   690
hold off catastrophe."

Enter HAIMON.

LEADER
(to KREON)
There's Haimon,
the youngest of your sons.
Does he come here enraged
that you've condemned Antigone,
the bride he's been promised,
or in shock that his hopes
for marriage have been crushed?

KREON
We'll soon have an answer
better than any prophet's.   700
My son, now that you've heard
my formal condemnation
of your bride, have you come here
to attack your father?
Or will I be dear to you still,
no matter what I do?

HAIMON
I'm yours, Father. I respect your wisdom.
Show me the straight path, and I'll take it.
I couldn't value any marriage more
than the excellent guidance you give me.   710

KREON

Son, that's exactly how you need to think:
follow your father's orders in all things.
It's the reason men pray for loyal sons
to be born and raised in their houses—
so they can harm their father's enemies
and show his friends respect to match his own.
If a man produces worthless children,
what has he spawned? His grief, his rivals' glee.

Don't throw away your judgment, son,
for the pleasure this woman offers.   720
You'll feel her turn ice-cold in your arms—
you'll feel her scorn in the bedroom. No wound
cuts deeper than poisonous love. So spit
this girl out like the enemy she is.
Let her find a mate in Hades.
I caught her in open defiance—
she alone in the whole city—and I will take
her life, just as I promised. I will not
show myself as a liar to my people.
It is useless for her to harp on the Zeus   730
of family life: if I indulge my own
family in rebelliousness,
I must indulge it everywhere.

A man who keeps his own house in order
will be perceived as righteous by his city.
But if anyone steps out of line, breaks

our laws, thinks he can dictate to his king,
he shouldn't expect any praise from me.
Citizens must obey men in office
appointed by the city, both in minor matters   740
and in the great questions of what is just—
even when they think an action unjust.
Obedient men lead ably and serve well.
Caught in a squall of spears, they hold their ground.
They make brave soldiers you can trust.
Insubordination is our worst crime.
It wrecks cities and empties homes. It breaks
and routs even allies who fight beside us.
Discipline is what saves the lives of all
good people who stay out of trouble.   750
And to make sure we enforce discipline—
never let a woman overwhelm a king.
Better to be driven from power, if it
comes to that, by a man. Then nobody
can say you were beaten by some female.

LEADER

Unless the years have sapped my wits, King,
what you have just said was wisely said.

HAIMON

Father, the gods instill reason in men.
It's the most valuable thing we possess.
I don't have the skill—nor do I want it—   760
to contradict all the things you have said.

Though someone else's perspective might help.
Look, it's not in your nature to notice
what people say and do—and what they don't like.
That harsh look on your face makes men afraid—
no one tells you what you'd rather not hear.
But I hear, unobserved, what people think.
Listen. Thebes aches for this girl. *No person
ever*, they're saying, *less deserved to die—
no one's ever been so unjustly killed*   770
*for actions as magnificent as hers.
When her own brother died in that bloodbath
she kept him from lying out there unburied,
fair game for flesh-eating dogs and vultures.
Hasn't she earned*, they ask, *golden honor?*
Those are the words they whisper in the shadows.

There's nothing I prize more, Father,
than your welfare.
                    What makes a son prouder
than a father's thriving reputation?
Don't fathers feel the same about their sons?   780

Attitudes are like clothes; you can change them.
Don't think that what you say is always right.
Whoever thinks that he alone is wise,
that he's got a superior tongue and brain,
open him up and you'll find him a blank.
It's never shameful for even a wise man
to keep on learning new things all his life.

Be flexible, not rigid. Think of trees
caught in a raging winter torrent: Those
that bend will survive with all their limbs   790
intact. Those that resist are swept away.
Or take a captain who cleats his mainsheet
down hard, never easing off in a blow—
he'll capsize his ship and go right on sailing,
his rowing benches where his keel should be.
Step back from your anger. Let yourself change.

If I, as a younger man, can offer
a thought, it's this: Yes, it would be better
if men were born with perfect understanding.
But things don't work that way. The best response   800
to worthy advice is to learn from it.

LEADER

King, if he has said anything to ease
this crisis, you had better learn from it.
Haimon, you do the same. You both spoke well.

KREON

So men my age should learn from one of yours?

HAIMON

If I happen to be right, yes! Don't look
at my youth, look at what I've accomplished.

KREON

What? Backing rebels makes you proud?

HAIMON

I'm not about to condone wrongdoing.

KREON

Hasn't *she* been attacked by that disease?   810

HAIMON

Your fellow citizens would deny it.

KREON

Shall Thebans dictate how I should govern?

HAIMON

Listen to yourself. You talk like a boy.

KREON

Should I yield to them—or rule Thebes myself?

HAIMON

It's not a *city* if one man owns it.

KREON

Don't we say men in power *own* their cities?

HAIMON

You'd make a first-rate king of a wasteland.

KREON

It seems this *boy* fights on the woman's side.

HAIMON

Only if you're the woman. You're my concern.

KREON

Then why do you make open war on me?   820

HAIMON

What I attack is your abuse of power.

KREON

Is protecting my interest an abuse?

HAIMON

What is it you protect by scorning the gods?

KREON

Look at yourself! A woman overpowers you.

HAIMON

But no disgraceful impulse ever will.

KREON

Your every word supports that woman.

HAIMON

And you, and me, and the gods of this earth.

KREON

You will not marry her while she's *on* this earth.

HAIMON

Then she will die and, dead, kill someone else.

KREON

You are brazen enough to threaten me?   830

HAIMON

What threatens you is hearing what I think.

KREON

Your mindless attack on me threatens *you*.

HAIMON

I'd question *your* mind if you weren't my father.

KREON

Stop your snide deference! You are her slave.

HAIMON

You're talking at me, but you don't hear me.

KREON

Really? By Olympos above, I hear you.
And I can assure you, you're going to
suffer the consequences of your attacks.

KREON speaks to his Men.

Bring out the odious creature. Let her
die at once in his presence. Let him watch,   840
this bridegroom, as she's killed beside him.

Two of Kreon's Men enter the palace.

HAIMON

Watch her die next to me? You think I'd do that?
Your eyes won't see my face, ever again.
Go on raving to friends who can stand you.

Exit HAIMON.

LEADER

King, the young man's fury hurls him out.
Rage makes a man his age utterly reckless.

KREON

Let him imagine he's superhuman.
He'll never save the lives of those two girls.

LEADER

Then you intend to execute them both?

KREON

Not the one with clean hands.   850
I think you're right about her.

LEADER

The one you plan to kill—how will you do it?

KREON

I will lead her along a deserted road,
and hide her, alive, in a hollow cave.
I'll leave her just enough food to evade
defilement—so the city won't be infected.
She can pray there to Hades, the one god
whom she respects. Maybe he will spare her!
Though she's more likely to learn, in her last hours,
that she's thrown her life away on the dead.   860

*KREON remains onstage during the next choral ode, possibly retiring into
the background.*

ELDERS

Love, you win all
your battles!—raising
havoc with our herds,
dwelling all night
on a girl's soft cheeks,
cruising the oceans,
invading homes
deep in the wilds!
No god can outlast you,
no mortal outrun you.   870
And those you seize go mad.

You wrench even good men's minds
so far off course they crash in ruins.
Now you ignite hatred in men

of the same blood—but allure flashing
from the keen eyes of the bride
always wins, for Desire wields
all the power of ancient law:
Aphrodite the implacable
plays cruel games with our lives.   880

Enter ANTIGONE, dressed in purple as a bride, guarded by Kreon's Men.

LEADER

This sight also drives *me*
outside the law. I can't stop
my own tears flowing when I see
Antigone on her way
to the bridal chamber,
where we all lie down in death.

ANTIGONE

Citizens of our fatherland, you see me
begin my last journey. I take one last look
at sunlight that I'll never see again.
Hades, who chills each one of us to sleep,   890
will guide me down to Acheron's shore.
I'll go hearing no wedding hymn
to carry me to my bridal chamber, or songs
girls sing when flowers crown a bride's hair.
I'm going to marry the River of Pain.

LEADER

Don't praise and glory go with you
to the deep caverns of the dead?
You haven't been wasted by disease.
You've helped no sword earn its keep.
No, you have chosen of your own free will   900
to enter Hades while you're still alive.
No one else has ever done that.

ANTIGONE

I once heard that a Phrygian stranger,
Niobe, the daughter of Tantalos,
died a hideous death on Mount Sipylos.
Living rock, clinging like ivy,
crushed her. Now, people say,
she erodes—rainwater and snow
never leave her alone—they keep on
pouring like tears from her eyes,   910
drenching the clefts of her body.
My death will be like hers,
when the god at last lets me sleep.

LEADER

You forget, child, she was a goddess,
with gods for parents, not a mortal
begotten by mortals like ourselves.
It's no small honor—for a mere woman
to suffer so godlike a fate, in both
how she has lived and the way she will die.

ANTIGONE

Now I'm being laughed at!   920
In the name of our fathers' gods,
wait till I'm gone! Don't mock me
while I stand here in plain sight—
all you rich citizens of this town!

At least I can trust you,
headwaters of the river
Dirke, and you, holy
plains around Thebes, home
of our great chariot-fleet,
to bear me witness: watch them   930
march me off to my strange tomb,
my heaped-up rock-bound prison,
without a friend to mourn me
or any law to protect me—

me, a miserable woman
with no home here on earth
and none down with the dead,
not quite alive, not yet a corpse.

LEADER

You took the ultimate risk when you smashed
yourself against the throne of Justice.   940
But the stiff price you're paying, daughter,
is one you inherit from your father.

ANTIGONE

You've touched my worst grief,
the fate of my father, which I
keep turning over in my mind.
We all were doomed, the whole
grand house of Labdakos,
by my mother's horrendous,
incestuous, coupling with her son.
From what kind of parents was I born?   950

I'm going to them now.
I'm dying unmarried.

And brother Polyneikes,
wasn't yours too a deadly
marriage? And when you
were slaughtered, so was I.

LEADER

Your pious conduct might deserve some praise,
but no assault on power will ever
be tolerated by him who wields it.
It was your own hotheaded   960
willfulness that destroyed you.

ANTIGONE

No friends, no mourners, no wedding songs
go with me. They push me down a road
that runs through sadness.

They have prepared it for me, alone.
Soon I will lose sight of the sun's holy eye,
wretched, with no one to love me,
no one to grieve.

*KREON moves forward from the shadows, speaking first to ANTIGONE, then
to his Men.*

KREON
You realize, don't you, that singing
and wailing would go on forever—if   970
they did the dying any good?

Hurry up now, take her away.
And when you've finished
sealing her off, just as I've ordered,
inside the cave's vault,
leave her there—absolutely
isolated—to decide whether
she wants to die at once, or go
on living in that black hole.
So we'll be pure as far as she's concerned.   980
In either case, today will be the last
she'll ever spend above the ground.

ANTIGONE
My tomb, my bridal bedroom, my home
dug from rock, where they'll keep me forever—
I'll join my family there, so many of us dead,

already welcomed by Persephone.
I'll be the last to arrive, and the worst off,
going down with most of my life unlived.
I hope my coming will please my father,
comfort my mother, and bring joy   990
to you, brother, because I washed your dead
bodies, dressed you with my hands, and poured
blessèd offerings of drink on your graves.
Now, because I honored your corpse,
Polyneikes, *this* is how I'm repaid!
I honored you as wise men would think right.
But I wouldn't have taken that task on
had I been a mother who lost her child,
or if my husband were rotting out there.
For them, I would never defy my city.   1000
You want to know what law lets me say this?
If my husband were dead, I could remarry.
A new husband could give me a new child.
But with my father and mother in Hades,
a new brother could never bloom for me.
That is the law that made me die for you,
Polyneikes. But Kreon says I'm wrong,
terribly wrong. And now I'm his captive.
He pulls me by the wrist to no bride's bed.
I won't hear bridal songs, or feel the joy   1010
of married love, and I will have no share
in raising children. No, I will go grieving,
friendless, and alive to a hollow tomb.
Tell me, gods, which of *your* laws did I break?

I'm too far gone to expect your help.
But whose strength can I count on, when acts
of blessing are considered blasphemy?
If the gods are happy I'm sentenced to die,
I hope one day I'll discover
what divine law I have broken.   1020
But if my judges are at fault, I want *them*
to suffer the pain they inflict on me now.

LEADER

She's still driven by raw gusts
raging through her mind.

KREON

I have no patience with such outbursts.
And none for men who drag their feet.

ANTIGONE

I think you mean my death is near.

KREON

It will be carried out. Don't think otherwise.

ANTIGONE

I leave you, Thebes, city of my fathers.
I leave you, ancient gods. This very moment,   1030
I'm being led away. They cannot wait!

ANTIGONE pulls the veil off her face and shakes her hair free.

Look at me, princely citizens of Thebes:
I'm the last daughter of the kings who ruled you.
Look at what's done to me, and by whom
it's done, to punish me for keeping faith.

Kreon's Men lead ANTIGONE *offstage.*

ELDERS

Like you, lovely Danaë
endured her loss
of heavenly sunlight
in a brass-bound cell—
a prison secret as a tomb.   1040
Night and day she was watched.
Like yours, my daughter,
her family was a great one.
The seed of Zeus, which fell
on her as golden rain,
she treasured in her womb.
Fate is strange and powerful.
Wealth cannot protect us,
nor can war, high city towers,
or storm-beaten black ships.   1050

Impounded too, was Lycurgos,
short-tempered son of Dryas,
King of Edonia: to pay
him back for insulting
defiance, Dionysos shut

him up in a rocky cell.
There his surging madness ebbed.
He learned too late how mad
he was to taunt this god
with derisive laughter.   1060
When he tried to suppress
Bakkhanalian torches
and women fired by their god,
he angered the Muses,
who love the oboe's song.

By waters off the Black Rocks,
a current joins two seas—
the Bosphoros' channel
follows the Thracian
shoreline of Salmydessos.   1070
Ares from his nearby city
saw this wild assault—
the savage wife of Phineus
attacking his two sons:
her stab-wounds darkened
their vengeance-craving eyes,
burst with a pointed shuttle
gripped in her blood-drenched hands.

Broken spirits, they howled
in their pain—these sons   1080
of a woman unhappy
in her marriage, this daughter

descended from the ancient
Erektheids. Nursed in caves
among her father's storm winds,
this daughter of the gods,
this child of Boreas,
rode swift horses over the mountains—
yet Fate broke her brutally, my child.

Enter TIRESIAS and the Lad who guides him.

TIRESIAS

Theban lords, we walk here side by side,   1090
one pair of eyes looking out for us both.
Blind men must travel with somebody's help.

KREON

What news do you bring, old man Tiresias?

TIRESIAS

I'll tell you. Then you must trust this prophet.

KREON

I've never questioned the advice you've given.

TIRESIAS

And it helped you keep Thebes on a straight course?

KREON

I know your value. I learned it firsthand.

TIRESIAS

Take care.
You're standing on the knife edge of fate.

KREON

What do you mean? That makes me shudder.   1100

TIRESIAS

You'll comprehend when you hear the warnings
issued by my art. When I took my seat
at my accustomed post of augury,
birds from everywhere fluttering nearby,
I heard a strange sound coming from their midst.
They screeched with such mindless ferocity,
any meaning their song possessed was drowned out.
I knew the birds were tearing at each other
with lethal talons. The hovering beats
of thrashing wings could have meant nothing else.   1110
Alarmed, I lit a sacrificial fire,
but the god failed to keep his flames alive.
Then from charred thighbones came a rancid slime,
smoking and sputtering, oozing out
into the ashes. The gallbladder burst open.
Liquefying thighs slid free from the strips
of fat enfolding them.
                            But my attempt
at prophecy failed. The signs I had sought
never appeared—this I learned from my lad.
He's my guide, as I am the guide for others.   1120

Kreon, your mind has sickened Thebes.
Our city's altars, and our city's braziers,
have been defiled, all of them, by dogs
and birds, with flesh torn from the wretched
corpse of Oedipus' fallen son.
Because of this, the gods will not accept
our prayers or the offerings of burnt meat
that come from our hands. No bird now sings
a clear omen—their keen cries have been garbled
by the taste of a slain man's thickened blood.   1130
Think about these facts, son.

                        All men go wrong.
But when a man blunders, he won't be stripped
of his wits and his strength if he corrects
the error he's committed and then ends
his stubborn ways. Stubbornness, you well know,
will bring on charges of stupidity.
Respect the dead. Don't spear the fallen.
How much courage does it take
to kill a dead man?

                  Let me
help you. My counsel is sound and well meant.   1140
No advice is sweeter than that from a wise
source who has only your interests at heart.

KREON

Old man, like archers at target practice,
you all aim arrows at me. And now you
stoop to using prophecy against me.

For a long time I have been merchandise
sold far and wide by you omen-mongers.
Go, make your money, strike your deals, import
silver from Sardis, gold from India,
if it suits you. But you won't hide that corpse   1150
under the earth! Never—even if Zeus'
own eagles fly scraps of flesh to his throne.

Defilement isn't something I fear. It won't
persuade me to order this burial.
I don't accept that men can defile gods.
But even the cleverest of mortals,
venerable Tiresias, will be brought
down hard, if, hoping to turn a profit,
they clothe ugly ideas in handsome words.

TIRESIAS

Does any man grasp . . . does he realize . . .   1160

KREON

Realize . . . what? What point are you making?

TIRESIAS

. . . that no possession is worth more than good sense?

KREON

Just as its absence is our worst disease.

TIRESIAS

But hasn't that disease infected you?

KREON

I won't trade insults with you, prophet.

TIRESIAS

You do when you call my prophecies false.

KREON

Your profession has always loved money.

TIRESIAS

And tyrants have a penchant for corruption.

KREON

You know you're abusing a king in power?

TIRESIAS

You hold power because I helped you save Thebes.   1170

KREON

You're a shrewd prophet. But you love to cause harm.

TIRESIAS

You'll force me to say what's clenched in my heart.

KREON

Say it. Unless you've been paid to say it.

TIRESIAS

I don't think it will pay you to hear it.

KREON

Get one thing straight: my conscience can't be bought.

TIRESIAS

Then tell your conscience this. You will not live
for many circuits of the chariot sun
before you trade a child born from your loins
for all the corpses whose deaths you have caused.
You have thrown children from the sunlight   1180
down to the shades of Hades, ruthlessly
housing a living person in a tomb,
while you detain here, among us, something
that belongs to the gods who live below
our world—the naked unwept corpse you've robbed
of the solemn grieving we owe our dead.
None of this should have been any concern
of yours—or of the Olympian gods—
but you have involved them in your outrage!
Therefore, avengers wait to ambush you—   1190
the Furies sent by Hades and its gods
will punish you for the crimes I have named.

Do you think someone hired me to tell you this?
It won't be long before wailing breaks out
from the women and men in your own house.
And hatred against you will surge in all

the countries whose sons, in mangled pieces,
received their rites of burial
from dogs, wild beasts, or flapping birds
who have carried the stench of defilement   1200
to the homelands and the hearths of the dead.

Since you've provoked me, these are the arrows
I have shot in anger, like a bowman,
straight at your heart—arrows you cannot dodge,
and whose pain you will feel.
                              Lad, take me home—
let this man turn his anger on younger
people. That might teach him to hold his tongue,
and to think more wisely than he does now.

Exit TIRESIAS led by the Lad.

LEADER

This old man leaves stark prophecies behind.
Never once, while my hair has gone from black   1210
to white, has this prophet told Thebes a lie.

KREON

I'm well aware of that. It unnerves me.
Surrender would be devastating,
but if I stand firm, I could be destroyed.

LEADER

What you need is some very clear advice,
son of Menoikeus.

KREON

What must I do?
If you have such advice, give it to me.

LEADER

Free the girl from her underground prison.
Build a tomb for the corpse you have let rot.

KREON

That's your advice? I should surrender?   1220

LEADER

Yes, King. Do it now. For the gods
act quickly to abort human folly.

KREON

I can hardly say this. But I'll give up
convictions I hold passionately—
and do what you ask. We can't fight
the raw power of destiny.

LEADER

Then go!
Yourself. Delegate this to no one.

KREON

I'll go just as I am. Move out, men. Now!
All of you, bring axes and run toward
that rising ground. You can see it from here.   1230
Because I'm the one who has changed, I who

locked her away will go there to free her.
My heart is telling me we must obey
established law until the day we die.

Exit KREON and his Men toward open country.

ELDERS
God with myriad names—
lustrous child
of Kadmos' daughter,
son of thundering Zeus—
you govern fabled Italy,
you preside at Eleusis,   1240
secluded Valley of Demeter
that welcomes all pilgrims.
O Bakkhos! Thebes
is your homeland,
mother city of maenads
on the quietly flowing
Ismenos, where the dragon's
teeth were sown.

Now you stand on the ridges rising
up the twin peaks of Parnassos.   1250
There through the wavering
smoke-haze your torches flare.
There walk your devotees,
the nymphs of Korykia,
beside Kastalia's fountains.

Thick-woven ivy on Nysa's sloping hills,
grape-clusters ripe on verdant shorelines
propel you here, while voices
of more than human power
sing "Evohoi!"—your name divine—   1260
when the streets of Thebes
are your final destination.

By honoring Thebes
beyond all cities,
you honor your mother
whom the lightning killed.
Now a plague
ravages our city. Come home
on healing footsteps—down
the slopes of Parnassos,   1270
or over the howling channel.
Stars breathing their gentle fire
shine joy on you as they rise,
O master of nocturnal voices!
Take shape before our eyes, Bakkhos,
son of Zeus our king, let the Thyiads
come with you, let them climb
the mad heights of frenzy
as you, Iakkhos, the bountiful,
watch them   1280
dance through the night.

Enter MESSENGER.

MESSENGER

Neighbors, who live not far from the grand
old houses of Amphion and Kadmos,
you can't trust anything in a person's life—
praiseworthy or shameful—never to change.
Fate lifts up—and Fate cuts down—both the lucky
and the unlucky, day in and day out.
No prophet can tell us what happens next.
Kreon always seemed someone to envy,
to me at least. He saved from attack   1290
the homeland where we sons of Kadmos live.
This won him absolute power. He was
the brilliant father of patrician children.
Now it has all slipped away. For when things
that give pleasure and meaning to our lives
desert a man, he's not a human being
anymore—he becomes a breathing corpse.
Amass wealth if you can, show off your house.
Display the panache of a great monarch.
But if joy disappears from your life,   1300
I wouldn't give the shadow cast by smoke
for all you possess. Only happiness matters.

LEADER

Should our masters expect more grief? What's happened?

MESSENGER

Death. And the killer is alive.

LEADER

Name the murderer. Name the dead. Tell us.

MESSENGER

Haimon is dead. The hand that killed him was his own . . .

LEADER

. . . father's? Or do you mean he killed himself?

MESSENGER

He killed himself. Raging at his killer father.

LEADER

Tiresias, you spoke the truth.

MESSENGER

You know the facts. Now you must cope with them.   1310

Enter EURYDIKE.

LEADER

I see Eurydike, soon to be crushed,
approaching from inside the house.
She may have heard what's happened to her son.

EURYDIKE

I heard all of you speaking as I came out—
on my way to offer prayers to Athena.
I happened to unlatch the gate,

to open it, when words of our disaster
carried to my ears. I fainted, terrified
and dumbstruck, in the arms of my servant.
Please tell me your news. Tell me all of it.   1320
I'm someone who has lived through misfortune.

MESSENGER

O my dear Queen, I will spare you nothing.
I'll tell you truthfully what I've just seen.
Why should I say something to soothe you
that will later prove me a liar?
Straight talk is always best.
I traveled with your husband to the far
edge of the plain where Polyneikes' corpse,
mangled by wild dogs, lay still uncared for.

We prayed for mercy to the Goddess   1330
of Roadways, and to Pluto, asking them
to restrain their anger. We washed his remains
with purified water. Using boughs stripped
from nearby bushes, we burned what was left,
then mounded a tomb from his native earth.

After that we turned toward the girl's deadly
wedding cavern—with its bed of cold stone.
Still far off, we heard an enormous wail
coming from somewhere near the unhallowed
portico—so we turned back to tell Kreon.   1340
As the king arrived, these incoherent

despairing shouts echoed all around him.
First he groaned, then he yelled out in raw pain,

"Am I a prophet? Will my worst fears come true?
Am I walking down the bitterest street
of my life? That's my son's voice greeting me!

"Move quickly, men. Run through that narrow gap
where the stones have been pulled loose from the wall.
Go where the cavern opens out. Tell me
the truth—is that Haimon's voice I'm hearing,   1350
or have the gods played some trick on my ears?"

Following orders from our despondent
master, we stared in. At the tomb's far end
there she was, hanging by the neck, a noose
of finely woven linen holding her aloft.
Haimon fell against her, hugging her waist,
grieving for the bride he'd lost to Hades,
for his father's acts, for his own doomed love.

When Kreon saw all this he stepped inside,
groaned horribly, and called out to his son: 1360
"My desperate child! What have you done? What
did you think you were doing? When did the gods
destroy your reason? Come out of there, son.
I beg you."
                        His son then glared straight at him
with savage eyes, spat in his face, spoke not

one word in answer, but drew his two-edged sword.
His father leapt back. Haimon missed his thrust.
Then this raging youth—with no warning—turned
on himself, tensed his body to the sword,
and drove half its length deep into his side.   1370
Still conscious, he clung to her with limp arms,
gasping for breath, spurts of his blood pulsing
onto her white cheek.

            Then he lay there, his dead
body embracing hers, married at last,
poor man—not up here, but somewhere
in Hades—proving that of all mankind's
evils, thoughtless violence is the worst.

Exit EURYDIKE.

LEADER

What do you make of that? She turns and leaves
without saying one word, brave or bitter.

MESSENGER

I don't like it. I hope that having heard   1380
the sorry way her son died, she won't grieve
for him in public. Maybe she's gone
to ask her maids to mourn him in the house.
This woman never loses her composure.

LEADER

I'm not so sure. To me this strange silence
seems ominous as an outburst of grief.

MESSENGER

I'll go in and find out.

She could have disguised the real

intent of her impassioned heart.

But I agree: her silence is alarming.   1390

Exit MESSENGER into the palace; KREON enters carrying the body of HAIMON
wrapped in cloth; his Men follow, bringing a bier on which KREON will lay his
son in due course.

LEADER

Here comes our king, burdened

with a message all too clear:

this wasn't caused by anyone's vengeance—

may I say it?—but by his own father's blunders.

KREON

Oh, what errors of the mind I have made!

Deadly, bullheaded blunders.

You all see it—the man

who murdered, and the son

who's dead. What I did

was blind and wrong!   1400

You died so young, my son.

Your death happened so fast!

Your life was cut short

not through your mad acts,

but through mine.

LEADER

You saw the right course of action
but took it far too late.

KREON

I've learned that lesson now—
in all its bitterness.
Sometime back, a god struck   1410
my head an immense blow,
it drove me
to act in brutal ways,
ways that stamped out
all my happiness.
What burdens and what pain
men suffer and endure.

Enter MESSENGER from the palace.

MESSENGER

Master, your hands are full of sorrow,
you bear its full weight.
But other sorrows are in store—   1420
you'll face them soon, inside your house.

KREON

Can any new
calamity make
what's happened worse?

MESSENGER

Your wife is dead—so much
a loving mother to your son,
poor woman, that she died
of wounds just now inflicted.

KREON

Oh Hades, you are hard
to appease! We flood   1430
your harbor. You want more.
Why are you trying
to destroy me?
(turning to MESSENGER)
What have you to tell me
this time?—you who bring
nothing but deadly news.
I was hardly alive, and now, my young friend,
you've come back to kill me again.
Son, what are you telling me?
What is this newest message   1440

—the palace doors open; EURYDIKE's corpse is revealed; KREON sighs—

that buries me? My wife is dead.
Slaughter after slaughter.

LEADER

Now you see it. Your house no longer hides it.

KREON

I see one more violent death. With what
else can Fate punish me? I have

just held my dead son in my arms—
now I see another dear body.
Ahhh. Unhappy mother, oh my son.

MESSENGER

There, at the altar, she pierced
herself with a sharp blade.   1450
Her eyes went quietly dark
and she closed them.
She had first mourned aloud
the empty marriage bed
of her dead son Megareus.
Then with her last breath
she cursed you, Kreon,
killer of your own son.

KREON

Ahhh! That sends fear
surging through me.   1460
Why hasn't someone
driven a two-edged
sword through my heart?
I'm a wretched coward,
awash with terror.

MESSENGER

The woman whose corpse you see
condemns you for the deaths of her sons.

KREON

Tell me how she did it.

MESSENGER

She drove the blade below her liver,
so she could suffer the same wound   1470
that killed Haimon, for whom she mourns.

KREON

There's no one I can blame,
no other mortal.
I am the only one.

*KREON looks at and touches the body of HAIMON as his Men assemble to
escort him offstage.*

I killed you, that's the reality.
Men, take me inside.
I'm less than nothing now.

LEADER

You are doing what's right,
if any right can be found
among all these misfortunes.   1480
Better to say little
in the face of evil.

KREON

Let it come, let it happen now—
let my own kindest fate

make this my final day on earth.
That would be kindness itself.
Let it happen, let it come.
Never let me see
tomorrow's dawn.

LEADER

That's in the future. We   1490
must deal with the present.
The future will be shaped
by those who control it.

KREON

My deepest desires are in that prayer.

LEADER

Stop your prayers.
No human being
evades calamity
once it has struck.

KREON puts his hand on HAIMON's corpse.

KREON

Take me from this place.
A foolish, impulsive man   1500
who killed you, my son, mindlessly,
killed you as well, my wife.
I'm truly cursed! I don't know

where to rest my eyes,
or on whose shoulders
I can lean my weight.
My hands warp
all they touch.

KREON, *still touching* HAIMON*'s corpse, looks toward* EURYDIKE*'s, then lifts
his hand and moves off toward the palace.*

And over there,
Fate's avalanche   1510
pounds my head.

LEADER
Good sense is crucial
to human happiness.
Never fail to respect the gods,
for the huge claims of proud men
are always hugely punished—
by blows that, as the proud grow old,
pound wisdom through their minds.

ALL *leave.*

NOTES TO THE PLAYS

AIAS

TEKMESSA *concubine/wife of Aias* Nominally Tekmessa is Aias's concubine, a "spear-taken" woman, but substantively she is his wife.

7 *where all is saved or lost* Literally, "the post at the end of the line." The outermost posts, being most vulnerable, are key. At Troy they were held by Achilles and by Aias.

25 *I can't see you* Athena is invisible to Odysseus, as Odysseus is invisible to Aias. Aias does see Athena, however.

28 *like a bronze-mouthed trumpet* ". . . the trumpet was invented for the Etruscans by Athena" (Garvie, 126).

151–152 *That foxfucker you ask me / about* him? The Greek *kinados* is a 'coarse' Sicilian word for fox. It is not gender specific. The epithet not only characterizes Odysseus but registers Aias's revulsion at the mere mention of his name. "Fox," in itself, carries some of the meaning but little of the weight, and even less the edge, of the original—nor do conventional qualifications such as "stinking," "cunning," "slippery," or "villainous." The key circumstance is that Aias is out of his mind, "screaming curses so awful no man could think them," as Tekmessa reports, adding that it must have been "a god came wailing *through* him" (308–312). Foxfucker has a suitably infamous *aural* lineage, the dead metaphor of "motherfucker" having metastasized into (or been metastasized from) like-sounding toxic epithets.

189 *Son of Telamon, rock of Salamis* Telamon, the father of Aias, was the first Greek warrior to scale the walls of Troy during the earlier expedition led by Herakles. Salamis is an island near Athens.

212 *only the great they envy after* "After" traces the submerged metaphor of the original Greek, where envy "creeps."

226–227 *as when the huge / bearded vulture* The Greek is "vulture." Yet vultures, as scavengers, eat only carrion, which here doesn't make sense. Some have conjectured that "most probably the Greeks made no clear distinction between vultures and eagles" (Garvie, 141–142). Others take the vulture to be a lammergeier, or bearded vulture, which is not a true vulture but a raptor. "Bearded vulture" seems sufficiently ominous—also, not likely to raise dramatically irrelevant questions as to how a scavenger could possibly threaten live Greek warriors.

230–232 *That* mother *of a rumor . . . Artemis riding a bull* Artemis Tauropolis, the bull rider, often associated with madness. Aias, as a hunter, has of course slaughtered animals, including bulls.

238 *and you gave nothing back?* Speculation that Aias may have cheated Artemis—either not giving her a share of the war spoil, or withholding her share of game he had gotten while hunting.

239 *bronze-armored War God* Ares. Speculation that Aias is being punished for not having acknowledged the help Ares gave him in battle.

284 *Carcass corpses* He has killed animals (carcasses) under the delusion that they were human beings (corpses). This gloss, of what is only implicit in the Greek, highlights the enormity of Aias's crime. The slaughter is a transgression not only of social and political order—as a Greek hero, by definition individualistic, Aias has destroyed the common property of the entire Greek army—but of the far greater natural order he will invoke later as he contemplates the bind he is in. If "Great natural forces know their place / in the greater scheme of things," he asks, why can't he do the same? (816–817)

457 *Go find somewhere else!* Literally, "Go off back again as to your foot to pasture." i.e., Go graze in some other pasture. To preclude contemporary misreadings of this idiomatic phrase (Aias is *not* dismissing Tekmessa as a metaphorical cow) the present translation cuts the line to its essence.

464 *noble goats* Literal translation. Aias, in the depths of self-degradation, has a heightened sense of the dignity of these animals.

522 *River Skamander* One of the two main rivers in the Troad, the area around Troy, which is today the northwestern part of Anatolia, Turkey.

522–523 *River Skamander, so kindly unkind / to all the Greeks* The Skamander's affective relation to the Greeks has been translated in mutually exclusive ways. Positive: (a) "so kindly to the Argives," (b) "kindly to the Greeks," (c) "Friendly

Skamander / river we love!" Negative: (a) "hostile to the Greeks," (b) "inimical to the Greeks," (c) "river that hates all Greeks." Yet another translation has it that the Skamander is "kinder to other Greeks" than it is to Aias himself. The present translation joins the difference—if only because, dramatically, it makes both objective and subjective sense. The Skamander has been "kindly unkind" in that it *is* the Skamander, the river of an enemy territory the Greeks are bogged down in, and yet the river *as* river has served them in various ways, not least as drinking water. Here the Skamander is the mirror in which Aias sees, memorializes, and takes leave of himself.

523 *this is one soldier* Speaking of himself in the third person, Aias already sees himself as a dead man.

533–539 Aiai! *My very name, Aias, / is a cry . . . my name in pieces* Much is made of Aias's name. Here he refers it back to AI, AI, the letters of lament marking the petals of the hyacinth, the flower that sprang from the blood of Hyacinthus, beloved of Apollo, when he was killed by the jealous wind god Zephyrus.

550 *procured them* He accuses Agamemnon and Menelaos of buying the votes by which Odysseus was awarded Achilles' armor.

555–556 hustled / *away from* Literally, "rushed away from." In being rushed away from his intended human targets, he has been hustled (rushed *plus* deceived, as in a scam) by Athena into attacking and destroying the war spoil of the Greeks.

558–559 *yet the stone-eyed / look of the unbending daughter of Zeus* Athena. Literally, "Gorgon-eyed." Whoever looked

on the Gorgon Medusa was turned to stone. "Unbending":
the Greek could read as "unconquerable" or "unwedded."

658 *When I had that... problem? Or what?* Aias and Tekmessa, usually so direct about their realities and anxieties,
tread lightly when referring to Eurysakes. Neither knows
how far Aias's madness might have taken him.

675–677 *trained / in the savage discipline... his nature* It's
customary to translate "savage discipline" euphemistically.
"Savage" becomes "rugged," "rough," or "harsh" and so
loses its edge. "Discipline" settles down into "ways." But
the Greek *ômos* means "savage," with all the rawness and
cruelty that word implies. And what are called "ways," as
though this were simply habitual, is the more purposeful
nomos. *Nomos* could mean "ways," but the greater part of
its semantic range is explicitly socially conditioned, referring
to law, custom (habitual or self-consciously chosen mores),
or rule. In a military context, it may refer to a discipline.
That Eurysakes must be broken in, "trained" to become as
his father, indicates that the warrior way of being is not simply a matter of temperament, nor something one happens to
fall into. In Aias's world, one is trained in a discipline until
it becomes his nature. That's why Aias can say to Tekmessa:
"Isn't it foolish to think / you can teach me, now, to change
my nature?" (738–739) The key word is "now."

729 *Don't worry at me!* Aias is *really* annoyed, hence the "at."
Originally, "worrying" was what dogs or wolves did to
sheep (from the Middle English *wirien*, to harass). In modern usage, "worry" in and of itself, without further emphasis, isn't strong enough to communicate the hair-trigger

intensity of Aias's reaction to Tekmessa's persistence in challenging him.

845 Ooo *I've got goose bumps; I'm so* The Greek describes "the prickling or shuddering of the flesh under strong emotion" followed by "the soaring effect of that emotion" (Garvie, 192).

861 *Ares dissolves his blood-dark threat!* Ares, the god of war, allows for peace when he ceases to destroy. The image is of a cloud-darkened sky breaking up.

865–866 *Aias . . . goes, in good faith* They think he will reaffirm the oath by which he committed himself to go to Troy, making a sacrifice to the gods. They do not anticipate that the sacrifice will be Aias himself.

894 *He wasn't to be let go out* The onus is on Aias's allies. Yet *any* attempt to restrain Aias from doing what he wants to do would be impossible to enforce.

945 *whose life is misery!* Cf. 637ff. Tekmessa: "All I have is you. With nowhere / to turn to. Backed by fate your spear . . ."

1006–1008 *the deathless virgins . . . the dread / ever-overtaking Furies* The Furies, or Erinyes. Goddesses of vengeance, relentless and merciless, who pursue justice not only through this world but on into the next. They are also called Eumenides, the Kindly Ones, either to mollify them or to acknowledge that by punishing offenses against the foundations of human society they become benefactors of society.

1015 *Helios, chariot wheels climbing the sky* The sun.

1069ff. *Nooo! We'll never get home!* The Chorus's first concern is how Aias's death will affect them. The same holds for everyone who has depended on Aias, including Tekmessa, when Aias is contemplating suicide, and Teukros, when he arrives on the scene of Aias's death. It testifies to the extraordinary web of relations and lives—including those of the Greek army and its commanders—that have depended on the towering figure of Aias.

1086 *the blood gasping up through his nostrils* Usually the blood is described as "spurting," i.e., pumped by the heart. But Aias is dead. His heart is stopped. The phrase must refer, then, to the postmortem pressure of gases and fluids set loose in the thorax as the body, on its own, resettles into itself. "Gasping" also intimates what expiring gases mingled with blood sound like. A related case has been made, on linguistic grounds, that the language here "resembles that at Aeschylus, Eumenides 248–9, where . . . Orestes, the prey of the Furies, gasps out his guts" (Garvie, 212).

1190 *the bastard of a captive girl* Teukros's mother was Hesione, the daughter of King Laomedon of Troy. Telamon 'won' her during the first Trojan war (1473–80).

1205–1206 *With the war belt / Aias gave him, Hektor was gripped* Reference to the customary reciprocity of gifts, including between enemies. In this version of the story, which differs from that in Homer, Hektor was tied to his chariot by Achilles (using the war belt Aias had given Hektor) and dragged to death. Now Aias has met his own death on the sword given him by Hektor.

1259–1262 *But in a city of no respect, just / insolence and willfulness . . . Fear is in order.* Menelaos's prescript for effective governance, and his attitude toward the *demôs*, is that of an oligarch.

1270–1272 *You've set down right-minded precepts . . . outraging the dead.* Menelaos has said the right thing, but in leaving Aias's corpse unburied he violates his own precepts.

1292–1293 *because of an oath . . . shell of a man.* See *Philoktetes*, 81–82.

1300 *The archer, far from blood dust, thinks he's something* Archery was considered less honorable than front line fighting with a sword or spear—though this attitude had less to do with military effectiveness than with 'class' distinctions. Frequently archers were archers (or slingers) because they couldn't afford hoplite armor. They were social inferiors (Hanson, 149). "The Scythian archers who formed the police force were slaves" (Garvie, 227). Eventually archers and cavalry became more decisive than hoplites, who with their breastplates, shields, and tight formations were too ponderous and inflexible to cope with ambushes or shifts in the direction of battle.

1301 *I'm very good at what I do* Discussed in the General Introduction, p. xx.

1350ff. *Press your hand on him, clutching locks of hair* As suppliants under the protection of Zeus, the boy and his mother will be safe. The dead Aias, "a few moments ago . . . so helpless, is now, even before he is buried, in a position to protect his dependents" even as they protect him (Garvie, 231). It is most telling that Eurysakes, who has been named after his father's shield, effectively *becomes* his father's shield, but in a way that Aias himself could not have envisioned. They form a telling tableau of survival based on interdependence—Eurysakes,

Tekmessa, Teukros, and the remains of Aias, in concert with Zeus—as distinguished from the old, now obsolete model whereby the survival of all depended on one towering, heroic individual.

1372–1373 *who taught Greeks / to combine forces* Not an imprecation against war in general, but against what Jebb calls "public war" (179), implicitly contrasting this with tribal or *polis* wars, essentially defensive wars fought largely on home or neighboring grounds. The Trojan War, however, involves an alliance among different Greek entities to fight an expeditionary war under a semiautonomous military command that is neither tribe- nor *polis*-based. This alliance, whereby the Greeks have been taught "how to league in war" (Lloyd-Jones, 143), more nearly resembles the organization of modern international warfare. The Greek "league" as presented in the *Iliad* is relatively primitive and ad hoc, based largely on opportunism, oaths, and standing allegiances to lords. Actual fifth-century alliances were nearer our own, but they were not, as in our own time, bureaucratized and 'legalized.' There is *no* qualitative comparison with present-day NATO—which, with its power to call upon the military forces of numerous, far-flung countries, is the global apotheosis of a composite expeditionary force. Nonetheless a rough comparison does throw light on the *specificity* of the Greek warriors' concerns.

1418 *a clear majority* Given the assumption that the vote was rigged, this may be a reminder that even a hands-on electoral republic (by implication Athens itself) is susceptible to bribery and other manipulation. A *dêmokratia* is no guarantee that power will reside in the hands of the *dêmos* (the common people).

1424 *but those with brains* i.e., Odysseus.

1463–1472 *Where are you looking? at what . . . in the silence of fishes* Pelops came from Phrygia, which is part of Troy. It therefore follows that Agamemnon, who is related to the enemy Trojans, is himself a barbarian. Agamemnon's father, Atreus, on discovering his wife had committed adultery with his brother, Thyestes, invited Thyestes to a banquet at which he fed Thyestes his own sons. The father of Agamemnon's mother (Aerope, from Crete) caught her with a slave lover. He sent her to King Nauplius to be drowned. She was spared, however, and (as we are now reminded) lived to be Agamemnon's mother.

1488 *Or was it your brother's wife?* Helen. Teukros either pretends he doesn't know or care which wife has been the cause of this war, or he insinuates that Agamemnon as well as Menelaos has bedded Helen. Either way, the insult may not be casual. If Helen is truly the cause of this war, she's not a valid nor a sufficient one.

WOMEN OF TRAKHIS

1 *saying* Herodotus (20–21) attributes the saying to Solon.

9 *Pleuron* A town in Aetolia over which Oeneus, Deianeira's father, was a powerful lord.

12 *a river lusted for me* The word *potamos* connotes both river and river god.

13 *Achelous* A river, still the mightiest in Greece and now called the Aspropotamo (White River), that has its source in the Pindus Mountains of northern Greece and flows to the Ionian Sea.

15 *each time in a different shape* This creature who can change its shape was represented in Greek art, notably on red-figured vases. Each of the three shapes has a man's face and beard attached to an animal body, in the same way a centaur does.

23 *son of Alkmene and Zeus* See introduction to play (p. 99) for Herakles' lineage and history.

30 *Zeus the battle god* From *agonios* "decider of the contest"— "an epithet applied to any of the gods who presided over [athletic] games" (Easterling 1982, 76). Boxing matches were held in honor of the river god in this part of Greece. Sophocles may be alluding to this here.

39 *sowing his seed, reaping the harvest* "Sowing" (*speiron*) is appropriate to describe the reproductive activity of both farmer and father.

41 *this one man* Deianeira refuses to use his name, because of the role this man plays in her continuing misery. He is Eurystheus, the king of Argos, who was charged with assigning Herakles his canonical twelve labors.

44 *Iphitus* Herakles killed Iphitus, the son of Eurytus, by sneaking up behind him and hurling him off a cliff, as punishment for Eurytus, who had banished the drunken Herakles from his house.

61 *Hyllos* The eldest of Herakles and Deianeira's four sons.

76 *Lydian woman* Queen Omphale. As punishment for deceitfully killing Iphitus, Zeus assigned Herakles to work for her for one year, with payment going to Eurytus.

82 *Eurytus* Ruler of Euboea.

85 *prophecies* Deianeira's memory has been stirred by the word "Euboea," since that is the place referred to (in the prophecies she's about to recall) as the site of Herakles' final combat.

103 *Chorus* A group of local women arrive singing an "entry song," a fixture in Greek plays that serves many purposes. Here it allows the women to state their concern for the welfare of both Herakles and Deianeira and to speculate on their difficulties.

114 *Alkmene's child* Herakles was born in Thebes but was not a descendant of Kadmos, since he was fathered by Zeus with Amphytrion's wife, Alkmene.

158 *Bear* The constellation we call Ursa Major. The Greeks animated the skies with mythological figures, human and animal, each with its own story. Because of their seasonal migrations ("starpaths") across the sky, constellations became a reliable source of information about seasonal change, including sowing and harvest times. The more fixed stars provided guidance for both sailors and foot travelers.

175–177 *thrive . . . glory* A young girl's life is here implicitly compared to the life of a delicate plant whose seclusion protects it from harsh weather.

186 *message carved on wood* This tablet was first mentioned at 51 and contains prophecies, written out by Herakles, that will be elaborated later in the play.

193 *widow's share* Deianeira's dowry, which would return to her at Herakles' death, together with any other property he has given to her during their marriage. His specific bequests

to her and their children were not inscribed on the tablet, but relayed orally to Deianeira when he explained the prophecies on it.

196–197 *fifteen / months* The exact figure for Herakles' current absence is significant because it ominously matches precisely the frightening prediction that he will either die or live on in peace after this date. The play's action takes place at this critical juncture, and both prophecies do come true.

203–205 *ancient oak . . . sibyls* Prophecies rendered by the oracle of Dodona originated in the rustling leaves of an oak tree, and were interpreted into Greek words by the shrine's two priestesses. The word I translate as "sibyls" is actually *peleiadon*, meaning "doves." Some scholars believe Sophocles used the word *peleiadon* simply as an affectionate alternative nickname for the priestesses; other scholars contend that he meant "doves" literally. If the latter is true, the doves would then need to somehow pass on the prophecy to the sibyls. To further complicate matters, very early texts imply that the trees' rustlings could be heard as actual human speech. Since a person would be needed to interpret what the leaves and/or the birds were trying to communicate, I've cut this particular Gordian tangle by calling the final interpreters "sibyls."

221 *laurel flowers* A crown of laurel leaves announced that a person was bringing good news.

243 *Malia* The plain between the rocky promontory, under the mountains on which the town of Trakhis sits, and the Gulf of Malia. The Malians on the plain below have swarmed around Likhas, who is bringing news of Herakles.

255ff. *Let the house* The Trakhinian women invite the men and women in the house and from the neighborhood to join them in a song to celebrate Herakles' imminent return. In the original production, singing extras might have arrived onstage to join the Chorus.

262 *Apollo* A god who has multiple functions; here he is, appropriately enough, addressed as the "protector of roads."

268–271 *Artemis . . . quail* Artemis is given the epithet here of *Ortigyian,* which refers to her association with quails and islands named for quails. Since quails were believed to be excellent mothers, the epithet may have to do with Artemis as the goddess of childbirth. There is no certain explanatory translation. Since all the actions proposed for gods in this ode are athletic, happen outdoors, and are exuberant, the chorus would think it natural to address her as Ortigyian while she hunts deer.

277 *I'm soaring!* The sudden shift from first person plural to first person singular signals an inrush of Bakkhic spirit as the choristers praise and call upon the god of ecstasy. In ancient productions, these words could be sung in unison— as one—which would reflect a principle of Dionysiac religion: that a group filled with the spirit of Bakkhos feels itself united within the body of the god.

280–286 *Ivy . . . Bakkhos!* As Jebb (1882) so lucidly explains: The "Trachinian maidens imagine themselves to be bacchanals; the music of the [flute] suggests the spell of the [ivy]: and they speak as if the ivy on their brows was sending its mystic power through their whole frames, stirring them to the dance."

305 *Euboea* Large island off the coast of Trakhis.

310 *the vow* Herakles had either made a prior vow before attacking Eurytus' city, or was acting on the advice of an oracle that told him it was prudent to make a sacrifice to Zeus and set up a shrine to him after plundering it.

326 *Omphale* According to a complex arrangement commanded by Zeus, Omphale paid Eurytus for Herakles' services.

339 *arrows* Theocritos (24, 106ff.) wrote that Eurytus taught Herakles to use a bow. If so, it would make sense that as a novice archer, Herakles had trouble besting Eurytus' well-schooled archer sons. The arrows Herakles was using were presumed to be unerring because Apollo provided them. Perhaps the arrows could not maintain their accuracy if the shooter was intoxicated, as Herakles evidently was while Eurytus' guest.

360 *Gods don't appreciate insolence* The gods' lack of appreciation for insolence (or hubris) applies to both Herakles and Eurytus.

384 *Zeus . . . battles* The most appropriate god to invoke here, since he was responsible for the plight of slaves.

DEIANEIRA approaches Iole. Iole is the daughter of Eurytus and the sister of Iphitus.

433 *it was Love* Eros the love god dominated Herakles at this moment, not, for instance, Ares the war god.

582–585 *Hades . . . Zeus . . . Kronos . . . Poseidon* Kronos is the father of Hades (the ruler of the underworld), Zeus (god of the sky and the ruler of Olympus), and Poseidon (god of the sea).

653 *Nessus* A famous centaur well known to be an exceptionally violent member of his species.

656 *Evenus* A fierce swift mountain river that has its source on Oita's western slope, from which it flows into the Gulf of Korinth.

669 *Hydra of Lerna* A snake with many heads, all of which regenerated as soon as Herakles cut them off. Lerna was the swamp in which the Hydra lived.

678 *rash acts* Here a twinge of conscience is fused with self-justification, enabling Sophocles to suggest the irony of Deianeira's action. She boasts that unlike some women, who maliciously harm a rival or a spouse, all she does is find a benign way to heighten Herakles' desire for her. Far from benign, her way will prove more deadly than malice.

717 *Hermes' craft* The messenger's craft: to deliver messages promptly, securely, and without garbling them.

730 *All of you living* The beat of the song and the instruments should be appropriately joyful.

756 *twelve months* Actually, according to Deianiera, they've been waiting fifteen months. An unaccountable mistake.

773 *power which burns* The text seems very likely corrupt here. I rely on Haupt's conjecture, *pharos* replacing the text's *theros*, which would correct the literal meaning of the phrase at issue to mean "on the pretext of the robe." Jebb interprets this phrase to mean that the *robe* was the *pretext* for using the love-charm (*pharmakon*) (Jebb 1882, 103). Whatever word Sophocles actually used here, the Chorus is focused on the artificial (chemical) *power to persuade* now inherent in the robe. The somewhat strained syntax and vocabulary of 660–662 hints that Sophocles sought to fuse metaphorically the lethal and burning properties of Nessus' poison with the warm intimate hopes of Deianeira.

775 *Persuasion* The Chorus invokes the goddess who gets people to do what they're reluctant to do.

803 *the moment it's smeared on* Deianeira omits mention of Herakles as the ultimate target for the potion; similarly, at 38, she neglects to name Eurytus.

874 *flawless bulls* To honor a god properly, at least twelve of the animals must be in prime condition.

876 *hundred animals* A hecatomb was a standard number of bulls used to complete a festival. Hyllos is guessing here, not counting.

880 *resin-soaked pine logs* Heat and sweat were required to activate the poison, hence both Nessus and Deianeira's specific instructions; Herakles was accustomed to following orders precisely.

920 *Vengeance and the Furies* Hyllos invokes the god of justice and the Furies because he believes his mother has committed an act of kin murder, the sentence for which is death. Significantly, Hyllos does not immediately carry out the punishment, but waits for her response, which comes not in words but in walking away. When she leaves the stage, the curse he actually delivers is simply that she suffer.

DEIANEIRA . . . walks toward the house without a word It was a convention of Athenian drama that a character intending to commit suicide would not respond to the speech or circumstances that provoked the decision.

935ff. *O sisters* The function of this chorus is to tie up loose ends and make deductions. The singers trace the guilt of Herakles' death all the way back to the Hydra and the centaur he killed; Deianeira is absolved in their minds; they sympathize in retrospect with her resort to the deadly charm, which they had approved when she asked them if they thought it was a good idea. They also correctly interpret the prophecy that had stumped Herakles. Their final casting of blame is upon the Cyprian, or Aphrodite, who, far from the hideous scene to come, caused it.

938 *twelfth year* Herakles' death occurs during the twelfth year following the oracle of Dodona's prophecy.

1085 *nightingale's voice* The bird who gives voice to irremediable harm and grief.

1155 *Athena* Pallas Athena, who during Herakles' lifetime was his mentor and protector.

1176–1177 *this net / of the Furies* A net was the Greeks' all-purpose image for a situation from which there is no escape. Herakles imagines that Hades and the Furies have made this net because (as Easterling 1982, 206, suggests) it puts him in the same class with Aias, who was killed with Hector's sword, forged by the same infernal prayer to be irresistible.

1187 *army of giants* Herakles fought against the giants on the side of the gods. His recounting of his many battles in which he was on the side of civilization and its hierarchies serves to declare his grievances against those who suddenly have abandoned him and to reassure himself of his own value.

1320–1321 *Now hear . . . prophecy / makes sense* The reader and audience will have grasped the sense in which both prophecies summarized earlier in the play have proven true. Herakles will be freed into peacefulness by his own death.

1375 *If burning me appalls you, do the rest* For a Greek to kill his own father, even as an act commanded by the father, would pollute the son irreparably. Thus Herakles agrees not to force Hyllos to build the fire or light it. Beyond the scope

of the play, as we learn in *Philoktetes*, it was Philoktetes who
set Herakles' pyre burning.

1392 *Marry her. Agree to it* As J. C. Kamerbeek puts it: "It
is in keeping with this unhuman or superhuman character
[Herakles] . . . for whom nothing is of any interest except
his own glorious deeds, his own excessive desires and his
divine descent that he requires his son to comply with this
shocking wish" (247).

1437–1450 *But look at the cruelty . . . you've seen nothing that
is not Zeus* Many scholars, wishing to protect both the reputations of Zeus and Sophocles, have pointed out that with
the reckless impiety of Hyllos' speech, Sophocles intended to
attribute Hyllos' sentiments to his youth and his grief. But
Hyllos shows intelligence and courage in resisting his father
to the extent he does. Sophocles carries his characterization
of Herakles and Zeus to the logical conclusion voiced by
Hyllos.

PHILOKTETES

NEOPTOLEMOS Son of Achilles. A neophyte, new to war
and to the world.

2 *Lemnos* Lemnos, as staged, is desolate, though historically
the island was inhabited. Here the fable-like setting, unclut-
tered by the lumber of insignificant descriptive detail, allows
the psychological and physiological drama to be projected
with near hallucinatory clarity. It deepens Philoktetes' iso-
lation from the world—cut off not only from human com-
panionship, but from human history. With Neoptolemos's
arrival, however, he is plunged back into the midst of both.

5–7 *as you're truly the son / of Achilles . . . listen to me* Odysseus uses Neoptolemos's pedigree as a 'hook' to enlist him in a scheme that contradicts everything his breeding stands for. (There's no "as" or "listen to me" in the Greek. This is a framing device, signaling that Odysseus's studied identification of Neoptolemos is not 'dead exposition' for an audience needing background information. Rather, the passage has a dramatic function that an ancient Greek audience, unlike a modern one, would have recognized without prompting. It is directed at Neoptolemos himself—to get him to associate this questionable undertaking with the heroic legacy of his father, Achilles.)

9 *the Malian, son of Poias* Philoktetes' lineage confirms his nobility. Malis is under Mount Oita, where Philoktetes, in an act of mercy, put the torch to Herakles' funeral pyre.

10 *under orders from the chiefs* Odysseus cites extenuating circumstances to explain away his past abandonment of Philoktetes. He was acting under orders. Philoktetes' odor and screams were unbearable to the army, they interfered with religious rituals, etc.

19–20 *my scheme / to take him is wasted* The Odysseus of the post–Homeric Epic Cycle, unlike the Odysseus of Homer, is known for his cunning and unscrupulousness. This negative portrayal extends into the classical era of Sophocles' own time. The exemplary Odysseus of *Aias*—who averts, if he does not resolve, the highly charged sociopolitical impasse dramatized in that play—is a rare exception.

21 *it's your job to help me carry this out* Odysseus, tightening his grip on Neoptolemos, lets the young man know he's not

a fellow-warrior on a mission but a subordinate under military command.

50 *scrounging for food* The Greek phrase implies that Philoktetes forages for food more like an animal than a human being.

51 *Send your man to watch out* The unseen sailor who trailed them as they made their way up the cliff.

60 *Some plan you haven't heard yet* Having positioned Neoptolemos to do what he (thought he) would never do, Odysseus keeps drawing the young man in, by stages deepening his involvement.

65 *reach into his soul. / Take it!* A literal translation. This is well-designed to appeal to Neoptolemos. Even as it counters his putative ethic of always acting 'aboveboard,' rhetorically it is pitched to his instinctive tendency, as a young and eager warrior, to *act*.

70 *they'd begged you, prayed you, to leave your home* "They" are Odysseus and Phoinix.

71 *you were their only hope of taking Troy* What Odysseus has not said, yet, is that as much as they need Neoptolemos, they also need Philoktetes and the bow given to him by Herakles.

74–75 *Instead / they handed them over to* Odysseus Cf. *Aias*.

81–82 You *didn't / come to Troy bound by an oath* Unlike Philoktetes, Odysseus did not go to Troy voluntarily. He and other suitors of Helen were bound by an oath to her father, Tyndareus, to help her husband (who has turned out to be Menelaos) if she were seduced or abducted by another man. When Helen went off with Paris, Odysseus did everything he could to avoid going to war. He pretended to be mad, harnessing a donkey and an ox—which have different stride lengths—to his plow. But when the Greeks put his young son Telemachus in front of the plow, Odysseus veered to save him, proving his sanity. The irony of Odysseus the conscript coming to dragoon Philoktetes, who had volunteered to fight in the war, is not incidental. Resolutions in this world, as in ours, are not necessarily nor even ordinarily based on what is fair or just. As mandated by Herakles, the demands of a temporal justice based on the individual must be set aside when the enduring good of the collectivity is at stake. What's more, this will benefit the individual as well. (e.g., The 'good' Odysseus in *Aias* insists that even though Aias has been an enemy, he should be given a proper burial. Because, as Odysseus says: "One day I will have the same need.")

90 *O . . . I know, it's not like you* Odysseus knows the still-green Neoptolemos inside out. That will change, however, as Neoptolemos, getting a 'crash course' experience of the world from Philoktetes, becomes more complex and less predictable.

94–95 *Give yourself . . . one short, shameless / stretch of day* Having drawn Neoptolemos this far in, rather than mask or excuse the shamelessness of the deception, Odysseus flaunts it—but speaks as though the shamelessness could be limited to the duration of the act itself.

96–97 *Then, forever after . . . the very soul of honor* A cynical rationale informed by considerable realism and truth. The capture of Troy could well 'put paid' any lingering sense of shame.

99–100 *It's not in me . . . in my father* Neoptolemos's certainty of his own rectitude comes not from experience but confidence in his breeding.

105–106 *I'd rather do / what's right, and fail* As Neoptolemos's idealistic, untested morality teeters amidst the complexity and confusion of life-in-the-world, his moral posture grows increasingly assertive and abstract.

110–111 *learned it's words / that move people, not deeds* A scholiast (an ancient interpreter of classical texts) identified this as a slander directed against contemporary Athenian politicians.

118 *Arrows definite as the death they deliver* Sophocles reproduces the Homeric tendency to 'personify' weapons as though they were self-acting. This short, sharp exchange between Odysseus and Neoptolemos is an instance of *stichomythia*, a technique for increasing dramatic intensity by assigning alternating lines or 'rows' of speech to two characters, often with the alternating lines linked by a single word. (Neoptolemos: "Won't the *look* on my face give me away?" Odysseus: "*Look* to what's in it for you.")

122–123 *Not if lying gets us through this / dragged-out war* Literally, "Not if the lie brings deliverance." This is not about deliverance in general, however, but about breaking the specific impasse the Homeric Greeks have found themselves at. Fifth-century Greeks would have had that impasse (we'd use metaphors such as 'bogged down' or 'quagmire') firmly in mind. It's less likely that modern audiences will have a comparable awareness.

128 *not going to take Troy? Like you said?* Plural "you." Cf. 390–391.

135–136 *what I told you then? Understood? . . . I've said
I would* This is the only place where Sophocles uses end
rhyme to close off a passage of *stichomythia*. Odysseus is
making sure that Neoptolemos understands not only what
he's supposed to do, but its implications.

146–148 *May Hermes . . . Defender of Athens* Hermes, the god
who speeds things along, is also associated with thievery
and deception. Athena, the patron of Odysseus, is identified
here as Athena Polias (the Defender of Athens). Sophocles
invokes Athena's relationship to Athens to link *Odysseus*
with Athens—thus reconceiving him, anachronistically, as
a representative of the Athenian polity. Homer's Odysseus
had no relation to Athens. This then is a critical political
interpolation by Sophocles.

160–161 You, *still in youth, / have had this passed down to you*
"The whole ancestral power of Achilles' family" is now in
the hands of Neoptolemos (Webster, 80).

187 *I feel sorry for him* Here the sailors feel for Philoktetes.
Yet when he's lying helpless, they'll be eager to capture
him. This doesn't mean they're self-contradictory or insincere. They feel what they're free to feel, or what their own
interests compel them to feel, depending on what the moment and the circumstances allow for.

203 *dappled or shaggy beasts* Someone has remarked on Sophocles' "careful imprecision." The "beasts" could be spotted
deer and shaggy goats, but we'll never know. Nor should
we. We're not supposed to get caught up in such details.
Sophocles, having another order of 'truth' in view, needs

to keep the fabulous or otherworldly aspect of Lemnos—
it's so *purely* what it is—intact.

206–208 *Echo . . . crying back at him his own crying* Rather
than lessen his solitude, Echo compounds it.

211 *the vicious Chrysē* The serpent guarding the shrine of
Chrysē, an obscure, localized deity, has bitten and infected
Philoktetes. The gods allowed this to happen, but only to
put off the destined fall of Troy until the time was right.
Foreknowledge of this comes from Helenos, the Trojan seer
captured by Odysseus.

214 *his almighty bow* The bow Herakles gave Philoktetes.

242 *this desolate island* In the plays (now lost) that Aeschylus
and Euripides wrote about Philoktetes, the island was inhabited. The choruses were made up of Lemnians.

249 *if you really come as friends* Time and again Philoktetes'
desperate hopes for deliverance are hedged by his own justi-
fiable suspicions.

269 *your grandfather Lykomedes* Neoptolemos's grandfather
on his mother's side.

281 *Not one word of me abandoned here* A crushing blow to
his pride as a warrior.

287–288 *my disease / flourishes its worst, and spreads* As is
typical of Philoktetes, he conceives his disease as having a
life of its own.

293 *two commanders and Odysseus* The Greek text doesn't
name Odysseus but refers to him by his title: Lord of Kephallenia. The island of Kephallenia was part of Odysseus's
domain.

296–297 *vicious . . . vicious* The repetition occurs in the original text. The story itself needed no elaboration, as the audience would have been familiar with it.

298 *Sickness I was left alone with* Another 'personification,' or
self-acting entity.

305–306 *some rags . . . Me too they left* Implicitly equating
Philoktetes with the rags.

319–320 *I made do / myself. Had to.* Philoktetes is a lord, not a
generic warrior. He was not prepared, emotionally or prac-
tically, to live a 'make-do' life. His hands are made for his
bow, not for menial nor craft work. e.g., His wooden cup is
"rough, poorly made."

368 *You said it, boy!* "Philoktetes, excited by the boy's words,
turns colloquial. The exclamation . . . does not recur [in the
canon of classical tragedies]" (Ussher, 122).

387 *the great Odysseus* Sarcastic, in keeping with Odysseus's
instructions to say "anything you want about me. Nothing's
too nasty" (76).

395–396 *I wanted so to see my father / unburied* Neoptolemos,
born the day Achilles left for Troy, has never seen his father.

397 *Then too, they promised me* Neoptolemos's ambition for
success as a warrior never leaves him. Herakles in his part-
ing words will allude to this.

401 *still painful Sigeion* "Painful" because it's where he first
landed at Troy. The soldiers crowding round, swearing that
in Neoptolemos "the dead Achilles lived again," brought
home to him the *felt* reality of his father's death.

431–433 *An army, like a city, depends . . . from their leaders* Popular wisdom cast as a *gnōmē*, a moral aphorism or

proverb. N.B. Homilies or 'old sayings' crop up from time to time, especially among the Chorus. The *dramatic* utility of this maxim, as distinguished from its substance, is that it's canned. It serves as a convenient device for Neoptolemos to put the minefield of his improvised story behind him—to seal it off with a truism, thus precluding further discussion or questioning. As with any drama, it's necessary to recognize not only what is said, but what the saying is *doing*. In dramatic as in social context, even a cliché may reveal something having little or nothing to do with its ostensible meaning. This particular *gnōmē* may have an extratheatrical function as well. According to Jebb: "This play was brought out in the spring of 409 B.C. The Revolution of the Four Hundred in the summer of 411 B.C. was emphatically a case in which Peisander and his fellow oligarchs had corrupted or intimidated the polis. Thus, to the ears of an Athenian audience, [Sophocles'] verses might well suggest a lightly-hinted apology for those citizens who, against their will, had been compromised by the conspirators" (1898, 69–70). When we put all this together, Neoptolemos's patchwork 'saying' becomes rich soil indeed.

436–442 *Goddess of Mountains . . . Wondrous Mother* The Chorus invokes a goddess who has the features of Mother Earth and Kybele, "a Phrygian goddess identified with the Greek Rhea, mother of Zeus" (Schein, 37). Effectively, the sailors, with their invocation of the goddess and their criticism of the sons of Atreus, are lending atmospheric support to Neoptolemos's deception.

467 *the bastard Sisyphos begot then sold to Laertes* Sisyphos was notorious for his cunning. Anticleia, made pregnant by

Sisyphos, was carrying Odysseus when Laertes bought her with 'many gifts.'

471 *Nestor of Pylos* King of Pylos. His son, Antilochos, was a leading warrior and a friend of Achilles.

483 *Patroklos* Achilles' lover. He was killed by Hektor, who was in turn killed by Achilles.

487–488 *war doesn't single out evil men, but in general kills the good* A common saying.

493 *Thersites* An ugly, lame, quarrelsome man who reputedly taunted Achilles, who then killed him. In the *Iliad*, as a self-appointed representative of the *dêmos*, the common people, Thersites is a caricature. There he's pitted against Odysseus, who embodies the dominant monarchic/aristocratic order and perspective informing the *Iliad* (Cartledge, 33–37).

499–500 *keeping / the slick smooth ones out of Hades* e.g., Sisyphos.

507 *O son of an Oitan father* Reminder of Philoktetes' link to Herakles.

513 *rockbound Skyros* Neoptolemos's home island.

547 *Chalkedon in Euboea* A contemporary of Philoktetes' father, Poias.

570–571 *if it were me I'd turn / their evils to his advantage* Even as the Chorus gives Neoptolemos (sometimes impassioned) advice, the sailors are not about to press the matter. After all, he's still their master.

585–587 *Just pray . . . wherever we're going* The indefinition of Neoptolemos's "wherever" does double duty: it allows him to avoid being presumptuous, which would offend the gods, and it allows Philoktetes to persist in the delusion that they're going to take him home.

MERCHANT The charade orchestrated by Odysseus to hasten Philoktetes' departure from the island. In this play-within-a-play-within-a-play, the fake merchant speaks in a progressively 'confidential' tone, whereas Neoptolemos, playing to Philoktetes, grows louder and louder.

605–606 *vineyards / of Peparethos* A small island famous for its wine. The 'Merchant' supplies wine to the Greek forces at the siege of Troy. He'll peddle anything to anyone, wine or information, provided there's money in it. This gives the faux merchant an air of authenticity. Possibly it gave the audience a bit of extracurricular amusement as well.

617 *and the sons of Theseus* Theseus was the legendary founder of Athens. Akamas and Demophon, his sons, are obscure figures known mainly from post-Homeric poems about the sack of Troy. They do not appear in the *Iliad*. But then, *all* male Athenians are in a sense 'sons of Theseus.' This seemingly offhand allusion is one of many intimations or reminders that *Philoktetes* is, among other things—and especially as regards the ethos of Odysseus—also a comment on contemporary Athens.

630–631 *a man who . . . but first, who is that over there?* An interruption intended to rekindle Philoketes' fears and hasten his departure from Lemnos.

682 *That bottomless pit of a man* Literally, "that utter devil" (Ussher, 61) or "utter plague" (Lloyd-Jones, 315) or something on the order of "he's a complete loss" (Webster, 108). The Greek is an abusive phrase that Ussher (131) thinks may

be colloquial, though it seems not to exist in Greek comedy. The problem is that ritual imprecations such as these can't be taken seriously. "Bottomless pit" is, then, a shot in the dark of Hades—which Odysseus's father, Sisyphos, had already tested to its limits (see below).

683–687 *He'd persuade me . . . to rise . . . like his own father did* The dying Sisyphos instructed his wife not to bury him. When he arrived in the underworld, he asked that Hades return him to earth—to punish her for not doing her duty and burying him. Hades consented, and Sisyphos returned to the world until fate in the guise of Necessity (*anangke*) put him under for good.

713 *To tame this vicious wound* Philoktetes regards the wound as a wild beast (Ussher, 132). That is, he objectifies the wound by 'animating' but *not* anthropomorphizing it. The wound remains 'other.' This is not so with personification as we ordinarily, and correctly, understand that term: as a means of appropriating or absorbing what is 'other,' or projecting that 'other' as an expression of one's self.

740–741 *Whoever knows how to pay back / kindness* A *gnōmē* or maxim.

746–747 *the man who tried to slip into / Zeus' wife's bed* As punishment for his grievous violation of the laws of hospitality, Ixion was bound forever to a wheel of fire.

790–791 *will bring him to his own / ancestral home* They feel for Philoktetes in his misery, yet embellish the deception that Neoptolemos will return him to his home in Oita.

793–796 *bronze-shielded Herakles / rose in flames . . . high above Oita* Cf. *Women of Trakhis.*

832 *this wandering disease* Literally, "wanderer": an ancient medical term for intermittent fever (Ussher, 136).

856–857 *wherever / the heavens send us* Again, Neoptolemos's piety hides his purposeful ambiguity. He knows full well where 'the heavens' are sending them.

869 *Oooodysseus, my friend* Odysseus is not named in the Greek text, where he's called "the Kephallenian."

884 *Lemnian fire* Mount Mosychlos, associated with Hephestos.

889 *Where are you?* Literally, "Where are you [in your thinking]?" The "where" is idiomatic, as in "Where're you at?" or "Where's your mind at?" Compare this with the exchange (997–1000) that begins when Philoktetes, troubled that a suddenly disoriented Neoptolemos has started talking to himself, asks: "Where're you getting at?" At that juncture the highly adaptable, idiomatic "where" metamorphoses into a revelatory road metaphor.

898 *Not that I'd ask you to swear to that* Philoktetes is not asking for a solemn oath but simply a "hand pledge" or handshake. Cf. 900: "Your hand on that! Give it."

902–904 *Now. Up there. Take me . . . Up up . . .* Apparently referring to the volcano, Mount Mosychlos. In his agony, Philoktetes wants, like Herakles, to be consumed by fire.

910 *You'll kill me holding me like that* This is resonant given Sophocles' hands-on involvement in medicine and practical health care. But the full implications of these words, their 'teaching message,' are not exhausted by their use in a medical context. Clearly, it is necessary but not sufficient to do

the right thing. It must also be done *in the right way*. So Herakles, later, not only predicts that Neoptolemos and Philoktetes will take Troy but also warns that they must do it in the proper way: "with piety toward all things / relating to the gods."

914 *sleep will grip him soon* Another 'personification.' Note that the onset of sleep, unlike sleep itself, has a preemptive character. Neoptolemos characterizes it as an *event*. This differs markedly from the Chorus's softer-edged evocation of sleep as a beatific state of being.

919–926 *Sweet sleep that feels . . . Come* Lullaby. Sleep identified as a healing agent.

923 *this most serene glow* The daughter of Asklepios, the god of healing, is Aigla, the "gleam of serenity" that healing brings.

930–932 *The Right Moment is . . . victory* A common saying. It's not that they don't feel for Philoktetes, they do, but they have a task to accomplish. N.B. Though the sailors serve under Neoptolemos, they will on occasion question or (obliquely) correct him. Unlike soldiers in modern military structures, they have a complex historical relation to their lord, including as retainers. They do not operate, as is the norm now, within a relatively freestanding, codified chain of command.

935 *He's the victory trophy* Neoptolemos must bring not only the bow but Philoktetes himself back to Troy.

940 *sick men sleep sleepless, they pick up on things* Literal: "all men's sleep is keen of sight in sickness" (Ussher, 39).

947–956 *But now, my boy, the wind . . . quickly, without warning* As conceived in this translation, the Chorus is a collectivity in which several voices, at times with individual inflections, express common perspectives or concerns. e.g., The voice coming from the Chorus in 952 ("Strengthless he is, like one laid at the edge of Hades") is different from that of the practical-minded Leader. The same sententious voice is heard in 195–197 ("Dark are the doings of the gods . . . short of their doom"). Not that these distinctions need be observed, but in contemporary (maskless) production they're available as a dramatic resource.

969–970 *you're / naturally noble* Belief in the efficacy of breeding, or bloodline, is a given.

1036 *you filthy piece of work!* Literal: "you contrivance of villainy" (Ussher, 142).

1093–1094 *You learned this / from truly evil teachers* Cf. Neoptolemos' words at 430–433.

1099–1101 *You won't get back / here and / give me that bow?* A negative future question posed as a command. The phrasing reflects a common Greek construction. The difficulty, in English, is in keeping it from sounding like a plea. It may help to deliver 1100–1101 in a heavy-footed way, hence the gaps between the words.

1116 *Let that man drag me off?* Emphasis to indicate that "drag" is literal, not metaphorical. Philoktetes will be forced, not led, away.

1119–1121 *ZEUS rules . . . I carry out his orders* That Odysseus is cynical doesn't preclude his having beliefs. "Odysseus—whatever his interpretation of it—is concerned to bring a prophecy, in which he believes, to fulfillment" (Ussher, 145).

1140–1142 *hands . . . now / together, held helpless* His hands are held down by the guards on either side of him.

1225 *The two of us* Neoptolemos speaking as though he and Odysseus were still of one mind in this mission.

1233–1234 *O forlorn space, all echoed up / reeking with my pain* The Greek mingles "both the groaning and the stench" (Webster, 136).

1372 *would you be so* kind *as to say* why Aggressive (faux) politeness.

1404 *You will be* Odysseus's line has been lost. "You will be" is the translator's interpolation.

1418 *But you, son of Poias* Removed, awkward phrasing. Neoptolemos is apprehensive, uncertain what reception he'll get.

1523 *And O my eyes* Literally, "orbs." In the remarkable phrase of T. B. L. Webster: "The lonely man's eyes have a life of their own . . ." (152).

1532–1534 *Men whose souls / have conceived, once . . . evils* Another *gnōmē*.

1562 *You, I should imagine* Neoptolemos "dismisses the question (with light irony) as one that cannot seriously be intended" (Ussher, 160).

1595–1596 *Not till you've heard / what* I *will say* As Herakles speaks from a cultural and historical context that is fundamental, and more comprehensive, than any contained within personal or otherwise partial perspectives, his word is authoritative.

1619 *spoils such as common soldiers get* See introduction to this play (187).

1631ff. *Yet remember, when / you sack Troy show piety* Implicitly, though unmistakably, an admonition to Neoptolemos.

1669–1670 *the god . . . subduing everything* Zeus.

1673 *the nymphs of the sea* The Nereids, patrons of sailors and fishermen.

ELEKTRA

6–13 *Hallowed country . . . house of Pelops* The Elder quickly evokes legendary and contemporary Argos and Mycenae, and the horrific legacy of the house of Pelops and Atreus. His is not a guidebook's pinpointing of sights, but an evocative gathering of legendary aspects of Mycenae.

7 *horsefly hounded Io* Zeus seduced Io, whereupon Zeus' wife Hera turned her into a cow and arranged to have her chased over the countryside by a giant buzzing horsefly.

9 *outdoor market* The market square, dedicated to Apollo, and Hera's temple were the city's most famous landmarks, though the temple would not be visible from the actual heights where the trio pauses.

13 *Pelops* The house of Pelops, whose name was given to the entire region still known as the Peloponnesus, began with Pelops' father Tantalos, who offered his son to Zeus and the god's divine cohorts as the entrée at a banquet brazenly intended to test the gods' powers of perception. Zeus, not fooled or pleased, restored Pelops to life. Pelops fathered Atreus, who became king of Mycenae, and eventually adopted his grandsons, Agamemnon and Menelaus. Through further episodes of cannibalism, incest, adultery, and kin murder, this dynastic family continued to foster the hatred and treachery we see as the play opens.

21 *Pylades* The son of Strophios, king of Phokis, and Anaxibia, the sister of Agamemnon, with whom Orestes lived while

growing to manhood and preparing to return to Argos and avenge his father.

29–30 *My best friend . . . mentor* The initial role of the "Pae-dogogus," as he is named in the Greek manuscripts, was to oversee Orestes' education, but he has assumed the duties of a friend and adviser as Orestes reached maturity.

40 *I went to Delphi* Orestes had determined to kill Klytem-nestra and Aegisthus before consulting the sibyl at Delphi; he did not ask Apollo whether to do so was advisable. He simply asked how best to carry out the murders. Apollo sup-plied a plan and made no effort to discourage him.

76 *Why should this omen bother me* Ambiguous words or physical signs that suggested worst-case scenarios frequently spooked the superstitious Greeks. Here Orestes briefly fears that his feigned death might invite his actual death. He reas-sures himself by remembering that famous travelers and war veterans were known to feign death as a ploy to enhance their reputations as survivors.

ORESTES and his companions descend from their hilltop In the original staging, it was likely that the trio appeared atop the roof of the skenê behind the façade of the palace, to rep-resent their excellent vantage. After Orestes completed his long speech, they would have descended and entered the or-chestra from stage right.

122–123 *when he fought / barbarians* Elektra wishes that if Agamemnon was fated to die a violent death, he had died fighting the Trojans (whom she considers barbarians). She regrets that Ares, the war god, deprived her father of such an honorable death.

124–126 *my mother / and . . . Aegisthus, / laid open* Sophocles
envisions the murder of Agamemnon as having occurred
while he was reclining at dinner on his first night home from
Troy and thus unable to see his killers approaching from
behind. So positioned, his head would be an easy target for
a swung ax.

136 *I'm like the nightingale* Elektra compares herself to Prokne,
who killed her own son, Itys, and served him to her husband,
Tereus, who had raped her sister Philomela and cut out her
tongue to prevent her from exposing him. When vengeful
Tereus pursued both sisters, Zeus changed all three to birds,
Tereus to a hoopoe, and the two women to a swallow and a
nightingale respectively. The resemblance to a bird whose sole
powers of complaint are musical suits the fact that the passage
in which the metaphor occurs is sung.

140 *Hades! Persephone! Hermes!* All gods of the underworld:
respectively, the ruler of the underworld, his semicaptive
wife who divides her time each year between the living
world and the world of the dead, and the nimble messenger
god, one of whose duties is to lead dead souls into Hades'
kingdom.

143 *You Curses who can kill!* The Greeks of the Homeric era
believed an emphatically uttered curse had the power to kill
or damage its target. Note that Elektra takes this verbal
power literally though her brother does not.

144 *And you Furies* The (female) Furies were tasked with pursuing murderers of kin until the kin of their victims killed
them or the murderers committed suicide. Though Elektra
asks them to intervene, the traditional Furies do not appear

in the play. Sophocles, however, suggests at several places that Orestes, Pylades, and Elektra have become human embodiments of Furies and are fulfilling their ancient function in the course of killing Klytemnestra and Aegisthus.

190–193 *Littlewheel!* . . . *Niobe* Another appropriate mythological counterpart to express Elektra's inconsolable bereavement. Niobe was the daughter of King Tantalos of Lydia. She married Amphion, a king of Thebes, and bore six sons and six daughters to him, according to Homer. She infuriated the goddess Leto by claiming to be a better mother than the goddess, having given birth to twelve children compared to Leto's two. Unfortunately for Niobe, Leto instructed her children (Apollo and Artemis) to murder Niobe's children. Niobe wept for nine days and nights, and the Olympian gods turned her to stone on a cliff of Mount Sipylos, the home of her father, where her rock face continued to drip with tears. "Littlewheel" may refer to Prokne's dead child Itys, whose name in Greek could mean small wheel or circle.

199 *Chrysòthomis and Iphianassa* Elektra's living sisters. Iphianassa does not figure in the play.

231 *Acheron* The river and marsh surrounding the underworld.

364 *hold off a bit* After Agamemnon's murder, Elektra acted swiftly, entrusting the Elder with her brother, Orestes, giving the man instructions to keep the boy safe in another part of Greece, and to train him to return to Mycenae and kill his father's murderers.

444–445 *shut you up / in a cave* A mode of execution that avoided the polluting effect on perpetrators who inflicted outright kin murder with their own hands or through direct orders. See the similar use of death by entombment and starvation in *Antigone*.

476 *reacting, I think, to a nightmare* Dreams and nightmares were believed to be sent into sleeping minds by the gods, but they needed to be accurately interpreted to illuminate a situation or to become prophecies.

508 *hacked off his extremities* This phrase translates the Greek verb *emascalisthe* (which also appears in two passages from Aeschylus) and refers to the practice of murderers who would cut off the arms and legs and then tie them around the necks of their victims. Though the English word "emasculate" derives from the same root, Sophocles did not necessarily mean that Klytemnestra emasculated Agamemnon. What she did was terrible enough. The word also referred to the military practice of amputating an enemy's arms and/or legs after death to humiliate him in the underworld.

539 *Justice* The Chorus refers to Diké, whom they assume sent Klytemnestra the dream as a warning that this goddess was about to strike a deadlier blow.

563–564 *the chariot race / Pelops ran* A moment of treachery that began the curse afflicting the House of Pelops. In order to win Hippodamia as a bride, Pelops bested her father, Oenomaus, in a chariot race. But Pelops had cheated and needed to cover up his malfeasance. He had bribed Oenomaus' chariot-mechanic Myrtilos to ensure a wreck (by removing the chariot's linchpin) that killed his master during the race. Later, Myrtilos and Pelops fell out. While both were aboard an airborne chariot (a gift from Poseidon), Pelops hurled Myrtilos to his death. Dying, Myrtilos cursed Pelops so potently that his malice inflicted grotesque acts of revenge on every subsequent generation of the Pelops clan. This origin myth suggests it is no coincidence that Orestes (i.e., Sophocles) chose a chariot race as the setting for the Elder's false story of Orestes' death. When she heard it, Klytemnestra might have been pleased and reassured by the irony: a curse that began with one chariot race conveniently ends with another.

617–618 *ask how impartial . . . before you condemn* This spirited and savage debate in which Klytemnestra seizes the first rounds is a good example of Athenian legal argumentation. Such confrontations suggest that hostility was a constant of this household's daily life. The two women counter each other's positions, but they remain oblivious to the weakness of their own assumptions and red herrings. To kill one's daughter is horrific from any point of view, and Klytemnestra clearly is right in saying that her husband has committed the serious crime of kin murder. But her suggestion that it would have been more appropriate for one of Menelaus' children to have been sacrificed is irrelevant, since it is from Agamemnon that Artemis seeks redress. Klytemnestra's urging Elektra to evaluate the 'justice' of her own argument before responding is wishful thinking.

630–631 *You were seduced / to murder him* Here Elektra nails what (she thinks) was her mother's true motivation for killing Agamemnon. But her speech veers opportunistically from resentment to resentment in a way that such real-life confrontations usually do. Blundell's exacting analysis of their opposing arguments (*Helping Friends and Harming Enemies*, 157–72) demonstrates that Sophocles was in control and aware himself of his two antagonists' valid points and each one's shortcomings. The dramatic function of this showdown is more to expose a snarl of longstanding hostilities than to ask us to adjudicate the matter.

641 *whooping a boast* An inadvisable provocation, though Artemis' wrath seems out of proportion to the offense.

642–647 *becalmed the Greek fleet . . . Otherwise . . . marooned* Perhaps Artemis raised the stakes for the Greek's getting to Troy to dissuade the Atreus brothers from throwing good men after a bad wife.

658–660 *If you invent a law . . . won't it / inflict guilt . . . back on you?* A valid point, one Klytemnestra brushes off. Her actual rejoinder will be to ignore Elektra and appeal to Apollo to weigh in on her side.

737–739 *Promise me . . . If signs I saw . . . seem harmless* A conventional self-protective formula in situations where one cannot be sure that the dreamer is correctly interpreting the intent of the god who inspired the dream.

748–749 *Spare the offspring . . . Lose those* More obliquity. She implies that Chrysòthemis should be spared but not Elektra or Orestes.

782 *That's why I'm here. To tell it all.* The Elder must have spent his offstage time composing this remarkably detailed speech. The Orestes it imagines is far more impressive than the Orestes who speaks and acts within the play. Blundell (174) suggests the speech represents Elektra's idealized version of her brother. The speech also contrasts the Orestes of the play with the man he might have become.

835 *Orestes cut the pillars close* The race stewards assigned
positions at the start line by drawing lots. Orestes has drawn
the inmost position, which, as Kells (144) notes, explains
his racing strategy (identical to that Nestor gave his son in
the *Iliad*): stay in your lane; if other drivers pass you, they
will tire from covering more distance; you'll be able to catch
them on the last of the twelve laps. The chariots are racing
counterclockwise. Rounding them on the innermost lane requires a 180-degree reversal of direction, hence cornering is
a highly dangerous maneuver if the charioteer cuts the posts
close in order to catch the leader. The forward momentum
of the standing driver will naturally throw him forward in
front of the chariot when it loses a wheel and drags an axle.

896 *birthing a child* A line that dramatizes the maternal reflexes
Klytemnestra feels and then suppresses. She quickly recovers
her animosity toward Orestes. The line also nods in passing
to the Greeks' belief the mother-child relation is a sacred
one. As shrewdly noted by Kells (138–139), the extreme realism of the Elder's account has a profound effect on Klytemnestra: "she is presented with a picture of Orestes whom she
only remembers as a little boy, now grown to manhood, dis-
tinguishing himself . . . now behaving as a son *of whom she
might be proud. . . .* Only such an account . . . could have
moved . . . the mother's heart to that . . . amazing *peripeteia*
of emotion 896–898 represents."

1012 *Nemesis!* The goddess of payback. An instance of the
Greek sense that *all gods* listen to all human speech and
react to offenses within their spheres of intervention.

1050 *Where is the Sun* One of the Sun's roles was to expose the
guilty so that Zeus knew where to aim his thunderbolts.

1055 *Don't scream at* Them! The Olympian gods, whom Elektra accuses of failing to punish the guilty.

1062–1063 *Amphiaraos—whose wife, / bribed with a golden necklace* Elektra will react hostilely to this invocation of Amphiaraos' fate. He was a seer whose wife contrived to get him killed during the attack on Thebes by the armies of seven cities, as described in *Antigone*. Polyneikes had given Amphiaraos' wife Eriphyle a golden necklace in exchange for shaming her husband into joining the ill-fated expedition. The gods spared him (as a good man betrayed) death by slaughter and instead had him swallowed by the Earth in a manner similar to Oedipus' entry into the afterlife. After death, Amphiaraos' seer-craft did not desert him; he ended up as a ruler of the dead. The implication is that the gods and the dead will treat Orestes with similar respect.

1071 *Aaagggh indeed* As Jebb (1894, 121) interprets this cryptic exchange, Elektra's scream arises from the fact that Amphiaraos' wife was punished for killing him, but her father, Agamemnon, remains unavenged. The Leader takes Elektra's cry to mean, "So much for Eriphyle's treachery," and responds, in effect, "Yes, yes!" The chorus starts to say, "for the murderess," intending to continue, "who killed her husband!" Elektra, however, can think only of the difference between the two outcomes, interjecting, "was brought down." I have adjusted the translation to maintain the rapid-fire quality of the exchange.

1299–1300 *airborne birds / instinctively cherish the parents* The bird referred to here is probably the stork, whose example of parent-child reciprocity was noted by Aristotle *Av.* 1355. (Jebb, *Elektra*, 145)

1306 *Themis* The goddess of justice, religious observance, and right action.

1321 *tirelessly, like a nightingale* The nightingale of the Prokne myth. This species became an apt choice to represent cease-less mourning because it sings all night long.

1324–1325 *twin / Furies* Aegisthus and Klytemnestra.

Aide carrying . . . urn It may be without a lid, but could contain real ashes to allow the actress to show her tenderness toward Orestes' remains.

1420 *When you raced on that terrible circuit* Many scholars interpret this line to refer to Orestes' outward journey into exile in Attica, only to return as ashes. The lines seem also, perhaps even more appropriately, to refer to his fatal circuit of the racecourse at Delphi.

1432 *What should I say?* Orestes is conflicted here. Should he reveal who he is and thus risk that his reckless sister will give him away? Or should he respond to her by relieving her of her misery?

1629 *Even things that might not seem fine at all* The Elder might mean that Klytemnestra has resumed grieving for Orestes, now that she's holding his ashes, and therefore is distracted and not on her guard. (See Kells, 213.)

kneeling at the ELDER's feet The gesture emphasizes Elektra's delusional confusion of the Elder with her dead father.

1681 *relentless hounds tracking evil* A phrase that fuses Orestes and Pylades with the invisible Furies who inhabit them as they kill Klytemnestra.

1688–1690 *the edge of his vengeance / newly-honed ahead of him, / while Hermes* Hermes, earlier invoked by Elektra, and whose function is to usher the doomed into death, ar-rives to encourage the pair on their deadly mission.

1710–1711 *The destiny that shadowed you . . . done now* The
Chorus believes the curse on the House of Atreus has run its
course. Though this chorus is more perceptive than many in
Sophocles' plays, the unresolved exchange at play's end suggest they might be mistaken here.

1713–1714 *Stab her again— / if you have the strength* Elektra's
great moment. Why she thinks Orestes might be incapable
of stabbing Klytemnestra again is puzzling. Perhaps her
chilling encouragement is meant to discourage any revulsion
or second thoughts on her brother's part.

1717 *The Curses work!* See earlier comment about Curses as
viable weapons for line 143.

1728–1729 *It went well. If / Apollo oracled well* The line suggests a certain detachment on Orestes' part. He carried out
the killings according to Apollo's instructions. If Apollo sup-
plied them sincerely, then everything did go well. If Apollo's
terse words concealed a hidden danger, further trouble may
be in the wings. Or Orestes may simply refer here to the un-
finished business of killing Aegisthus.

1770–1771 *Time has taught / me to join . . . those stronger than me* Elektra's capacity for irony is fully exercised
throughout her exchange with Aegisthus. Here she implies
for Aegisthus' benefit that she's yielding to his dominance,
but by "those stronger" she clearly means Orestes and Pylades.

1790–1791 *Haven't you realized by now "the dead" . . .* are
alive? Orestes' taunt ties in with the Chorus's apprehension
that Orestes and Pylades pursue Klytemnestra and Aegisthus into the palace as if they were ancient "Furies" and in
doing so act on behalf of the "dead" Agamemnon.

1817–1818 *Must this house witness all the murders / our family's suffered—and those still to come?* Aegisthus' response to Orestes' declaration of finality is to predict (twice) that the curse on the House of Atreus has yet to run its course.

1831–1832 *Justice dealt by the sword / will keep evil in check* Orestes implicitly claims that justice, achieved by his punishing the latest kin murderers, will put an end to intrafamilial feuds.

1833–1835 *House of Atreus . . . what's been / accomplished today sets you free* The Chorus takes Orestes at his word. Does Sophocles?

OEDIPUS THE KING

1–7 *My children . . . Healing God?* These first lines in the Greek are compressed—dense with mythic, dramatic, and ironic significance. Oedipus emerges from the palace to confront a sea of green branches—the olive boughs his agitated Theban subjects have brought to him in supplication (see note to 4). He plays on that image—"fresh green life / old Kadmos nurtures and protects"—to acknowledge the citizens' ancestry: they are the latest crop, the newest descendants of Kadmos, Thebes' legendary founder and its first king, who seeded the ground with dragon's teeth from which sprang fully armed soldiers. That Oedipus invokes Kadmos as the still-fathering source of Thebes' newest generation registers the power enduring paternal bloodlines held for fifth-century Greeks. By referring to the delegation as *trophê*—an abstract noun used here to mean "those cared for" or "those protected" by Kadmos—Oedipus seems briefly to be puzzled as to why the delegation appeals to him for help, rather than to the city's divinities. He tries to shift responsibility for their welfare away from himself to Kadmos. But the compassion he extends to them in his first words—by calling them his "children," as though he were related by blood—turns out to be more than a metaphoric gesture when Oedipus discovers that Kadmos is his ancestor as well.

4 *with your wool-strung boughs* Suppliants left branches of laurel or olive, with tufts of wool tied on to them, at the altars of gods to whom they appealed for help. But here the use of suppliant boughs to seek help from a mortal man is highly unusual. Oedipus' initial puzzlement as to why he is being petitioned with ritual emblems of supplication also suggests his reluctance to get involved, perhaps his sense of inadequacy. This momentary doubt vanishes as he feels his subjects' need and as his strength and competence recover. He has indeed, we soon learn, been totally aware of Thebes' widespread devastation.

6–7 *prayers . . . Healing God* Literally, "paeans." A paean was a hymn to Apollo as a healer of disease, one of the god's many roles. Although the oracle that predicted the plague was given by Apollo—and Homer's *Iliad* tells us he could send a plague as well as cure one—nothing in the text implicates him as the cause of the plague now inflicting Thebes.

26–27 *river shrine . . . ashes . . . prophecy* Literally, "prophetic embers of Ismenos." A temple on the shores of the Ismenos, one of the two Theban rivers, was dedicated to Apollo. Embers in the temple smoldered under a sacrificed animal

whose burnt remains could be read to interpret the will of a
god, in this case Apollo's.

31 *Plague* The plague that had struck Thebes was general, destroying crops, animals, and people. The fiery heat characteristic of the fever is referred to again at 227–228 (see note
to 224–239). The resemblance between the plague in this
play and the Athenian plague of 430 BCE as described by
Thucydides has led some scholars to date the play shortly
after 429. See especially Bernard Knox, "The Date of the
Oedipus Tyrannus of Sophocles," in *American Journal of
Philology* 77, no. 2 (1956).

34 *A burning god* The Greeks assumed a god to be responsible
for a general and devastating plague. At 224 the Chorus
names Ares, symbol of violence or destructiveness, as the
responsible divinity.

37 *Hades* The god who presides over the underworld.

38–41 *We haven't come . . . confronting gods* The Priest explains why he, a man who himself has access to the gods,
comes to Oedipus, a political leader, for help in this crisis;
Oedipus has proven his ability to act effectively in situations
requiring direct contact with a divinity.

42–44 *freed us . . . rasping Singer* The "rasping Singer" is the
Sphinx, pictured by Greek artists of Sophocles' time with a lion's body, a woman's head and breasts, and wings. She arrived
in Thebes shortly after Laios' departure and destroyed young
Thebans ("the tax we paid with our lives") by posing a riddle
that resulted in the death of those who answered incorrectly.
(In some versions of the myth, the victims were thrown from
a cliff, and in others they were strangled, perhaps in some

sexual embrace; the word "Sphinx" is related to the Greek verb meaning "to strangle.") Oedipus triumphed by solving the riddle and killing the Sphinx, thus liberating Thebes from a reign of terror. One version of the riddle follows; it appears in myth in slightly different formulations: "There exists on land a thing with two feet and four feet, with a single voice, that has three feet as well. It changes shape alone among the things that move on land or in the air or down through the sea. Yet during periods when it is supported by the largest number of feet, then is the speed in its limbs the feeblest of all" (Gould 1970, 19). By answering "man," Oedipus demonstrated his lifelong attribute, intellectual resourcefulness in harrowing circumstances. Sophocles refrains from presenting the riddle itself, perhaps because its folk-tale cleverness seemed too insufficient a proof of real intelligence.

51 *god's intimation* A prophetic voice, an oracle or augury, or a divine signal of some kind.

62 *a bird from god* Birdlife was a major medium of communication between gods and mortals. Prophets and seers divined messages from birds' songs and flight patterns. Oedipus himself is ironically seen here as a favorable birdlike omen. See *Antigone*, note to 463–464.

62 *good luck* The first of many invocations of the Greek concept of *tyche*, which can mean "luck," "chance," or "fate." I generally translate "luck" when the speaker is gratified, "chance" when the outcome seems uncertain or unfortunate, and "fate" when a divinity seems involved.

69 *I know what need* Oedipus' grasp of the situation might seem contradictory to his initial professed ignorance of the

suppliants' appeal. In his first speech, he was simply searching for new developments and urging his people to voice fears and needs. Here he reveals his continued concern and reports specific actions he has taken.

69 *this sickness* Oedipus refers both to the literal "sickness" of the suppliants, all victims in some respect of the plague, and to his own metaphoric sickness—his mental suffering for his fellow Thebans. But the Greek audience understood that the "sickness" that affects Oedipus, of which he is unaware, is not metaphoric at all but a literal pollution of his entire being. Sophocles will continue to reveal how characters' metaphoric speech turns out to be unexpectedly and horrifyingly literal.

81 *Phoibos* Apollo.

85 *He takes too long* The Pythoness at Delphi delivered answers to questioners only once a month, and the shortest possible elapsed time for a trip from Thebes to Delphi and back would be about four or five days.

90 *Lord Apollo* This exclamation could be as much an impromptu prayer as an oath. The stage might contain a statue of Apollo to which Oedipus turns or nods as he speaks these lines.

91–92 *Luck so bright . . . see it* I follow the interpretation of these lines given by Lowell Edmunds in "Sophocles' *Oedipus Tyrannus*," in *Harvard Studies in Classical Philology* 80–81 (1976): 41–44, who disputes the traditional interpretation: "May his radiant look prove the herald of good news." Arguing that Sophocles uses an idiom dependent on a suppressed preposition, Edmunds believes *eu* should be

understood before *ommati* and the lines literally be translated as "May he come bright with saving fortune as he is
bright to view."

laurel crown A laurel crown customarily signified that a pil-
grimage to a shrine or an oracle had been a success.

96 *Menoikeos* One of the "Sown Men" who grew up instantly
and fully armed in Thebes when Kadmos seeded the earth
with dragon's teeth. Pronounced "Me-NEE-kius."

98–99 *A good one . . . will be fine* A deliberately obscure answer. Kreon here resists revealing, until directed by Oedipus, the shocking nature of the oracle he has received. The
lines also suggest Kreon's annoying use of a Sophist's quib-
bling idiom.

102–103 *in front . . . go inside* Kreon gives Oedipus the option
of keeping Thebes in the dark about the oracle's disturbing
accusations.

107 *very clear* Kreon remarks on the lack of evasion or surface
difficulty in this new oracle. Oracles (frequently delivered
in lines of hexameter verse) were sometimes cryptic and de-
manded interpretation. The oracles to Oedipus are among
the rare ones in Greek myth that mean exactly what they
literally say.

113 *banishing . . . killing* Apollo offers Thebes two choices for
purging itself of Laios' murderer: death or exile. This choice
comes up again when Oedipus charges Kreon with the crime
and when Oedipus and Kreon debate Oedipus' ultimate fate.

113–114 *blood— / kin murder* The presence in a city of a person who had shed the blood of someone in his own family
was absolutely horrifying and unacceptable to a Greek. Even

in the late fifth century, lawyers made dramatic use of this horror when prosecuting murderers.

120 *own hands* The first of many references to hands, especially hands that shed blood. In Greek law the hands of a person who committed a crime retained the pollution inherent in that crime, regardless of motive or intent. Here Oedipus' avenging hands are paired rhetorically with the hands that murdered Laios. The two pairs of hands will be shown to be only one pair, Oedipus' own.

129–130 *journey . . . god's presence* The Greek word so translated is *theoros*, literally, a spectator of (or witness to) a divine rite or event. We know from Euripides' *Phoenician Women* (Grene and Lattimore, vol. IV, 1959, 462) that Laios was on his way to Delphi to ask the Pythoness whether or not the son he had exposed was really dead. But by not specifically naming Laios' destination, Sophocles permits Oedipus to postpone facing the possibility that Laios and he were traveling on the same road at the same time.

141 *bandit* Though Kreon clearly used the plural in 138, Oedipus speaks of a single bandit with chilling, unconscious accuracy. But because his sentence is a hypothetical question, it is logically proper.

144–145 *new troubles . . . no avenger* Kreon evokes a rapid sequence of events: Laios' departure; news of his death; attack by the Sphinx; arrival of Oedipus; death of the Sphinx. The elapsed time might have been only a few days, or at most a week or two.

147 *blocked* The Greek word so translated, *empodon*, refers to stumbling, tripping, or impeding the legs.

150 *at our feet* Kreon continues the foot imagery, which may carry a reference to Oedipus' own swollen feet.

160 *exacting vengeance* Oedipus strangely imagines himself the victim of a second crime by Laios' original murderer. That this should be an act of "vengeance" is hard to explain given the state of Oedipus' knowledge, but it will indeed be an act of vengeance when the same hands that killed Laios blind Oedipus.

164 *people of Kadmos* Theban citizens. When they arrive, the Chorus will represent the "people of Kadmos."

173 *Voice from Zeus* Though Apollo was the resident deity who issued his prophecies through the Pythoness at Delphi, the Chorus here attributes the commands to Zeus, the ultimate source of knowledge and power.

179 *Delos* The island at the center of the Cyclades, birthplace of Apollo, was said to be the navel of the sea, as Delphi was the navel of the Earth. Gods communicated with mortals through both connections.

181 *new threat . . . old doom* The Chorus distinguishes between a curse that has been known for some years and one that has newly emerged. The Voice of Zeus will invoke an old curse against the murderer of Laios.

186–191 *Athena . . . Artemis . . . Apollo* The Chorus, not knowing which god will be the truly relevant one, prays to three divinities to focus their powers on rescuing Thebes.

208 *Deathgod* Hades.

224–239 *Ares . . . who kills us* The war god Ares is not associated with the plague in myth, but Sophocles probably alludes to the plague's spread in Athens during the Spartan attacks of 430–425. The image of Ares as a murderer "without armor now" reflects the fifth-century Greeks' lack of knowledge about infectious diseases. Throngs of rural Greeks, assuming Athens a safe haven from the Spartans, flocked to the city; there the overcrowded conditions facilitated the plague's swift and deadly spread. In Aeschylus' *Suppliants* (Grene and Lattimore, vol. I, 1959, 201), Ares personifies the plague or destruction itself.

229–230 *vast sea-room / of Amphitritê* Literally, "great hall of Amphitritê." Amphitritê was a sea nymph whose home was the Atlantic Ocean, hence her name became synonymous with that body of water.

232 *jagged harbors* Literally, "welcomeless anchorage."

233 *seas off Thrace* The Black Sea. The Thracians, who lived on its shores, were warlike; Ares was their primary god.

233–235 *If night ... finish it* The meaning is obscure, but Gould (1970, 39) suggests "if the night lets anything survive, the day moves in to finish it."

240 *lord of the morning light* Literally, "Lycean Lord." Lycean was one of Apollo's epithets and could suggest either "light" or "wolf." The Chorus surely calls on him here in his protective, light-bringing aspect.

246 *morning hills* Literally, "Lycian hills," in southwestern Asia Minor, where Artemis was worshipped, with her brother Apollo, as a fire deity. Sophocles puns on the similarity between Lycean and Lycian to stress the light-bringing character of the sibling gods.

250 *Bakkhos* An alternate name for Dionysos, the god of wine and other forms of intoxication and ecstasy. He was a native Theban, the son of Zeus and Semele, Kadmos' daughter.

251 *maenads* Literally, "madwomen." Revelers loyal to Dionysos.

263 *I'm a stranger* According to Athenian law, a blood relative of a slain person should act to interdict the murderer. Unknowingly, Oedipus is in fact such a relative, though here he acts as a representative of the state speaking for the next of kin, who is presumed to be absent.

265 *mesh some clue* The word translated as "clue" is *symbolon*, a fragment of some larger object, typically a potsherd. When matched to fit its other half, it established the identity of a messenger or long-lost parent or relative.

268 *come late* Oedipus arrived in Thebes after the report of Laios' death had reached the city.

273 *Labdakos* An earlier king of Thebes.

286–289 *roof . . . speak . . . pray . . . sacrifice . . . pour* The prohibitions in Oedipus' decree reveal the extreme aversion felt by a Greek of Sophocles' time to any contact with a person whose hands had committed a defiling act. See *Kolonos*, note to 1029.

316–317 *Laios / had no luck . . . children* An example of words whose second meaning will be grasped when the true facts of Oedipus' life are known. Oedipus means to say that Laios was childless, but the words also suggest that any child Laios fathered was the *source* of his ill fortune.

318 *came down on his head* This idiom through which Oedipus explains Laios' death is uncannily appropriate to the way in

which Laios actually died: from a blow to the head, struck by Oedipus himself.

324 *all our kings* My gloss added to explain Oedipus' list.

335 *None of us is the killer* The blunt denial is understandable, because Oedipus has addressed the Chorus as if it potentially harbored Laios' killer.

343 *Tiresias* The blind Theban prophet, who figures in many of the most famous myths of his native city. His association with the god Apollo, and his access to the god's knowledge, are crucial here, because Apollo is the source of the oracles that predicted Oedipus' incest and patricide.

348 *Kreon's urging* An important point. Later, when Tiresias accuses Oedipus of causing the pollution, Oedipus remembers that it was Kreon who advised consulting the seer. Kreon's involvement thus lends plausibility to Oedipus' countercharges.

352 *travelers* The Leader substitutes a word that is nearer the truth than Kreon's "bandits." Oedipus does not react to the difference.

354 *who did it* Here I accept an anonymous emendation cited by Burton in Jebb (1883, 50). The manuscripts literally say "the one who saw it no one sees." But the emendation fits the context of the next three speeches, which concern not the eyewitness, but the killer, the one who did it.

390–391 *lawful . . . guidance* Greek cities were morally, if not legally, entitled to benefit from the wisdom of an acknowledged prophet. Here, at first, Oedipus' remonstrance is gentle. (See Jebb 1883, 54.)

393–394 *What you've said . . . happen to me* Tiresias refers here most probably to the part of Oedipus' speech that curses Laios' murderer. Less probably, he might be referring to the plea with which Oedipus greets him. The manuscripts contain a possible variant of these lines, which Gould translates, "I see your understanding comes to you inopportunely. So that won't happen to me . . ." (1970, 54). This variant makes sense in the larger context of Oedipus' discovery of his true past. I have, however, translated the line to make the most sense in the immediate context.

399 *You know and won't help?* Tiresias' scornful refusal to respond seems not only inexplicable to Oedipus but unacceptable. Tiresias must be made to tell what the city needs to know for its survival. Oedipus' fury may be justified as necessary to force the truth from him.

406 *rage* A cunning double meaning. Tiresias speaks of "rage" (*orgei*, a feminine noun in Greek) as something Oedipus "cohabits" or "dwells" with and of which he is ignorant. Oedipus thinks he is being accused of possessing a violent nature. But because this "rage" is also spoken of as a sexual partner, Tiresias' words could mean as well that Oedipus is ignorant of the identity of his own wife. Sophocles has the Messenger describe the last frantic actions of Jokasta, after she knows Oedipus is her son, as *orge*, or raging (1406). The characterization of Oedipus' whole family by rage is prominent in Aeschylus and even earlier writers.

425–426 *charge . . . flushed out* The metaphor is from hunting and suggests, first, that the accusation is like an animal driven from its cover and, second, that Tiresias himself has become an animal fleeing Oedipus' wrath.

440–441 *living . . . intimacy* This phrase normally means "to live under the same roof," but it also frequently means "to have sexual intercourse with."

442 *nearest and most loving kin* The most frequent reference of this phrase (*philatoi*) is to one's blood kin; less often it refers to those whom one loves, regardless of blood relationship. Tiresias' lines seem to Oedipus an astonishing insult because their true import, that his wife is his closest blood relative, is unthinkable. See introduction to *Antigone*, passim.

451 *You can't harm me* This phrase could also mean "I shall not harm you." My translation is governed by acceptance of Brunck's emendation in the next speech, as cited in Jebb (1883, 61).

453 *I'm not the one who will bring you down* All but one of the manuscripts give, "It's not my fate to be struck down by you." If this version is sound, the rest of Tiresias' speech makes little sense. If, however, Brunck's emendation of a fourteenth-century manuscript is correct, as most modern editors believe, Apollo's involvement in Oedipus' downfall follows quite logically.

455 *Or was it Kreon?* In seeking an explanation for what he sees as false and treasonous accusations by Tiresias, Oedipus connects Kreon's recommendation to call in Tiresias with the fact that banishing Oedipus would leave Kreon in position to assume the throne. This sudden accusation against Kreon suggests not only Oedipus' quick mind, but the suspiciousness and ruthless initiative required of a

tyrannos (see note to 1006–1007). Gould has drawn a useful distinction between Tiresias and Oedipus under duress (1970, 60). While Oedipus sharpens his ability to make inferences, Tiresias can only clarify and elaborate on Oedipus' guilt with an intuitive vision. The prophet is unreasonable but correct, Oedipus plausible but wrong.

465 *bogus beggar-priest* The Greeks used the word *magus* to refer to what they considered an unreliable and corruptible breed of fortune-tellers from Persia.

476 *the know-nothing* Oedipus himself stresses the difference between his ability to solve problems intellectually and Tiresias' failure to solve them using the arts of prophecy. Oedipus smugly boasts of his "ignorance" but is in fact truly and desperately ignorant of the hidden facts that will ruin him.

506 *terror-stricken feet* The phrase may mean that the curse pursuing Oedipus is itself "terrible footed." But the sound of the word for "terrible footed," *deinopous*, echoes Oedipus' name (literally, "Swollenfoot") so as to suggest that Oedipus' scarred feet, which were pinned together when he was exposed at birth, are in some way terrible or terrified.

511 *Kithairon* The mountain on which Oedipus, as an infant, was left to die.

517 *bring you down to what you are* This sentence is obscure in Greek. Jebb suggests that it means Oedipus will be leveled, i.e., "equal" to his true self by being revealed as Laios' son, and "equal" to his own children, all of whom have the same mother, Jokasta (1883, 67).

520 *warning spoken through my mouth* This seeming circumlocution conveys the fact that Tiresias is not the source of

his prophecies, but the transmitter of Apollo's messages. The word *stoma*, or "mouth," also means the message spoken by the mouth.

531 *Who was my father?* Literally, "the one who gave me birth." The word is masculine, indicating that Oedipus asks who his male parent is.

557 *father's seed and his seed* Literally, "seed fellow to his father." The word *homosporos* names one who impregnates the same woman as his father, but it also carries the suggestion of blood relationship to the father.

571 *Fates* The *Keres*, who execute the will of Zeus and Apollo.

574 *Parnassos* The mountain home of the Muses, visible from Thebes.

582 *Earth . . . mouth* Literally, "from Earth's mid-navel." The navel was a white stone at Delphi, at the spot where oracles or "dooms" such as those mentioned here were spoken. The navel, or *omphalos*, was an avenue of communication to the wisdom of the earth. See note to 179.

585 *man who reads birds* Tiresias.

589–597 *doubt . . . no proof* The Chorus faces a hard choice. Either they must abandon their trust in divine oracles or they must accuse Oedipus of the death of Laios. They decide that before joining with Tiresias, they must have some proof (literally, a "touchstone," *basanos*, which streaks black when rubbed with true gold) to remove their doubt. Because no metaphoric touchstone exists—no feud or crime that set the Korinthian royal house against the Theban House of Kadmos—they withhold their accusation.

608–609 *charges / proved against him* Here again the word "touchstone" is used, this time as a verb.

637 *master's murderer* Oedipus' language is perhaps purposely ambiguous. He proleptically accuses Kreon of murdering him, but the phrase could accuse Kreon of Laios' murder.

664 *Laios?* Kreon has not yet heard Tiresias' charges, hence his surprise.

671 *hunt down the killer* Oedipus may be hinting that the investigation of Laios' murder was less than thorough.

688 *rationally* Kreon's pedantic reasonableness contrasts sharply with Oedipus' impatient quickness. His laborious catalog of the disadvantages of kingship may be heartfelt, but its pompous rhetorical expression generates suspicion in Oedipus.

696 *To be king* These protestations should be compared with Kreon's later implicit acceptance of the kingship at 1730–1732.

707 *Nor would I join someone* This oblique reference is probably to Tiresias. Kreon accepts the possibility that Tiresias is treasonous in his accusations; he clearly does not believe such accusations against Oedipus to be valid.

732 *your death* Oedipus chooses the harsher penalty of the two, death or exile, that the Delphi oracle promised Kreon would cure Thebes at 113. But Oedipus may have in mind that execution was the normal punishment for treason.

733 *Then start by defining "betrayal"* The text, in the judgment of many scholars, may be corrupt at this point. Editors have attempted to preserve continuous sense by reassigning the lines to other speakers and by positing a line to bridge

the gap in logic after Gr. 625 (734). Gould, however, argues plausibly that Kreon's proclivity for verbal analysis and Socratic love of general laws may explain his apparent non sequitur, which attempts to deflect Oedipus from violence into philosophical debate (1970, 84). I accept Gould's defense of the manuscripts and translate the text as received.

755 *or to have me killed* Kreon reverts to the choice of banishment or death proposed by the oracle he himself brought from Delphi. He also may have assumed Oedipus' recent threat of death to be hyperbole.

757 *False prophecy* Literally, "evil arts." This implies that Kreon has employed Tiresias to make false charges disguised as prophecy to destroy Oedipus. Such treacherous use of prophecy was a part of fifth-century Greek political life.

758 *I ask the gods* Kreon makes a formal declaration of innocence that invokes the gods; his innocence is instantly respected as valid by all but Oedipus.

763–812 *Give in . . . luck* These lines are a *kommos*, a sung expression of grief or strong emotion in which the Leader joins one or more of the main characters. To judge by the root meaning of *kommos* (which is "beat"), this portion must have had a more strongly accented rhythm than the rest of the dialogue. Here the emotion might stem from the realization, by all present, of increasingly grave circumstances.

775 *No! We ask neither* Though the Chorus reveres Oedipus for the success and prosperity of his kingship, it does not accept either of the harsh alternatives his quick mind suggests:

Oedipus sees that if Kreon's conspiracy is not stamped out, it will lead ultimately to his own destruction. The Chorus gropes for a less severe outcome and gradually refrains from identifying with Oedipus as the events of his life are revealed to them.

776 *the Sun* The Sun frequently appears as the source of final appeal in tragedy, as it will later at 1617 when Kreon orders Oedipus out of its "life-giving flame."

782 *let him go* That Oedipus yields, however grudgingly, shows that his stubbornness and self-confidence are not immune to persuasion, nor is he insensitive to the wishes of those close to him.

818 *He says I murdered Laios* Kreon did not say this, of course. Because Oedipus so passionately believes in the truth of his inference—that Kreon is responsible for Tiresias' charges—he puts Tiresias' words in Kreon's mouth.

827 *I don't say Apollo himself sent it* This qualification both absolves Apollo from false prophecy and expresses skepticism concerning oracles, skepticism that must have been shared widely in a world where oracles were constantly put to dubious political use. The Chorus has the strongest commitment to the divine authority of oracles. Oedipus' belief is conditioned by experience and changes with events.

829–830 *destined to die / at the hands of* In Jokasta's version, the oracle to Laios was unqualified and not meant as a punishment. Gould notes that by omitting the aspect of punishment present in earlier versions of the myth, Sophocles establishes the pure and unexplained malice of Apollo's destruction of Oedipus.

832 *three roads meet* This is the detail that disturbs Oedipus, and the one he reverts to as soon as Jokasta ends her speech. The actor playing Oedipus must make a gesture of recognition to account for Jokasta's question at 846. Sophocles might have meant such a pointed reaction to explain why Oedipus was distracted from picking up another fact with direct bearing on his identity: Jokasta's child's feet had been "pierced and pinned" together, as Oedipus' own had been, to produce the swollen scars that gave him his name. However, the weight to be given Oedipus' crippled feet may not be as conclusive as some commentators think. If exposure of children was common, Oedipus might not be expected to connect himself instantly and absolutely with Laios' son, even if he had heard Jokasta's words.

841–843 *god wants . . . showing what he's done* Literally, "Of what things the god hunts the use, he reveals easily himself." Allusions to hunting appear also at 267, 426, and 671. The words here conjure the image of god seizing his prey and then displaying it.

846 *What fear made you turn* Jokasta could refer either to a movement by Oedipus at 844–845 or earlier, at 832.

851–852 *Phokis . . . Daulis* Towns near Delphi.

854 *before you came to power* For the sequence of events leading to Oedipus' assumption of power in Thebes, see this play's introduction.

858 *Was he a young man* Oedipus poses as the first alternative the one he must hope is true: that Laios was not an older man of an age to be his father. In her response, Jokasta not

only dashes this hope but suggests a physical resemblance between Laios and Oedipus.

862 *that savage curse* Oedipus declared this interdiction against Laios' murderer at 290–303.

869 *a herald* The presence of a herald might have indicated to Oedipus that the party contained a prince or ruler.

876 *touched . . . begged* A touch on the arm, like clasping a person's knees, was a formal supplication, an appeal to piety in hope of achieving a favorable response.

883 *I've said too much* What Oedipus means here is uncertain. Most likely, as Gould suggests, he regrets the curse pronounced against himself—the curse to which he has already referred at 862 (1970, 98).

890 *know the risks* Literally, "while I cross through this chance [*tyche*]."

891–892 *Polybos . . . Merope* Are we to understand that Oedipus has never before named his parents or his origins to Jokasta? Although such extreme reticence is possible, it is much more likely that Sophocles uses here an epic convention whereby a hero begins a piece of consequential autobiography by formally naming his homeland and immediate ancestors.

893–894 *Chance . . . blow* An excellent instance of Sophocles' practice of having Oedipus label as chance or luck an event that, seen in retrospect, becomes part of the pattern of his ruin created by Apollo.

904 *the rumor still rankled; it hounded me* The Greek word *hupheppe* could mean either that the rumor "crept abroad"

or that "the memory recurred." I have tried to translate the phrase so as to include both possibilities.

905 *with no word to my parents* Had Oedipus informed his parents of the mission to Delphi, they presumably would have intervened. By seeking assurance of his birth beyond his parents' word, Oedipus placed himself in the hands of the god Apollo. It was both a conventional and a rational act, because Delphi could serve as a locator of lost kin, and because Oedipus had no reason to suspect the god held any enmity toward him.

907 *god would not honor me* What was the question Oedipus put to the Pythoness? "Who are my true parents?" or "Is Polybos my true father?" For the oracle not to answer such a question seems to Oedipus a violation of the normal treatment a pilgrim could expect from the god (literally, "Phoibos," or Apollo) at Delphi.

909–910 *his words flashed . . . horrible, wretched things* The phrase is so vivid some scholars have questioned its authenticity. It does fit both Oedipus' present mental condition, in which he sees himself as a target for strange malice, and the verbs of leaping and striking that Sophocles uses for actions attributable to Apollo. The oracle given Oedipus is not an answer to his question, but an attack on Oedipus—not a clarification, but a condemnation that impacts Oedipus with a shock or flash. His reaction, to flee Korinth and his parents, is entirely comprehensible and in no way morally flawed. An oracle might be fulfilled in a metaphorical or oblique manner; in real life, some oracles were never fulfilled, a frequent event in the experience of Sophocles' audience. In tragedy, however, the audience would expect all oracles to be completed. Many readers think that Oedipus ought eventually to have considered the oracle's broader implications. (Could the oracle be telling me that Polybos is not my father? Had I better avoid killing anyone old enough to be my father or marrying a woman old enough to be my mother?) But Sophocles gave his audience no opportunity in the play's swift action to consider such questions; the speed with which he shows us the oracle's completion fits with the consistent image of the god leaping or striking at Oedipus.

926 *man out front* Presumably the herald.

929–936 *I smash . . . kill them all* Oedipus uses the historical present tense in these lines. Although the events happened some twenty years earlier, they are vivid and immediate in his mind (Segal 2001, 90).

933–934 *staff / this hand holds* The hand was the instrument that retained the defilement of its acts. The actor might have raised his hand at this point, as he might have at other times when his hand is named. In Athenian law, acts committed by an agent's own hand, even if involuntarily, resulted in pollution, but masterminding or delegating the act escaped such stigma.

936 *kill them all* Said in pride, perhaps, but not in boastfulness. Laios' men would have attacked him; only by killing or disabling all would he have survived. In fact, Oedipus killed only four; the fifth (the herald) escaped, or perhaps recovered from a wound after being left for dead.

937 *stranger and Laios . . . were the same blood* In Greek, the word for stranger, *xenos*, could apply to Oedipus himself.

938 *triumph* The Greek word so translated is *athlios*, a superlative form of *athlon*, a contest or combat.

949 *utter filth* The Greek word so translated is *anagnos*, meaning "guilty," "unclean," or "unholy," and is usually translated as "polluted," which I avoid to escape confusion with modern uses of that word.

955 *brought me up and gave me birth* By reversing the natural order—birth followed by nurture— Sophocles reminds us that Polybos "gave birth" to Oedipus only by bringing him up and falsely claiming him as his own son.

965 *eyewitness* Literally, "person who was there."

976 *braving the road alone* The Greek word here is somewhat mysterious and might be translated literally as "with solitary belt." The word appears nowhere else in surviving Greek. It may mean simply "dressed as a traveler."

978 *evidence will drag me down* Literally, "the balance tips toward me." The metaphor is from scales for weighing, a typical one in judicial contexts. See *Oedipus at Kolonos*, note to 1652.

986 *poor doomed child* Literally, "unhappy person" (*dystanos*). Here Jokasta is thinking of the short, doomed life of her baby and uses the most common word for "unfortunate one." In her final speeches to Oedipus (at 1214 and 1217), she will use the same word to sum up his life.

989 *look right, then left* Literally, "shoot frightened glances right and left" (Gould 1970, 106). Ancient Greeks, who habitually took actions and made decisions based on signs and omens from the divinities, interpreted the sudden presence of a person or bird as hopeful (if it appeared on the right)

and dangerous (if it appeared on the left). Jokasta has abandoned such precautions.

996 *sky-walking laws* Literally, "sky-footed." The laws to which the Chorus refers here are those whose origins go as far back as human consciousness does, laws inseparable from our instinctive behavior. The laws forbidding incest and kin murder would be those most on the Chorus's mind.

1006–1007 *A violent will / fathers the tyrant* Literally, "*hubris* plants the seed of the *tyrannos*." *Hubris*, a general word for violence, outrage, and moral insubordination, sums up the actions of a person who exercises pure will without constraint, and thus applies most exactly to a Greek *tyrannos*. The name *tyrannos* was given to powerful rulers from the late seventh to the early fifth centuries who "emerged from the aristocratic oligarchy as sole rulers of their city-states, responsible only to themselves. . . . They were necessarily energetic, intelligent, confident, ambitious, and aggressive; they also had to be ruthless and suspicious of plots to overthrow their sometimes precarious position" (Segal 2001, 6). The term did not acquire our pejorative meaning of "tyrant" until Plato, in the fourth century. Throughout the play Sophocles uses *tyrannos* in the more neutral sense of a *basileus*, or king, except at 1007, where the modern sense of the tyrant is surely intended.

1039–1041 *Delphi . . . Olympia . . . Abai* All are holy shrines and destinations of religious pilgrimages. See note to 179.

1049 *the gods lose force* Literally, "the things pertaining to divinity slowly depart."

1080 *isthmus* The Isthmus of Korinth connects the Peloponnesus to the Greek mainland.

1104 *scour Pythian smoke* Literally, "scrutinize the Pythian hearth." The Pythoness delivered the prophecies from within a basement cell inside the temple of Apollo in Delphi, located on the slopes of Mount Parnassos. The smoky vapors that rose from the temple floor were reputed to put her in a trance. Recent geological studies of the soil around Delphi suggest that the fumes from its underlying rock structure contained ethylene—a sweet-smelling gas, once used as an anesthetic, that produces a pleasant euphoria. (See William J. Broad, "For Delphic Oracle, Fumes and Visions," *New York Times,* 19 March 2002, late ed.: F1.)

1131 *shines a great light* Literally, "great eye." The Greeks believed eyes projected powerful rays toward the people and the objects they looked at. Other uses of this metaphor in Greek literature suggest that a "great eye" was a sign of wonderful good hope or good luck.

1155 *unforgivable harm* Literally, "Lest you receive a religious pollution from those who planted you."

1214 *You poor child!* Jokasta calls Oedipus *dystanos,* the same word she called her child who was exposed and presumed dead (see note to 986). She now knows that child is Oedipus, and will call him *dystanos* once more at 1217. In his next speech, Oedipus will disclaim all human mothering and claim Luck (*Tyche*) for his parent (1226); he sees only the good in his situation at the moment.

1248 *Pan* A god holy to rural people, Pan was a patron of shepherds and herdsmen, as well as a fertility god amorous to both sexes. The mountain he roves is Kithairon, the mountain on which Oedipus' parents instructed the shepherd to let him die.

1253–1256 *Hermes . . . Kyllene . . . Helikon* Like Pan, Hermes was a god well known to country people for playing childish tricks. Zeus made him his messenger and gave him the wide-brimmed hat, winged sandals, and *kerykeion* (or *caduceus* in Latin, meaning herald's staff) with which he is often shown. Because of his association with roads, Hermes is known as the patron of wayfarers—traders, travelers, and thieves. The Chorus's mention of him might allude to the crossroads, the place at which Oedipus killed Laios. Kyllene, a haunt of both Pan and Hermes, is a mountain in Arcadia in the central Peloponnesus, the largest peninsula south of Attica, connected to the mainland only by the Isthmus of Korinth. The Muses inhabited a sanctuary on Helikon, a mountain south of Thebes.

1288 *Arcturos* A star near the Big Dipper that, when it appeared in September, signaled the end of summer in Greece.

1326 *Kill her own child?* The Greek phrase so translated, *tlemon tekousa* (literally, "poor woman, she who gave birth"), "shows how difficult it is to translate Sophocles' density and richness of meaning" (Segal 2001, 103). Here Sophocles implies that Jokasta found herself doing something utterly horrible for a mother to do: killing her own child.

1350 *Your fate teaches* Literally, "with your example [or "paradigm," *paradigmos*] before us."

1351–1352 *the story / god spoke* Literally, "with your *daimon* before us." See the introduction to this play for a discussion of *daimon*.

1358 *who sang the god's dark oracles* Literally, "singer of oracles." Presumably a reference to the Sphinx's riddles, but
the word "oracle" usually refers to divinely sanctioned responses such as those given by Delphi. Sophocles may here
be connecting the Sphinx to the other instances of divine
intervention in Oedipus' life.

1371 *tumbling* The Greek word so translated, *pesein*, literally
means to "fall on," or "attack," and can refer in one usage
to a baby falling between the legs of a woman squatted or
seated in childbirth. E. A. Havelock (in Gould 1970, 138)
suggests another meaning for the verb—to mount sexually,
in which case there is an overtone of violence. A variation of
the same verb, *empiptein*, used at 1431, I translate as "burst
into" to describe Oedipus' entry into Jokasta's bedroom
after she's committed suicide. (See also note for 1419.)

1391 *Danube . . . Rion* The river Danube was called the Ister in
the ancient world. The Rion, the modern name of the Phasis,
is a river in the Caucasus, on the edge of what was then the
known world.

1394 *not involuntary evil. It was willed* The Servant refers to
Jokasta's suicide and Oedipus' self-blinding; he contrasts
these conscious and willed actions with the ones Jokasta
and Oedipus made without understanding their true consequences, such as their own marriage. Although Oedipus
knew what he was doing when he blinded himself, the action was just as fated as the patricide and incest; Tiresias
had predicted Oedipus' blindness earlier. When the Servant
says that voluntary evils are more painful, he cannot mean
that they are more blameworthy or more serious but that

they are done in horror and desperation—in contrast to the earlier evils, such as the marriage, committed in optimism and confidence.

1415 *doubled lives* The reference is to Oedipus' "double" (*diplos*) relationship to Jokasta, as her son and husband. The word appears again at 1429 with a comparable allusion, as Oedipus enters the "double doors" of their bedroom. Another significant image of doubled action appears in the piercing of Oedipus' ankles and the striking out of his own eyes.

1419 *burst in* The Greek word so translated is *eisepaiein*, an unusual compound (from *eis*, "into," and *paiein*, "to strike") that might have been a colloquial word for intercourse recognizable by the audience (Gould 1970, 47). It is used here to compare Oedipus' violent action to a sexual attack, and thus to link it both to incest and to parricide.

1424–1425 *furrowed twice-mothering Earth . . . children sprang* The Messenger reports that Oedipus identifies Jokasta with an *aroura*, or furrowed field, as the source or origin of both Oedipus himself and the children he conceived with her. The image of Mother Earth figures significantly in the *Kolonos*. (See *Kolonos*, lines 1818–1820, and its introduction, p. 501.)

1431 *burst into* Again, the word *empiptein* (see note to 1371), used to refer to Oedipus' violation of Jokasta's "harbor" and her "furrow."

1512–1514 *Apollo . . . made evil, consummate evil / out of my life* Literally, "it was Apollo, friends, Apollo who brought to completion these, my evils [*pathea*]." A *pathos* (singular)

is here, as often in Greek literature, an unmerited suffering
sent by a god.

1516 *these eyes* Sophocles uses a pronoun (*nin*) for eyes, not a
noun, and one that is the same for any gender, plural, dual,
or singular. The ambiguity is surely deliberate but cannot
be translated. Its inclusiveness, however, implies that *all* the
blows that made his life evil, though struck by Oedipus himself, were caused by Apollo.

1724 *you will have your wish* Some scholars believe that Kreon
is agreeing to Oedipus' plea to be exiled. But it is more likely
that the words are noncommittal in the usual way of politicians.

1733–1746 *Thebans . . . god's victim* Some scholars question
the authenticity of these lines, partly because of the difficulty in making sense of several of them, and partly because
of their suspicious resemblance to the ending of Euripides'
Phoenician Women. Modern audiences object to them
mainly because they seem less than climactic. This objection
is illegitimate. Greek dramatists did not place strong emphasis on concluding lines the way modern dramatists do, but
often used them to facilitate the departure of the Chorus.

1746 *never having been god's victim* Literally, "having been
made to undergo no anguish." The final word of the play,
pathon, "having been made to undergo," is the same noun
used at 1471 in a phrase I translate as "pure, helpless anguish." Oedipus also used *pathos* at 1513 when he explained
that Apollo was the god who reduced him to misery. The
word is often used as a technical phrase for the suffering of
the *heros* in hero cults. The Latin translation is *passio*, which

gives us in its Christian context the "passion" of Christ. The word appears in the concluding lines of two of Aeschylus' plays, *The Libation Bearers* and *Prometheus Bound*, as well as in the last sentence of Sophocles' *Elektra*. It does not figure in the conclusion of any of Euripides' surviving plays.

OEDIPUS AT KOLONOS

2 *Have we come to a town?* It's clear from the exchange at 28–29 that Oedipus and Antigone know they're approaching Athens. Oedipus wants to know both what place (*koros*) or piece of open ground they're near and what town (*polis*). The word *polis* normally means city, but here it more likely refers to a smaller inhabited entity. The eventual answer to Oedipus' last question is: Kolonos.

11 *on public land, or in a grove* Oedipus is so tired that he doesn't care whether he and Antigone rest in a public space or risk trespassing, which they will shortly do, into a sacred grove (or precinct) from which unauthorized folk are excluded.

23 *nightingales* Nightingales symbolize death. This is the first allusion to the "holy place" where Oedipus will die.

25 *Be my lookout* Antigone maintains a sentinel's alertness throughout, spotting in turn the Stranger, the Old Men, Ismene, Kreon, and Polyneikes just before each enters.

37 *Stranger* The word *xenos*, translated usually throughout the text as "stranger," can also mean, and is sometimes translated as, "host" or "guest" depending on the context. The character called the Stranger in the surviving texts would most probably be a local farmer.

44–50 *fearsome goddesses . . . harsher names* The fearsome
   goddesses (literally, *emphoboi theai*) are the Eumenides,
   chthonian (or Earth) powers associated with death and
   the underworld (as opposed to Olympian, the heavenly or
   sky gods). Originally known as the Erinys, or Furies, they
   avenge wrongs done to family members—disrespect for elders, for instance, but especially kin murder. They were
   worshipped under a variety of names. Thebans, including
   Oedipus in this play, address them as "Ladies." In Athens
   their cult name was "Solemn Ones" (*Semnai*). Those who
   called them Kindly Ones did so to deflect their ire. In 50
   (literally, "other places have different names"), I translate
   the euphemistic "different" as "harsher" to highlight the
   Stranger's subtext, which is that these goddesses are dangerous. See note to 92.

51 *suppliant* Oedipus claims his formal status as a suppliant,
   one who makes a specific request of a higher authority, usually a god or his representative, or a ruler. Suppliants generally expected and were granted divine protection, though
   there were horrific exceptions, particularly during times of
   war or civil strife, in which suppliants were granted safety
   and then slaughtered.

54 here *is where I meet my fate* Oedipus' words in Greek are
   compact and mysterious. They may also be translated: "It's
   the sign of my destiny." The Greek word *synthema*, if translated literally as "sign," means a particular agreed-upon
   token, signal, or code word (Jebb 1986, 19). Oedipus could
   be saying that the name "Eumenides" is the sign foretold to
   him by Apollo's priestess at Delphi. Or he could mean that

his intended prayer or the grove itself is the sign. In any case, Apollo had promised that when Oedipus arrived at the grove of the Eumenides he would find rest at last. When Oedipus suddenly hears the name of the presiding goddesses, "the Kindly Ones," he turns brusquely decisive. He's arrived on promised ground and will not be moved.

62–64 *This entire grove . . . shrine here* Sacred groves in ancient Greece could harbor more than one divinity. This grove's major god is Poseidon, whose affinity with horses and the sea made him important to the Athenians, since navy and cavalry were crucial to their military prowess. The grove also contains shrines to Prometheus, and to the Eumenides, the grove's resident deities described in the note to 44–50.

65 *brass-footed threshold* In Sophocles' era, a well-known grove was located in Kolonos about a mile north of the Acropolis on the main route into Athens. Somewhere near the grove was a steeply descending rift or cavern in the rock, perhaps reinforced with brass to forms "steps." Jebb calls them "the *stay* of Athens: a phrase in which the idea of a physical basis is joined to that of a religious safeguard" (1886, 57n). The ancient audience would have understood the grove's rich mythical and historical associations and connected them to the area "on stage." See notes 1746–47 and 1748–50.

68 *We've all taken his name* Inhabitants commonly added their hometowns to their given names; e.g., Sophocles of Kolonos; Ion of Chios.

76 *Theseus* Theseus was a legendary hero who arrived in Athens as a formidable teenager after killing many human

and bestial adversaries on the way from his birthplace in
Troezen. He was unaware that the reigning king of Athens
was actually his father, Aigeus (though in some versions of
the myth Poseidon had actually sired him). Theseus' great
political accomplishment was the unification of Attica under
Athenian leadership.

81 *My words . . . can see* Oedipus claims here only the immediate cogency of his speech, but his confident assertion suggests the prophetic power his words will acquire and project
during the course of the play.

84 *down on your luck* Literally, *daimon*, a personal deity who
directs the events of an individual's life. At this point the
Stranger doesn't realize the full implication of the *daimon*
impacting Oedipus' life. See introduction to *Oedipus the
King* passim.

92 *eyes we dread* Literally, *deinopes*, or "dread-eyed." The
Kindly Ones were dreaded for their power to "see everything," especially all kinds of malfeasance. That power en-
abled them to detect and punish intrafamilial abuse.

95 *Apollo* Apollo, one of the twelve Olympian gods, was a
symbol of light and sometimes associated with Helios,
god of the sun. Apollo's primary epithet, *Phoibos*, means
"shining." He also oversaw the sites, the practice, and the
profession of prophecy. As revealed in *Oedipus the King*,
Apollo's priestess, the Pythoness at Delphi, prophesied Oedipus' fate: that Oedipus would kill his father and marry
his mother.

107–108 *sober man . . . spurn wine* Most Greek divinities received wine as an offering; the Eumenides were an exception. While Oedipus' sobriety might result from the recent

austere circumstances of his life, it also alludes to the frightening countenance he shares with the goddesses. See note to 155.

127–187 *Look for him . . . keep quiet* These lines comprise the *parodos* or entry song of the chorus, or Old Men, and like the choral odes to follow, were sung and accompanied by an oboe-like instrument, the *aulos*. This entry song is unusual in its utilitarian purpose; instead of reporting an event, it enacts an event: the search for and discovery of the grove's invader. The Old Men operate here and later as "security guards" who protect the sacred grove and the community of Kolonos. Oedipus addresses them as "guardians."

147–151 *We've heard . . . hiding place* The Leader and the Old Men, by interchangeably referring to themselves as "I" or "we," reinforce their collective nature.

155 *The sight of you . . . appalls us* Literally, "dreadful" [*deinos*] to see, dreadful to hear." Oedipus used the word *deinos* to refer to the Eumenides at 92.

234 *The horror I was born to* Oedipus' life. He refers to the fate assigned him before birth by Apollo, a fate he began living as soon as he was born.

242–244 *Laios' son . . . house of Labdakos* Laios was Oedipus' father, the man he killed without knowing his true identity; Labdakos, an earlier king of Thebes, was Laios' father.

259–260 *burden / our city . . . deadly contagion* Literally, "place a heavy obligation on the city." The obligation here is a *miasma*, or pollution. Ancient Greeks believed that those who murdered blood kin carried with them a contagion that would inflict damage on those in contact with the murderer.

At the beginning of *Oedipus the King*, Thebes suffers from such a contagion, which causes deadly disease, crop failure, and rampant miscarriage.

287–288 *Athens ... haven for persecuted strangers* Athens' reputation as a haven for exiles in distress was prominent in myth and the dramas derived from myth. Athens sheltered Orestes when he was pursued by the Furies; both the children of Herakles, who were persecuted by King Eurystheus; and the crazed Herakles himself after he had murdered his wife and children. Athens maintained that reputation in Sophocles' era by welcoming and granting legal status to immigrants as *metics*, allowing them to work and take part in some civic activities.

303–304 *those who tried / to murder me* Oedipus here refers to Jokasta and Laios, his true parents. When they heard an oracle's prophecy that doomed their son to kill his father and marry his mother, they pinned the infant's ankles together and left him to die. See *Oedipus the King*, 1173–1179.

335 *busy with foot traffic* The main road north from Athens passed through Kolonos. The implication is that Oedipus' disclosure of his identity to the Old Men would soon be bruited among the travelers heading toward Athens, and that Theseus would hear it from them as he moved north.

362 *two wretched lives!* Literally, "twice-wretched." Ismene reacts to the grim appearance of her father and sister. But "twice-wretched" also refers to the doubling of roles, in which his two sisters are also Oedipus' children, and thus adds psychic wretchedness to their physical and social misery.

371 *Those two boys imitate the Egyptians* The Greeks' cultural
     norm for the division of labor between the sexes was totally
     reversed in the lives of their Egyptian peers. Oedipus' sneer-
     ing judgment of his sons reveals the tendency of Greeks to
     consider foreigners as barbarians, morally and intellectually
     inferior to themselves. Sophocles was possibly influenced
     here by the section of Herodotus' *Histories* (2.35) that docu-
     mented Egyptian customs and manners.

386 *the latest oracles to your father* After Oedipus' banish-
     ment, Ismene became her father's informant—as Antigone,
     in a similarly helpful role, became his companion and senti-
     nel. Ismene brought Oedipus both Theban news and oracles
     involving him. Since she was in effect a spy, she was living
     dangerously. Ismene also volunteers to perform the purifica-
     tion ritual required of Oedipus by the "dread goddesses,"
     during which she's kidnapped.

398 *They were keen, at first, to let Kreon rule* The decision to
     allow Kreon to succeed Oedipus was prudent—both broth-
     ers realized the curse on their family might harm Thebes
     again, as it had during Oedipus' reign. But they changed
     their minds and contested the kingship, thus activating the
     curse. They had agreed to alternating terms. First Polynei-
     kes ruled Thebes, but then Eteokles, who succeeded him,
     refused to step down, apparently with the approval of the
     Theban population. See note to 930.

405 *that hothead* Eteokles inherited Oedipus' impetuousness
     without his father's intelligence and judgment.

410 *Argos* An area in the northeastern part of the Peloponnesus.

410 *married power* After his exile from Thebes, Polyneikes'
     marriage to the daughter of Adrastos, king of Argos, gave

him access to the Argive warrior class, which he persuaded
to lay siege to Thebes. Antigone calls her brother's marriage
"deadly" (*Antigone*, 954–955) because it led to the attack
that doomed both him and her.

422 *I have new oracles* It appears from the plural that Ismene has learned of two distinct oracles (probably sought
by Eteokles and/or Kreon). One identified Oedipus, living
or dead, as a magical defensive barrier that would protect
Thebes from attack. Another promised that Oedipus himself would be transformed into a *heros* whose powers would
extend beyond his physical death (see 424–435).

428 *When I'm nothing . . . be a man* Oedipus does not yet
know he has been tapped for heroization. In the course of
his next long speech (458–498), he realizes the power he's
been granted and begins to wield it.

435 *Theban frontier* There were no exact, demarcated borders
between Greek city-states like the ones that exist between
modern contiguous countries. Thebans would therefore
be making a judgment call when choosing the place near
Thebes in which to hold Oedipus; it had to be far enough
away so that Thebes wouldn't be contaminated by his pat-
ricidal guilt but close enough to the city to interfere with an
Athenian attack force.

439 *serious trouble* The trouble might refer to the possibility of
placing Oedipus' future Theban tomb in the wrong location
or to some other form of neglect, such as failing to honor the
dead king with libations of wine and honey.

448 *Your rage . . . your tomb* In their new oracles, the gods promise that Oedipus' crucial power will be manifest in his rage.

The scene envisioned in this line probably refers to Oedipus' tomb should it be located in Athens. The Thebans would deploy around it and be overwhelmed by the Athenian defenders as they fight; the dead *heros'* rage would add firepower to the attack against his former countrymen. Sophocles might allude here to the Theban raiding party that Athenian forces repulsed at Kolonos a few years before he wrote the play.

450 *Sacred envoys* Literally, *theoron,* a spectator or witness of a sacred rite or event. In this line, Sophocles specifically mentions that the envoys went to Delphi. In *Oedipus the King,* he uses the same word (*theoros,* a different grammatical case) to explain Laios' journey "into god's presence"—but he purposely withholds the king's destination. See *Oedipus the King,* note to 129–130.

450 *Delphic hearth* Apollo's oracle resided at Delphi. The hearth refers to the smoky fire that enveloped the Pythoness as she delivered her versified answer to the questions posed to her by envoys. See *Oedipus the King,* note to 1104.

458–461 *Gods, don't interfere . . . dead set* Oedipus here frames the wish that his sons both die as a request to the gods; later, at 1495–1520, he will himself deliver the same malevolence as both curse and prophecy.

464–465 *When I was driven . . . no move to stop it or help me.* At the end of *Oedipus the King,* Oedipus had asked Kreon to exile him, but Kreon refused. As implied in the *Kolonos,* Oedipus had become reconciled to Thebes and wished to remain there. Here he refers to his sons' failure to honor that wish, as well as to their dereliction of a duty fundamental in Greek law: to care for, support, and protect an aged parent.

470 *far-off day when my fury seethed* Oedipus refers to the day
he became aware of the incest and patricide he had unwittingly committed—the day on which he blinded himself and
asked Kreon to banish him from Thebes. See *Oedipus the
King,* 1629–1630.

489 *I recalled some prophecies* Without explaining the specif-
ics, Oedipus makes clear that he now sees the connection
between the two new prophecies brought by Ismene—that
he will be transformed at death and that his dead body will
have military potency—and the much earlier prophecy at
Delphi, which said he would find a final home in the Eumenides' grove.

503 *Whatever my host wants done* Oedipus addresses the
Leader in his specific role as adviser to strangers on the
local laws and customs. As Oedipus grows more and more
alienated from (and obstinate in) his relationships with his
sons, the Old Men, and Kreon, he becomes increasingly ac-
quiescent in his position as a suppliant—and he gains in divine authority.

504–531 *Ask atonement . . . If you don't . . . I'm afraid for
you.* This lengthy passage, in which the Leader specifies the
procedure that Oedipus, as suppliant, must follow in his ritual offering to the Eumenides, serves a dramatic purpose: Ismene, by volunteering to perform the rituals, is sent offstage
long enough to be kidnapped by Kreon. But the passage also
marks the beginning of Oedipus' religious involvement mentioned in the note to 503.

519 *Just pure water* The Eumenides differed from other gods
because they did not receive offerings of wine. See note to
107–108.

529 *without looking back, leave* It was customary when making offerings to most gods, and especially these "dread-eyed goddesses," to avert one's eyes from the actual shrine while pouring the offerings, to pray quietly, and then to leave the shrine "without looking back."

549–603 *Unpleasant it may be . . . ignorance* This colloquy in which the Old Men press Oedipus to confess to his incest and patricide, and during which Oedipus both admits to the facts but defends the innocence of his motives, is a choral ode and was set in the ancient productions to music and sung.

562–566 *I suffered anguish . . . I chose to do none* In this coolly rational defense of his moral innocence, Oedipus focuses on the huge imbalance between the misery he's suffered and his lack of culpability for actions he committed in ignorance. In successive restatements he will add passion to his logic, especially when replying to Kreon's accusations.

568–569 *Thebes married me . . . woman who would destroy me* The Thebans, who were grateful that Oedipus had saved them from the Sphinx, rewarded him with the throne—and Laios' widow, Jokasta, who became his wife. See introduction to *Oedipus the King*.

575 *scourges* Literally, *ata*, or "curses." Oedipus does not mean that his two much-loved daughters are literally curses, but rather that they are constant reminders of the defilement and pain his acts have caused. Speaking metaphorically, no matter how deeply they care for him, his daughters are constant scourges who pursue him in order to punish his incest and patricide. (See also note for 945–951.)

One of Theseus' Men enters I infer this stage direction to make
 sense of the Leader's next lines, in which he seems certain
 that Theseus intends to help Oedipus.

619 *I was also raised in exile* Theseus, raised by his mother
 Aethra, a princess of Troezen, in the Peloponnesus, grew
 up without knowing that his father was King Aigeus of
 Athens. As a young man, Theseus learned the truth and
 traveled to his father's home, performing many heroic feats
 along the way. Similarly, Oedipus, who was raised in Korinth by Polybos without knowing that his natural father
 was Laios, king of Thebes, suffered great hardship after
 the discovery of his true identity—and is still suffering at
 this point in the play.

656 *Then what superhuman pain* do *you suffer?* Sophocles
 might allude here to Oedipus' imminent transformation to
 a *heros.*

661 *God's voice* The oracle. Its words, from the Pythoness of
 Apollo, made clear to the Thebans that not bringing Oedipus home put their city at risk.

666–667 *All powerful / Time ravages the rest* Oedipus reminds Theseus of a lesson he first learned in *Oedipus the
 King*: the only thing man can be certain of is the unstable
 nature of all human relationships—including political alliances between cities. Oedipus elaborates his first reference
 to Time, or *Kronos*, as a teacher of acquiescence (7–8); he
 now sees time as a continuum that destroys and revives
 relationships. The idea is analogous to his own transformation by the gods from great king to blind beggar to honored
 heros.

679–680 *Then my dead body . . . will drink their hot blood*
Oedipus extrapolates from the oracle he heard from Ismene:
that the Thebans will be defeated in battle while they are
mustered near his tomb.

690 *kindness* The Greek word *eumeneia*, translated as "kindness," often refers to the goodwill of the gods. Here it echoes
the name of the Eumenides, or Kindly Ones, and also alludes to a bond between Oedipus and the goddesses.

692 *our wartime ally* Some scholars, including Blundell, think
this refers to a preexisting military alliance, while others,
including Knox, say that it means nothing so specific or
formal, but rather a traditional courtesy extended between
royal houses.

697–698 *I'll settle him . . . rights of a citizen* A much-disputed
line that depends upon whether one reads a Greek word at
637 in the ancient manuscripts as *empalin* or *empolin*. The
line could mean respectively *"on the contrary I'll settle him
in our land"* or, as I believe, and as Jebb translates, *"but will
establish him as a citizen* in the land" (1886, 109). The issue
is important because the granting of the highly prized Athenian citizenship rights to a foreigner like Oedipus would be
a more striking demonstration of Theseus' *charis*, or grace,
toward him than would his simply offering Oedipus a place
to live.

728–787 *You've come, stranger . . . Nereid's skittering feet* This
ode of welcome to Oedipus as an Athenian citizen touches
on many visual features of the splendid Kolonian landscape.
Its intent, however, is to celebrate the mythical and practical
advantages for Athens inherent in these visual images. For

an excellent discussion of the ode as both a hymn of praise to the pinnacle of Athens' greatness and as a requiem for the city's dying power, see Knox (1964, 154–156).

728 *shining Kolonos* The epithet "shining" may derive from the light, chalky color of Kolonos' soil, which has persisted to this day.

741–743 *Dionysos . . . maenads* Dionysos, the god associated with wine and revelry, was the son of Zeus and Semele, the daughter of Kadmos, king of Thebes. In the version of the myth adapted by Euripides in *The Bakkhai*, Semele tried to test the godliness of Zeus by challenging him to appear to her in his true shape. He did—and she was struck by lightning and thunderbolts, the symbols of his divine power. Zeus then snatched the unborn Dionysos from her body, hid him in his thigh, and took him to be brought up by nymphs, or maenads, on Mount Nysa in India. There Dionysos was schooled in the joys of wine by Silenus and the satyrs; he also cultivated a following of maenads (bacchants) who eventually traveled with him through Asia and into Greece.

749–750 *Persephone and Demeter . . . golden crocus* Demeter, the corn goddess, traveled into the underworld to find her daughter Persephone, who had been carried there (where she was forced to spend half the year) by Hades. Both goddesses are associated with death and the mysteries, which promise their initiates rebirth through the purification of death. The crocus and the nightingale also symbolize death and are fitting reminders that Oedipus will die in this grove.

751 *Bountiful . . . Kephisos* While other rivers in Attica ran dry in the summer heat, the Kephisos flowed abundantly all year.

758–759 *Goddess of Love / with golden reins in her hands* Aphrodite, the goddess of erotic desire, was often portrayed driving a chariot drawn by sparrows, swans, or doves.

761 *Asia* The Greeks used "Asia" to refer to what is now called the Middle East.

761–773 *A tree not found . . . guard it with tireless glare.* Although olive trees did grow in "Asia" and the peninsula known as Peloponnesus, the first olive tree was said to have sprung up from the Acropolis at Athena's command. This sacred tree, burned during the Persian wars, was also said to have miraculously come back to life ("a tree born from itself") and, because it was protected by Athena, to have deflected later invaders ("a terror to enemy spears"). "Zeus of the Olive Groves" translates Zeus *Morios*, his title as "co-protector" of the sacred olives. Sophocles might be using the olive tree to symbolize more than Athens' military resilience and the divine protection it receives. The Athenians believed their race was autochthonic, i.e., they were born directly from the land. Their political system, democracy, was similarly homegrown. The olive tree, which Sophocles enjoins Athenian men (both young and old) not to shatter and destroy, might symbolize the democratic institutions at the heart of Athens' past glory.

787 *fifty Nereids* The daughters of the sea god Nereus are sometimes portrayed escorting ships through the high seas. Sophocles' image suggests that the Nereids' presence is

visible in the rhythmic circular ripples made by the oars as
they dip into the water.

809 *fellow Kadmeans* Thebans were called Kadmeans after
Kadmos, the mythical son of Agenor and founder of Thebes.
Kadmos seeded the earth with dragon's teeth from which
the Thebans grew (see *Oedipus the King*, note to 96).

819 *first vulgar lout who comes along* Kreon himself will soon
live up to this description when he orders his troops to abduct Antigone and attempt to take her back to Thebes. But a
darker irony in this passage harks back to *Antigone*, which
Sophocles wrote some decades earlier, in which she is betrothed to Kreon's son Haimon.

834 *That would cause me unendurable pain* Oedipus knows
that if he went back to Thebes, Kreon would refuse to bury
his corpse; because he has committed patricide and incest,
burial rites are forbidden him.

838 *you refused me* When Oedipus first pleaded to be exiled
(see *Oedipus the King*, 1629–1630), Kreon refused, saying
he needed first to consult the gods. Here Oedipus suggests
that Kreon acted arbitrarily without such a consultation.

909 *She's mine* Oedipus asked Kreon to assume guardianship
of Antigone and Ismene in *Oedipus the King*, but Antigone
has hardly been under his protection, since for many years
she's been wandering with Oedipus, more or less acting as
his guardian.

921–922 *My city, / our city is attacked!* The issue here is not a
physical attack by the Theban raiding party but the violation and abduction of Antigone, who, like Oedipus, is a suppliant under Attic protection.

927 *daughters for crutches* The word translated as crutches, *skeptroin*, literally means scepters. Blundell writes, "Since scepter is in origin a staff or walking stick, the same word in Greek is used for both. Sophocles exploits this ambiguity to create a pathetic contrast between Oedipus' helplessness (here and at [Greek] l. 1109) and his sons' bid for the royal scepter of Thebes ([Greek] 425, 449, 1354). There is also a nice dramatic irony in [K]reon's words, since as it turns out, Oedipus will not need the support of these 'scepters' any longer" (1990, 55). At 462, 484, and 1416, I translate *skeptroin* in its singular form as "scepter," "power and a kingdom," and "your throne and your power," respectively.

930 *though I remain their king* The kingship of Thebes remains unclear throughout the play. We're told earlier that Eteokles has reneged on his agreement with Polyneikes to relinquish the throne. But does Eteokles still rule? Kreon seems to assert here that he's in power, as we assumed he would be at the end of *Oedipus the King*. See note to 398.

933–935 *turned your back . . . self-destructive fury* In *Oedipus the King*, Sophocles portrays Oedipus as full of rage and fury, a man who quickly turns in anger on his friends (especially at 760–790, where Kreon, Jokasta, and the Leader attempt to calm him down to no avail). Undoubtedly, Oedipus' two most self-destructive acts are the killing of Laios and his own self-blinding. In the *Kolonos*, Oedipus' anger loses its self-destructive power as it's transformed into a power that helps his new friends the Athenians and harms his enemies, a category that now includes both his sons.

943 *You might—unless our king stops you* Some scholars
and translators attribute this line to Kreon, changing
"our" to "your" as justifiably sarcastic under the circumstances.

945–951 *Goddesses...the curse...as miserable as my
own* When Oedipus invokes the Eumenides in their role
as guarantors of curses, he avoids calling them Kindly
Ones (see 1109 and 1521). Ancient Greeks commonly
cursed their enemies with the same "evils" that had been
inflicted on them. The Greek word *ata* means both prayer
and curse; a curse was simply a malicious or retaliatory
prayer. At the end of Antigone's life, she asks that her oppressors suffer a punishment equivalent to hers (*Antigone*,
1021–1022).

949 *Let the Sun, who sees all there is* Helios, the sun god, sometimes associated with Apollo, rode a golden chariot across
the sky, a perfect vantage point from which to take in everything that happens on Earth.

978 *the two I have left* At this point, having disowned his sons,
he's effectively given them up as dead. Antigone will similarly treat Ismene as nonexistent after she refuses to help
bury Polyneikes (*Antigone*, 95ff.).

1017 *permanent residence* Theseus makes Kreon an offer he
can't refuse: bring the girls back unless he wants to be taken
prisoner.

1029 *morally toxic father-killer* The Greek word translated
"morally toxic" is *anagnon*, which in Jebb's words "refers
to the taint of murder aggravated by union with the wife of
the slain" (1886, 152). Kreon implies that Oedipus' crimes
are present in his physical person and contagious. Oedipus

himself agrees; at 1241 he will shrink back from his own instinctual gesture to shake Theseus' hand.

1031 *Council of Mount Ares* The ancient Athenian Council of Areopagos, which met on a hill near the Acropolis, had jurisdiction over murder and matters of impiety; it imposed penalties including fines, exile with loss of property, and death, and its judgments were final.

1048–1050 *none of which / I chose . . . whole life* Oedipus continues with increasing conviction to plead his case: because he was ignorant of the identity of his father and mother when he committed patricide and incest he believes that he is not responsible for or guilty of the crimes.

1050 *ancestors* The House of Labdakos. See note to 242–244.

1145–1202 *Oh let us . . . help this land and our people!* In this rousing ode, the Old Men imagine the action and outcome of the skirmish that ensues when Theseus and his troops set out to free Antigone and Ismene from the Thebans.

1148 *Pythian shore* The Old Men name two possible points, both on the Bay of Eleusis, where Theseus' horsemen could overtake Kreon's men, who had fled with the kidnapped daughters. The first, the "Pythian shore," would be reached via Daphni, a town in a mountain pass about six miles from Kolonos. Daphni was the site of a temple to Apollo, who is sometimes called Pythian.

1149–1154 *torch-lit beaches . . . rites for the dead* The second interception point would be at the sacred town of Eleusis, where an annual torch-lit procession was held in honor of Demeter and Persephone—the "two great queens" of the underworld (see note to 749–750). Eleusis was about five miles south of the Pythian shore. The Eleusinian rites, known as

the Mysteries, were tightly guarded secrets kept from all
but initiates. The priests who carried out the initiations and
enforced the pledge of secrecy were always members of the
family of Eumolpidae.

1162–1163 *snowy / rock in the town of Oea* The Old Men now
propose a third escape route for Kreon's men. Jebb cites
an ancient scholiast who identifies the "snowy rock" as an
outcrop of Mount Aigaleos near the Athenian rural district
or *deme* of Oea, several miles northwest of Kolonos (1886,
1059n).

1172 *Athena* Athena, also a goddess of horses, shared an altar
at Kolonos with Poseidon, presumably the altar where Theseus has been making sacrifices.

1175 *goddess Rhea* Poseidon was the son of Kronos and Rhea.

1198–1199 *Apollo, / bring Artemis* Apollo, the god whose
weapon of choice was the bow and arrow, was the brother
of Artemis, the goddess of hunting.

1294–1316 *Father, please hear me . . . repay it.* Antigone's substantial speech is noteworthy in several respects. It demonstrates her intense sisterly concern for Polyneikes. In asking
her father to show compassion, she invokes the damage the
family curse has inflicted by having parents punish their
children. Antigone fears that Oedipus' cruelty will affect
others besides Polyneikes. She's right; Oedipus rejection of
Polyneikes will have a role in Antigone's own death.

1326–1369 *Anyone who craves . . . northern mountains* In this
starkly unsentimental and keenly detailed picture of aging,
the Old Men remind the audience of an implied alternative to accepting one's painful final years. Death and the

ultimate home of the dead, Hades, become a wished-for release. The outlook resembles that of Hamlet's "To be or not
to be" soliloquy.

1344–1350 *By any measure . . . place he came from* The sentiments in this famously pessimistic Greek proverb—the story
goes back at least to the archaic period—belong to Silenus,
the leader of the satyrs in Dionysos' band of revelers. When
asked (while drunk), "What's best?" he answered, "Never
to be born at all." Second best, if one was unlucky enough to
be born, was to go back wherever one came from as quickly
as possible. Easterling (52–53) writes, "Death never ceased
to be a defining feature of tragedy in Greek tradition; it is
perhaps not an accident that the presiding deity of the festivals which included tragedy [i.e., Dionysos] should have such
strong connexions with the world of the dead." See translators' introduction passim for examples of the Dionysiac
influence on Athens' great theater festival.

1389 *Respect* In the Greek, *aidos.* Many scholars and translators use "Mercy" here, but I follow Blundell in interpreting Respect as the goddess that Polyneikes personifies as an
attendant of Zeus (1990). The tenor of Polyneikes' speech
suggests that he is appealing precisely for respect rather than
begging for mercy. Oedipus counters and rejects Polyneikes'
invocation by personifying Justice as Zeus' attendant at
1508.

1395 *Will you deny me with silent contempt?* As a suppliant,
Polyneikes is due the honor of an answer to a request, but
as both Theseus and Antigone explain, at 1291–1293 and
1294–1316, Oedipus is not bound to grant the request.

Oedipus might be silent for the moment, but he unleashes his wrath at 1480ff.

1415–1416 *elder son . . . to inherit your throne* Since primogeniture was not customary in ancient Greece, Polyneikes' argument loses some of its force.

1420 *persuaded Thebes to back him* Polyneikes implies that Eteokles manipulated the Thebans into backing him—a tactic, writes Blundell, that democrats in Sophocles' time would have approved of (1990, 139n). The word literally translated as persuade, *peisas*, often euphemistically connotes bribery, writes Knox (1982, 1467n).

1421–1422 *the Fury who stalks you / strengthened his case* Polyneikes, with characteristic tactlessness, blames the ancient curse on Oedipus for the quarrel between the brothers.

1428–1429 *seven companies / of spearmen to fight Thebes* Polyneikes has convinced six Argive warlords to join his attack on the seven gates of Thebes and put him back in power. They will not succeed. Here Polyneikes presents his strategy for the assault, presumably hoping for his father's approval. The most colorful of the seven participants are noted below. Also see *Antigone*, note to line 20.

1435 *Amphiaraos* Amphiaraos, once the king of Argos, was a seer who refused to take part in the ill-fated siege against Thebes until his wife Eriphyle shamed him to join the battle. (Polyneikes had bribed her to do so with a golden heirloom necklace that belonged to his family.)

1441 *Kapaneus* Kapaneus, who boasted that nothing could stop him from scaling the walls of Thebes to set its houses on fire, was struck down for his arrogance by a thunderbolt from Zeus. See *Antigone*, 148ff.

1444 *Atalanta* Atalanta, the late-life mother of Parthenopaios, was disowned by her father and raised in the woods by a she-bear in Arcadia. She swore never to marry unless the successful suitor outran her in a footrace. In some versions of the myth, Milanion, who fathered her son, met Atalanta's conditions by dropping three golden apples along the route of a race, each of which she stopped to pick up. He thereby overtook her.

1457 *fountains of home* Springs, the source of fresh water essential for life, were considered symbolic of the land and often protected by nymphs.

1459–1460 *I'm a beggar . . . but so are you* Polyneikes overlooks a crucial difference between Oedipus' status as beggar and exile and his own: Oedipus brings with him a helpful "gift" for his benefactor; Polyneikes only pleads for help.

1498–1499 *The blood you shed will defile you . . . as he dies* Oedipus means that the brothers will defile each other by committing simultaneous fratricide.

1500–1522 *I cursed you both . . . Ares the Destroyer* Oedipus imagines his curses (in the Greek, *arai*) almost as having physical force. He speaks of them as allies, as fellow fighters in his campaign to teach his sons to respect their parents. Jebb writes, "The *arai,* when they have once passed the father's lips, are henceforth personal agencies of vengeance" (1886, 1375n). Tartaros is the part of the underworld where evildoers are punished for their crimes. The native spirits Oedipus summons are the Eumenides in their punitive mode.

1508 *Justice* Oedipus responds to Polyneikes' personification of Respect at 1389 by invoking Justice, a goddess
who can be expected to carry out Zeus' will without
mitigation.

1538–1539 *don't dishonor me . . . Perform the rituals* In *Antigone*, she will honor her brother by performing the burial
rites he requests, but by doing so she risks her own life.

1580–1628 *We've just seen . . . Zeus!* In this choral ode, the
gods begin their final and benign intervention in Oedipus'
life. The heightened musical energy from song and wind instruments accompanies Oedipus' understanding and acceptance that he is being called to his death.

1594 *That was thunder! O Zeus!* In Apollo's original oracle,
thunder and lightning were two of the three signs that would
announce Oedipus' death and transformation.

1652 *My life is weighted to sink down* This ancient image is of
a balance scale in which Zeus decides the outcome of life-
or-death matters by weighting the scale so that it sinks the
doomed person or people.

1698 *Hermes* As the messenger of Zeus, one of Hermes' duties
was to escort the souls of the dead to the underworld.

1708 *unseen goddess* Persephone, queen of the underworld, was
called the unseen goddess, perhaps because her husband's
name, Hades, literally means "unseen."

1711 *Aidoneus* Aidoneus is a longer version of Hades' name.
The Old Men address him tentatively because he is notori-
ously resistant to prayer. See *Antigone*, 857, where Kreon
makes a jibe at Antigone by snidely suggesting she pray to
Hades to save her life.

1715 *house of Styx* A reference to the River Styx that runs through the underworld.

1719 *Earth Goddesses!* The Eumenides.

1721 *Savage guard-dog!* Cerberus, the monstrous three-headed dog who stands guard at the entrance to the underworld, was said to be docile to those who entered but to devour all who attempted to leave.

1743 *steep brass steps* See note to 65.

1744 *a maze of crossing paths* This might allude to the crossroads where Oedipus killed Laios and to the maze of fated events in his life.

1746–1747 *immortal pact that Theseus / made with Peirithous* Before attempting to rescue Persephone from the underworld, Theseus and his friend Peirithous pledged their everlasting friendship at a place "where a bowl had been hollowed from a rock shelf." But Hades trapped and detained them both. In most versions of the myth, Herakles rescued Theseus but left Peirithous to suffer the torments of the criminal dead.

1748–1750 *rock / of Thoricos . . . stone tomb* These local landmarks (and their significance) would have been familiar to Sophocles' audience. Although the exact location of the spot where Oedipus is transformed must remain a secret, the detailed geographical description adds credibility to the miraculous destination of Oedipus' final journey.

1758–1759 *washed . . . white clothes customary* Literally, "gave him the bath and the prescribed clothing." Greek burial rituals included washing the corpse and dressing it in white garments. See *Antigone* introduction.

1762 *Zeus of the Underworld thundered* A reference to Hades.
Both Hades and the Olympian Zeus are the supreme gods
of their respective realms below and above the Earth. The
earthquake is the third and last of the signs that Apollo told
Oedipus would signal his imminent death.

1778 *enormous voice called him* Blundell suggests that the god
who beckons Oedipus might be identified with Hermes,
Persephone, or perhaps Hades himself (1990, 190n), but the
anonymity of the god's voice adds to the mystery.

1818–1820 *Earth's lower world . . . welcoming kindness* For
a discussion of this passage, see *Kolonos* introduction, pp.
500–501.

1924–1925 *the Earth Powers / have shown us all so much grace*
Theseus reminds the grieving Antigone and Ismene that by allowing their father to die a painless death in this sacred grove,
the gods of Hades have blessed both Oedipus and Athens.

1936 *Horkos* The son of Eris, or Strife. His role is to witness
and enforce oaths, and therefore to end contention and war
by bringing mortals together in binding agreements.

ANTIGONE

Scene Antigone's awareness of Kreon's decree and Polyneikes'
unburied corpse suggests that she had left the palace to visit
the city (and perhaps the battlefield). If so, she would enter
from outside the palace gates.

1–2 *Born . . . womb* The Greek word *autadelphon*, translated
with *koinon* (kindred) as a single phrase "born like me from
that same womb," literally means "selfsame womb." *Koinon*,
subsumed into the phrase as "like me," may also be rendered

as "kindred" (Jebb) or "linked to me" (Lloyd-Jones). Antigone's first words to Ismene thus strike a chord that reverberates throughout the drama: their shared family inheritance includes horrific misfortunes that go back to their conceptions and births. The Greek word *kara* is translated with the endearment "love." Tyrrell and Bennett write, "Sophocles' avoidance of a usual word for sister may also point to Ismene as less important to Antigone in that capacity than as a 'wombmate' . . . and also suggests the excessive closeness brought about by Oedipus, their common father and brother" (31).

5–8 our lives . . . *you and I haven't seen and shared* Antigone speaks of her sister and herself as united by common interests, as well as blood, until 94. After Ismene refuses to help bury Polyneikes (95–96), Antigone stops referring to herself and Ismene as a pair.

9 *new command* Kreon, the girls' uncle, Thebes' military leader, or *strategos*, and now its new king, presumably declared this edict only hours earlier, as soon as the Argive army's retreat was apparent.

15 *as if they were our enemies!* This suggests that the bodies of all the dead Argive attackers have been left unburied. We later learn from Tiresias that this is indeed the case. Polyneikes fits both the category of *philos*, loved one or family member, and that of *ekthros*, enemy.

20 *the double blow* After Oedipus departed Thebes in exile to Athens, his sons Eteokles and Polyneikes agreed to alternate as king. But Eteokles refused to step down at the end of his year and banished his brother. Polyneikes moved to Argos, married King Adrastos' daughter, and solicited support for a campaign

to regain power in his home city. He and six other Argive captains attacked the seven gates of Thebes. During the battle, the brothers apparently struck each other with simultaneous deadly spear thrusts, a mode of death that fulfilled the curse against his sons delivered by Oedipus in the *Kolonos*. (Aspects of this war are the subject of Aeschylus' *Seven Against Thebes* and Euripides' *Phoenician Women* and *The Suppliants*.)

24 *past the gates* Refers to the house gates, not the outer palace gates that lead to the town.

32 *The dead will respect him* According to fifth-century Greek religious belief, failure to mound earth over a dead family member and perform the required funeral rituals would cause those already dead in Hades to shun and scorn such a dishonored shade (ghost) when it arrived among them.

43 *stoned to death* Since communal stoning by many citizens would have been an appropriate method of execution for Polyneikes, a traitor to his own people, a citizen who defied the city to bury a traitor would be fittingly sentenced to the same method of execution.

48–49 *yanking the knot . . . pry it loose* The image comes from weaving, strictly a woman's occupation for the Greeks. Ismene might be sarcastically asking her sister how her weaving skills could be of any use in burying Polyneikes and confronting Kreon.

52 *lift his body* To cover Polyneikes' heavy body with the substantial mounding of earth that Antigone envisions at 97–98, she will need Ismene's help. Without that help she would be forced to perform a more limited ceremony—a dusting with earth, a poured libation, screams of grief—such as the Guard will soon describe.

58–70 *our father's / destruction . . . kin murder!* Ismene recalls
the gods' savage punishment of their parents to highlight the
difference between Oedipus' and Jokasta's "horrible deeds"
and the lesser matter of a failed ritual, which she hopes the
gods and the dead ("the Spirits," 78) will understand and
forgive.

71–72 *how much worse / our own deaths* Ismene imagines the
threatened stoning as a much harsher method of death than
their mother's hanging, but "much worse" could also refer
to the fact that there are no women left in the family to
perform the sacred burial rituals mentioned in the note to
52—rituals that only women could perform. See *Antigone*
introduction, pp. 621–622.

87–88 *lie down / next to* The Greek word Antigone uses here
for lying down, *keisomai*, would be equally appropriate to
describe lying in death (either before burial or in Hades) or
having sexual relations with a lover (Blundell 1989, 110).
The words used to describe their kinship, *philê* with *philou*,
(translated here as "I who love him" next to "him who loves
me") accentuate both the emotional bond and the physical
proximity of the bodies (Griffith, 135).

89 *criminal conduct* The Greek words *hosia panourgesas*
(literally, "sacred transgressions") refer primarily to the
outlawed act of burying her "traitor" brother, but they
also allude, given the way they are embedded in the sentence, to the incestuous love Antigone might feel for Polyneikes.

107 *those who matter* Most likely the gods; perhaps also Polyneikes. See 487–508, an elaboration of Antigone's intention
to please Hades and the gods of the underworld.

Exit ANTIGONE She leaves abruptly to look for Polyneikes'
  body on the battlefield, ignoring Ismene's warning and concern.

121–122 *Morning sunlight . . . on seven-gated Thebes!* The Elders begin a song that celebrates Thebes' victory over Argos.
  Notably missing from the song is any reference to what pre-
  occupies Kreon: punishing the dead body of Polyneikes. Joy
  and celebration, gratitude to Dionysos, Ares, and all the
  other gods, are paramount.

124 *Dirke* One of two rivers flowing through Thebes. The other
  is the Ismenos.

127 *white shield* The name of the region from which the attacking army comes, Argos, suggests silvery or shining white-
  ness.

128 *sharp piercing bit* The Argive army is portrayed as a wild
  vicious horse and the defending Thebans as the horse tamer
  who subdues it—by using a particularly nasty bit that digs
  into the horse's jaw.

131 *quarrelsome* A pun, since Polyneikes' name means literally
  "serial battler."

133 *white-feathered Eagle* An emblem of Argos.

141–142 *Firegod's / incendiary pine tar* Literally, "Hephestos'
  pine-fed flame." Balls of pine pitch were set afire and lobbed
  via catapult over defensive walls and onto wooden houses in
  besieged cities.

146 *Dragon* The ancestral "snake" with whom Thebans identified. See *Oedipus the King*, note to 96.

148 *Zeus hates a proud tongue* A reference to Kapaneus. See
  Kolonos, note to 1441.

169–170 *trophies / for Zeus* At the end of a battle, the armor of
the defeated troops was collected and fastened to totem-like
structures in honor of Zeus.

174 *Victory* The wingèd goddess Niké.

181 *each god's temple* With the fighting over and victory secured, every god who might have played a part in helping
Thebes win must be honored in his or her own temple, hence
the festive midnight rounds.

183–184 *Bakkhos, the god whose dancing / rocks Thebes*
Bakkhos, an alternate name for Dionysos, is characteristi-
cally worshipped by song and a drum-accompanied dance.
He often makes his presence felt by causing an earthquake.
See *Oedipus the King*, note to 250.

185–191 *our new king . . . Council of the Wise* This will be
Kreon's first consultation with this body of seasoned politicians since his assumption of power the previous day. It will
turn out that he neither solicits nor welcomes their opinions.

204 *defiled by his own brother's blood* Kin murder had been
for centuries an intensely feared crime, since it inflicted infamy and uncleanness on the guilty; such defilement was difficult to cleanse. In this case, it will be impossible because
the guilty brothers are both dead.

207–212 *character, / policies . . . sound advice* By setting stan-
dards according to which a ruler should be judged, Kreon
focuses attention on his coming failures and blunders as a
leader.

222–223 *It's only on board . . . true friends* Kreon's assess-
ment of friendship, for him defined in the context of loyalty

to one's city, differs startlingly from Antigone's. She believes that friends are made only at birth, an indication of her strong ties to family. The Greek word used in both of their assessments of "friendship" is *philia*. See note to 567–568.

239 *ugly . . . disgrace* The practice of refusing burial to dead enemies was a contentious political issue in fifth-century Greece that was dramatized in two other surviving plays, *The Suppliants* of Aeschylus and *The Suppliant Women* of Euripides.

266 *talking annihilation* I follow here Griffith's interpretation of the Greek line 234 and his suggestion that a translation of the phrase *to medon exerô* should express the Guard's fear that his story might turn him into "nothing"—i.e., get him killed.

279–280 *thirsty / dust . . . rituals* Polyneikes' body was not buried or entombed as would have been customary, but appears to have received a minimal ritual from a source unknown. See note to 310.

310 *inspired by the gods?* The mysterious circumstances of the burial described by the Guard—no tracks, no footprints— suggest to the Leader that the gods have either performed or otherwise prompted the minimal burial of Polyneikes. If so, punishing a human agent would be dangerously offensive to the gods who have intervened on Polyneikes' behalf.

340 *strung up—and you'll hang* Kreon, with characteristic bluster, threatens to torture and kill anyone within earshot who refuses to track down and hand over the person who buried Polyneikes.

352 *since you were born* Implies that the Guard is a household
servant or slave with whom Kreon has been long acquainted.

364–365 *Wonders abound . . . astounding than man!* Literally,
"There are many wonders / terrors but none as wonderful /
terrible as man." The Greek word *ta deina* can mean either
"wonderful" or "terrible." Most scholars and translators
stress both the positive and negative capacities of humans
in the context of this ode (364–413). I omit the "terrifying"
dimension in 364 because, on inspection, virtually all the
examples of humankind's activity in the ode contributed to
the development of civilization. But my choice of the word
"astounding" in 365 alludes to the human capacity for evil.
At the end of the ode, when humankind's "terrifying" or
destructive aspect does surface, the Elders condemn it. The
city's banishment of an isolated "reckless and corrupt" over-
reacher reflects the Elders' final judgment.

373 *stallion-sired mules* Literally, "the children of horses."
Mules were the preferred draft animals used on Greek farms.

404–405 *follow the laws / Earth teaches him* With these
lines, Sophocles reminds us that Kreon and Antigone not
only differ about which laws and which gods to obey, but
that they understand "earth" in very different terms: "for
Kreon, earth is the political territory of Thebes, defined
by human law; for Antigone, it is the realm of the gods
below, who protect the rites of the dead" (Segal 2003,
130–131).

463–464 *piercing scream . . . nest robbed* Grieving women
were often compared to mother birds robbed of their nest-
lings. But here Sophocles' simile suggests that Antigone is,

in the traditional Greek sense, a bird as omen, thus a vehicle for delivering the gods' will. Images of Polyneikes' corpse, exposed as human carrion, intensify the significance. Other readings are equally pertinent and foreboding: the empty nest recalls the children who might have been born to Antigone and Haimon; Polyneikes' empty grave, the result of battle and marriage to King Adrastos' daughter Argeia (see note to 954–955); and the empty nest of Kreon after the suicide of his son and wife. See Tyrrell and Bennett, 66–67. (Also cf. Sophocles' use of the metaphor in *Oedipus the King* [62] when the Priest calls Oedipus "a bird from god.")

469 *three cool swallows* As a part of funeral ritual, ancient Greeks poured libations directly onto the grave for a dead relative to drink.

471–473 *charged her . . . now this one. / Didn't deny a thing* Sophoclean scholars have long debated whether Antigone performed only the second or both "burials" of Polyneikes, especially since the first burial, according to the Guard, seems to have been performed by a being who left no evidence behind, and might well be a divine or other airborne creature. Here Antigone accepts blame for both burials. The difficulties in believing Antigone was the first duster of the body, however, are considerable: how did she do it without leaving a trace? The gods were entirely capable of intervening to *protect* Polyneikes' body from animals until it could be given a proper honoring. (In Homer's *Iliad* gods protected both Sarpedon and Hector.) What the gods cannot do is perform full burial rites, which are the responsibility of blood kin alone. For a most interesting and persuasive discussion of this issue, see Tyrrell and Bennett (54–62).

492 *unwritten and infallible laws* Such laws were a part of both legal and religious thought. Examples of unwritten laws include the imperative to bury the dead according to precise ancient customs, the prohibition against killing blood kin, and the permanent defilement of kin-slayers.

509–510 *girl's nature . . . her father's* In both his Theban and Athenian incarnations (in *Oedipus the King* and the *Kolonos*), Sophocles' character Oedipus displays a reckless and hasty violence in thought and action that the Leader now finds in Antigone. Antigone's "savage" (or *oumós*, "raw") nature primarily attacks Kreon and the politics he represents, and Ismene for her refusal to help perform Polyneikes' burial rituals. Griffith notes that *oumós* "is a very strong term to apply to anyone, esp. a young woman (elsewhere in tragedy used only of men)" (204). Segal notes that the word is reserved for the worst crimes and especially strong taboos pertaining to family (1981, 34). It might therefore be interpreted to include her incestuous feeling for Polyneikes implied at 87–88.

531 *screaming, hysterical, deranged* Ismene's fit could be the result of fear for Antigone's recklessness or of distress at her own refusal to help her sister bury Polyneikes. It is surely not what Kreon assumes: a fit of guilt as she contemplates treachery.

550 *bite their tongues* The verb Antigone uses here, *upillousin*, which I translate as "bite," refers to the way in which a cowering dog clamps its tail between its legs.

563 *Hades . . . rituals* Antigone insists Hades makes no distinctions or exceptions among the dead. He demands they all be honored and buried.

567–568 *I made no enemies . . . friends* Traditionally this line has been translated as Jebb has it: "'Tis not my nature to join in hating, only in loving" (1888, 102). Lloyd-Jones and Wilson, however, state that *physis*, which Jebb translates as "nature," must refer in this context to "one's birth." They argue that the Greeks believed one can make *friends* by birth, but never *enemies* (126). So translated in this context, the line makes clearer sense of Antigone's conduct in the drama, since the Greeks' sense of "hating," and certainly our own, is evident throughout in Antigone's temperament and her words. Lloyd-Jones and Wilson's solution spares scholars many an interpretive contortion. Those producing the play who believe Antigone is referring to her loving nature might substitute: "It's my nature to share love, not hatred."

594 *sprang to his defense* At 56 Ismene admitted she was afraid of betraying Kreon, and at 95–96 she declared her refusal to defy the city.

602 *Some think you're right* Those who agree with Ismene are living, principally Kreon; those who agree with Antigone, her dead family and the underworld gods, are in Hades.

603 *equally wrong* They can't be equally wrong—at least in the gods' eyes: Hades' demand that kin be buried is confirmed in the resolution of the drama.

615 *field to plow* The metaphor of a woman's body as a field or furrow for plowing, common in ancient Greece, echoes

Athenian marriage contracts (Blundell 1989, 120). Athenian audiences would not have normally found Kreon's use of it offensive, but his insensitivity to both Antigone and Haimon could have struck them as obscene (Tyrrell and Bennett, 78–79).

628–691 *Lucky are those . . . catastrophe* The particular evil the Elders have in mind in this ode is peculiar to families, and it cannot be evaded or defeated by any action or virtue of a family member. The ray of hope suggested by Antigone's character and vigor as "the last rootstock" is snuffed out by her insistence on burying her brother and by Kreon's "reckless talk" and mental "Furies," but the failure of a generation to "protect its own youth" also applies to Kreon and Haimon as well. The ode offers a more general theory of human futility in its latter section: the gods punish humankind for achievement itself, and though hope sometimes is justified, it's usually delusive and deadly. Also, the foolish can't distinguish evil from noble motives; catastrophe results. If Kreon (onstage in the background) hears this ode, he seems unaware that it targets him.

644 *Labdakids* Oedipus' ancestral family.

657 *blood-drenched dust* The image recalls the latest act committed by a member of the doomed House of Labdakos—Antigone's sprinkling of dust over Polyneikes. But it also evokes the brothers' dead bodies on the battlefield and, perhaps, the dust storm that swirled when Antigone performed the burial rites.

658 *death gods* Hades, Acheron, Persephone, Hermes.

660 *Furies in the mind* The goddesses called Furies—also referred to as the Erinys—typically punish the conscience for

crimes committed against the family, especially kin murder, and they are often credited with unbalancing a person's judgment. The Furies first "appear" in ancient tragedy (in Aeschylus' *Libation Bearers*) to punish Orestes for killing his mother. Although the audience realizes that the goddesses have manifested themselves in Orestes' mind, none of the other characters onstage is aware of their presence. For more on their role in *Kolonos*, where they preside in their more benevolent incarnation as the Eumenides, see notes to 44–50 and 92 in that play.

670 *Olympos* The mountain, visible from ancient Thebes, was the home base of the Olympian gods, from Zeus through Hephestos.

686–691 *"Evil seems noble . . . hold off catastrophe"* These words of wisdom refer to the ancient Greeks' belief that the gods "destroy the judgment of a person bent on evil and destruction. As we might phrase it in our more psychologizing terms, the gods collaborate with the evil tendencies of the prospective criminal to lead him to his ruin" (Segal 2003, 140–141).

693 *youngest of your sons* Haimon has an older brother, Megareus. See note to 1095.

721 *turn ice-cold in your arms* Here Kreon's words foreshadow how Haimon will wrap his arms around Antigone not long after she commits suicide, at 1371. Sophocles intensifies the irony with Kreon's avowal at 699–700 that "we'll soon have an answer" as to whether Haimon will defend his bride or support Kreon's sentencing her to death—an answer that is "better than any prophet's."

730–731 *Zeus / of family life* Zeus Herkeios, literally, Zeus of
   the Fence (*herkos*), is a manifestation of Zeus who protects
   an extended family's welfare. He was worshipped within the
   boundaries of the house, usually at an inner courtyard shrine.
   Kreon implies that this "household" Zeus would disapprove
   of Antigone's burial of Polyneikes (and her invocation of kinship law as the motive behind it), since the god would not
   approve a family member's rebellion against the head of its
   household.

756 *sapped my wits* The Leader alludes ironically to Kreon's
   earlier insult at 312, where he accused the Leader of sounding old and senile.

785 *open him up* Haimon compares his father to a clay writing
   tablet that opened and closed like a book or laptop com-
   puter. Kreon, says his son, has nothing inside him.

828 *You will not marry her while she's* on *this earth* Another
   example of the irony in Kreon's "prophetic" powers. The
   "marriage" of Haimon and Antigone will indeed take place
   after her death. See 1373–1375.

855–856 *enough food to evade / defilement* The city would be
   defiled if Antigone, Kreon's blood relative, were executed at
   his command. By leaving enough food to sustain her for a
   while, Kreon might hope that she'll commit suicide in despair, as indeed she will, and thus relieve Thebes of defilement. But Kreon was wrong to think his conduct could elude
   the defilement that will harm all Thebes. See Tiresias' denunciation of Kreon at 1176–1208.

857 *pray there to Hades* Since Hades is Antigone's favored
   deity, he would logically be the one she turns to in a desperate situation. But Hades has no reputation for saving lives.

By saying "Maybe he will spare her" Kreon sneers at Antigone's self-delusion.

861–880 *Love, you win . . . our lives* The Elders sing a brief celebration of Aphrodite and her son Eros, gods of Love—the emotion that Kreon leaves out of his calculations. He may remain onstage to hear the Elders enumerate Love's power over humans and beasts, and to hear them give Love its rightful place among the ancient powers and laws, written or unwritten. The ode presents a double paradox: The allure of the bride is both irresistible and destructive, as Antigone's allure for Haimon will prove to be. And what humans consider to be disastrous, the gods of Love deem as play or even mockery. (See Griffith, 260.)

863 *havoc with our herds* A literal translation. The word translated as "herds," *ktemasi*, can also refer to what the herds represent economically: wealth. The line could mean something like "love who . . . impoverishes us." I interpret it with Griffith (257) to mean that erotic power also drives animals into frenzy.

872–873 *wrench men's minds . . . off course* The image is of a chariot overturning on a race course. Love at the intensity the Elders register here made even the ancients unsafe drivers.

dressed in purple as a bride Throughout her final scene, Antigone conducts herself as if she were preparing for her wedding. Her spoken and sung speeches are dense with allusions, both ironic and plaintive, to a bride's expectations. Having her appear in a traditional Greek purple bridal costume would visually reinforce Sophocles' verbal imagery. Indeed, wedding and funeral rituals were deeply associative of each other in Athenian culture; they both signified a similar transition in life. Upon leaving her father's house, the bride entered the house of another man and perished as a virgin; the dead entered Hades' house, never to return (Tyrrell and Bennett, 98). Sophocles' audience would have been attuned to the visual and verbal clues that connected the rituals of marriage and death.

891 *Acheron* The river god of a stream that flows through Hades.

895 *River of Pain* A literal rendering of the meaning of Acheron.

901 *enter Hades . . . still alive* A bit of sophistry on the Elders' part. Antigone will be imprisoned below ground, thus in proximity to Hades, and she will still be alive. But only the truly dead ever enter the real place. The Elders probably want to emphasize Antigone's exercise of free choice in committing the act that led to her death sentence.

903–905 *Phrygian stranger . . . Mount Sipylos* The Phyrigian stranger, or Niobe, was the daughter of King Tantalos of Lydia. She married Amphion, a king of Thebes, and bore him an equal number of sons and daughters (six of each, according to Homer; other versions of the myth say seven, nine, or ten). After Niobe boasted that she was superior to the goddess Leto, who had only one of each, Leto sent her children, who just happened to be Apollo and Artemis, to kill Niobe's. Niobe wept for nine days and nights, after which the Olympian gods turned her to a stone face embedded on a cliff on Mount Sipylos (where her father lived). The rain and snow eternally dripping from this stone image were seen as tears. In other versions of the myth, Niobe is a mortal whose boast of being superior to a divinity provoked her punishment. Sophocles' audience would have recognized his artistic license in making her a god. Tyrrell and Bennett suggest that Sophocles' purpose was to accentuate Antigone's own likening of herself to a god, considered by fifth-century Greeks as "boastfulness beyond the pale" (107). Sophocles also could have intended to soften the Leader's reproach at 914–919, where he calls her godlike fate "no small honor."

906 *Living rock* In Niobe's case, the metaphor of a body turned to stone alludes to the end of her fertility; in Antigone's case, the allusion is first to her never-to-be-penetrated virgin body. Seaford interprets the stone in both cases as enclosing them with their natal families (Seaford 1994, 351).

932 *heaped-up rock-bound prison* Suggests that Antigone's "tomb" was not a geologically formed cave but man-made, with earth piled above a hollowed lower chamber.

933 *without a friend* Antigone may have admirers in Thebes (as Haimon insists), but none comes forward to grieve for her, presumably out of fear. And of course Antigone no longer considers her sister Ismene to be a *philê*, or family member, thus she is not a possible mourner.

943–956 *You've touched . . . so was I* In this lyric, Antigone traces her family curse not to Laios' original disobedience of Apollo, but to her mother's incest. (The focus on her mother's responsibility echoes her opening words to Ismene, "born . . . from that same womb.") As Segal notes, "kinship as a function of female procreative power [was] embedded in Greek culture" (1998, 183). Throughout this meditation, Antigone sees marriage as a maker of defilement and death, not of children and life (see note to 954–955 and the counterpart to her speech, Oedipus' howl of pain against marriages in *Oedipus the King*, 1591–1596).

954–955 *deadly / marriage* By marrying Argeia, the daughter of the Argive king Adrastos, Polyneikes gained the military support he needed to attack Thebes; thus his marriage contributed to his death in battle.

980 *pure as far as she's concerned* Kreon assumes his precautions—leaving her a small ration of food and enclosing her in a tomb away from the city—will be enough to evade the defilement of kin murder.

983–984 *My tomb . . . dug from rock* The tomb has three identities for Antigone: it is the grave Kreon sentenced her to in punishment for attempting to violate his decree; it is the nuptial bedroom in which she will wed Hades; and it is the hollow in which she will dwell with her parents and dead brothers (Tyrrell and Bennett, 111).

996–1013 *I honored you . . . hollow tomb* The authenticity of these lines has been questioned at least since Goethe (in 1827) famously expressed the hope that some classical scholar would prove them spurious. Though many editors and critics have impugned the lines, including Jebb and Winnington-Ingram, confidence in their genuineness has grown in recent years. On the one hand, Lloyd-Jones and Wilson correctly state that objections to them are invariably subjective. On the other hand, contemporary scholars, e.g., Tyrrell and Bennett, and Griffith, have argued that their content conforms to Antigone's understanding of both herself and the duties to kin as prescribed by divine law. For those producing the play and unconvinced of their authenticity, or who believe including them would divert audience attention into seemingly arid and arcane matters, these lines can be omitted en bloc without disrupting the flow and logic of the remaining lines.

1009 *he pulls me by the wrist* After the wedding feast, the bride was traditionally pulled by the wrist (from a table with other women) in a symbolic act of abduction and led away by the bridegroom. Although Antigone imagines Hades as her bridegroom, she seems here to allude to Kreon as the person who prevents her from a marriage on earth. Kreon does not actually lead Antigone away himself but delegates the act to his men.

1021–1022 *I want* them / *to suffer the pain* Antigone's call for vengeance might be directed at the citizens of Thebes who did not defend her and her cause, but Kreon is her primary target. Not having any *philoi* left to mourn her or to take vengeance on Kreon, she must depend on the gods, she thinks, and she appeals to them directly.

1032 *Look at me, princely citizens* In the moments before she gives herself to Hades, Antigone enacts her own version of *anakalyptêria*, the bride's traditional lifting of her veil for the first time among men. The penetration of the men's eyes was symbolic of her imminent loss of virginity. The gesture of showing her face, as made by a Greek bride whose passivity was taken for granted, was a speechless invitation. But here Antigone acts aggressively, as she did in performing burial rituals for Polyneikes, and calls out to the Elders.

1036 *Danaë* Danaë's father, Akrisios, king of Argos, locked her in a bronze tower because an oracle prophesied that a son of hers would someday kill him. Zeus impregnated her with a shower of gold, and she gave birth to Perseus, who did in fact kill Akrisios accidentally while throwing a discus. Two other mythological characters in this ode were in some way imprisoned; see notes to 1051 and 1081–1084.

1051 *Lycurgos* According to Homer's *Iliad* (6.130ff.) Lycurgos attacked Dionysos, forcing the young god and his nurses to take refuge in the sea. Soon after Dionysos retaliated by blinding him, Lycurgos died. Sophocles likely knew other versions of the myth, and seems to draw here on the versions of Apollodorus (I. 35) and Hyginus (*Fab.* 132), in which Dionysos drives Lycurgos mad.

1066–1068 *Black Rocks . . . Bosphoros' channel* The Bosphoros, a narrow strait that joined the Black Sea with the Sea of Marmara and the Mediterranean, divided Asia and Europe; the Black Rocks, over which a swift current passed, have been worn away over the past 2,400 years.

1071 *Ares* The god of cruel bloodshed, considered to be of Thracian origin, was unpopular in the ancient world, and important only in Thebes and perhaps Athens. In mythology he is nearly always portrayed as an instigator of violence or a tempestuous lover; he never develops a moral function, as do Zeus, Apollo, and Dionysos, on his own terms, as the people's god.

1073 *savage wife of Phineus* When Phineus, a Thracian king, cast off his wife Kleopatra—who was the daughter of Boreas, the North Wind—he married Eidothea, who blinded Phineus' two sons (for reasons unclear in the various versions of the myth).

1081–1084 *a woman unhappy . . . Erektheids* The unhappy woman, distraught because her marriage ended, is

Kleopatra, the mother of Phineus' blinded sons. Her mother was Oreithyia, daughter of Erektheus, a king of Athens. Sophocles supposed Kleopatra's story to be familiar to his audience—although he doesn't mention it here, she was imprisoned by Phineas—and clearly means to connect her fate to Antigone's (Jebb 1888, 966n).

TIRESIAS . . . Lad Thebes' resident prophet, always accompanied by a young boy, also appears at critical moments in Oedipus the King and Euripides' Bakkhai.

1095 questioned the advice This may be a reference to advice Tiresias had given within the last few days concerning how best to divinely protect Thebes against the Argive onslaught (see note to 20). In one version of the myth of the Seven Against Thebes, Tiresias advises Kreon to sacrifice his eldest son, Megareus, mentioned at 1455, in order for Thebes to prevail.

1096 straight course Tiresias' use of "straight," or orthos, echoes Kreon's repeated use of the word in various forms to characterize his statesmanlike virtues of being upright and on course. His obsession with "straightness" carries over to manipulating people as expertly as one might steer a ship.

1106–1107 They screeched . . . was drowned out Birds were a major medium of communication between gods and mortals. Because the birds' angry screeching has made their songs unintelligible, Tiresias interprets the screeching itself as a sign of the gods' extreme displeasure with Kreon's recent acts and decrees. See note to 463–464.

1111 sacrificial fire Tiresias burns a large animal in the god's honor in order to regain his good will. Hephestos, god of fire, snuffs it out, thus blocking the gesture. At this point, Tiresias' prophetic drill shifts to examining the inner organs of the animal for useful omens.

1113–1117 *charred thighbones . . . fat enfolding them* Tiresias recounts how the sacrifice failed. The offering, probably the meat of an ox, should have gone up in flames when it was ignited—the fragrant smoke ascending like a prayer to the gods above. Instead, the fire smoldered, fat oozed into the ashes, and the gallbladder burst its stench into the air. The "vivid and repulsive description . . . [suggests] the putrescent corpse of Polyneikes" (Griffith, 299).

1117–1118 *attempt / at prophecy failed* Neither the animal's organs nor the sacrifice seeking divine advice yields any readable communications from the gods. Tiresias instead gives Kreon sensible advice of his own, unsanctioned by Apollo.

1122–1123 *city's altars . . . defiled* Because neither Polyneikes nor the Argive soldiers were properly mourned and buried, their dishonored flesh, spread throughout the city by dogs and birds, defiles Thebes.

1129–1130 *keen cries . . . garbled / by . . . thickened blood* Tiresias makes a direct connection between the city's defilement and the gods' displeasure at the city's leader.

1149 *silver from Sardis* Literally, silver-gold (an alloy).

1155 *men can defile gods* Kreon distorts Tiresias' explanation of his wrongdoing. The point is not whether men defile gods, but that Thebans and Kreon have defiled themselves.

1191 *Furies sent by Hades* Presumably the Eumenides, who will punish Kreon for his impiety by attacking his family. See *Kolonos*, notes to 44–50.

1227 *Delegate this to no one* The Leader might be alluding to
the fact that Kreon, after boasting that he'd lead Antigone to
her tomb himself, assigned his soldiers to the task.

1231–1232 *I who / locked her away will . . . free her* At
1218–1219, the Leader advised Kreon to free Antigone from
her tomb and then to bury Polyneikes. Kreon makes tending to Polyneikes' body his first priority. Though going first
to Antigone might not have saved her life, Kreon's mindless
reversal of the logical priority further damns him.

1235–1281 *God with myriad names . . . night* Just before the
worst calamity occurs (or is announced) in each of the three
Oedipus plays, the Chorus members sing their appeal for
help to Dionysos. This ode presents a vivid picture of the or-
giastic worship of the god on Parnassos, a mountain north-
east of Delphi that was traditionally sacred to Apollo and
the muses. In the winter months, Apollo ceded his shrine
at Delphi to Dionysos and his cult; a festival was held every
two years and attended by a sanctioned band of maenads.
(See Guthrie, 178, 202.)

1237 *Kadmos' daughter* Semele. See *Kolonos*, notes to 741–743.

1240–1241 *Eleusis . . . Demeter* See *Kolonos*, notes to 749–750
and 1149–1154.

1254–1255 *nymphs of Korykia . . . Kastalia's fountains*
Nymphs, young female spirits representing the divine powers of nature, were named specifically for their function or
the locale in which they resided. Korykia, a stalactite cavern
in Mount Parnassos, was an ancient place of sacrifice. The
Kastalia is a stream that flows from the fissure of a high cliff
in the mountain.

1256 *Nysa's sloping hills* The mountain where Dionysos was born in some versions of myth. See *Kolonos,* notes to 741–743.

1260 *Evohoi!* A shout made by Dionysos' worshippers to signal that the god was among them.

1265–1266 *mother / whom the lightning killed* Semele.

1271 *howling channel* The windy straits between the Greek mainland and the island of Euboea.

1276 *Thyiads* A troop of Attic women sent to join the revels of their Delphic sisters in the winter worship of Dionysos.

1279 *Iakkhos* A secondary cult name of Bakkhos or Dionysos.

Messenger From his demeanor, he is an educated and trusted palace servant.

1283 *Amphion and Kadmos* Early kings of Thebes.

Eurydike Kreon's wife. Within days, she has seen both her sons die as a result of choices made by her husband. Her name means "wide" (*eury*) "justice/penalty/satisfaction" (*dike*), which she will fittingly exact from Kreon by leaving him without a female family member to mourn his son (or, when he dies, himself).

1321 *lived through misfortune* This could be a reference to the (possibly) sacrificial murder of her son, Megareus, as well as to the events of Oedipus' reign. See note to 1095.

1330–1331 *Goddess / of Roadways . . . Pluto* The goddess Hekate was worshipped at crossroads in the form of a statue with three heads or three bodies. Her mention brings to mind the crossroads where Oedipus killed Laios (see *Oedipus the King,* 832). Pluto is another name for Hades.

1344 *Am I a prophet?* Kreon has unwittingly predicted the tragic outcome of his son's relationship to Antigone. See note to 721.

1354–1357 *hanging . . . he'd lost to Hades* The image of Haimon embracing Antigone around the waist as she hangs from a noose of linen (perhaps made from the veil she lifted in her bridal procession) evokes another Attic wedding ritual that has been depicted in vase paintings. After the groom leads the bride by the wrist from the feast, he lifts her bolt upright into the mule cart that will carry the couple to their nuptial bed. The groom demonstrates his physical strength and dominance over the bride; the bride submits in compliance and dignity by remaining rigidly in the posture (Tyrrell and Bennett, 142).

1365 *spat in his face* Literally, *ptúsas prosopoi*. This gesture reminds us of the crude advice Kreon gave his son at 723–724: "spit this girl out like the enemy she is"; in the Greek, *ptúsas osei te dusmene*. Sophoclean irony shows Kreon once again as a man whose arrogant behavior comes back to haunt him. The metaphorical usage of 723–724 is not found elsewhere in tragedy but is common in epic and lyric; for this reason, and perhaps because genteel Victorian scholars refrained from translating literally such an ungentlemanly act as spitting, Jebb and others of his era focus on the loathing and contempt implicit in the passages. (See Griffith, 236, 338.)

1366 *two-edged* Literally, *diplos*, or "double." The blade kills Haimon the son and Haimon the potential father. See *Oedipus the King*, note to 1415.

1371–1374 *he clung to her . . . married at last* The "marriage" is consummated with *oxeian*, literally, "spurts," of Haimon's blood, not Antigone's.

1425–1426 *so much / a loving mother to your son* Literally,
"the *pammêtôr* of the corpse," or, in the scholiast's understanding, "the mother in all respects." *Pammêtôr* connotes
the great Mother Earth, Gaia, the true mother of all things.
Gaia repeatedly defends her offspring throughout the for-
mative period of the universe against male aggressors who
attempt to control her children or usurp her procreativity.
Sophocles' use of the term here draws on Panhellenic myth
in which the goddess unleashes her vengeance as a subordinate of Zeus. Eurydike's violent suicide presents Kreon with
the silenced woman he wanted in Antigone, and it gives Antigone the vengeance she sought against Kreon—a silent funeral (Tyrrell and Bennett, 149–51).

1430–1431 *we flood / your harbor* The dead arrive in Hades'
realm by a boat that transports them across the River Styx.
Kreon imagines his own dead family as a sacrifice made to
Hades, but one that fails to win the gods' goodwill.

WORKS CITED AND CONSULTED

Aeschylus. *The Complete Greek Tragedies.* Trans. Richmond Lattimore, ed. David Grene and Richmond Lattimore. Chicago: University of Chicago Press, 1959.

Aristotle. *Aristotle's Poetics.* Trans. Leon Golden. Tallahassee: Florida State University Press, 1981.

———. *The Art of Rhetoric.* Trans. John Henry Freese. Loeb Classical Library 193. Cambridge, MA: Harvard University Press, 1967.

Berlin, Normand. *The Secret Cause: A Discussion of Tragedy.* Amherst: University of Massachusetts Press, 1981.

Benardete, Seth. *Sacred Transgressions: A Reading of Sophocles' "Antigone."* South Bend, IN: St. Augustine's Press, 1999.

Blundell, Mary Whitlock. *Helping Friends and Harming Enemies: A Study in Sophocles and Greek Ethics.* Cambridge: Cambridge University Press, 1989.

———, trans. *Antigone.* By Sophocles. Focus Classical Library. Newburyport, MA: Focus Information Group, 1998.

———, trans. *Oedipus at Colonus.* By Sophocles. Focus Classical Library. Newburyport, MA: Focus Information Group, 1990.

Boegehold, Alan L. *When a Gesture Was Expected*. Princeton, NJ: Princeton University Press, 1999.

Carpenter, Thomas H., and Christopher A. Faraone, eds. *Masks of Dionysus*. Ithaca, NY: Cornell University Press, 1993.

Cartledge, Paul. *Ancient Greek Political Thought in Practice*. Cambridge: Cambridge University Press, 2009.

Csapo, Eric, and William J. Slater. *The Context of Ancient Drama*. Ann Arbor: University of Michigan Press, 1994.

Davidson, John N. *Courtesans and Fishcakes: The Consuming Passions of Classical Athens*. New York: St. Martin's Press, 1998.

Eagleton, Terry. *Sweet Violence: The Idea of the Tragic*. Malden, MA: Blackwell, 2003.

Easterling, P. E., ed. *The Cambridge Companion to Greek Tragedy*. Cambridge: Cambridge University Press, 1997.

———, ed. *Trachiniae*. By Sophocles. Cambridge: Cambridge University Press, 1982.

Edmunds, Lowell. *Theatrical Space and Historical Place in Sophocles' "Oedipus at Colonus."* Lanham, MD: Rowman & Littlefield, 1996.

Else, Gerald F. *The Origin and Early Form of Greek Tragedy*. New York: Norton, 1965.

Euripides. *Euripides*. The Complete Greek Tragedies, vol. 4. Ed. David Grene and Richmond Lattimore. Chicago: University of Chicago Press, 1959.

Foley, Helene P. *Female Acts in Greek Tragedy*. Princeton, NJ: Princeton University Press, 2001.

Garland, Robert. *The Greek Way of Death*. Ithaca, NY: Cornell University Press, 1985.

————. *The Greek Way of Life*. Ithaca, NY: Cornell University Press, 1990.

Garvie, A. F., ed. and trans. *Ajax*. By Sophocles. Warminster, UK: Aris & Phillips, 1998.

Golder, Herbert, and Richard Pevear, trans. *Aias (Ajax)*. By Sophocles. New York: Oxford University Press, 1999.

Goldhill, Simon. *Reading Greek Tragedy*. Cambridge: Cambridge University Press, 1986.

Gould, Thomas. *The Ancient Quarrel Between Poetry and Philosophy*. Princeton, NJ: Princeton University Press, 1990.

————, trans. *"Oedipus the King": A Translation with Commentary*. By Sophocles. Englewood Cliffs, NJ: Prentice-Hall, 1970.

Grene, David, trans. *Sophocles 1*. 2nd ed. The Complete Greek Tragedies. Ed. David Grene and Richmond Lattimore. Chicago: University of Chicago Press, 1991.

Griffith, Mark, ed. *Antigone*. By Sophocles. Cambridge: Cambridge University Press, 1999.

Guthrie, W. K. C. *The Greeks and Their Gods*. Boston: Beacon Press, 1950.

Hanson, Victor Davis. *A War Like No Other*. New York: Random House, 2005.

Herodotus. *The Landmark Herodotus: The Histories*. Ed. Robert B. Strassler. New York: Pantheon Books, 2007.

Hesk, Jon. *Sophocles: Ajax*. London: Gerald Duckworth & Co., 2003.

Hughes, Bettany. *The Hemlock Cup: Socrates, Athens and the Search for the Good Life*. New York: Knopf, 2010.

Jebb, R. C., trans. *Antigone.* By Sophocles. Cambridge: Cambridge University Press, 1928. (Originally published 1888.)

———, trans. *Ajax.* By Sophocles. Cambridge: Cambridge University, 1896.

———, trans. *Electra.* By Sophocles. Cambridge: Cambridge University, 1894.

———, trans. *Oedipus Coloneus.* By Sophocles. Cambridge: Cambridge University, 1886.

———, trans. *Philoctetes.* By Sophocles. Cambridge: Cambridge University, 1898.

———, trans. *Oedipus Tyrannus.* By Sophocles. Cambridge: Cambridge University, 1883.

———, trans. *Trachiniae.* By Sophocles. Cambridge: Cambridge University, 1892.

Kagan, Donald. *Pericles of Athens and the Birth of Democracy.* New York: Touchstone–Simon & Schuster, 1991.

Kamerbeek, J. C. *The Trachiniae.* The Plays of Sophocles: Commentaries, vol. 2. Leiden, Netherlands: E. J. Brill, 1959.

Kells, J. H., ed. *Electra.* By Sophocles. Cambridge: Cambridge University Press, 1973.

Kirkwood, G. M. *A Study of Sophoclean Drama.* Cornell Studies in Classical Philology 31. Ithaca, NY: Cornell University Press, 1994.

Knox, Bernard M. W. *Essays: Ancient and Modern.* Baltimore: Johns Hopkins University Press, 1989.

———. *The Heroic Temper: Studies in Sophoclean Tragedy.* Berkeley: University of California Press, 1964.

———. *Oedipus at Thebes.* New Haven, CT: Yale University Press, 1957.

———. Introduction and notes to *The Three Theban Plays*. By Sophocles. Trans. Robert Fagles. New York: Viking, 1982.

Lefkowitz, Mary R. *The Lives of Greek Poets*. Baltimore: Johns Hopkins University Press, 1981.

Levett, Brad. *Sophocles: Women of Trachis*. London: Gerald Duckworth & Co., 2004.

Lloyd, Michael. *Sophocles: Electra*. London: Gerald Duckworth & Co., 2005.

Lloyd-Jones, Hugh, trans. *Antigone*. By Sophocles. Loeb Classical Library 20. Cambridge, MA: Harvard University Press, 1994.

———, trans. *Oedipus at Colonus*. By Sophocles. Loeb Classical Library 21. Cambridge, MA: Harvard University Press, 1994.

———, trans. *Oedipus Tyrannus*. By Sophocles. Loeb Classical Library 20. Cambridge, MA: Harvard University Press, 1994.

Lloyd-Jones, Hugh, and N. G. Wilson. *Sophoclea: Studies on the Text of Sophocles*. Oxford: Clarendon Press, 1990.

Moore, J. A., trans. *Selections from the Greek Elegiac, Iambic, and Lyric Poets*. Cambridge, MA: Harvard University Press, 1947.

Phillips, Carl, trans. Introduction and notes by Diskin Clay. *Philoctetes*. By Sophocles. New York: Oxford University Press, 2003.

Pickard-Cambridge, Arthur. *The Dramatic Festivals of Athens*. 2nd ed. Revised with a new supplement by John Gould and D. M. Lewis. Oxford: Clarendon Press, 1988.

Plutarch. *The Rise and Fall of Athens: Nine Greek Lives*. Trans. Ian Scott-Kilvert. London: Penguin, 1960.

Radice, Betty. *Who's Who in the Ancient World*. London: Penguin, 1971.

Rehm, Rush. *The Play of Space: Spatial Transformation in Greek Tragedy*. Princeton, NJ: Princeton University Press, 2002.

Reinhardt, Karl. *Sophocles*. New York: Barnes & Noble–Harper & Row, 1979.

Roisman, Hanna M. *Sophocles: Philoctetes*. London: Gerald Duckworth & Co., 2005.

Seaford, Richard. *Reciprocity and Ritual: Homer and Tragedy in the Developing City-State*. Oxford: Clarendon Press, 1994.

Segal, Charles. Notes to *Antigone*. By Sophocles. Trans. Reginald Gibbons and Charles Segal. New York: Oxford University Press, 2003.

———. *"Oedipus Tyrannus": Tragic Heroism and the Limits of Knowledge*. 2nd ed. New York: Oxford University Press, 2001.

———. *Sophocles' Tragic World: Divinity, Nature, Society*. Cambridge, MA: Harvard University Press, 1995.

———. *Tragedy and Civilization: An Interpretation of Sophocles*. Cambridge, MA: Harvard University Press, 1981.

Steiner, George. *Antigones*. New Haven, CT: Yale University Press, 1996.

Taplin, Oliver. *Greek Tragedy in Action*. Berkeley: University of California Press, 1978.

Thucydides. *The Landmark Thucydides: A Comprehensive Guide to the Peloponnesian War*. Ed. Robert B. Strassler. New York: Touchstone–Simon & Schuster, 1996.

Tyrrell, Wm. Blake, and Larry J. Bennett. *Recapturing Sophocles' "Antigone."* Lanham, MD: Rowman & Littlefield, 1998.

Ussher, R. G., ed. and trans. *Philoctetes.* By Sophocles. Warminster, UK: Aris & Phillips, 1990.

Vernant, Jean-Pierre, ed. *The Greeks.* Trans. Charles Lambert and Teresa Lavender Fagan. Chicago: University of Chicago Press, 1995.

Vernant, Jean-Pierre, and Pierre Vidal-Naquet. *Myth and Tragedy in Ancient Greece.* Trans. Janet Lloyd. New York: Zone Books, 1990.

Webster, T. B. L., ed. *Philoctetes.* By Sophocles. Cambridge: Cambridge University Press, 1970.

Whitman, C. E. *Sophocles.* Cambridge, MA: Harvard University Press, 1951.

Wiles, David. *Greek Theatre Performances: An Introduction.* Cambridge: Cambridge University Press, 2000.

———. *Tragedy in Athens: Performance Space and Theatrical Meaning.* Cambridge: Cambridge University Press, 1997.

Winkler, John J., and Froma I. Zeitlin, eds. *Nothing to Do with Dionysos?: Athenian Drama in Its Social Context.* Princeton, NJ: Princeton University Press, 1990.

Winnington-Ingram, R. P. *Sophocles: An Interpretation.* Cambridge: Cambridge University Press, 1980.

Zimmern, Alfred. *The Greek Commonwealth: Politics and Economics in Fifth-Century Greece.* 5th ed. New York: Modern Library, 1931.